Libertine Love

At first, he simply held her against his shoulder, stroking her bare arm and whispering endearments against her hair to allay her fears. When Aurora relaxed and slid her arm around his waist, he began kissing her, slowly, luxuriantly, his hot mouth touching her forehead, her eyes, her lips, before trailing down the slender column of her throat.

Aurora surrendered to the pleasure he aroused in her until she felt as though she were being devoured by flames. Only one man could make her burn with such desire. . . .

THRILL TO THE DARK PASSIONS OF SIGNET'S HISTORICAL ROMANTIC GOTHICS

Sapphire
and
Silk

by
Leslie O'Grady

AN ONYX BOOK

NEW AMERICAN LIBRARY

NAL BOOKS ARE AVAILABLE AT QUANTITY DISCOUNTS
WHEN USED TO PROMOTE PRODUCTS OR SERVICES.
FOR INFORMATION PLEASE WRITE TO PREMIUM MARKETING DIVISION.
NEW AMERICAN LIBRARY. 1633 BROADWAY.
NEW YORK. NEW YORK 10019.

PUBLISHER'S NOTE

Onyx is a trademark of NAL PENGUIN INC.

SIGNET, SIGNET CLASSIC, MENTOR, ONYX, PLUME, MERIDIAN
and NAL BOOKS are published by NAL PENGUIN INC.,
1633 Broadway, New York, New York 10019

First Printing, July, 1987

1 2 3 4 5 6 7 8 9

PRINTED IN THE UNITED STATES OF AMERICA

1

BY the feeble light of dawn, a restless Lord Silverblade left his mistress sleeping in the summerhouse and strolled outside into the secluded clearing. He inhaled the scent of mossy earth and looked around, shivering as the damp morning air chilled the bare flesh of his arms and chest. Towering oak trees and a tangled jungle of shrubs and vines surrounded him like an impenetrable fortress. Even where the trees thinned and parted, revealing a steep hill and green fields divided by low stone walls, this private place was still guarded from prying eyes.

Nicholas stopped at the edge of the clearing to survey his vast domain, noticing how hushed and tranquil the May morning was. Not a leaf rustled, not a bird sang. He smiled lazily as he turned and looked back at the summerhouse, a fanciful bit of architecture with tightly closed shutters and an upturned red tile roof. Now, not even a low moan of contentment from Pamela disturbed the serenity of this enchanted place, though last night . . . He grinned, for the memory was still fresh in his mind.

Suddenly the stillness was shattered by the drumming of hooves. Nicholas scowled in consternation and listened. The distant rumble kept growing louder and closer, and within seconds he felt the first faint tremors in the earth beneath his feet. It would not be long now. He waited, eager to confront the intruder.

His patience was soon rewarded. A magnificent chestnut horse came flying over the crest of a nearby hill, his glossy red-gold coat turned to fire by the rising sun and jets of white steam puffing from his flared nostrils.

A fire-breathing dragon ravaging the peaceful Surrey countryside, Nicholas thought.

However, it was not the spirited animal that caught and held his attention, but the rider crouched low over the horse's arched neck. The lad was so small in comparison to his strapping mount that he looked as insignificant as a burr caught in the horse's mane.

At first Nicholas dismissed the stripling as some undergroom out exercising one of his master's thoroughbreds, but as the pair drew closer, his cold gray eyes narrowed suspiciously. Despite the fact that the slender youth wore fitted buff-colored breeches and rode astride, a man of Nicholas' considerable experience was not fooled. He would have known the chestnut's rider was a woman even if her white lawn shirt weren't clinging so provocatively to her small, softly rounded breasts.

When the woman reached the foot of the hill, she reined in her mount effortlessly and stared up at the man standing there watching her so intently. At first she hesitated, as if debating the wisdom of approaching a stranger. Then, with a reckless shrug, she touched her heel to her mount's ribs and urged him up the slope.

Horse and rider drew closer. Nicholas noticed that the woman's thick, curling hair matched the rich copper-gold fire of her mount's coat. Even though she had tied her mane out of the way with a narrow black ribbon, soft, wispy tendrils had escaped to frame her delicate oval face in a most feminine manner.

Still cautious, the woman halted her horse a prudent distance away, where the high-strung animal proceeded to dance in place, his head bobbing up and down, his bit jingling impatiently. But when his rider placed a hand on his foam-flecked neck and murmured something, he quieted right down, obviously soothed by her gentle touch and soft voice. Then she eyed the man mistrustfully.

Nicholas really couldn't blame her, for he was half-naked, clad only in the breeches he had hastily pulled on after rising. A lovely woman cavorting about the countryside without the protection of a groom couldn't be too careful of strangers, he thought wryly, especially half-dressed men.

To put her at ease, he granted her one of his most disarming smiles. "Ah, Diana herself . . ."

Two huge, guileless blue eyes stared down at him in puzzlement. "But I am not Diana," she said in a clear, sweet voice, "I am Aurora."

He bowed deferentially. "Perhaps goddess of the dawn is more appropriate after all."

Suddenly comprehension lit her face and she laughed, a delightful, melodic trill that bubbled up from deep within her and more than compensated for the lack of birdsong. "Oh, now I understand. I suppose I should be flattered to be compared to a goddess, but Aurora is actually my name. Aurora Falconet."

Falconet . . . Nicholas' smile suddenly died at a particularly sharp and painful memory and he stared, searching her face for any resemblance to the Falconet he had once loved as a brother. He cursed himself for not seeing it immediately—the pale blue eyes with their challenging gleam, the strong, stubborn chin, the defiant tilt of the head.

She even had her brother's quick intuitiveness as well, for her finely arched brows came together in a scowl. "Is something wrong? You looked at me quite oddly just then."

Nicholas recovered his composure and smiled again. "I'm assuming you are Diana Falconet's sister, staying with her at Overton Manor." His eyes narrowed as they roved over the red mountain of excitable horseflesh, now as docile as a lapdog. "Isn't that Lord Overton's new stallion, the one that broke the head groom's arm and kicked three ostlers senseless?"

Aurora's face was the picture of affronted innocence. "Firelight?" she said incredulously. "This gentle lamb? This sweet baby? Lies, all lies."

"Are they, now? From what I've heard, that 'sweet

baby' would just as soon throw you and trample you as look at you."

Aurora slapped the animal's neck, then reached over to scratch him between the ears, causing him to close his eyes and whicker softly in equine contentment.

"Firelight wouldn't do that to me, would you, boy?" she crooned. "We understand each other. I know what's in his heart and mind, don't I, my sweet baby?"

But Nicholas was not convinced and suddenly feared for her safety. "Miss Falconet, I insist that you dismount at once!" He stepped forward, his arm outstretched to grasp the bridle and hold the horse's head steady so its rider could dismount.

When the sudden movement caused Firelight to whistle a warning as he began prancing again, Nicholas jumped back out of harm's way. Miss Falconet, however, remained steadfast in the saddle.

Now she was glaring down at him scornfully, that determined chin outthrust. "I can assure you your fears for my safety are groundless. I am an excellent rider. And I'll thank you not to frighten Firelight again. He's skittish around strangers. Now, if you'll kindly give me directions to Overton Manor, I shall be on my way."

Before Nicholas could reply, he was distracted by the sound of the summerhouse door creaking open, followed by a languid, sleepy voice calling his name.

Then Pamela emerged, her tousled golden hair tumbling about her shoulders in wild abandon, her wrinkled gown looking as though she had hastily dragged it on without assistance. When she saw Lord Silverblade in the company of what appeared to be another young gentleman, she froze for a second, then visibly began to preen. Pamela tossed her hair out of her eyes with a coquettish gesture, tugged at the waist of her gown to adjust it, then shrugged herself into the bodice in a belated attempt at modesty.

Nicholas turned to find Aurora gawking at Pamela in frank bewilderment. Gradually comprehension dawned and Aurora's pale, freckled face grew rosy with embarrassment.

"If you'll kindly give me directions to Overton

Manor," she said, quickly looking away from the half-dressed woman gliding toward them, "I shall be on my way."

Nicholas pointed off to his right. "Just ride up that rise, turn left, and follow the stone wall for approximately five miles. You'll soon come to Overton land."

Aurora mumbled her thanks, leaned forward, and made a clicking sound that caused Firelight to bolt as if he had been shot from a cannon.

For a moment Nicholas just stood and watched with his heart in his mouth as horse and rider charged down the hill at breakneck speed, gathering momentum with every long stride. If Firelight should step into a hidden rabbit hole it would spell certain death for both of them, but Aurora Falconet seemed oblivious of the danger as she urged her horse on.

Nicholas felt Pamela's hand rest lightly on his arm, and when he looked down at her, he somehow wasn't surprised to find her attention riveted on the horseman galloping away.

"Nicholas, who was that handsome young gentleman?" she asked in her throaty voice.

He chuckled. "I wish you could see the expression on your face, my dear. You look as though you'd like to devour the lad whole. You should also never express interest in another man while in my presence, or I fear I shall become wildly jealous and challenge him to a duel."

"Nicholas, stop teasing me!" Pamela said with a stamp of her tiny bare foot. "I may be scandalously unfaithful to my doddering old fool of a husband, but you know I would never be unfaithful to you. I was merely curious, that's all."

He reached over to pluck out a bit of dried brown leaf tangled in her hair. "Oh, I know that, my lovely Pamela, especially," he added, glancing at the horseman one last time, "not with that particular young gentleman. You see," Nicholas whispered into her ear, "that *he* is a *she*."

Pamela's head jerked back and her eyes widened in surprise. "Whatever is a young woman doing traipsing about the countryside dressed as a man?"

Nicholas shrugged. "Presumably she is an eccentric. She probably keeps seventy cats and allows them all to sleep in her bed every night."

Pamela scoffed at that. "I doubt if she shares her bed with seventy cats, my lord. She is far too beautiful. And she rides well."

Nicholas raised his brows at such faint praise. "Rides *well*, you say? She rides as though she were part horse herself. A veritable centaur."

"Did this object of your boundless admiration tell you who she is?"

"Her name is Aurora Falconet and she is Diana Falconet's sister."

Pamela glanced at him. "Then she's Tim Falconet's sister as well."

When Nicholas made no reply and his playful mood abruptly vanished with the quickness of a cloud moving over the sun, Pamela sensed the change in him at once.

"She is so like him," Nicholas mused, his eyes following the horse and rider as they miraculously reached the foot of the slope unscathed. "Bold, reckless . . .

Pamela noticed the look of pain that passed so fleetingly over his face and she rushed to ease it the only way she knew how.

"Nicholas," she murmured, turning her back to him and lifting her hair, "would you mind hooking up my gown the rest of the way? I'm all thumbs when it comes to dressing myself, as you well know."

One look at her creamy white back was enough to divert him. "Then next time," he said, brushing his lips against the nape of her neck as his fingers worked to unhook her instead, "we shall ask your maid to join us."

"Nicholas!" Pamela cried in mock indignation. "What an improper suggestion!"

He grinned as he unfastened the last hook. "Haven't I always taught you that variety is the spice of life, my wanton Pamela?"

"You handsome, incorrigible, irresistible rogue."

"I'll take that as a compliment."

His work done, Nicholas turned his mistress to face

him. As always, Pamela's perfect beauty took his breath away and caused his heart to hammer violently against his ribs. Even after making love to her all night, he could still take her again.

Now, as Nicholas cupped her heart-shaped face between his palms, savoring the smooth, silken feel of her skin as he stroked her cheeks with his thumbs, Pamela was regarding him hungrily out of half-closed eyes, her pink lips slightly parted and waiting for his kiss.

Instead, he let his fingertips trail lightly down the long column of her neck and across her collarbone.

Pamela closed her eyes and sighed raggedly in surrender. "Oh, Nicholas . . ."

Then he slipped his hands beneath the fabric of her gown and pushed. The bodice fell away, baring Pamela's high white breasts, the erect nipples like twin rosy pearls ready for his touch. Nicholas felt the familiar, immediate tightening in his loins even before he reached out to fondle one warm, heavy breast possessively, testing its weight as it filled his hand.

Pamela groaned softly and swayed toward him. "Please, Nicholas . . ."

He only released her so he could tug at her gown and strip her completely. Pamela's eyes flew open in surprise and she quickly looked around at the fields beyond, but made no attempt to conceal her unabashed nakedness.

She shivered. "Nicholas, someone will see us."

"You sound almost hopeful, my lady of the perfect ivory body."

Nicholas swung her effortlessly into his arms and dropped a fierce, proprietary kiss on her rosy, pouting mouth, causing her to whimper in anticipation. But as he carried Pamela back to the privacy of the summerhouse to resume their dalliance, he couldn't resist glancing across the fields one last time. To his keen disappointment, Aurora Falconet and her headstrong stallion had vanished from sight.

He kicked open the door with a bang and carried Pamela inside. Soon Aurora Falconet was forgotten.

*   *   *

When Aurora reached the top of the rise, she halted Firelight and looked back. Although too far away to see the two figures very clearly, she was close enough to discern the man undressing his companion and carrying her back toward the Chinese summerhouse.

"Well, Firelight," she muttered, patting the animal's smooth neck, "we certainly know what those two are about, don't we?"

The horse nodded his head and pawed the earth, uprooting clumps of grass and sending them flying through the air.

"We happened upon a lovers' tryst." Aurora stared at the grove for a moment, then shrugged and touched her heel to Firelight's side. "None of our affair."

Her lithe body easily synchronized itself with her horse's smooth, rocking canter and she rode off in the direction that would lead her to Overton Manor. Try as she might, Aurora couldn't get the stranger out of her mind. She hadn't expected to meet anyone abroad this early in the morning, save for farmers working their fields, so she was startled to come upon a half-dressed man brazenly watching her as he stood in the middle of a clearing.

She guessed him to be old—perhaps all of thirty—but his body had intrigued her, for the stranger was tall, broad-shouldered, and slender, his naked torso as sleek and well-muscled as Firelight. And he was scarred.

Aurora's curiosity was aroused as she recalled the long smooth scar on his left breast, just above his heart. Perhaps he had been just a split second too slow to evade the sharp point of an opponent's slashing sword. And what of the livid ridged scar plowing through the pale flesh of his narrow waist, just above his right hipbone? That could have been made only by a ball fired from a pistol. The fresh red scratches she had noticed on his back, however, were doubtless from a battle of quite a different kind.

He was obviously a man who was not afraid to fight; she had to say that for him.

As her horse's breakneck speed whipped the wind into her eyes, Aurora tried to put the stranger out of

her mind. To her chagrin, his strong, distinct features
lingered in her memory, as tormenting as a burr under
the saddle. Unlike most men, he did not wear a wig or
powder his black hair, and like his scars, a broken
nose that veered off at the tip was also a testament to
battles won or lost.

But it was the stranger's eyes that had made Aurora
shiver with uneasiness. They were a haunting shade of
gray, cold as rapier steel and just as merciless in their
thorough scrutiny of her.

"Now, there is a man who is full of his own importance, Firelight," she declared as she slowed her horse
to a sedate walk. "He acts just like God, and the
world be damned. I may be a better judge of horseflesh than I am of people, but I don't like him, and I
hope we never meet again. And as for his companion
. . ." Aurora snickered unkindly. "She was very beautiful, Firelight, but obviously a woman of the basest
character and reputation. She's probably his doxy."

The moment the words slipped out of her mouth,
Aurora was overcome by shame. She knew she shouldn't
be so quick to judge and condemn the blond woman
without knowing her, for wasn't her own sister living
with a man not her husband?

"But it's not the same," Aurora assured Firelight,
who cocked one ear back to listen. "Diana's been
Overton's mistress for so long, I am sure they are
married in the eyes of God if not in the laws of man."

Suddenly Aurora topped the crest of another hill,
and sure enough, there, as the stranger had promised,
was Overton Manor nestled in a valley. Impatient to
be back in his stall with a breakfast of hot mash
awaiting him, Firelight surged forward, but Aurora
held him back, for she didn't want to return just yet.
She needed some time to be alone, to come to terms
with her new home.

If it hadn't been for her father, Aurora would still
be living at Falconstown, her beloved home in Ireland.

She squeezed her eyes shut to fight back tears that
still welled up too easily. She could remember too clearly
that black, sorrowful night a little over two months
ago when her father had come staggering into the

main hall, his mouth slack and his glazed eyes enormous as he kept muttering, "Lost it all. Everything. Gone," over and over in a bizarre litany of despair.

When Aurora tried to help him, he looked right through her, shoved her away, and lurched up the stairs to his room. Once inside, he bolted the door from the inside and wouldn't open it. Tearful and panic-stricken, Aurora sobbed and pleaded with him, pounding on the door until her fists were red and bleeding.

How could she ever forget the sight that greeted her eyes when several footmen later broke down the door? There was her beloved father swinging from a rope, his face mercifully averted, the flickering candlelight causing his elongated shadow to jump and dance grotesquely on the opposite wall.

They carried her out bodily, kicking and screaming, before she could see her father's face. All she saw was the note he had scrawled just before he stood on a chair and stepped off into oblivion. All it said was, "I'm sorry for failing my beautiful Aurora, and hope she will one day find it in her heart to forgive me."

Aurora didn't learn just how miserably her father had failed her until a week after his funeral, when one of their neighbors, Lord Fitzhugh, came to call and she received him in the drawing room. In a chilling, gloating voice he informed her that her father had been gambling heavily with some cronies the evening of his death, and he had lost virtually everything he owned to Lord Fitzhugh.

Although still numb with grief and shocked by this latest disclosure, Aurora did not dishonor herself by throwing herself on Lord Fitzhugh's mercy and begging him to cancel the debts. She gathered all the dignity and self-possession she could muster, faced him squarely, and told him that she would leave Falconstown as soon as she could find another place to live.

And then Lord Fitzhugh boldly tendered a proposition that would allow Aurora to remain in the home she loved. But at a price. All she had to do was agree to marry him.

To her credit, she resisted the impulse to laugh at the bowlegged little man and instead gravely informed him that she would consider his proposal. And she did. She thought of the thirty years' difference in their ages, and the three wives he had already buried. She thought of his watery, protruding eyes, his razor-sharp nose, and his rotting brown teeth that befouled his every breath. She thought of enduring his intimacies in the marriage bed.

Aurora politely refused Lord Fitzhugh the next day. Then she wrote to her estranged sister, informed her of their father's death, and begged her for sanctuary.

Two weeks later, the sister she hadn't seen for seven years, since 1743, came to Falconstown herself to take Aurora back to England and Overton Manor.

Now, as she surveyed the large Elizabethan manor house of warm red brick surrounded by verdant lawns and carefully laid out gardens, Aurora sighed in contentment, sure that she had made the right choice. Both Diana and Overton had made her feel so welcome, and within a week Aurora felt as though she had been living there all her life. Ireland and her father's death belonged to the past.

Beneath her, Firelight began to prance and snort impatiently.

"All right, all right," Aurora murmured.

She gave the red-gold stallion his head, and together they raced like the wind for home.

When Aurora finally finished scrubbing the pungent odor of horse from her body, she stepped shivering out of her bath and dried herself with a soft lavender-scented towel. Then she slipped on her gold silk wrapping gown, shook out her damp unruly hair, and summoned her maid to dress her. Aurora resented the heavy linen corset, but she allowed herself to be laced in; then she stepped into an underskirt and stood still while the maid pulled a pretty gown of green flowered lawn down over her head.

No sooner did the maid finish dressing her hair than there came a knock at the door, and Diana came sweeping into the room.

Aurora regarded her beautiful older sister in frank admiration and just a touch of envy. Diana was tall and graceful, with a smooth ivory complexion unblemished by freckles and soft light brown hair that did what it was told. With her thin nose, rosebud mouth, and eyes the compelling blue of sapphires, Diana was the uncontested beauty of the family.

She nodded briefly at the maid and smiled warmly at her sister. "Good morning, Aurora. Have you had breakfast yet?"

Aurora rose from her dressing table to kiss her sister on the cheek. "Good morning, Diana. No, I haven't."

"Well, neither have I, so why don't we share a cup of cocoa, shall we? Sarah, will you go down to the kitchen and have cook make us some cocoa and toast?"

After the maid left, Diana said, "My, aren't you one for rising with the lark!" She delicately stifled a yawn with the back of her hand. "I must confess I am a lazy creature and seldom rise before ten myself."

Aurora stared at her sister in puzzlement. Diana looked anything but lazy, her eyes bright and alert, her expression lively.

"I usually rise at dawn to go riding," Aurora explained.

"Is that where you were this morning, out riding?"

"Yes. I rode Firelight."

"Oh," was all Diana said in a quelling tone. "And did you have Halley's permission to do so?"

Aurora swallowed hard, shook her head, and hung it in shame.

Diana made an exasperated noise and shook her head. Then she grasped her sister's hands and held them tightly. "Aurora, look at me."

Aurora opened her eyes to find Diana regarding her gravely.

"You should have asked Halley's permission before you rode that horse," Diana said. "The animal is dangerous. You could have been seriously injured or even killed."

"But, Diana," she protested, "you know there isn't a horse alive that I can't ride."

. Diana smiled at some cherished long-ago memory. "I remember. Tim and I used to call you our Gypsy changeling because of the mysterious power you had over animals. All you had to do was whisper in their ears and they did whatever you asked."

Aurora's eyes shone with pride. "And I haven't lost that power. Firelight was as docile as a baby. He—"

"It makes no difference whatsoever." Diana became stern again. "You shouldn't have ridden the horse without Halley's permission. He was furious when he saw you come cantering across the lawn this morning."

Privately Diana thought that Halley was not upset with Aurora for having ridden the animal, only that she had done so without his permission. She had flouted his supreme authority, and as Diana well knew, no one dared do that to Lord Overton.

"I . . . I'm sorry," Aurora said. "I won't let it happen again."

"See that you don't." Diana dropped her sister's hands and walked over to the chair where Aurora's breeches and shirt lay neatly folded. She wrinkled her nose contemptuously. "And I would suggest you put these away while you're living here at Overton Manor. Halley was scandalized when he saw you in these, and I can't say that I blame him."

Rebellion flared deep in Aurora's breast like a sudden flame. "But, Diana, Father always let me dress as a man when I went riding."

"Father was far too lenient with you. If our mother had still been alive when you moved to Ireland, I'm sure you would have had a proper upbringing like a proper gentlewoman. You're a young lady of seventeen, Aurora, and you should act like one."

Aurora bristled at any implied criticism of her father, and her eyes flashed dangerously. "I won't hear a word spoken against him, Diana."

Diana sighed and wished she hadn't spoken so hastily, for she knew how much Aurora revered their father and always sprang to his defense. Diana had no wish to disillusion her, but their father was far from the saint Aurora thought him to be. It was too soon after Josiah Falconet's death to enlighten Aurora about a few matters, so Diana wisely held her tongue.

Instead, she extended her hand toward the silk striped settee. "Please sit down, Aurora. I must explain something to you."

No sooner did they sit down than they were interrupted by the maid bearing a huge silver tray with a pot of steaming hot chocolate, delicate porcelain cups, and a rack of toast. After setting down the tray, she bobbed a curtsy and left the two sisters alone once again. Once the chocolate was poured, Diana resumed speaking.

"If I were Halley's wife," she began, "I wouldn't care if you went riding dressed as a . . . a nun." When Aurora finished stifling a giggle, Diana went on with, "But I am not his wife, I am his mistress. Halley can send me packing if I displease him. I am certain that he never will," she added hastily, seeing her sister's shocked expression, "but I must be realistic. There is always that possibility."

Diana set down her cup and toyed with the blond lace trimming her blue silk gown. "I am begging you not to spoil my situation by your unconventional behavior. Halley is the Viscount Overton, a gentleman and a peer of the realm. He has a position to uphold in society. As he warned me just this morning, he won't have you disgracing him by challenging one of his neighbors to a duel."

Aurora thought everyone was making much too much of her morning ride, but she held her tongue for she knew she owed her sister and Viscount Overton a great deal. If they hadn't agreed to take her in, she would have had to marry the odious Lord Fitzhugh or find herself a protector.

Diana said, "I'm giving you fair warning, Aurora. If you disgrace Overton in any way, he will withdraw his generous offer and send you away. Then where would you go? What would you do?"

"I'm sorry I upset everyone, Diana," she said, bowing her head contritely. "I don't want you to think I'm ungrateful. I promise not to disgrace you or Overton ever again."

Diana gave an inaudible sigh of relief. "I knew you would be sensible, Aurora."

Aurora fell silent as she ate her toast and drank her chocolate, but her thoughts were on Diana, the sister who had been a stranger to her for so long. Aurora had been only ten years old when Diana suddenly disappeared from her life, remaining in England while Aurora and their father went off to live on the Irish estate. Aurora missed her older sister so much she often cried herself to sleep night after night. But when she begged her father to bring Diana to her, he would glower and mutter, "Diana has brought scandal and shame to the Falconet family, and you'll never see her again as long as I'm alive."

Aurora was fourteen years old when she finally understood the reason for her father's callous attitude. One of her many governesses, a slattern more fond of the bottle than of her charge, informed her that her beloved Diana was no better than a whore, living with a man without benefit of matrimony. She had disgraced her family and her good name; that's why her father wanted nothing to do with her.

But after her father's death, a panic-stricken Aurora could think of no one else to turn to, and Diana did not disappoint her. She welcomed Aurora with a loving and open heart.

After finishing her second slice of toast, Aurora brushed the crumbs from her fingertips and said, "I think Father was wrong about you and Overton, Diana. Since I've been here, I've seen how much you really love him."

"You don't know how much it means to me to hear you say that, Aurora." Diana's voice shook slightly and her eyes were bright with unshed tears. "You'll never know how hurt I was when Father disowned me. But he just refused to understand how much I loved Halley and needed to be with him, no matter what the cost."

Privately Aurora wondered what her sister saw in Lord Overton to inspire such steadfast devotion, but she wisely held her tongue. Instead, she told Diana about the man she had seen on her ride that morning and asked her if she knew him.

Diana nodded. "The man you describe could only be Nicholas Devenish, the Marquess of Silverblade. He owns the neighboring estate that bears his name." She paused, then added, "Tell me, what did you think of him?"

Aurora frowned in distaste. "He struck me as arrogant and cold, ordering me about as though he were my master. I didn't like him at all."

Diana chuckled at that. "You must be the only woman in England, then. Most of the unmarried women I know would sell their souls to become his marchioness, and those that are already married would gladly leave their husbands for a liaison with him."

Aurora regarded her sister curiously. "Well, if you find him so attractive, Diana, why haven't you set your cap for him yourself?" The minute the words were out of her mouth, Aurora realized she had spoken without thinking once again.

But Diana didn't take offense by inferring that Aurora found Halley lacking in some way. "I love Halley," she explained simply. "Besides, I am far below Nicholas Devenish's touch. All of his women have been extraordinary in some way, either extremely beautiful or formidably intelligent, and often both. I am neither, I'm afraid."

"That's not true, Diana!"

Her sister smiled over the brim of her cup. "I do appreciate your loyalty." She sipped her chocolate. "I have always liked Nicholas. He has a special gift for making any woman feel beautiful and desirable, even if she is as plain as a pikestaff or past her prime. But I must warn you, Aurora, he runs with a fast set and does have quite an unsavory reputation as a rake. I would not be alone with him, if I were you."

Aurora thought of his lovely blond companion and said, "Oh, I have no intention of ever being alone with Lord Silverblade. You can be sure of that."

"Splendid," Diana said, finished her cocoa, and took her leave.

Once she was alone again, Aurora went to the carved

oak chest at the foot of her bed, lifted the lid, and took out her father's sword. After sliding it from its scabbard, she held it in her hand, savoring its perfect balance and the way the steel blade captured the light and gleamed.

"I shall hate to give you up, old friend," she murmured. Aurora reluctantly slipped it back into the scabbard, then put it away.

Next she lifted out a shallow mahogany case. Inside, fitted into a bed of green baize, was a pair of flintlock pistols that had belonged to her father. They belonged to her now. She ran her fingers reverentially over the exquisite silver-wire inlays and the silver butt cap carved in the shape of a Gorgon's head.

She understood why her father had chosen to hang himself rather than shoot himself with one of his pistols. He believed these weapons should be used for honorable purposes only, and not be dishonored by taking their owner's life.

Aurora closed the box and hugged it to her chest for one brief moment. "I promise to use them only in honor, Father. I promise."

But use them she would, no matter what Diana or Halley said.

2

LADY Vivien Devenish, the dowager Marchioness of Silverblade, sat in her cozy drawing room and waited for callers who never came. These days, her only companions were the three ancient spaniels snoring loudly at her feet, the young West Indian page seated on a stool and playing with his pet monkey, and the six chirping canaries in a big brass birdcage.

She sighed as she shifted her brittle old bones into a more comfortable position on the settee.

"It's terrible to be so old, Juma," she muttered to the page in a querulous, scratchy voice that sounded like the rustling of dried leaves in an autumn wind. "No one comes to call anymore. No one listens to the wisdom of the old. They just shut us away and forget us."

Juma, dressed in sumptuous gold and silver brocades and a turban like some miniature Oriental pasha, regarded his mistress out of black eyes too wise for their years. "It is their loss, milady."

Lady Vivien chuckled at that and patted his shoulder with a withered, spotted hand. "I may be old, my boy, but I am not witless. I can still tell the difference between truth and flattery."

The page grinned back. They understood each other so well, the old lady and her young servant.

Still, she had much to be thankful for. At least her hair was still her own, albeit pure white, and so were her teeth, though stained yellow with age. And she could walk unaided without stumbling and shuffling about.

Suddenly, to her surprise, there came a loud knock on the drawing-room door. Immediately the brown-and-white spaniels awoke with a start. They rose in unison and went tottering and grunting across the room.

"Juma, see who it is." Lady Vivien adjusted her wool shawl about her shoulders and sat up straight.

When the page opened the door, he bowed toward the marchioness and said, "Mr. Wesley Devenish, milady."

Lady Vivien, whose faded gray eyes were just as sharp as her mind, despite her seventy years, beamed at her favorite grandson. "Why, Wesley, my dear boy. How good of you to call on your poor old grandmother."

Wesley stood in the doorway for a moment, giving the dogs a chance to sniff at his buckled shoes. When they lumbered back to their places at their mistress's feet, he followed them.

As her grandson walked toward her, Lady Vivien wished for the thousandth time that Wesley were as well-favored as his cousin Nicholas. But he wasn't. Where Nicholas was tall with a lithe, perfectly proportioned body, Wesley was tall with a boxy torso set on spindly legs. His eyes were small and feral, a large red-veined nose dominated his face, and his lips were just a bit too fleshy to be attractive.

It just wasn't fair, she thought. Nicholas was the one everyone sought out and remembered. He was the handsome one, the accomplished one, and Wesley was his pallid shadow, always unnoticed in a crowd and quickly forgotten.

Yet it was Nicholas who had turned his own grandmother out of her home, while considerate, faithful Wesley never failed to court her and pay the respect that was her due.

"Good afternoon, Grandmother," Wesley said in his soft, slow voice, precisely enunciating every word. "And how have you been keeping?"

"You know full well I haven't been myself ever since Nicholas exiled me to the dower house," she

grumbled as Wesley seated himself across from her.
"If I didn't have my Juma and my animals, I would
surely expire from loneliness. I ask you . . . what have
I done to deserve such shabby treatment at the hands
of my own grandson?"

Before Wesley could comment, she answered her
own question. "I know why. He wants to play his
lascivious games in private, that's the reason he sent
me packing."

With an irritated wave of her beringed hand, Lady
Vivien dismissed Juma, for she never discussed family
in front of the servants, no matter how fond she was of
them. There were one or two things she had to say
about Nicholas that were for Wesley's ears alone.

"The goings-on at Silverblade are simply scandalous, Wesley, simply scandalous, an affront to God and
man. Cavorting in that garden in broad daylight . . .
sleeping with a different woman every night. Nicholas
and his friends rival the monks of Medmanham in
their debaucheries." The old lady shook her snowy
head in disgust. "Nicholas' father—God rest his soul—
must be turning over in his grave."

Wesley's small gray eyes widened as much as they
dared. "I know Cousin Nick is known in certain circles
as a rake, Grandmother, but surely you can't believe—"

"But it's true, Wesley," the marchioness insisted. "I
have my spies back at Silverblade and they are very
well informed. Why, do you know he is entertaining
two actresses there this week? Actresses!" she scoffed.
"Everyone knows they are nothing more than whores."

Wesley sighed. "I had hoped to spare you, Grandmother."

"I know you are a good, kind man who is reluctant
to believe the worst of anyone," she said, "but I am
telling you the truth."

"I know you are. Regrettably, I hear much of the
same in London."

Her jaw worked in anger and her eyes narrowed,
adding new lines to her well-wrinkled face. "Something must be done, and soon, before the Silverblade
name is tarnished irreparably."

"And what do you propose to do, Grandmother?"

"Nicholas must marry," she replied emphatically. "With a suitable young woman of quality installed at Silverblade, there won't be any question of his entertaining such people. If he wants a doxy, he shall have to keep her discreetly in London, just like everyone else."

"I must warn you that you may be facing an impossible task."

"Why is that?"

Wesley rubbed the side of his nose with his forefinger, a gesture that had always annoyed Lady Vivien. "I'm not sure any gentleman of quality will want his daughter wed to the notorious Lord Silverblade."

"Someone will," she declared vehemently, "if only for his title and fortune. Nicholas needs a wife to provide an heir for Silverblade, otherwise you will inherit it all."

Much to Lady Vivien's surprise, Wesley shot her a venomous glance just before jumping to his feet and striding across the room, startling the canaries as he passed. He stopped before one of the tall windows facing the garden and waited until the birds' frenzied chirping died before he spoke.

"And would it be so objectionable if I did inherit Silverblade?"

Lady Vivien turned in her seat and stared at her grandson's rigid back for a long, silent minute. This was the first time Wesley had ever mentioned the possibility of wanting to inherit Silverblade. She had always assumed he wasn't interested.

Now he whirled around, his face still bearing vestiges of anger. "And why shouldn't I inherit Silverblade if my cousin should have no heir? I am just as much a Devenish as he is. And if my father had been born first, I would now be the Marquess of Silverblade, not Nick."

"I am not questioning your claim, Wesley," Lady Vivien said soothingly. "I was merely stating a fact."

That seemed to placate him, for he returned to his seat, patting her shoulder as he passed. "Do forgive me for my outburst, Grandmother. But I do resent it when people forget that I am just as much a Devenish as Cousin Nick." He sat back and smiled. "Now, tell me. How do you propose to find my cousin a wife?"

Relieved that Wes' anger had passed, Lady Vivien leaned forward. "I may be an old woman, Wesley, but I am not without influence. Although it is true that I may seem to have been forgotten as I rusticate in the Surrey countryside, I do have many friends in positions of power. And these friends have eligible granddaughters."

"And you hope to find Nicholas' wife among them?"

"I do."

Wesley smiled and shook his head. "You are truly formidable, grandmother, truly formidable."

"Your cousin hasn't yet discovered how truly formidable I can be."

At that very moment, the object of such plans was sitting in Silverblade's salon, waiting for his guests to come down. He was thinking of Aurora Falconet.

Nicholas could still see her in his mind's eye, galloping that huge, mettlesome stallion across the open fields, riding like no other woman he had ever known, a huntress utterly fearless and unconcerned for her own safety. She was either very brave or very foolish, and being Tim Falconet's sister, Nicholas suspected it was the former.

Stretching his long legs out before him, he stared up at several of the new paintings he had bought in Italy last year, and thought of Tim with a keen pang of regret and loss.

Tim had been a good friend and companion, always ready to be a part of any prank Nicholas could suggest, and quick to suggest a few of his own, no matter how outrageous or dangerous, no matter what the consequences. Now he wished Tim hadn't been so quick to suggest they impersonate highwaymen, for on that particular night, the consequences were very high indeed.

Nicholas found himself wondering if Aurora Falconet knew he had been with her brother the night he was shot. Surely her father had told her by now. Nicholas smiled ruefully to himself. Old Josiah Falconet had been all too ready to blame him for his only son's untimely death. What did it matter that one more person in the world thought ill of him? It was a rake's lot, after all, to be misunderstood and despised.

Suddenly his reverie was interrupted by light, quick footsteps, and he rose languidly to his feet just as Pamela came floating into the room. Her delicate ivory-and-gold beauty made Aurora Falconet's wild autumnal coloring seem startling and even garish by comparison. Surely Aurora's straight, boyish body couldn't bestow pleasure the way Pamela's lush, softly curved figure did.

The wanton of the summerhouse had been replaced by the demure gentlewoman. Pamela's glossy golden hair was now free of twigs and bits of leaves, brushed smooth off her brow, and nearly hidden beneath a prim mobcap with kissing strings untied so invitingly. Her pink dress of flowered dimity had a square bodice cut just low enough across her full breasts to entice without being immodest. She looked radiant and so desirable.

Pamela stifled a dainty yawn with her fingertips. "Good gracious, Nicholas, what time is it?"

"Nearly two in the afternoon, my dear," he replied, capturing her free hand and drawing it to his lips.

Pamela beamed up at him. "Surely you can't blame me for being exhausted, when you are responsible for keeping me up all night?"

"And I fully intend to do so again."

He caught at the kissing strings, using them to hold Pamela's head still so he could touch her mouth with his own in a brief, possessive kiss.

Pamela groaned and leaned toward him, ever greedy for his exciting touch, but Nicholas set her away with a light, teasing laugh. "I hear footsteps approaching. I think the rest of our party is up and about at long last."

Pamela pouted, then stepped back just as four chattering, exquisitely dressed young gentlemen, each with a woman on his arm, came filing into the salon.

"Good morning, one and all," Nicholas greeted them when they were all assembled, "or should I say, good

afternoon?" When the chuckling died down, he raised
an eyebrow at them and said, "I trust you all . . . slept
well?"

Enthusiastic nods and a ripple of ribald laughter
told him that they had.

Suddenly portly Lord Blackburn Oliver stepped forward, his dark eyes sparkling mischievously. "Umm,
Silverblade, may I have your kind permission to address our gathering on a subject of extreme importance?"

Nicholas bowed his head. "Why, of course, Ollie."

Everyone fell silent.

Ollie's round red cheeks were more flushed than
usual. "Umm, I have a special diversion planned for
this evening, but it requires the cooperation and approval of the ladies present."

Bess, the buxom black-haired actress who was his
mistress, scoffed. "The last time you planned a diversion, Ollie, you wanted us to ride through the village
dressed as Lady Godiva!"

As everyone chuckled, Ollie gave her a look of
chagrin. "My dear Bess, my new conception has nothing to do with that at all." He reached into his waistcoat pocket and drew out a pendant, a small, highly
polished golden apple swinging from a heavy gold
chain.

All of the women present suddenly surged forward
and crowded around, eager to examine the beautiful
bauble.

"I propose a Pageant of Venus," Ollie announced.
"Whichever of you fair ladies is judged as being the
most beautiful will be presented with this golden apple, just as Helen of Troy was given a golden apple by
Paris."

Suddenly Lord Effingham, who would wager on the
outcome of any contest, said, "Let's make this wager
interesting, shall we not? I propose each gentleman
wagers at least a hundred pounds on his lady."

Felicity, another actress and the current inamorata
of Lord Cox, said, "Who is to be the judge? Won't
every gentleman here cast his vote for his own ladylove?"

"If he knows what's good for him, he will!" Cox
piped up with a ribald wink at Felicity.

Ollie looked quite flustered and reached up to scratch beneath his periwig. "Ummm, I hadn't thought of that." Then he turned to Nicholas in appeal. "You're our host, Silverblade, and a renowned connoisseur of feminine beauty. You be the judge."

As assent rippled around the room, Nicholas rose and held up his hands in protest. "It is precisely because I am your host that I must refuse. No, we need an impartial judge, or perhaps several."

When no one came forth to volunteer, it looked as though Ollie's Pageant of Venus was doomed. Grumbling to himself, he crossed the room to stand before one of the salon's tall windows. Suddenly something outside caused his florid face to light up, and he turned back to the assembled guests with an exultant grin.

"Look who is coming up the drive, Old Immortality himself. Why don't we ask him to be our judge?"

Pamela let out a tinkling peal of laughter as she rushed over to Ollie's side. "Old Immortality? Why, it's common knowledge he's never displayed an interest in women. How do you expect him to be any judge of feminine beauty?"

Everyone laughed, until Lord Haze, the youngest and newest member of Silverblade's fast set, asked, "Who in the world is Old Immortality?"

Nicholas looked out the window and saw a familiar figure astride a docile hack come trotting down the circular drive. "Old Immortality is the name we have given my cousin, Wesley Devenish," he explained. "Wesley, you see, fears death."

Lord Haze looked puzzled. "But we all fear death."

A faint smile touched Nicholas' mouth. "True, but Wesley goes to extremes to ensure that he will live forever, hence the name. He never attends funerals or hangings. In fact, several years ago, he ran off to the Continent on some pretext or other just so he wouldn't have to attend his own father's funeral. The mere sight of a hearse or a graveyard is enough to instill terror into him, and he is scrupulous about never offending anyone because he's afraid of being challenged to a duel."

"And," Ollie added, "he never wears black like

most members of the merchant class because it's the
color of mourning."

"Why is he so afraid of death?" Bess wanted to
know.

Nicholas replied, "When he was just a boy, some
village children locked him in the church crypt. By the
time they told anyone what they had done, several
days had passed. Wesley almost starved to death and
nearly went mad from sheer terror, and ever since
then . . ." Nicholas shrugged expressively.

"How horrible!" Bess exclaimed.

Ollie exchanged a conspiratorial look with Silverblade.
"Tell them about the night we invited Old Immortality
to his own funeral."

"I'd rather not, Ollie." Nicholas' gray eyes darkened with reproach. "You'll shock my guests, and
they shall think me a coldhearted blackguard."

It had been one of the cruelest pranks Nicholas had
ever played as a hot-blooded young buck of twenty,
and he was reluctant to recount it to his guests, for it
was not something he was especially proud of. Over
the years, he had tried to forget it.

But Ollie, not known for his tact, said, "If you
won't, then I will. We're all friends here, and I know
what I'm about to say won't go beyond this room."

Nicholas knew it was pointless to argue, so he said
nothing as his friend addressed the rapt assembly.

"One night," Ollie began, "Nick and some friends
decided to have some sport with Cousin Wesley. Six of
us dressed in black monks' cowls and carried an empty
coffin to his London house. We surprised him in bed,
tied him hand and foot and gagged him, then put him
in the coffin.

"You should have seen his face!" Ollie exclaimed,
laughing so hard that his shoulders shook and tears
formed in his eyes. "Then we carried the coffin down
to his drawing room and held a mock funeral service
for him."

When Nicholas thought of his poor cousin's muffled
screams, his bulging eyes mirroring stark, mindless
terror, he was overcome by shame at his own callous
behavior.

"You were just having a bit of sport," Lord Haze said, rising to his friend's defense.

"Nothing wrong with that," Lord Cox added sympathetically. "We've all gone on a lark or two ourselves and done things we've later regretted."

Bess, however, was appalled. "If someone played such a prank on me, I should be hard-pressed ever to forgive him."

Nicholas smiled over at her. "Even though I don't deserve it, my cousin is a most forgiving man. After I apologized, the incident was forgotten. We are on the best of terms today."

He looked up and through the open salon door to see Wesley bobbing down the hall in his short, mincing stride. "Here he comes now. You can see for yourself."

Wesley entered the salon with a bow and a soft, "Good afternoon, everyone."

Nicholas greeted him with his most charming smile. "Wesley, how good of you to call."

"I just stopped by to call upon our grandmother, and thought I would pay my respects to you and Aunt Mary before I return to London." He was forever glancing about as if he feared something were chasing him.

"Mother always enjoys your company," Nicholas said. Then he added, "You know everyone here, I trust?"

"Of course," Wesley said smoothly, glancing around the assembled company.

Ollie came forward. "Umm, Devenish, we have a favor to ask of you."

"I am yours to command," Wesley said graciously.

When Ollie finished reciting what that favor would be, Wesley quickly agreed to judge the Pageant of Venus.

"Good fellow," Ollie said, beaming.

"But on one condition," Wesley added.

"What is that?" Ollie asked suspiciously.

"That the losers' consorts do not challenge me to a duel."

Good-natured laughter followed as all the men present agreed to his terms.

Then Nicholas drew his cousin into the group, offered him some refreshment, and soon the guests excused themselves and began drifting off. Some left to avail themselves of their host's well-stocked stables, while others strolled around the grounds or read the latest periodicals in the huge library.

Finally, when only the two cousins were left, Nicholas said to Wesley, "Come. Perhaps Mother is out in her cutting garden today. I know she always looks forward to your visits."

The cutting garden was situated behind the main house and perfumed the summer air with the sweet scents of long-stemmed flowers. But Lady Mary Devenish was nowhere to be found.

Nicholas frowned and made a soft sound of consternation. "All of my guests must have frightened Mother off today. She does so hate guests."

Wesley smiled and said, "Well, what are you supposed to do, deprive yourself of such pleasant company just because your mother chooses to be a recluse?"

A look of pain flitted across Nicholas' features as he thought of his mother, who left her own apartments only once a day, to come down to the cutting garden. But he had been only a child of ten when tragedy devastated her and she withdrew from life.

Nicholas smiled wanly. "I had been hoping that by having guests at Silverblade, Mother could be persuaded to come out of her self-imposed exile, but it hasn't succeeded. If anything, she's more reclusive than ever, except with certain family members."

"Perhaps if you invited Grandmother back to Silverblade, she could help Aunt Mary."

Nicholas thought of his elderly grandmother, a disagreeable woman who alternated between being a whining, petulant child and a sharp-tongued termagant. She had been the bane of his existence until, taxed to the limits of his patience, he had exiled her to the dower house at the other side of the park. How peaceful Silverblade had been for the past year without the old lady's caustic reproaches and constant meddling.

Nicholas shook his head, his mouth tightening in a determined line. "That is not the solution to this par-

ticular problem, cousin. You know full well that Grandmother and I cannot tolerate each other, let alone live
under the same roof. She would be trying to run my
life as well as the lives of everyone else who lives at
Silverblade. All she does is upset Mother unnecessarily."

He shook his head. "No, Wesley, I have done my
duty to our grandmother. The dower house is comfortable, and she has her own staff of servants, as well as a
liberal allowance of pocket money. She has her animals and her page for company, and I see to it that
she wants for nothing. All I ask is that she leave me in
peace."

"Oh, I'm not suggesting that you have neglected
Grandmother in any way," Wesley said hastily, ever
eager to placate when he thought he had given offense. "You have been most generous to her. It's just
that whenever I go to call upon her, she begs me to
intercede for her. She complains that she is lonely and
that no one listens to her anymore."

"And whose fault is that? She makes everyone's life
a living hell with her adder's tongue," Nicholas said.
"She's always made it quite clear that she thinks me
nothing more than a libertine, and she always insults
my guests."

Wesley sighed. "She just feels it's time you married
and settled down."

"To a suitable woman of her choosing, no doubt,"
Nicholas muttered bitterly.

Suddenly tiring of discussing their grandmother, he
abruptly changed the subject. "And how is the mer-
cantile trade these days?"

Wesley lifted one thin shoulder in an offhand shrug.
"It could be better. I just received word that I lost a
ship to a storm in the Indian Ocean, but three more
arrived safely with their cargoes." His smile was a
shade too bright and falsely optimistic. "I'm sure I'll
weather this storm as I have all the others."

"I'm sure you will, cousin," Nicholas agreed politely, but privately he wasn't so sure, for it was common knowledge that Wesley lacked his late father's
aptitude for trade and had made several disastrous
decisions concerning the running of his company.

Nicholas had always admired his uncle. When Nicholas' father became the Marquess of Silverblade, inheriting the great estate of Silverblade as well as the family fortune, his younger brother—Wesley's father—had scandalized the family by turning his back on his own class and becoming a merchant. To everyone's astonishment, he excelled at it, and the family was certain that his son would as well.

Oh, Wesley tried. But during the past five years since his father's death, the fortunes of the shipping company he had inherited had been fluctuating wildly. After several years of prosperity, matters were now steadily worsening, and Nicholas had heard rumors that his cousin might even be forced to sell his own small country house located not far from Silverblade if he were going to keep his ships afloat.

Nicholas looked back at his ancestral home with its many windows reflecting the afternoon sun like a row of diamonds, and he wondered how he would feel if his own father had been born the second son. Would he resent having to work for a living after growing up in a splendid manor house and wanting for nothing? Would he resent those relatives who had more than he? He wondered.

Suddenly a high-pitched giggle caught Nicholas' attention, and he realized they were approaching the entrance to the Garden of Eros, which was guarded by a life-size marble statue set on a high pedestal.

He grinned at Wesley. "I think the garden is occupied at the moment. Perhaps it would be best if we returned to the house and left my guests to their . . . diversions."

Wesley gave his cousin a conspiratorial smirk. "Yes, I think that would be most prudent." Then he looked up at the statue, which had been carved with a grotesque face and anatomical proportions no human male had ever possessed. He sighed regretfully. "Oh, to be so well-endowed."

The remark was so unlike Wesley that Nicholas was momentarily taken aback. Then he let out a whoop of ribald laughter. "That is my fervent wish as well."

The two cousins fell into companionable silence as

they cut short their stroll and started back toward the house.

The clock had just struck two in the morning when a weary, red-eyed Nicholas came staggering up the stairs to his own apartments on the second floor.

The moment he entered his bedchamber, called the Sabine Room because of the huge mural painted on the ceiling, the light from the single candle he carried flickered and danced, creating eerie shadows and making the figures come alive.

As Nicholas set his silver candlestick down and began undressing himself without the usual assistance of his valet, he fancied several of the Roman soldiers were leering down at him as they carried off their hapless Sabine conquests. He had slept and sported beneath the mural for so long, he fancied he knew each one of the conquerors personally. Nicholas chuckled at his own imagination, heightened by a decanter of claret and the late hour.

When he was down to his breeches, the heavy crimson damask drapes surrounding his huge four-poster bed suddenly parted, and a tousled fair head peeked out from between them.

"Nicholas, is that you?" a familiar voice called.

"Since I am the only man who sleeps in this particular chamber, I think it is safe to assume that it is I."

Pamela rewarded him with a drowsy smile. "I am relieved."

Nicholas grinned at her as he unbuttoned his breeches and let them fall to the floor. "You know that I am not accustomed to sharing what is mine."

Pamela eyed him appreciatively as she lay back to expose her waiting naked body. "I've been keeping the bed warm for you."

Nicholas crossed the room and slid in beside her. "My wanton Pamela . . . how very thoughtful of you."

As she curled her warm, pliant body against his, Pamela asked, "Were you successful at the tables tonight, my lord?"

"It was not one of my better nights," he admitted, breathing in the fresh, clean scent of her hair.

"At least Ollie's pageant was a great success."

Nicholas leaned back against the pillows. "Do you think so? I think his Bess was a little annoyed that she won't be wearing the golden apple."

Pamela shrugged one smooth bare shoulder, her breast brushing against her lover's chest provocatively. "All of the women who didn't win were disappointed, but I think the judging was fair."

"Oh, I quite agree. Very clever of Wes to choose neither my lover nor Ollie's for the honor. That's Wes, always careful never to offend. He would have made a brilliant politician."

"Well, it was only a harmless entertainment, after all. The women who lost didn't scratch each other's eyes out, and—"

Nicholas effectively silenced her with a kiss. "Enough chatter," he growled.

Then he closed the draperies to protect them from the harmful night air.

Later, after he rolled off Pamela with a contented sigh, an exhausted Nicholas parted the draperies, leaned back, and studied the mural out of sleepy, half-closed eyes. Suddenly the features of one of the soldiers blurred, and Nicholas found himself looking at a mirror image of himself. To his surprise, the struggling woman slung over his shoulder suspiciously resembled Aurora Falconet, her mouth open in a silent scream, her blue eyes filled with terror at the prospect of imminent ravishment.

Nicholas smiled at his own heightened imagination, closed his eyes, and slept.

3

THE following morning, Aurora dressed herself quickly and slipped out of the house unobserved, her father's pistols, powder flask, and shot concealed under the voluminous folds of her cloak. She repressed the urge to run, and instead forced herself to walk across the lawn sedately, so that if any servants happened to see her, they would think she was just out for a morning stroll, nothing more. But when she passed the stables without attracting the attention of the ostlers, and the house disappeared behind a grove of stately oaks, she could restrain herself no longer. Her heart hammering with anticipation, Aurora threw caution to the winds and started running down the narrow path, her cloak billowing out behind her.

When she finally reached her destination, a small field far from the house, she took off the cloak, spread it on the damp grass, then carefully set down her pistols and ammunition. She cautiously looked around to see if anyone had followed her. Satisfied that she was alone, Aurora knelt down and began to load one of the pistols with practiced ease.

"Let's see how well you do today," she murmured as she stroked the pistol butt lovingly and rose to find a suitable target.

She squinted in concentration as she looked around the field, and a towering old oak tree not thirty feet away caught her attention. One of its long, gnarled limbs was low to the ground, and several smaller branches were growing out of it.

"I think those will make worthy targets for you," she muttered affectionately to the pistol, for like her father, she tended to think of the weapons as endowed with human characteristics and foibles.

With the pistol primed and held at her side, Aurora concentrated on one of the slender branches as though she could will the ball to hit it. Then she planted her feet firmly on the ground and braced herself for the weapon's kick. When she was ready, she swung her arm up in a smooth arc until the pistol was at eye level; then she took careful aim and squeezed the trigger.

First came a puff of white smoke, followed a split second later by the main charge. The roar startled a flock of blackbirds roosting nearby, sending them fluttering high into the air, squawking in raucous alarm. The shot also momentarily deafened Aurora, leaving her ears ringing and filling her nostrils with the acrid scent of burning powder. When the smoke cleared and the ringing died away, she strode across the clearing to see if she had hit her target.

The branch had been shot clean off. Only a stump remained.

Aurora let out an unladylike whoop of elation, then turned and went back to fire another round from the first pistol's twin. So intent was she on the ritual of firing and reloading the pistols that she failed to hear the snapping of a dry twig and the rustling of underbrush in the woods behind her.

Lord Overton froze behind his concealing bush, waiting for Aurora to realize she was being watched, but she was too absorbed in her shooting to notice him. Perhaps it was just as well, for then she would have seen just how furious he was with her.

His handsome face contorted into a livid mask of rage as he watched her blithely defying him once again. Here she was, brazenly shooting like a man, where anyone might happen upon her and be scandalized. Overton's palm itched to take the rebellious child over his knee and spank her until she begged for mercy.

Suddenly the thought of touching Aurora so intimately, even to administer well-deserved punishment, cooled Overton's anger and unexpectedly aroused warmer thoughts of quite a different nature. He found himself studying Diana's sister as though really seeing her for the first time.

Overton's countenance was the picture of affability as he came out of hiding and strolled onto the field.

"A fine shot," he said.

The moment Aurora heard someone speak, she started like a guilty child caught stealing hot pies from the kitchen window ledge and whirled around to come face-to-face with the elegant personage of Lord Overton. She felt her cheeks turn hot with mortification, and she could not look him in the eye.

"L-Lord Overton . . ." she stammered, wishing the earth would split open beneath her feet and devour her. Then she swallowed hard and prepared herself to accept her inevitable punishment like a man.

However, the anticipated scolding never came.

Overton surprised her by smiling benignly. "I was just getting ready to try my hand at Firelight again when I heard the sounds of gunshots. I thought there might be poachers on my property, so I came to investigate. Imagine my surprise to find you here, Aurora, practicing your marksmanship."

She moistened her lips, which had suddenly gone quite dry from sheer terror. "I . . . I know I promised Diana that I would mend my hoydenish ways, Lord Overton, but—"

"Those pistols really are quite fine," he mused, ignoring her attempts at explanations as he extended his hand. "May I examine one more closely?"

"Of . . . of course." As she handed him the hot, smoking pistol, Aurora watched Overton's face for any sign of anger, but his features were a carefully composed mask and revealed nothing.

He was too handsome for Aurora's taste, with a profile a Greek god would envy and melting hazel eyes. He also seemed to care more for his extensive wardrobe than he did for Diana. Wherever a mirror could be found, there was Lord Overton smiling at his reflection as he inspected the cut and fit of his jacket.

Now he was testing the pistol's weight in his hand. Then he nodded in approval. "A fine pistol, fine indeed."

"They belonged to my father," Aurora replied. "I couldn't allow Lord Fitzhugh to take them along with everything else, so I brought them with me to England."

"I don't blame you. They are beautifully made. German, I would say. Was it your father who taught you how to shoot? I'm surprised you have enough strength to pull the trigger."

Aurora regarded him out of wary eyes, for she had expected anger from Overton, not uncharacteristic sympathy. But perhaps she had misjudged him, so she smiled brightly. "Yes, he did. He missed not having a son, you see."

Overton smiled, revealing a flash of strong white teeth. "And are you a good shot?"

"I am an excellent shot. Come with me, and I'll show you just how good I am."

When she showed Overton how well she had done, he nodded in approval. "You put most men I know to shame."

She blushed with pleasure at the compliment, for Lord Overton rarely praised anyone. Then suddenly she became somber. "I . . . I do apologize for being such a trial to you and Diana, Lord Overton. You have so kindly offered to take me in, and here I am repaying that kindness with willful disobedience. It won't happen again."

To her surprise, he patted her on the shoulder like a benevolent older brother. "I know you must think us ogres—"

"Oh no, not at all!" She was unaware that her face contradicted her.

"But your sister and I really have your best interests at heart, as I'm sure she has told you." Suddenly Overton's soft eyes sparkled mischievously. "However, I think we can reach a compromise."

"Compromise?"

"If you agree not to go riding about the countryside

dressed as a stableboy, you may continue to practice your markmanship—discreetly, of course."

Aurora just stared at Overton in dumbfounded silence, unable to believe he was willing to let her continue her shooting.

"Do you mean it, Lord Overton?" she asked in disbelief.

"On one condition."

Aurora's spirits sank until he grinned and added, "If you will stop calling me Lord Overton. My name is Halley."

Aurora felt her cheeks grow pink and she looked away shyly, for no gentleman had ever given her permission to use his Christian name before.

"Very well," she murmured.

When she looked up at Overton, Aurora thought she saw a look in his eyes that was anything but brotherly, for she was not as innocent as people supposed her to be. But the impression was so fleeting, she decided that she must have imagined it.

"Why don't you gather your pistols and powder and accompany me back to the house?" he said. "Breakfast is being served by now."

While Overton waited, Aurora set her things in the center of her cloak, then caught the ends together to form a bundle. She was intent on carrying it herself, but Overton took it from her, then extended his crooked arm to her with a brief nod.

They walked arm in arm back to the manor.

As Aurora and Overton approached the small summerhouse at the far end of the garden, a familiar figure seated inside rose and waved. Aurora smiled and waved back. Then Diana gathered the full skirts of her yellow dimity gown, swept down the steps, and glided toward them.

"Good morning," Aurora said when her sister drew closer.

Diana did not acknowledge the greeting immediately. Her gaze darted from Aurora to Overton and back to Aurora before her brows rose ever so slightly. Aurora caught that brief speculative look and felt compelled to withdraw her hand from Overton's arm lest her sister make false assumptions about why they were alone together.

Then Diana was smiling brightly, her expression benign and composed once again. "And where were the pair of you off to this morning?"

"Aurora and I were reaching an understanding," Overton replied cryptically.

Aurora noticed the way Diana's eyes suddenly hardened with suspicion, so she rushed to explain. "Halley has graciously agreed to let me practice my marksmanship if I agree not to ride around the countryside dressed as a groom."

Did she imagine it, or did her sister look vastly relieved?

"I'm pleased to see you've come to your senses," Diana said, smoothly placing herself between Aurora and Overton, "but I cannot say that I approve of your shooting."

"No harm can come of letting Aurora shoot at branches," Overton said as they started walking back to the house.

Diana reluctantly concurred. "As long as you approve, Halley . . ."

The three of them were silent as they strolled through the garden.

Suddenly Diana drew Aurora's arm through her own, then reached for Overton's arm with her left hand so the two sisters and one gentleman were linked companionably together.

She looked up at Overton and said, "Since my sister has agreed to mend her hoydenish ways, what do you think of our giving a ball in her honor?"

Overton was silent for a moment as he studied the ground; then he looked over at Aurora and said, "I think that would be a splendid idea."

Aurora was overwhelmed. "A ball in my honor?" Since her father hadn't been one for socializing at Falconstown, Aurora had been to only one ball in her entire life, a small affair given by a neighbor on Aurora's sixteenth birthday.

Diana nodded. "It would be the perfect opportunity to introduce you to all of our friends." She gave a little squeal of delight as she gripped Aurora's arm. "It will be such fun! We'll have to decide what to serve for supper, how the manor will be decorated, who will be invited . . . and of course you shall have a new gown, something elegant in a blue silk or damask perhaps, decorated with rows of ruffles on the skirt and bows running down the bodice."

That prospect delighted Aurora, for although her father had always been generous with her clothing allowance, she was sure nothing she had worn in Ireland would compare with the lavish creation Diana had planned for her. She found herself becoming caught up in her sister's excitement and enthusiasm.

Suddenly Overton said to Diana, "Send your mantua-maker to me. I shall select the material for your gowns."

Aurora stared at him in shock, for she wasn't sure it was proper for a gentleman to select a gown for a lady.

But Diana set her at ease with a quick smile. "Halley always selects my gowns, Aurora. I can assure you, his taste is impeccable. You won't be disappointed."

"I guarantee it," he added.

They reached the house and went inside to have breakfast together. As Aurora listened to an animated Diana plan the ball, she decided she must have imagined the look of annoyance and suspicion her sister had given her when she first saw Aurora and Halley walking together arm in arm. No, her sister was secure in Halley's love. She had nothing to fear from Aurora.

Aurora surprised the ostlers when she appeared at the stable the next morning for her ride. Gone were her trousers and lawn shirt, replaced by a tailored riding habit of bottle-green camlet. She looked every inch a lady in the fitted coat, long waistcoat, and skirt that nearly swept the ground, and atop her auburn curls was a small cocked hat set at a rakish angle.

She cast a wistful glance at Firelight pacing back and forth in his paddock, but she chose a docile bay mare named Molly to ride instead and ordered her saddled with a sidesaddle. Once she was mounted, Aurora further astounded the men by asking a groom to accompany her.

Half an hour later, after putting the mare through her paces, Aurora could have screamed from boredom. The sidesaddle made her feel as though she were sitting in a rocking chair, and the petticoat beneath her skirt was picking at her legs, making them itch. In a moment of devilry, she longed to swing her right leg over the side and ride astride, but of course that would hike her skirt above her knees immodestly. The groom trotting after her at a discreet distance would be sure to report her behavior to Halley.

Aurora patted the mare's neck absently as she stifled a yawn. "I'm sure you are a fine horse, Molly, but you're not much of a challenge, are you? Not like Firelight."

They rode through a stretch of woodland, following a narrow babbling brook until they came to a clearing of deep, cool shadows and dappled sunlight.

"Well, let's see how you jump," Aurora said, setting her mount at a low stone wall.

The bay mare heaved herself over it reluctantly. Aurora was about to give up and ride back to the manor in disgust when a horse and rider galloping across the opposite field caught her attention. Aurora stopped to watch.

The horse was a tall dappled gray, long-legged and built for speed, and as he came charging down the field toward her, Aurora grudgingly admitted he could be Firelight's equal. They were still too far away for her to discern the rider's face, but she had an uneasy feeling she had seen the man somewhere before.

As the horse drew closer and closer, and Aurora saw who his rider was, she felt like turning her mare right around and galloping back to Overton Manor. But she knew she could never hope to outrun that magnificent gray, so she glanced over her shoulder to make sure the groom was still within shouting distance, stood her ground, and waited.

Several yards away from her, the rider effortlessly reined in his horse and doffed his black cocked hat with a flourish. "Good morning, Miss Falconet."

"Good morning, Lord Silverblade," she replied tonelessly without returning his smile.

She had to admit he looked magnificent. He wore a somber gray velvet jacket left unbuttoned to reveal a cascade of snowy lace at his throat and a gray satin waistcoat richly embroidered with silver thread. His fitted breeches were of a pale oyster color and tucked into black boots as highly polished as onyx. Yet for all the elegance of his attire, Lord Silverblade seemed quite unaware of what a splendid picture he made.

Now those cold gray eyes seemed to be laughing as they regarded her steadily. "So you know who I am."

"My sister, Diana, told me."

He grinned. "I'm flattered you thought enough of me to inquire about my identity."

Aurora stiffened in the saddle, causing her mare to shake her head in alarm. "I was merely curious, that's all. Now, if you will excuse me, I shall be on my way."

She touched her heel to Molly's ribs, but before the animal could amble off, Lord Silverblade reached down and grasped the reins above the bit, effectively stopping her.

"Lord Silverblade!" Aurora glared up at him in indignation. "Release my horse this instant!"

"My, aren't we the prickly one?" he said, those eyes twinkling with humor. "One would think I meant to abduct you for my harem from the way you are carrying on." Then he grew serious. "I merely wish to ride with you, Miss Falconet, that is all." He released the mare's reins, adding, "Of course, that is if you're not afraid of me."

Aurora bristled at the implicit challenge in his voice. "I am afraid of nothing, Lord Silverblade. Even of you."

"I am not really such a fearsome fellow, you know." He nodded toward the groom standing at the edge of the clearing. "And with that fine stalwart fellow to protect you, you really have nothing to fear from me."

Aurora glanced back at the groom, a skinny, gawky lad who looked as though he'd blow over in the first strong wind. The thought of a contest between the two men was so absurd she burst out laughing in spite of herself.

"That's better," Lord Silverblade said.

As their horses fell into step, Lord Silverblade looked her up and down with a critical eye. "I must confess I almost didn't recognize you without your breeches." He flashed her a teasing smile. "Or was that your twin brother, Rory, I met the other day?"

Aurora chuckled at that. "No, I fear Aurora and Rory are one and the same."

"Where is that fire-breathing red monster of yours?"

She wore a woebegone expression. "How I dearly wish I were riding him now. Molly here is a dear, sweet creature, but she is nothing more than a rocking horse fit for a child."

"And truly unworthy of your skills as a horsewoman."

"I can tell you're laughing at me again, Lord Silverblade."

"I assure you I am not, Miss Falconet. And I quite agree. Your mount is solid and dependable, but she has all the spirit of toasted cheese."

Aurora smiled at the apt comparison, then let her eyes rove enviously over Silverblade's spirited stallion. "The same could not be said of your horse. What is his name?"

"Stormcloud."

Aurora nodded. "It suits him perfectly."

"And his temperament as well." Suddenly Silverblade reined in his horse and said, "Would you like to ride him? That is, if you think you can handle him."

"I can handle him," she replied with supreme confidence.

Thinking of sitting astride Silverblade's saddle, still warm from his body, Aurora experienced strange stirrings within herself that she had never felt before. She felt her breathing quicken of its own accord.

"But I . . . mustn't," she added lamely. "I am not dressed for riding astride today. And I did promise my sister that I would not behave like a wayward lad anymore."

Silverblade was undaunted. "We shall merely change

saddles, then. Surely your sister has no objection to your riding sidesaddle, does she?"

Aurora perked up at once. "What a splendid idea!"

"I thought you might approve."

Then Aurora slid off Molly in a flurry of petticoats, quite unaware that she had given Silverblade a glimpse of her neat booted ankles.

"Please, please, Miss Falconet," he admonished her good-naturedly when she began unsaddling Molly herself. "You must allow me to do that for you after I unsaddle Stormcloud. A gentleman does like to feel useful."

So while Lord Silverblade began unsaddling his horse, Aurora busied herself becoming acquainted with Stormcloud, who eyed her suspiciously out of a white-rimmed rolling eye as she slowly walked toward him.

"My, what a big boy you are!" She spoke in a soft, soothing voice, while slowly reaching into the skirt pocket of her riding habit. "What do we have here for you, Stormcloud?" She produced a carrot, which she held at arm's length toward the horse's quivering, inquisitive muzzle.

"You'll spoil him," Silverblade warned. He lifted the saddle from the stallion's back, set it on the ground, and went over to unsaddle Molly.

When the gray stallion craned his long arched neck to take the proffered carrot, Aurora grasped his bridle and began stroking his cheek, all the while crooning, "Stormcloud likes carrots, doesn't he? Yes. That's my boy." Then she blew gently into his nostrils as he nuzzled her palm in search of more carrots. Not finding any, he playfully butted her in the chest with his head. Aurora grinned and staggered back, but didn't lose her balance.

"All right, all right, you greedy beast." She took another carrot from her pocket.

"You seem to have an inexhaustible supply," Silverblade remarked as he carried the sidesaddle over and set it on his horse's back.

Aurora scratched the gray on his forehead. "Give a horse a carrot, and he becomes your slave."

Silverblade chuckled at that. "Well, that must be

true, for you've made a conquest of my irascible stallion. He doesn't let just anyone touch him, I'll have you know. He's the terror of my stables."

Aurora watched as he worked quickly and competently. His hands, she noticed as he tightened the girth, were strong, yet gentle, with long, graceful fingers. She could imagine them quieting a restive horse or holding a pistol steady. Suddenly another image of those same hands tugging the dress off his mistress's body flashed unbidden across Aurora's mind, leaving her all shivery inside. She breathed deeply to calm herself and averted her face, lest the man read her thoughts.

"Finished," he announced, and turned to her. "Ready?"

Aurora nodded excitedly, stood on tiptoe to whisper some secret into Stormcloud's ear, then slid her hand down his glossy neck and gathered the reins.

Just as she was about to hoist herself into the saddle, the man startled her by saying, "Allow me." Before Aurora knew what was happening, she felt those strong, sure hands grasp her by the ankle, enabling her to spring up and vault easily into the saddle.

Aurora blushed crimson, for Lord Silverblade's touch was making her stomach quiver oddly. To cover her embarrassment, she busied herself hooking her right leg over the sidesaddle's pommel and finding her seat as Stormcloud shifted uneasily beneath the light, unfamiliar weight.

Lord Silverblade stepped back. "Keep a tight rein on him. If he gets the bit between his teeth, nothing will stop him and he'll run home with you."

Aurora's reply was a breezy, "He can try."

With that, she nudged the stallion in the ribs with her heel. The horse squealed and leapt forward as though fired from a pistol, then arched his back and bucked once in a halfhearted attempt to unseat his determined rider. But Aurora was ready for him, and only her hat went tumbling to the ground.

Nicholas cried out her name in panic and fear, instantly regretting his impulsive offer to let Aurora ride his mettlesome stallion. Her exultant laugh came floating back to him as she and the horse galloped off.

He bent down to retrieve her hat and stood there watching her. As the horse circled the open field with long strides, Nicholas could see that Aurora was blatantly disregarding his advice by giving Stormcloud his head and letting him set his own pace. The stallion was running faster and faster now, excited by the wind whistling past him.

When horse and rider went bounding over a high hedge and disappeared from view, Nicholas just shook his head. "I warned the stubborn little chit. I told her Stormcloud would head for home if she didn't keep him on a tight rein."

He turned to Molly, who was grazing obliviously nearby, and wrinkled his nose. He was not looking forward to the smirks and snickers of his ostlers when he came riding into the stableyard on such a placid, bovine creature, his long legs dragging on the ground.

Suddenly he heard the sound of someone clearing his throat, and he looked up to see the gawky young groom staring at him.

"Excuse me, milord," the man said. "Should I go after the lady?"

Nicholas shook his head. "That won't be necessary. I shall go after her myself. You may return to Overton Manor."

The groom opened his mouth as if to speak, then turned his horse and did what he was told.

Alone now, Nicholas ran his hand absently down Molly's smooth, sleek rump. How quiet and empty the glade suddenly seemed without Aurora Falconet's irrepressible presence. She reminded him of sunlight glimpsed through trees—quick, bright, elusive.

Just as he was about to admit defeat and saddle Molly, he heard the thunder of hoofbeats and felt the ground tremble imperceptibly beneath his feet. He looked up in time to see Stormcloud come sailing back over the hedge at the opposite end of the field.

Nicholas chuckled to himself and shook his head in wonder as Aurora slowed the horse to a trot, then a walk.

"So he didn't run away with you after all," he said as she entered the glade.

Aurora looked down at him disdainfully. "Of course not."

"You did, however, lose your hat." Nicholas handed it up to her.

"Through no fault of my own." Aurora took it with one hand and set it firmly back on her head.

The moment Nicholas noticed her slip her left foot out of the stirrup, he reached up and grasped her around the waist to help her dismount.

Angry blue eyes stared down at him. "I am perfectly capable of dismounting myself, Lord Silverblade."

"Of course you are, since you are a very independent young lady," he said blandly. "But I am also a gentleman, and a gentleman doesn't allow a lady to dismount unaided, especially since you are a tiny thing, and it's a very long way to the ground."

Before Aurora could protest further, he lifted her bodily out of the saddle.

Nicholas' action forced her to place her hands on his shoulders to balance herself, and as he swung her down, Aurora's face was inches from his own for the briefest of moments. Nicholas found himself transfixed. Aurora's eyes were a light, clear blue, framed by thick auburn lashes, and the bridge of her nose had just a dusting of pale golden freckles. Her cheeks were flushed from the exertion of her wild ride, and her entire being glowed and crackled with vitality and youthful exuberance.

Aurora's feet touched the ground, and the spell was broken. Her hands slid off his shoulders and she moved away.

"Thank you for letting me ride Stormcloud, Lord Silverblade," she said as she turned to pat the horse's lathered neck. "Next to Firelight, he's the best horse I've ever ridden."

Nicholas raised an amused brow. "Next to Firelight? My dear Miss Falconet, no other horse can compare to Stormcloud. See, now you've offended him. He's going to brood all week."

Aurora giggled. "My sister was right. You are quite the wit, Lord Silverblade."

He acknowledged her compliment with a bow and a flourish. "It's just one of my many attributes, Miss Falconet."

Suddenly Aurora looked around, her pretty brow furrowed in puzzlement. "Wherever has my groom gone?"

"Oh, our gawky young friend . . ." Nicholas explained he had sent him back to Overton Manor and why.

"I must return, then," Aurora said, "before my sister sends men out looking for me."

Nicholas quickly saddled Molly for her, and he and Aurora started back to Overton Manor.

At first they rode in silence, for Aurora was still a little awkward in Lord Silverblade's presence.

Suddenly he broke that silence by saying, "Are you enjoying your stay with your sister, Miss Falconet?"

"Well enough," she replied after a brief silence.

"Your enthusiasm quite overwhelms me, Miss Falconet."

"I don't mean to appear ungrateful, Lord Silverblade. I owe my sister a great deal. But I miss the freedom of saying whatever I feel. At Overton Manor I am constantly on my guard lest I blurt out what's on my mind and offend someone."

"And do you do that often, Miss Falconet?" he asked with a teasing smile.

"More times than I care to remember, Lord Silverblade," she glumly replied.

He laughed at that. She really was a delightful, winsome creature.

"At least Lord Overton has agreed to let me practice my marksmanship," Aurora said, "though I doubt if he will agree to becoming my fencing partner."

Nicholas choked. "You shoot and fence as well as ride like the wind, Miss Falconet?"

"As well as any man." Her eyes narrowed. "I suspect you are laughing at me again, Lord Silverblade."

"I am not laughing at you. I was merely expressing my astonishment at your many talents, that's all."

Aurora sighed and plucked at Molly's mane. "I wish I were a man. Then I could be the master of my fate and wouldn't have to depend on others."

Lord Silverblade smiled indulgently. "But we all have to depend on others for something, Miss Falconet."

"And whom do you depend on, Lord Silverblade?"

The challenge in her voice disconcerted him, but only momentarily. "Why, my servants, of course. They make my life comfortable. I also depend on my friends for stimulating conversation and company." And Pamela for stimulation of quite a different nature, but he discreetly left that out.

"But you are still free to do as you please, Lord Silverblade. I am not. I am at the mercy of fate. If it hadn't been for a tragic set of circumstances, I would still be at Falconstown."

He was intrigued. "Falconstown . . . Where is that, pray tell?"

Aurora fought back treacherous tears. "In Ireland. My father and I used to live there. That is, until he lost the estate in a card game."

"I am sorry."

Despite her best intentions to remain aloof, Aurora found herself telling Lord Silverblade all about her father's suicide and its horrid aftermath. When she finished, he once again expressed his sympathies in a soft, heartfelt voice.

Aurora said bitterly, "Of course, none of this would have happened in the first place if it hadn't been for Viscount Havering."

Lord Silverblade gave her an odd look. "Viscount Havering? I don't understand . . ."

"Viscount Havering ruined my family," she said bluntly. When she thought of Tim, her voice shook. "I once had an older brother named Timothy, the finest brother any girl could have. He was handsome, intelligent, courageous . . . but he did not choose his friends well, a Falconet trait, I fear.

"One night Viscount Havering, one of those so-called friends, badgered Tim into playing highwaymen. The two of them went to Hounslow Heath and held up the first coach that passed." Aurora took a deep breath to keep from shaking. "The occupants of the carriage had pistols and began shooting. The cowardly Viscount Havering wheeled his horse around and fled, leaving my brother at the mercy of the men they had attacked. Tim was shot and left for dead, while Viscount Havering escaped without a scratch."

It was only when Lord Silverblade held out his handkerchief that Aurora realized she had been crying.

While she dabbed at her eyes, she added, "I was only ten years old at the time, but I was as devastated as the rest of my family. My father challenged Havering to a duel, to avenge Tim's honor, but the coward refused. Then, when Diana ran off with Overton, my father lost another child. That's when he took me and moved to our Irish estate of Falconstown."

Lord Silverblade looked grave as he rode by her side. "You mustn't be too hard on Viscount Havering, my dear."

Aurora shot him a venomous look. "He killed my brother, Lord Silverblade. If he hadn't goaded Tim into playing highwayman that night, my brother would still be alive. We would have never moved to Ireland, and my father would still be alive as well."

"I knew Havering in his youth," the marquess said. "He was a wild one, but then, most young gentlemen are. They take great enjoyment in posing as highwaymen, or riding through some village and shooting out windows, or stealing signs from public houses. I am sure he didn't intend for your brother to die."

"And I am equally sure he did!" Aurora snapped. She stared straight ahead, her back stiff with anger. "You go too far, Lord Silverblade. I will not hear that man defended in my presence."

"You strike me as a fair woman, Miss Falconet. I thought you should hear his side of it before you condemned him, that's all."

"My brother is dead, and Viscount Havering is alive. That's all I need to know."

By this time they had come to the gates of Overton Manor.

Aurora coolly nodded her head in Silverblade's general direction, but did not look him in the eye or smile. "Thank you for letting me ride Stormcloud, my lord. Good day."

Then she kicked Molly and sent the mare ambling away before Lord Silverblade could say another word.

Nicholas stared at Aurora Falconet's retreating figure in dismay, but he made no attempt to ride after her. She was furious with him for taking Viscount Havering's part. But there was nothing else he could do without condemning himself as a blackguard, for until he had assumed his father's title of Marquess of Silverblade six years ago, Viscount Havering had been none other than Nicholas himself.

4

DIANA stood back to admire her handiwork. "Aurora, you are sure to be the most beautiful woman at the ball."

Aurora grimaced at the white reflection staring back at her. "I think I look like a . . . a ghost!"

Just an hour ago her sister had ordered her into the powder closet to be painted for the ball tonight. Aurora had protested vociferously, but Diana had remained adamant. Every lady would be wearing cosmetics, and if Aurora didn't conform, she could just stay in her room for the rest of the evening and brood.

So Aurora submitted without a whimper while the powdering gown was draped over her and the hairdresser began combing sticky, sweet-smelling pomatum through her auburn curls. Soon they lost their fiery color beneath a dusting of fine gray powder that tickled Aurora's nose and made her sneeze repeatedly.

Next, thick white ceruse was spread not only on her face but also on her neck and chest. After blackening Aurora's eyebrows with a lead comb and dabbing Spanish red rouge on her cheeks, Diana pronounced her fit to enter polite society.

But Aurora was not so sure. To her, the dead white skin, black brows, and two bright red spots on her cheeks looked garish and grotesque. How could any woman possibly think she looked beautiful?

She shook her head. "I can't face anyone looking like this, Diana."

Her sister's expression turned stern, and she grasped Aurora firmly by the shoulders. "Now, listen to me, Aurora Falconet, you are no longer some ignorant country miss rusticating in Ireland. We have different customs here in England, and while you are here, you are expected to conform to them. I'll not have you disgracing Lord Overton. Or me, for that matter."

For once, Aurora couldn't mask her true feelings. "I wish I were back in Ireland! At least the women there don't go around like painted trollops!"

The moment she saw the stricken expression on Diana's face, Aurora could have bitten her tongue.

"I'm . . . I'm sorry, Diana. I didn't mean that. I spoke out of turn."

But it was too late. Diana's lower lip quivered and her face crumpled. "I offer you a home, I try to introduce you to society, and this is the thanks I get?" She sniffed noisily into a lace-edged handkerchief. "I never dreamed my own sister could be so thankless."

Aurora rushed over to her side and put an arm around her sister's shaking shoulders. "I don't mean to be so disagreeable, I really don't. It's just that my tongue gets away from me sometimes and I say things I don't mean. Please don't cry."

Diana dabbed at her eyes, which seemed suspiciously dry to Aurora. "And there will be no more talk of appearing at the ball tonight with an unpainted face?"

Aurora nodded in mute surrender, though she felt as though she had just sold her soul to the devil.

Diana's face brightened, now that she had bent her headstrong sister to her will. "You have so little experience in the ways of the world, Aurora. Other women are often like a flock of geese. As long as all the geese look and behave the same, everything is fine. But let a lovely swan enter their midst, and they will band together and attack it. You will see what I mean tonight."

Privately, Aurora wondered if her sister included herself in that low assessment of her own sex, but she was learning to think before she spoke, and wisely said nothing.

Diana smiled. "Well, now it's time for me to be painted, so I shall leave you to your own devices, dear sister."

So, while Diana disappeared into the powder closet, Aurora stared down at her new gown. She may not have been pleased with her painted face, but she thought her gown was the most exquisite garment she had ever owned.

She shook out the pale blue damask skirt, so full over the wide panniers, and delighted in the rich rustle it made. The bodice had been cut into a low square neckline, with a line of bows running down the front. The wide skirt fell open gracefully to reveal an under-skirt of soft blond lace, and the same lace trimmed the pagoda sleeves flaring out at her elbows.

With a small ruffle around her throat as her only ornamentation, Aurora thought she looked every inch the fine lady.

"Ah, Father," she murmured wistfully, "I wish you were still alive to see your Aurora now."

She fought against the tears that suddenly welled up in her eyes, for if they fell, they would surely leave tracks down her cheeks, thus spoiling the carefully applied paint. She didn't want to risk upsetting Diana again.

Growing impatient with standing around and waiting for Diana, Aurora decided to go downstairs and see if any of the two hundred expected guests had arrived yet.

A full moon hanging in the sky bathed the landscape with cool white light, making it easy for the coach-and-four to negotiate the narrow road that led to Overton Manor.

Inside, Nicholas leaned back against the soft leather squabs and tried not to look at Wesley or his grandmother seated across from him. He silently cursed himself for ever suggesting that Wesley share his carriage to Overton's ball, but how was he to know that his cousin would bring their grandmother and her page with him?

Looks were certainly deceiving, he thought as he regarded the dowager marchioness out of thoughtful, half-closed eyes. At first glance, she looked like a sweet, kindly old lady, with snow-white hair framing a face so angelic in repose. But let her open her mouth, and that angelic expression would instantly sharpen and twist to reveal an autocratic harridan with bile running through her veins instead of warm red blood.

She patted Wesley's hand and smiled at him. "How kind of you to invite me to the ball tonight. Getting out in society will do me a world of good." She sighed and glanced at Nicholas out of the corner of her eye to see if he were paying attention. "I grow so lonely at the dower house. People tend to forget you when you're old."

Nicholas refused to be baited. "Nonsense, Grand-mother. If you wish to visit Silverblade, all you have to do is have your coachman drive you up to the house. Mother and I are always pleased to receive you. And if you wish to call on anyone else, your coachman will drive you anywhere in England."

"I have so few friends," she muttered morosely. "Most of them are dead. I've outlived them all."

At the mention of death, Wesley squirmed in his seat and drummed his knees nervously with his fingers.

Nicholas said, "Well, then you should thank the good Lord that you're still alive and enjoying good health."

"Nicholas is right, Grandmother," Wesley added, earning him a rare scowl of disapproval.

Then she looked at Nicholas slyly. "I have one wish before I die."

"And what is that, Grandmother?"

"I want to see you married to a suitable young woman of a good family. The Silverblade line needs an heir. It's your responsibility."

Nicholas reached into his waistcoat pocket, took out a silver snuffbox, and after offering a pinch to Wesley, helped himself.

"Grandmother," he began wearily, "I am fully aware of my responsibilities. I will marry, all in good time."

She puffed up like a fighting cock ruffling its feathers just before a match. "Hmph. Not if you keep carrying on with your doxies and licentious friends."

Seeing the black look that suddenly settled on Nicholas' features, Wesley hurried to forestall a confrontation with a warning, "Grandmother—"

But once her tongue was at full career, nothing could stop Lady Vivien from speaking her mind. "Don't 'Grandmother' me, Wesley. Someone has to keep Nicholas from destroying the Silverblade heritage."

Nicholas sneezed and forced himself to keep his temper in check. There was no person in the world who could rattle him the way his grandmother could. But to snap back at her would be to give her the victory she craved, for the old harridan liked nothing better than to rile him.

So he merely gave her one of his lazy, infuriating smiles and said in decidedly bored tones, "Grandmother, you can say what you will, but you should know by now that I am going to do whatever I please."

The marchioness glared at him as though she would like to turn him into stone with one glance. Nicholas knew she bitterly resented the fact that she no longer wielded absolute power in the family.

Wesley tried to ease the palpable tension in the carriage by saying, "I understand the purpose of the ball tonight is to introduce Diana Falconet's sister into society."

Lady Vivien, for all her complaints about being lonely, nevertheless managed to know all the gossip in the neighborhood.

"Hmph," she muttered, "Diana Falconet should worry about finding a suitable husband for herself. That popinjay Overton will never marry her, and she's a fool if she thinks he'll ever come around. He's just like his father and his father before him. Both of them kept mistresses for twelve years before throwing them out and marrying someone more suitable. Young Halley will do the same, so Miss Diana Falconet ought to be on her guard."

But Nicholas barely heard her, for his thoughts had raced ahead to Aurora. After their last meeting all of two weeks ago, when she had coldly dismissed him for making excuses for Viscount Havering, he wondered if she would even speak to him tonight. He found himself hoping she had forgotten the incident.

Suddenly the carriage slowed, followed by the unmistakable crunch of carriage wheels rolling over gravel.

Wesley looked out the window. "We've arrived," he said.

Aurora stood beside Diana and Overton, smiling at the Duke-of-this and curtseying to the Duchess-of-that. Everyone looked so much alike in white wigs, powdered hair, and pastel satins and brocades that she found it difficult to match names with faces. She resigned herself to not even trying.

Then the Marquess of Silverblade and his party arrived.

The moment Aurora heard him announced, her gaze went to him of its own volition. He was so unlike any other man here tonight. Again, he flouted fashion by wearing no wig; his own glossy dark hair was pulled back and tied with a thin black satin bow. His coat, instead of being pastel blue or lavender, was a medium shade of lustrous gray satin, and the waistcoat was heavily embroidered with black and silver threads.

While conversation stopped for no one, it decreased markedly when Lord Silverblade sauntered into the room. He moved with languid grace, and if he was aware of the effect his presence was having, he didn't show it.

Aurora noticed the other man and the old lady with him and asked Diana who they were.

"The other man is Wesley Devenish, the marquess's cousin," Diana replied *sotto voce*, "and the woman is Lady Vivien Devenish, the dowager Marchioness of Silverblade, followed by her page."

Aurora tore her eyes away. She was still furious with the marquess for defending Viscount Havering, the man responsible for Tim's death, and she was sorry Diana had ever invited him to her ball.

She would have liked nothing better than to turn and disappear into the ballroom, but common courtesy dictated that she receive him.

So Aurora pasted a smile on her face when she was introduced first to the marchioness, a redoubtable old lady who still carried herself as straight as a queen, despite her advanced years. She was very gracious in a condescending way, but her sly, probing eyes made Aurora uneasy.

Next came the marquess's cousin. From the moment Aurora had set eyes on him, all she could think of was that he looked like a lackluster version of his cousin. If Lord Silverblade were a diamond, his cousin would be a lump of coal.

When Mr. Devenish took her hand in his cold, clammy grasp, Aurora wanted to pull away in revulsion. She prayed her face wouldn't betray her because she didn't want to hurt the man's feelings. Judging by the lavish compliments he was paying her, she had succeeded.

Then, before she was quite ready to receive Lord Silverblade, Wesley Devenish was moving on and his cousin was taking his place.

Seeing Aurora now, Nicholas was keenly disappointed. The young woman who stood before him was nothing more than a painted doll.

In all honesty, he could not bring himself to compliment her. "Good evening . . . er, it *is* Miss Falconet, is it not?"

Blue eyes stared back at him coldly as she curtsied stiffly. "And who else might I be?"

He shrugged. "If you are truly Miss Falconet, then where are your fiery curls?"

His bantering tone did not coax a smile out of her as he had hoped. Aurora raised her small pointed chin proudly and fixed him with a penetrating stare.

"If you will kindly excuse me, Lord Silverblade, there are other guests waiting."

Not wishing to cause a scene in the receiving line, Nicholas merely bowed and strolled off to the ballroom. He would bide his time and talk to the icy Miss Falconet later.

Aurora nearly gasped aloud when the next two guests stepped up to be introduced, for she recognized the woman immediately despite her powdered hair.

"Sir Francis Littlewood and his wife, Pamela," Diana said, "I'd like to present my sister, Aurora Falconet."

Aurora curtsied quickly, trying to maintain her composure, for all she could think of was the lovely Mrs. Littlewood being carried toward the summerhouse by Lord Silverblade.

She swallowed hard. "It is a pleasure to meet you."

Aurora fancied she saw a sudden spark of recognition in Mrs. Littlewood's deep blue eyes, followed by a piercing look of assessment and a patronizing smile of dismissal.

"The pleasure is all mine, Miss Falconet," she said in a silken voice lightly edged with laughter.

After her husband uttered a few pleasantries, Mrs. Littlewood quickly steered him in the direction of the ballroom.

When the couple was out of earshot, Diana said, "He has to be at least three times her age. It's obvious she married him for his fortune, which I understand is considerable."

I wonder if she would still smile so smugly if Mr. Littlewood knew of her trysts with Lord Silverblade, Aurora wondered as she watched the beautiful Mrs. Littlewood making a great show of doting on her husband.

Aurora was introduced to a dozen more guests, then Diana tapped her on the arm with her fan and said, "I think that accounts for everyone. Halley wants us to join our guests in the ballroom for a while, and then he'll start the dancing."

Aurora had never seen anything so splendid. The ballroom seemed to shimmer with color and light, as the candles from three huge crystal chandeliers overhead sparkled and danced off gleaming satins and brilliant jewels. The low hum of conversation filled the air, underscored by soft music. The festive atmosphere was contagious, and soon Aurora forgot about Lord

Silverblade and Mrs. Littlewood enough to enjoy herself.

She tried to follow Diana's example and mingle among her guests, complimenting the women on their gowns and encouraging the men to discuss their estates or life in London. Many of the younger men surprised her by lavishly complimenting her until she blushed.

Soon Aurora's jaw began to ache from making so much chitchat. Just as she debated disappearing for a few moments into the library, a lovely young woman in a peach-colored satin gown approached her and handed her a cup of punch.

"My dear Miss Falconet," she said with a sympathetic smile, "if you don't have some of this excellent punch, you are sure to expire before the dancing even begins."

Aurora recognized Katherine Crossways, the Duchess of Kilkenny, at once, and curtsied. "Thank you, your grace."

The duchess was only a few years older that Aurora, and quite beautiful, with unusual pale green eyes the color of peridots and a heart-shaped face. Unlike most of the other women here tonight, she had not painted her face, but left it bare, revealing the same warm, golden complexion that only a titian-haired beauty could possess.

Aurora regarded her unpainted face enviously, but then, as a duchess, Katherine Crossways could do as she pleased without inviting the wrath of the other women present.

"Please," the duchess said with a wave of her hand, "we mustn't stand on formality. From the moment I was introduced to you, Aurora—you don't mind if I call you that, do you? . . . I insist you call me Katherine— I knew that we were going to be great friends. I always go by my feelings, you see. And when someone told me that you have been living in Ireland for the past ten years . . ." She smiled brightly. "I knew it for a certainty."

Katherine, as Aurora soon discovered, was something of a prattler, but a most delightful one.

She guided Aurora over to a quiet corner of the ballroom. "Whereabouts did you live in Ireland? I meet so few of my countrymen in London."

When Aurora told her about Falconstown, the duchess raised her brows in astonishment. "Why, that is only in the next county! I am surprised we never met."

Aurora smiled. "I'm afraid my father was not one for socializing."

Then she told Katherine how he had lost his beloved Falconstown and later killed himself.

The other woman went quite pale and fanned herself rapidly. "How tragic for you."

"But Diana and Lord Overton have been very kind to me," she said.

"Well, you are not alone. I am your friend now, and you must feel free to come to me for anything," Katherine said, and meant it.

Aurora thanked her for her kindness. Katherine started chatting about Ireland and would have kept on for the entire evening if her doting, indulgent husband hadn't claimed her for the dancing that was about to start.

Suddenly Aurora found herself surrounded by young men, each eager to have her dance the first dance.

"Your little Miss Falconet is quite sought after," Pamela said, fanning herself against the heat of the ballroom and the tight lacings of the corset crushing the breath out of her.

"You surprise me, Pamela," Nicholas said, not taking his eyes off Aurora, who was swaying as gracefully as a reed to the strains of a minuet. He sipped his punch. "I've never known you to be jealous of another woman."

"Me? Jealous of that child?" Her laugh was strong and confident. "I merely called her 'your little Miss Falconet' because you haven't been able to stop talking about her."

"Haven't I?"

"No, Nicholas, you haven't. If I were a jealous woman, I'd say you have a *tendre* for her."

"You have nothing to worry about, my dear, nothing at all."

"I'm delighted to hear it." Pamela shivered. "You should have seen the expression on her face when her sister introduced Sir Francis and myself. She recognized me as the woman who was with you in the summerhouse that morning she came riding by. I was certain the foolish child would blurt something out and embarrass us all."

"But she didn't expose you to Littlewood, did she?"

"No, thank God. It seems she has more sense than I gave her credit for." When Nicholas made no comment, Pamela said, "Look at all the young men swarming about her like bees to the hive. But I am afraid all of the elaborate plans Diana Falconet has made for her sister will come to naught."

"And why is that?"

Pamela shrugged. "Why, because she is penniless, of course."

"Ah, that explains it."

"Granted, she is a lovely child and she does come from a good family, but we both know that without a suitable dowry, she will never make a suitable match."

Nicholas smiled sweetly. "But you were penniless, Pamela, and you made an outstanding match."

The irony of his tone was not lost on Pamela, for she gave him a wounded look. "I suppose I deserved that."

"Yes, you did, my dear," Nicholas agreed. "Such character assassination of another woman is unworthy of you." Before she could say anything more, he added, "I think you should return to Littlewood. We've been talking together for quite a long time and are sure to cause comment."

Pamela said, in a voice both hopeful and fearful, "Shall I see you tomorrow afternoon, if I can get away without arousing my husband's suspicions?"

Nicholas bowed over her hand. "Certainly, Mrs. Littlewood. I will look forward to it, as always."

"Lord Silverblade," Pamela murmured in relief.

As he watched her return to her husband, Nicholas found himself thinking what complex, curious creatures women were. Pamela had always been supremely confident of his affections, never jealous of another woman. But there was something about Aurora Falconet, the reckless child-woman, that threatened Pamela and forced her to reveal another side to her personality that was frankly repugnant to Nicholas.

The music stopped and the dancing ended. Nicholas watched Aurora curtsy to her partner, and they walked off the dance floor.

He found himself wondering just what it was about Aurora that could upset his mistress so. He decided to find out.

Aurora found herself a quiet corner far away from the persistent young men who clamored for another dance, and fanned herself. The seven dances she had danced in a row had left her breathless and her feet aching in their soft kid slippers. Now she was glad she had insisted her maid not lace her in too tightly; otherwise she surely would have fainted from such strenuous exercise.

Suddenly a deep, amused voice behind her said, "Ah, I've cornered you at last, Miss Falconet." She whirled around to come face-to-face with none other than Lord Silverblade.

His glittering gray eyes held hers. "One would think you were deliberately trying to avoid me." He made an indulgent clucking sound. "That will never do, I'm afraid. You must be hospitable to all of your guests."

Aurora glared at him. "I have deliberately been trying to avoid you, Lord Silverblade. I will not converse with anyone who defends my brother's murderer."

"Very well. Viscount Havering is a base, vile, black-hearted coward and murderer. Now are you satisfied?"

Aurora was not amused. "If there is one thing I cannot tolerate, it's a hypocrite."

Lord Silverblade's face darkened in anger and his smile died. "There is no pleasing you, is there?"

"I'm afraid not, so if you will excuse me . . ."

But he just stepped in front of her to block her escape. He was standing so close to her, the silver buttons of his coat nearly brushed the bodice of her gown, where her breasts were heaving in response to her quickened breathing. Aurora could even discern the scent of his shaving soap, spicy and fresh, not cloying like that of many of the men she had danced with that evening.

"And if there is one thing *I* cannot tolerate, Miss Falconet," he said in a low, silky voice, "it is someone who will not accept an apology when it is sincerely offered."

Aurora stepped back a pace. "You *should* apologize for defending a man like Viscount Havering!"

Lord Silverblade inclined his head gravely. "Then I do. I apologize for ever defending the man, and will break off our association immediately. I will never see him again, if it pleases you. I just want us to be friends again, Miss Falconet."

At first Aurora was just going to turn on her heel and walk away without another word. But while she would never forgive Havering for what he had done to her brother, she could not bring herself to extend her wrath to Lord Silverblade just because he had the misfortune to know the man.

Her angry gaze faltered, and she shrugged sheepishly. "Very well, Lord Silverblade. I shall accept your apology, provided you never mention Viscount Havering's name to me again."

He smiled, transforming the auster planes of his face into a pleasant expression. "Thank you, Miss Falconet. You are truly a good fellow."

Aurora beamed with pleasure, for she prided herself on having a sense of honor equal to any man's.

With apologies given and accepted, the tension eased between them.

"Are you enjoying the ball?" Lord Silverblade asked conversationally.

Aurora nodded. "I've met so many interesting people."

"That gown looks especially becoming."

"Thank you. Lord Overton selected it for me." Then she added, "What did you mean when you pretended not to know me in the receiving line?"

"I was referring to that mask you are wearing."

Aurora's hand flew to her cheek involuntarily. "Oh, you mean the paint."

Lord Silverblade nodded. "You really should not wear it, you know."

"I didn't want to, but Diana insisted. She said every other woman would be painted tonight, and it would not be seemly for me to be different."

Lord Silverblade glanced around the ballroom. "Well, as you can see, that simply is not true. The Duchess of Kilkenny never paints, and neither do several other ladies present."

Neither does Mrs. Littlewood, Aurora thought to herself, but caught herself before blurting it out.

He placed his arm beneath her elbow. "Come with me a moment. I would like to show you something."

He guided Aurora to the edge of the ballroom, where a large arrangement of flowers stood on a pedestal. "What do you think of this rose?" he asked.

"Why, it's beautiful."

"Would you dream of painting it?"

"Of course not. That would spoil its natural beauty."

"Precisely my point."

She realized at once that he was referring to her as well, and she smiled.

He returned the smile, and Aurora couldn't help thinking that he looked so much less forbidding when he smiled.

Suddenly the orchestra struck up another tune.

"Will you honor me with the next dance, Miss Falconet?" he asked.

Aurora smiled and nodded. When they walked out onto the floor together, both were unaware that they were objects of intense scrutiny.

Near the ballroom entrance, a group of four men including Overton stopped discussing politics long enough to watch a dozen couples dance.

"Seems Silverblade has taken quite an interest in your ward, Overton," one of them said.

Another added, "It looked like quite a little *tête-à-tête* they were having in the corner."

Overton smiled. "The man's merely being neighborly, nothing more. He may be a libertine, but all of us know he has no taste for children, especially penniless children."

Several of the men chuckled lasciviously.

"The Littlewood wench would vouch for that," the first man said, after the lady's husband walked slowly by, then drifted out of earshot.

All except Overton laughed again.

As he watched Aurora smile up at her partner, he wondered if Silverblade did indeed fancy Diana's sister for himself. Nothing sweetened the chase for Overton more than knowing someone else also coveted what he wanted. It made winning all the sweeter. And he was going to win. Before the month was out, Aurora was going to be his mistress.

On the other side of the ballroom, Diana tried to keep her attention focused on what the voluble Duchess of Kilkenny was saying, but her gaze kept wandering to Aurora and Lord Silverblade on the dance floor.

The rakehell lord and her virginal sister . . . now, that was an odd match if ever there was one! Diana smiled to herself. She would have preferred someone who lived as far away from Overton Manor as possible, but once Aurora was married to Lord Silverblade, she would present no threat to Diana. No threat at all.

She turned her attention back to the duchess.

Something was dreadfully wrong.

No sooner had Aurora traded Lord Silverblade for another earnest young dancing partner than her skin felt as though she were being stabbed with thousands of red-hot needles. She just wanted to throw good manners to the wind and scratch her itching cheeks like a common scullery maid with a rash.

She excused herself and managed to elude her admirers by slipping out through the French doors onto the flagstone terrace, where she sought to hide until supper was announced. Then she planned to escape up to her bedchamber while everyone was occupied and wash off every bit of paint.

Outside in the darkness, a cool summer's night breeze caressed her skin, easing its torment somewhat. Aurora walked to the very end of the terrace, where the lights from the ballroom and the sounds of people within didn't reach. She breathed deeply of the softly perfumed air coming from the garden, and when she heard the musical tinkling of a fountain, she raced down the steps toward it.

When she reached the fountain, she dipped her cupped hands into the cool water and splashed it on her face repeatedly, washing off the paint while soothing her scorched skin.

So intent was she on her task that she failed to hear the tapping of footsteps crossing the flagstone terrace and approaching her.

She heard nothing until a familiar voice said, "It's going to take more than water to wash all that paint off your face."

She straightened abruptly and spun around. "Lord Silverblade! You really shouldn't creep up on a person that way. You nearly caused my heart to stop."

He bowed from the waist. "Do forgive me, Miss Falconet, but I wished to escort you in to supper, and when I saw you disappear through the French doors, my natural curiosity got the better of me." Then he scowled, stared at Aurora with a frightful intensity, and took a step toward her. He caught her chin in his long fingers and tilted her face toward the moon. "Good Lord! What have you done to yourself?"

"Wh-what do you mean?"

Lord Silverblade's shoulders began shaking from suppressed laughter, though he managed to keep his face composed. "I'm afraid your careful ministrations have done you more harm than good, Miss Falconet. Instead of removing your paint, you've only succeeded in smearing the lead from your brows all over your face. I'm afraid you rather resemble Juma, my grandmother's blackamoor page."

Before the full import of Lord Silverblade's words had a chance to register, Aurora noticed two men appear on the terrace, whose voices carried.

"Where in the devil do you suppose she's gone?"

"Perhaps she's out here somewhere. I must find her so I can escort her to supper."

"Let's not fight over her. Whoever finds her first may escort her to supper."

"Agreed."

With a gasp of horror mingled with mortification, Aurora suddenly panicked. Her hands flew to her cheeks. "Dear God! Whatever am I to do? I can't let anyone see me like this."

Nicholas suddenly grabbed her hand. "Quickly! Follow me!"

He led Aurora through the garden, crouching behind tall shrubbery as he moved farther and farther away from the terrace and the two eager young gentlemen searching for their quarry.

Finally he pulled the panting and terrified Aurora behind one corner of the house.

"I think we're safe for now," he whispered, "but we've got to get you inside before someone else comes looking for you. Where is the kitchen door?"

"This way," Aurora replied, feeling her way.

As Nicholas expected, the kitchen was brightly lit and alive with the sounds of an army of servants preparing the food and transporting it out to the dining room. His mouth watered as the heady scents of roasting meat and baking bread tickled his nostrils, reminding him of how hungry he was. But this was no time to think of his stomach.

Aurora shrank back. "I can't go in there. Everyone will see me."

He grinned down at her. "Where is the fearless lad who rode Stormcloud the other day?"

His mocking words had the desired effect of goading her into action. Aurora scowled at him and said, "What do you want me to do?"

"Here is what we are going to do . . ."

A moment later, several cooks and serving girls stared openmouthed as the distinguished-looking gentleman came barging through their kitchen, leading a lady with a coat draped over her head, thus concealing her identity. He said not a word of explanation, for he was a gentleman, and they made not a word of inquiry, for they were servants and it was above their station to question the idiosyncrasies of their betters.

Even when the gentleman bellowed for a candle and demanded to be shown the servants' stairs, they complied with alacrity.

Nicholas led Aurora up the stairs, and did not remove his coat from her head until they were on the second floor landing. Then he set the candle down on the floor and put his coat back on.

Aurora leaned against the wall and gave a shaky sigh of relief. "Safe at last."

Nicholas stared at her. She may have looked like a bedraggled waif with her streaked, dirtied cheeks, but there was something touching in her utter lack of vanity. Aurora didn't shriek or put her hands to her face in an attempt to conceal it, as any other woman might have done. And he suddenly found himself overcome with desire.

"No, Miss Falconet," he said, his voice suddenly husky, "I'm afraid you are not safe at all."

Aurora's smile died and she grew very still. A little voice deep inside her head urged her to dart for the door, open it, and flee while there was still time. But much to her surprise, she didn't want to. She and the marquess had had a narrow escape and Aurora suddenly felt irresistibly drawn to him.

Now Lord Silverblade was standing before her, so tall and imposing that she had to tilt her head back to look at him. Those compelling eyes were dark and luminous on the shadowy, dimly lit landing. The promises she read in their depths took Aurora's breath away and sent a charge of anticipation running along her arms. Her heart stopped, then started again with a painful jolt. She stood there, dazzled, sensing she was on the verge of experiencing something both wonderful and frightening.

He looked right through her out of half-closed eyes, then slowly lowered his head. Aurora held her breath, knowing he was going to kiss her this time and powerless to stop him. She was afraid, excited, reluctant, and willing all at once.

Lord Silverblade's face came closer and closer. Aurora could feel the tip of his nose brush against hers tentatively, as if testing her response. When she didn't pull away, his lower lip began tracing the contours of her mouth in a slow, seductive dance, urging her lips to part. His teasing, feather-light touch was having the most unexpected effect on her.

A warm knot of pleasure began to form in the pit of her stomach, blossoming and suffusing through her until she trembled like a leaf in an autumn wind. The novel sensation blotted out the rest of the world and erased all conscious thought from her mind. There was nothing left except this unexpected, dizzying pleasure and the marquess's formidable will seeking to take possession of her.

Aurora sighed in surrender and swayed toward him, her arms slipping around his waist instinctively, boldly pulling him against her. She had never held a man this way before and was quite unprepared for her own body's response. Her nipples strained against the bodice of her gown as her breasts pressed against Silverblade's unyielding muscular chest. As he shifted his weight and braced himself with his feet apart, Aurora insinuated her leg between his to get as close as she dared. When she did, she felt something stir against her thigh.

This wasn't happening to her. It was all so unfamiliar, and so wicked and shocking, yet she didn't want it to stop, not for a minute, not ever.

Nicholas looked down at Aurora's upturned face, her eyes closed, her soft lips slightly parted, and he smiled in satisfaction. Never had he dreamed she would respond to him so willingly, with such fervor. He suspected, however, that she didn't quite realize the devastating effect her arousing gestures were having upon him, or what the ultimate consequence would be if she pushed him too far. He sensed she trusted him not to hurt her. He wondered fleetingly if he deserved it.

Aurora heard Lord Silverblade laugh softly before he took her in his arms and began kissing her in earnest. His sweet mouth was hot and insistent against hers, sapping her of any resistance. Aurora's lips willingly parted beneath his, and she whimpered in delight.

Suddenly Silverblade's kiss deepened passionately, his tongue darting into her mouth. Aurora reared back, alarmed as liquid fire bubbled in her veins and shot across her limbs, igniting her skin. Then she reveled in it, following his lead and meeting his searching tongue with her own.

She wanted him. She wanted those long, elegant fingers to tear off her gown as he had Mrs. Littlewood's that day. She wanted him to make love to her, to banish her innocence forever and reveal the woman hidden within.

Without warning, the sound of a door slamming caused him to wrench himself away from her.

"Damnation!" he growled, as lumbering footsteps came shuffling up the stairs, closer, ever closer.

Before they could be discovered, Lord Silverblade retrieved the candlestick, opened the door, and shoved Aurora through it. Then he closed it behind them.

Breathing heavily through his nose and looking most annoyed, he handed her the candlestick. "I suggest you go to your room at once and ring for your maid. I must return to the ballroom before I am missed."

Aurora tried to catch her breath. She felt as though she had just been pulled back away from the edge of a precipice. Yet why did she feel so . . . so disappointed?

"Thank you, Lord Silverblade, for saving me from such humiliation."

He sketched her a bow. "There's nothing I like better than rescuing a damsel in distress."

Then he disappeared back down the servants' stairs.

Aurora started to call him back, but his name died on her lips. She was alone now. The corridor was empty, quiet, and dark except for the feeble candle. Without Lord Silverblade to sustain it, the euphoria Aurora had felt gradually dissipated, and cold, harsh reality began reclaiming her senses. She fought to hang on to the magic, but it was no use. She came crashing back to earth.

"Why did I ever let him kiss me?" she asked herself indignantly. "He's Viscount Havering's friend, and I don't even like him!"

Then Aurora remembered the reason she had left the ball in the first place.

One hand flew to her face in horror; then she gathered her skirts and went running back to her bedchamber as fast as her legs would carry her. The moment she entered the room, she flew over to the mirror. The sight that greeted her eyes caused her to groan in anguish.

She did indeed resemble a blackamoor. To make matters worse, her skin was beginning to itch furiously again, and it took all of Aurora's strength of resolve to keep from scratching it raw.

"How could I have let a man kiss me, knowing I look like this!" she shrieked, and rang for her maid.

When Sarah answered the summons a few minutes later, her eyes widened in shock. "Why, Miss Aurora, whatever has happened? Your poor face . . ."

"Do something, Sarah!" Aurora cried in panic. "My skin feels like it's crawling with vermin."

The maid dragged Aurora to Diana's powder room, sat her down, and began smoothing a cream on the suffering girl's face and neck. Just as Sarah finished removing the last of the paint from Aurora's forehead, Diana came marching into the powder room.

"Aurora, why did you leave the ball?" she demanded peevishly. "Lord Silverblade said you had to, but he wouldn't say why. You're the guest of honor, for heaven's sake!" She peered over at her and clucked in dismay. "Why have you removed your paint?"

"Why? Because this itching skin is driving me to madness, that's why!" Aurora wailed, tears of frustration welling in her eyes.

The vehemence of Aurora's retort stunned Diana into momentary silence. When she finally spoke, it was to say, "Your skin must be sensitive to the white ceruse."

"I never should have agree to wear that horrid paint in the first place. My evening is ruined, Diana. Ruined!"

"Now, now, Aurora," Diana said soothingly, "don't you fret. Some herbal compresses will have you back to rights in no time. And then you really must return to the ball."

"But, Diana—"

"You're the guest of honor, Aurora. It would be most impolite of you to just disappear from your own ball. Besides, supper is to be served in fifteen minutes."

"I'll only go back downstairs if I don't have to paint again," Aurora said stubbornly.

Diana hesitated for a moment, then capitulated with a dramatic sigh. "Oh, all right. You won't have to paint again."

"Ever?"

"Ever."

Aurora smiled in triumph. She had won.

Fifteen minutes later, after the herbal compresses had relieved Aurora's itching skin, she returned to the ball.

The moment she walked into the ballroom, the two young gentlemen she had eluded with Lord Silverblade's help raced up to her and demanded that she choose one of them to escort her in to supper. Aurora won their hearts when she threw convention to the winds and sweetly insisted they both share that honor.

But once she was seated in the dining room and her two gallants went off to fill her plate from the sumptuous buffet, Aurora found herself scanning the sea of faces for any sign of Lord Silverblade. Then she saw him across the room, conversing with Mrs. Littlewood's husband.

Suddenly he raised his head and caught her staring.

Even across the crowded room, Aurora could feel the impact of his gaze as it caught and held her own boldly, without wavering. She thought of the way his clear gray eyes had warmed and darkened like smoke just before he kissed her on the landing, and she felt her cheeks suddenly turn warm as her breathing quickened of its own volition.

His lips curved into a smile as he suddenly raised his hand and drew a finger down his own cheek. Aurora knew he was referring to her now unpainted face, and she sensed he approved. She smiled shyly and nodded in return to acknowledge his compliment.

At that moment her two gallants suddenly returned,

one bearing a plate for Aurora and the other glasses of punch.

Throughout supper, Aurora found her gaze constantly straying over to Lord Silverblade, but she was never able to catch his attention again. Hours later, when the ball finally ended and Lord Silverblade was bidding her good night, he was so formal and distant that Aurora began to wonder if he had ever really kissed her at all.

5

THE dogcart, pulled by a sassy black pony, sped through the wrought-iron gate of the Silverblade estate, past the dower house, and disappeared into the densely wooded park.

Seated beside Diana, who was driving, Aurora plucked at her skirt nervously as she watched a herd of tame deer regard her with frank curiosity before flicking their tails and bounding away.

"Turn the cart around right this instant!" she demanded, her courage finally deserting her. "I don't want to have luncheon with Lord Silverblade!"

But her sister wouldn't obey. "Now, now, Aurora . . . Lord Silverblade very graciously invited us to have luncheon with him today, and I accepted for us."

"Well, you go ahead, and I'll walk back to the manor."

Diana gave her an exasperated look out of the corner of her eye. "He invited both of us, and we are both going. He's merely being neighborly, that's all."

But Aurora wasn't so sure. The night of the ball, when Lord Silverblade had taken her in his arms and brazenly kissed her, was still as fresh in her mind as if it had happened just yesterday instead of a week ago. When she thought of his warm, hard mouth crushed against hers and the way she had responded like a wanton, Aurora's cheeks turned rosy with shame. How could she possibly face the man again after such shocking behavior?

"Aurora," Diana was saying, "one would think you were going to your own hanging instead of a pleasant luncheon with a neighbor. What are you so afraid of?" Before Aurora could tell her, Diana continued with, "Your face no longer itches. In fact, you look quite fresh and lovely today."

Like a goose dressed for Christmas dinner, Aurora thought dismally.

Since Aurora had known Diana for so short a time, she often found it difficult to speak candidly with her about certain matters. But now she tried to put her fears and misgivings into words.

"It . . . it's just that Lord Silverblade makes me uncomfortable. I've heard such terrible things about him that I think I'm a bit afraid of him."

"Oh, Aurora," Diana said, her voice softening with sympathy. "I know how you must feel, really I do. You are very young, and you've led a sheltered life. But there is nothing to be afraid of. Nicholas Devenish is a fine man."

Aurora thought of the morning she had happened upon Mrs. Littlewood in Lord Silverblade's summerhouse, where they had obviously spent the night enjoying each other. A fine man indeed!

As if reading her thoughts, Diana conceded, "I will admit he is no saint, Aurora, but then, what man is? It's not what a man does before his marriage that counts, it's what he doesn't do afterward."

Aurora twisted in her seat, her eyes huge and round. "Marriage? Who said anything about my marrying Lord Silverblade?"

"No one," Diana amended hurriedly. "I was merely making a point."

That seemed to satisfy Aurora, for she said nothing and busied herself taking stock of her surroundings.

"This park is huge," she said in awe. "It seems like we've been driving for hours."

"Silverblade is one of the richest holdings in Surrey," Diana explained. "I've heard Overton say it's made up of several thousand acres of prime farmland.

You could ride for half a day and not come to the end of it."

Diana glanced at Aurora to see if her sister were suitably impressed, but she could tell at once that the child was not. Diana scowled in chagrin. England was filled with beautiful women who would sell their souls to be invited to dine with Nicholas Devenish, and here was Aurora worried about something as trifling as the man's reputation!

Diana raised the reins and clicked her tongue to make the pony go faster. She herself had wondered why Lord Silverblade had invited them today, but she hoped against hope that she hadn't misinterpreted his intentions.

It was obvious that he was interested in Aurora.

As the cart rounded a bend in the road, the trees on either side thinned and parted suddenly, revealing a long, lush lawn sweeping far beyond the park. At the end of the lawn stood the magnificent house of Silverblade, its gray stone walls gleaming softly in the noonday sun. The darkness of the park contrasted so sharply with the treeless plain beyond that it seemed to frame the house and grounds like a priceless painting.

Aurora gasped in wonder. "It . . . it's beautiful!"

"And quite large," Diana added. "Why, it's at least twice the size of Overton Manor, and the furnishings and paintings are priceless."

Then the cart started down the circular drive.

Nicholas stood before one of the salon's long windows, impatiently watching for any sign of his guests.

Behind him, his grandmother stirred and muttered disagreeably, "You've been staring out that window for the last hour. One would think someone important were coming to dine."

Nicholas sighed in exasperation. He was beginning to regret ever asking his grandmother to serve as hostess today, but since his mother had abdicated all social responsibilities years ago, there was no one else he could turn to. It was one thing to entertain Pamela alone, but quite another to entertain a gentlewoman like Aurora.

"The Falconet sisters are important, Grandmother," he replied. "They are our neighbors."

The old lady sniffed in disdain. "Common doxies, the pair of them."

Nicholas clenched his teeth together to keep his annoyance in check. "Whatever you may think of her sister, Miss Aurora is not a doxy. And I'll thank you to keep a civil tongue in your head while they are here, Grandmother, or you will no longer be welcome at Silverblade."

"Are you insinuating that I don't know how to behave properly in company?" she snapped.

Nicholas was spared a reply, for just at that moment a dogcart came out of the park and started down the drive.

"If you'll excuse me, Grandmother, I am going to receive my guests," Nicholas said, and went hurrying out of the salon.

He reached the front door just as the dogcart pulled up to the steps and a footman took the pony's head.

"Good day to you, ladies," Nicholas said, trotting down the steps so he could help the women to alight. "I'm so pleased you could join me today."

"How very kind of you to invite us," Diana said, taking his proffered hand and stepping down.

Then he turned back for Aurora.

She looked most comely today in a sack dress of green flowered silk, with her vibrant hair hidden beneath a plain white cap and tip-tilted straw hat. He was relieved to see that her face had survived its bout with white ceruse.

But as he offered her his hand, she took it shyly, without looking at him, and he sensed a nervousness about her that hadn't been there before.

"You look especially lovely today, Miss Falconet," he said, trying to put her at ease.

She started and gave her sister an alarmed look. Then she stammered, "Th-thank you, Lord Silverblade," like a shy young miss just out of the schoolroom.

Just as he began wondering whatever had happened to the spirited young woman he had known, Aurora added, "Your house is beautiful."

Once Aurora was out of the cart, Nicholas said, "It shall be my great pleasure to show it to you after luncheon."

Offering one arm to each sister, he said, "My grandmother has graciously offered to be my hostess today, and I'm sure you'll find her entertaining company. Now, if you'll follow me, ladies . . ."

The trio walked up the steps and into the house.

The luncheon was a disaster and it was all Aurora's fault.

During the entire meal, she merely took several bites of the succulent lobster, then toyed with the rest of her food as if she had lost her appetite. She hardly said two words, placing the burden of conversation on everyone else. When someone did address her, she would reply in a soft, reserved voice that hardly carried across the width of the long mahogany table.

Nicholas was relieved when the interminable meal was finally over.

When they all rose, he said, "Ladies, I promised to show you the rest of my house, so if you'll just follow me . . ."

Perhaps if Aurora were shown all the fine, rare books in his vast library, the priceless paintings he had collected in Italy, the intriguing art objects filling each and every room, she would lose her reticence and become the enchanting, delightful young woman from the ball.

So Nicholas proceeded to lay his treasures at her feet, to impress her and invite her admiration.

The books received a cursory glance, and each painting was duly stared at, eliciting only a polite "It's lovely." What did he have to do to please her? he wondered in annoyance. Give her Stormcloud?

Well, he wasn't about to do that, but recalling Aurora's partiality for horses gave him an idea.

"Grandmother," he said, "why don't you retire to the salon with Miss Diana while I show Miss Aurora the stables?" He turned to Aurora. "That is, if she is interested in seeing my horses and hounds."

Suddenly Aurora seemed to spring to life like a

drooping flower after a soft spring rain. "I would enjoy that very much, Lord Silverblade."

"I thought you might," he replied with a suppressed smile, and extended his arm to her.

Once outside, away from all the intimidating opulence of the house, Aurora found her confidence returning. "If all of your horses are the caliber of Stormcloud, I would say your stables were well-stocked, Lord Silverblade."

"I own forty horses, including my carriage horses," he replied absently, as though his mind were a million miles away. "But only a few of them are the caliber of Stormcloud."

They fell silent as they began strolling through the gardens, which, Aurora noticed, were on a grand scale, as was everything else at Silverblade.

Suddenly he stopped and looked down at her, his gray eyes mystified. "Why were you so reserved back at the house? I hardly recognized you as the charming, voluble, exasperating Aurora Falconet I remembered. You were quite the meek little mouse, not yourself at all."

Her cheeks reddened and she looked down at the ground. "I . . . I didn't want to come today."

"And why was that?" A smile hovered about Lord Silverblade's mouth. "Am I such an ogre that you could not bear my company?"

"It's not that I think you an ogre, it's just that I couldn't face you after . . . after what happened the night of the ball," she replied in a small voice.

"To what are you referring? The fact that you blackened your face, or the fact that I kissed you?"

She summoned the courage to look up at him, her heartbeat careening wildly. "Just why did you kiss me, Lord Silverblade?"

"Because I wanted to, and I suspect you wanted me to as well."

Aurora looked away and started walking again, embarrassed by his astuteness. "I think we should hurry to see the stables. I'm sure Diana will want to leave soon, and I don't want to keep her waiting."

She was relieved when Lord Silverblade matched her stride and began discussing his horses again.

Aurora was impressed with the fine array of horseflesh in the man's stables and told him so; then they proceeded to the kennels, where, Lord Silverblade explained, he was trying to breed a new species of foxhound.

"Come," he said, "I have something to show you."

The moment he opened the door to one of the pens, eight puppies came barreling out, barking and yipping as they jumped at Aurora's skirts. With a cry of delight she knelt down and tried to scoop up every wriggling bundle of fur into her arms.

"Careful, Miss Falconet," Nicholas warned her, "or they will dirty your gown and tear it."

But she didn't seem to hear, for her attention was captured by the smallest hound, who was being pushed out of the way by all of the others.

Nicholas shook his head as Aurora gathered the whimpering little fellow into her arms and held him against her shoulder. The runt of the litter. How had he known Aurora would choose that one to lavish her attentions upon?

"I like this one the best," she said.

"Why?" Nicholas asked. "He's smaller than the others and not as strong. He's always being pushed out of the way at mealtimes. Even his own mother regards him as a changeling."

"Don't malign him so! He has a great deal of . . . of character!"

The comical expression of affront on Aurora's face so touched Nicholas that he felt his heart give a queer little lurch.

"With you as his champion, I'm sure he'll distinguish himself in the hunting field," he said. "Now, why don't you put the puppy down and we'll return to the house? You may come whenever you like, to visit them."

"May I?" she asked, her eyes shining with eagerness.

"Anytime you wish."

As Aurora bent over to set the puppy down, one of the others suddenly leaped up, caught the brim of her straw hat in his mouth, and boldly tugged it right off her head. Then he proceeded to dash away with it, the others in hot pursuit.

Any other woman would have cried out in horror, but not Aurora. She merely dissolved into giggles, pulled off her white cap, and shook out her auburn curls until they tumbled to her shoulders in a shimmering russet veil. She looked as wild and carefree as a Gypsy maiden.

"Shall we return to the house, Lord Silverblade?" she said.

"But your hat . . ."

"I detested it anyway. The pups will get more enjoyment worrying it than I would out of wearing it."

Nicholas burst out laughing. "You are truly unlike any woman I have ever known, Miss Falconet."

His compliments seemed to make her uncomfortable, for she said nothing, just colored prettily. Suddenly she pointed to the statue of Priapus at the far end of the lawn and said, "What is that?"

Nicholas grabbed her arm and firmly steered her away from the Garden of Eros before she could satisfy her curiosity.

"Er, it's nothing, just a statue I bought in Rome several years ago. Very common and uninteresting as statues go, actually."

Much to his relief, she was not at all suspicious and accepted his explanation without question.

As they reentered the gardens toward the back of the house, Aurora was surprised to see a woman standing in the cutting garden, picking flowers and setting them in a basket over her arm. She scowled, for it was not Lord Silverblade's grandmother or Diana, and the woman was too well-dressed to be a servant.

The woman must have noticed them returning from the kennels, for suddenly she straightened and stared right at them. Aurora gasped in shock.

The woman's face was concealed by a black silk mask.

"Don't be alarmed, Miss Falconet," Lord Silverblade said hurriedly, his voice curiously flat and strained. "It is my mother. I shall ask her if she would like to be introduced to you, if you'll wait right here for one moment . . ."

Aurora remained rooted to the spot while her host began walking toward his mother. Suddenly she dropped the basket of flowers she had been holding, and with a quick backward glance over her shoulder, started running toward the house.

"Mother, please!" Lord Silverblade called to her, his hand extended beseechingly.

He stopped and his hand fell back to his side when she disappeared through a back door. He stood there for a moment, then turned and started back toward Aurora.

The pain in his eyes tore at Aurora's heart, but she couldn't think of anything appropriate to say, so she said nothing.

"You must forgive my mother for her strange behavior, Miss Falconet," he began in a voice low with shame. "She is a recluse, you see."

"I'm . . . I'm sorry."

Lord Silverblade viewed her through narrowed eyes as though debating whether to continue. Then he lifted one shoulder in a fatalistic shrug and murmured, "What can be the harm in telling you? Six years ago, she and my father contracted the dread smallpox. He died from it, but she recovered, though horribly scarred. I don't think she's ever been able to forgive herself for living, so she has shut herself away from the world and hides behind a mask. She comes out of her rooms only to pick flowers."

Then he smiled, a mere bitter grimace. "Do you know, I haven't seen her face in all that time? I've almost forgotten what she looks like."

His story was so moving that Aurora felt tears of pity well up in her eyes. She placed a comforting hand on his arm. "Nicholas, I am so, so sorry."

Her sudden and unexpected use of his Christian name took him by surprise. What an astonishing creature she was, a carefree child playing with puppies one moment and a wise, compassionate woman the next.

Nicholas rubbed his forehead with his fingertips. "It is my mother you should feel sorry for, not I."

Aurora's blue eyes flashed as her hand fell away. "But I do not feel sorry for her," she said sharply. "She has everything to live for—a fine home, a fine son, and no doubt many friends. Yet she chooses to remain hidden away from the world. Under the circumstances, I would be happy just to be alive."

Aurora's passionate, unexpected outburst took Nicholas aback. "Most people regard my mother as a tragic figure, an object of sympathy."

"Forgive me for saying this, but I'm afraid I find her behavior rather selfish."

He could only gape at her, dumbfounded. Not once, in all this time, had anyone realized how much his mother's withdrawal from life had hurt him. Never had anyone, except perhaps Ollie, guessed how much he had suffered from being shut out of her life so completely.

Aurora looked away. "I spoke out of turn. Forgive me. It is one of my many faults."

He placed his hands lightly on her shoulders and looked deeply into her eyes, so clear and trusting.

"I think your honesty is quite an endearing fault," he said softly, "and I also think you are quite remarkable, Aurora Falconet."

She caught her breath, and he could read the uncertainty in the depths of her eyes. So he hesitated for a moment to give her the opportunity to pull away and resist his embrace. But she didn't.

Encouraged, he reached up to caress her satin cheek with his fingertips. The freckles that dappled her skin warmed it, and the light blue of her eyes reminded him of the clear, shallow waters of the Mediterranean Sea and he wished he could drown himself in them. "You are so very beautiful as well."

He lowered his head slowly, giving her one final chance to flee, but to his delight, Aurora moved imperceptibly closer. She closed her eyes and tilted her face in bold expectation of his kiss.

Nicholas moved slowly and gently, not wanting to frighten her and betray her trust. While he slid one arm around her tiny waist, he reached up to cradle the back of her head in his hand. Her hair was so soft and silky he couldn't resist sifting his fingers through it.

He began kissing her ever so gently while pulling her against him. She was incredibly soft, the sweet scent of her filling his nostrils, sweeping him along on a rising tide of desire.

The soft, eager pressure of her lips against his fueled his hunger for her. Nicholas wanted to possess her mouth deeply with his tongue and feel her small, hard breast swell with excitement beneath his palm, but he restrained himself with superhuman effort. He knew instinctively that she wasn't ready for such ardent caresses.

Suddenly a throaty, bemused voice said, "I hope I am not intruding," bringing him down to earth with a jarring thud.

Aurora jumped out of his arms, and Nicholas turned to see none other than Pamela walking through the garden toward them.

"This is the second time we've been interrupted," he muttered savagely under his breath. Then he greeted Pamela in ill-disguised annoyance. "Ah, Mrs. Littlewood, how good of you to call."

Aurora blushed as the other woman regarded her with a small, frigid smile of amusement.

Mrs. Littlewood was attired in a riding habit of pale blue camlet that looked as though it had been sewn onto her lush figure. To Aurora's chagrin, there was not so much as a speck of lint on it, while her own dress was smudged and stained with dirty paw prints where the puppies had jumped on her. Her hair must have been flying every which way, making her feel like a stupid, unkempt child when compared with the elegant Mrs. Littlewood. Oh, how it rankled!

"I do apologize for the interruption," the woman said. "I did call at the house, but they said you were out here."

"The Falconet sisters were my guests for luncheon," Lord Silverblade said, but that was all the explanation he gave.

"Mrs. Littlewood," Aurora murmured by way of acknowledgment.

Mrs. Littlewood smiled at her briefly, then turned her attention to Lord Silverblade. "Do you mind if I join you? It is such a beautiful day for a walk."

The last thing Aurora wanted was to endure Mrs. Littlewood's patronizing company any longer. She said, "I'm afraid I must be getting back to my sister. We will be leaving shortly."

"What a shame," Mrs. Littlewood said.

To Aurora's satisfaction, Lord Silverblade looked crestfallen, but ever the gracious host, he said, "Let me escort you back to the house."

The three of them strolled back to the house together.

Later, after his other guests had been sent on their way and Nicholas was alone with Pamela, he could tell by the combative glint in his mistress's eye that she was furious with him for kissing Aurora Falconet. But Pamela also knew the folly of reproving him for his behavior, so she wisely said nothing about what she had seen in the garden.

"You have nothing to fear, my dear," he murmured huskily as he nuzzled her delectable neck. "I may steal a kiss from Aurora Falconet, but I share your bed. I will always share your bed."

Having reassured her, he pulled her into his arms and began showering insistent kisses on her face. Pamela closed her eyes and abandoned herself to the heat and unleashed passion of his embrace. She didn't mind finishing what Aurora Falconet had started.

She smiled to herself as Nicholas' deft fingers began undoing the hooks running down the back of her riding habit. Aurora Falconet may have been the recipient of Nicholas' chaste kisses, but she would never experience Nicholas' lovemaking.

Pamela was going to see to that.

Several days after her visit, Aurora went to call upon Lord Silverblade alone, ostensibly to see the foxhounds again.

Though she wouldn't admit it to herself, she was beginning to have feelings for him, deep feelings she was unable to control. The man preyed on her thoughts, especially the memory of his kisses that could still leave her feeling so vulnerable and shaken.

When she arrived at Silverblade, she was told that the master had gone out. Though greatly disappointed, Aurora decided to go down to the kennels to see the foxhound pups, just so her ride over to Silverblade would not be for naught.

The kennelmaster seemed startled to see her striding toward the pens by herself, but he smiled, proudly showed off his charges, and discussed their foibles and peculiarities with the knowledgeable Aurora. Then she started back to the house.

She had just come through the trees when the statue Lord Silverblade had so diligently steered her away from suddenly caught her eye. Aurora looked around furtively. She was alone. Not a gardener or a maid was about.

Burning with curiosity, she hurried across the lawn, but as she drew closer to the statue, she began to regret her hasty impulse to view it.

The statue was the most obscene thing she had ever seen. Aurora looked away, her face flaming with a mixture of disgust and embarrassment.

"His father must have been a stallion," she muttered to herself.

Noticing that the statue seemed to be standing guard at the entrance of another garden, Aurora's curiosity got the better of her once again, and she entered the area bounded by high hedges on either side. She was shocked to find more of the provocative statuary, depicting cupids, nymphs, and centaurs disporting themselves lasciviously in the secluded alcoves. When she discovered a woman's silk stocking caught on the branch of a shrub, she suddenly realized the purpose of this particular place.

"So what they say about him is true," she murmured, as disappointment welled up inside of her.

Throwing down the silk stocking, she ran from the garden as fast as she could.

During her wild ride back to Overton Manor, all she could think of was her startling discovery. She could visualize Lord Silverblade and Mrs. Littlewood together in that garden, and she felt herself consumed by irrational jealousy.

"What do I care how he conducts himself?" she told herself. "He's nothing more than a rake and a libertine. And his kisses mean nothing. Nothing!" The last word ended on a choked sob as her eyes filled with tears.

When she arrived back at Overton Manor, she flung herself off her horse and ran into the house. But when she passed the salon, the sound of voices made her stop in her tracks.

". . . and you would want to see Aurora married to Silverblade?" she heard Overton say incredulously.

Aurora moved closer to the open door and listened, not daring to breathe.

"Why not?" her sister replied. "He's handsome, wealthy, titled . . . everything a woman could ask for in a man. Aurora would be fortunate to find another so suitable, especially since she herself has no dowry. I think he's attracted to her as well." Diana lowered her voice, so Aurora had to strain to hear. "I saw them kissing in the garden the day we went for luncheon."

Aurora silently cursed herself for letting Lord Silverblade make a spectacle of her.

But Halley didn't sound as sure. "There is his reputation to consider as well, Diana."

"At least Aurora would have the protection of his name and the standing of a wife," Diana pointed out. "And once my sister presented him with an heir, they could go their separate ways. Many women do."

"But aren't you forgetting something?"

"And what is that?"

"Does Aurora know that Silverblade was the man who was with your brother the night he died?"

Aurora didn't hear Diana's reply. She felt as though a hand had suddenly grasped her heart and was squeezing it dry. For a moment the corridor seemed to swim before her eyes, and she heard a great roaring in her ears like the wind rushing overhead. She fought against the encroaching blackness and went staggering into the room.

"What do you mean, Lord Silverblade was with Tim

the night he died?" she demanded, her voice rising shrilly.

Diana started guiltily, and her smile was tremulous. "Why, Aurora . . . what are you doing here? We didn't expect you home so soon."

"What did he mean, Diana?" Aurora marched up to her sister, grasped her by the shoulders, and started shaking her. "Tell me this instant!"

It was Overton who pulled her away.

"Aurora, calm yourself! You're becoming overwrought."

Bosom heaving and eyes flashing, Aurora forced herself to speak slowly and clearly. "I want to know the truth, Diana. Now."

Diana reached up and began rubbing the shoulder that bore the red imprint of Aurora's fingers. "Silverblade was the man who accompanied Tim the night they masqueraded as highwaymen."

"That's impossible," Aurora snapped. "That man was named Havering, Viscount Havering, not Silverblade."

Overton looked at her strangely, then said, "But Viscount Havering is one of Nicholas Devenish's several other titles. Everyone knew him as Viscount Havering before his father died and he assumed the title of the Marquess of Silverblade."

Aurora was so stunned she couldn't speak. Her lips moved, but no words came out. She suddenly felt dizzy and would have fainted to the floor if Overton hadn't caught her and eased her into a chair. She sat there taking long, shuddering breaths to steady her shaking insides.

Finally she looked up and glared resentfully at her sister.

"Why didn't you tell me, Diana? How could you keep something like this from me?"

Diana shrugged lamely. "I . . . assumed you knew."

Aurora rose to her feet and grasped the back of the chair for support. "If I had known, do you think I would have even spoken to that evil man?" she cried. "Well, you may have forgotten that he killed your brother, but I certainly haven't!"

"What are you talking about?" Diana said, frowning. "Silverblade didn't kill Tim. In fact, he tried to dissuade him from posing as a highwayman that night."

This was just too much for Aurora to bear. Now her own sister was defending the man!

Aurora exploded. "That is a monstrous lie!"

And before Diana could say another word, Aurora ran blindly for the door, pausing only long enough to say, "And you call yourself my sister!" before dashing out.

Just as she started through the hallway, the sight of none other than Lord Silverblade himself brought her up short.

He had just finished setting his cocked hat on the hall table when he noticed her standing there. Unaware of what had just transpired, he smiled warmly and said, "Ah, Miss Falconet. I'm sorry I was out when you called earlier, but I—"

Aurora didn't give him a chance to finish. With a strangled cry of rage, she flew at him with upraised fists, shrieking, "Liar! Murderer!"

Nicholas was so astonished, that he didn't move fast enough, and suffered several painful blows about his chest and shoulders before he was able to capture Aurora's flailing fists and subdue her. She struggled wildly, screeching in fury as she tried to kick him in the shins, but he skillfully kept out of reach.

Finally, when she was too worn out and breathless to fight anymore, Nicholas said, "That's better. Now, will you kindly tell me the reason for your outburst, Miss Falconet?"

Her lip curled into a sneer. "As if you don't know, Viscount Havering!"

Suddenly Nicholas understood only too well.

With infinite regret he said, "So, you know."

"Yes, I do. And if I were a man, I'd challenge you to a duel. I'd make you pay with your life for what you did to Tim."

"Yes, I think you would enjoy putting a ball through my heart."

"It would be my greatest pleasure, Lord Silverblade."

Suddenly Diana came sweeping into the foyer with Overton not far behind.

"Lord Silverblade, I do apologize for my sister," Diana said, wringing her hands, "but she has had a great shock."

Aurora struggled again, but Nicholas tightened his grasp painfully. "How can you take his side?" she cried to Diana. "How can you allow this man in your house after what he did to your own brother?"

Nicholas looked over at Halley, who obviously found the altercation distasteful, judging from his bored expression. "Overton, is there somewhere Miss Falconet and I may talk undisturbed?"

"The library," he replied, sounding relieved.

Aurora was no match for Nicholas' superior strength. He dragged her, howling and balking in protest, through the foyer and down another corridor. She fought him mindlessly, until her breath came in painful gasps and only the strength of her hatred kept her from collapsing.

When they came to the library door, he shoved her inside, then slammed the door after them. He stood with his back against it, effectively barring her escape as he watched her out of wary eyes.

Aurora went over to the fireplace, as far away from him as possible, her slight frame tense and shuddering from her exertions. In their heated struggle, her hair had been shaken loose from its pins and now hung in tangles about her face, giving her the look of a madwoman.

Her face . . . Nicholas hardly recognized it, all tear-stained and twisted with bitterness and hate. He would give anything to see her smiling up at him so sweetly, her eyes filled with trust again.

"We have to talk," he said.

Aurora was regarding him with contempt as she rubbed her wrists, which bore red imprints of his fingers where he had gripped her. "You and I have nothing to say to each other."

"Oh, but we do. I'm going to tell you the truth about the night your brother died."

"The truth?" She flung back her head and laughed, a wild, frenzied sound that made Nicholas fear for her sanity. "You mean your version of the truth."

He shrugged. "You may choose to believe or disbelieve me as you wish, but neither of us is leaving this library until you hear me out."

"Very well," Aurora said. "The sooner I let you say your piece, the sooner I shall never have to suffer your company again."

She went over to a leather wing-back chair, sat herself down, folded her hands primly in her lap, and waited.

Nicholas went over to a decanter on a nearby table and poured brandy into a glass. He held it out to Aurora and said gently, "Drink this."

To his chagrin, her hand shot out and she pushed the glass away, splashing the liquid onto her skirt. "I don't want anything from you!"

Nicholas clenched his teeth to keep his temper in check, for he realized Aurora was in pain and expressing it by lashing out at the man she thought responsible. He set the glass down and moved away from her.

"Your brother and I were inseparable friends, Aurora," he began quietly. "We drank together, wenched together, and like most young men of our class, enjoyed releasing our high spirits by playing various pranks. One afternoon Tim suggested that we ride through Hounslow Heath and impersonate highwaymen."

"That's a lie!" Aurora cried, springing to her feet. "You were the one who kept baiting Tim until he agreed to your dangerous scheme."

Nicholas felt his temper soaring, and he took a menacing step forward. "If you don't stop interrupting me, I shall tie you to that chair and gag you."

Aurora reluctantly sat back down, but her entire being radiated loathing for him in a palpable wave.

Satisfied that she would remain quiet, Nicholas continued. "I though such a prank dangerous, and told him so, but Tim could be pigheaded on occasion, and he threatened to go alone if I didn't agree to accompany him. I couldn't allow him to do that, so that night we set out for the heath together."

Suddenly, he was there, reliving that terrible night. "We pulled up our black crepe masks, and when a carriage drew near, we fired our pistols into the air and cried, 'Stand and deliver!' Without warning, someone from inside the carriage fired through the window.''

He could see Aurora's shocked, pinched face, drained of all color as she gripped the arms of her chair and shook her head in wordless denial as she fought back tears. All Nicholas wanted to do was take her in his arms and hold her, but he knew she would resent any comfort he might offer.

"I screamed for the shooting to stop and identified myself. But it was too late for Tim. He took a ball in the chest and died in my arms."

"A touching story, Lord Silverblade," Aurora said tremulously, wiping at her eyes with the back of her hand, "but a lie."

His black brows came together in a scowl of impatience. "Oh? And just what is the truth, Miss Falconet?"

She looked him squarely in the eye. "I told you the truth the day we rode back to the manor together."

"Ah, yes, I remember now. I was the villain of the piece. You claimed I badgered your reluctant brother into riding that night, then hung back like the coward I am when the shooting started."

"It's the truth!"

"And who told you that?"

"My father."

Nicholas approached her chair. He tried to be as gentle as possible, for he knew what he was about to say would tarnish her sterling memories forever. "I know you revered your father, but I'm afraid he wasn't entirely truthful with you."

She rose and stood before him, her face only inches from his own. "Are you calling my father a liar, Lord Silverblade?"

"Must you twist my words around? I'm merely saying that he was a man in pain, angry and hurt by his only son's needless, tragic death. He needed someone to blame, and I was a convenient scapegoat. I felt so responsible that I offered to fight him, but he refused."

Before he realized what was happening, Aurora's hand went back and she struck him across the face with her open hand. The slap was so hard that Nicholas' head rocked to the side. He recoiled, momentarily stunned as tears sprang unbidden to his eyes.

Nicholas was too much of a gentleman to retaliate, though he felt Aurora could benefit from a good spanking. But he resisted the impulse and smiled wryly. "Feel better now, Miss Falconet?"

"My father was never a coward!" she cried. "If you challenged him to a duel, he would have fought you. And killed you."

Nicholas turned away, his cheek smarting. "You may ask anyone who was there. They will corroborate my story."

Aurora gave a snort of derision. "I would expect nothing less from your friends."

"It's the truth."

Aurora turned her back on him as if she couldn't bear the sight of him a moment longer.

"Aurora," he began gently, coming to stand behind her, "I want you to know that I'd give anything to bring Tim back for you, but I can't. And I know I should have told you sooner that I was Viscount Havering."

He ached to hold her, to share his strength, but the sight of her rigid back and her utter contempt for him made him hesitate. "I don't want us to be enemies."

"I hate you with all my heart, Lord Silverblade," she replied vehemently, without turning around to face him. "I have no wish to see you or speak with you ever again."

"Forever is a very long time, Aurora," he said kindly. "Are you sure you mean it?"

If he was expecting her to capitulate, to throw herself in his arms and seek comfort from him, he was mistaken. She merely nodded wordlessly.

"Very well. I will be most happy to comply." Without another word, Nicholas turned on his heel and strode out of the library, slamming the door behind him.

After his footsteps died away, Aurora slid back down into her chair, buried her face in her hands, and sobbed as if her heart were breaking.

*   *   *

Nicholas almost ran Stormcloud into the ground in his haste to return home.

He was furious with himself for not being honest with her and revealing his true identity sooner, and he was equally furious with her for not believing his version of what had happened that night. But what could he expect? She had lived most of her life with her father in Ireland, being spoon-fed his lies with her morning porridge. Why should she believe Nicholas' side of the story?

Yet he was oddly disappointed and hurt that she didn't. Up until now, Aurora had seemed to take pleasure in his company, even like him a little. And she certainly enjoyed his embraces, of that he was certain. But now she had only scorn for him.

When Nicholas arrived back at Silverblade, he found Pamela waiting for him.

Her brows arched in surprise. "And what is the matter with you, my lord? Your face is as dark as a thundercloud."

"I'm through with innocent waifs forever, my beauteous Pamela," he vowed between clenched teeth. "I think I shall go up to London and partake of more . . . sophisticated pleasures. Do you think you could persuade Littlewood to do likewise?"

Pamela smiled as she entwined her arms around his neck and offered her willing body to him. "I'm sure that can be arranged, my lord. Even though he hates the city, Littlewood can deny me nothing."

Even as he began tearing at her clothes, she found herself wondering what in the world the Falconet chit had done to infuriate him so. But not for long. Whatever it was, it had driven Nicholas right back to her arms, where she intended him to stay.

6

"LORD Silverblade has gone to London," Diana said to Aurora as the two were doing embroidery in the solarium.

"Good riddance," Aurora replied, spitefully jabbing her needle into the fabric. "At least now I'll be able to go riding in peace."

A week had passed since she had learned the terrible truth about the marquess, a week haunted by sleepless nights and dark, twisted nightmares of revenge. Aurora had lost count of the times she had taken her father's pistols and sword from the chest at the foot of her bed, and stared at them, wondering what it would feel like to send a ball or the tip of her sword right through Lord Silverblade's cold, black heart.

Then she would remember his strong, hard arms wrapped around her so tightly she couldn't breathe, the excitement of his urgent mouth against her own, and the sword would tremble in her hand and fall away.

Aurora flung her embroidery hoop down in disgust. Then she rose and went to the solarium's wall of windows overlooking the lawns beyond.

Through the corner of her eye, Aurora saw Diana rise, walk over to her chair, and examine the embroidery that Aurora had just discarded.

"You should make your stitches shorter and closer together," Diana said.

"I'm afraid I was never adept at embroidery," Aurora retorted waspishly. "Mother died when I was only six, and then you left four years later. Who was supposed to teach me such feminine accomplishments? Father?" she scoffed.

Diana was silent for a moment, then she said, "Are you blaming me because you can't do fine needlework, Aurora? Or do you blame me for taking Lord Silverblade's side in this dispute?"

Aurora sighed, suddenly contrite. "I'm sorry, Diana. I didn't mean to imply that you were to blame for my ineptitude with a needle and thread." She raised her head boldly. "But I'll never understand why you have remained friends with that man after all he has done to our family."

Diana regarded her solemnly, as though her sister baffled her. Then she said, "Please sit down and I shall tell you."

When they both were seated, Diana began. "You have to remember that you were only a child of ten when Tim was taken from us, Aurora. I was six years older than you, already a grown woman of sixteen. Tim was eighteen, and since we were closer in age, we shared more between us, matters you never knew about."

"What matters?" Aurora demanded suspiciously.

"Oh, the wooing of certain ladies. Tim was a great favorite with the ladies. He courted a different one every week. Or I'd listen to him recount some prank that Father knew nothing of. Tim was quite fond of pranks. You were still in the nursery, so you never met Tim's friends, a boisterous, hot-blooded lot if ever there was one. Tim was no angel, I'll have you know."

Diana leaned forward. "I think you should know that Tim always spoke of Nicholas Devenish with the utmost respect and affection. They were the closest of friends, often inseparable. In fact, people called them the Twins because they were so close. That's why I find it impossible to believe Lord Silverblade goaded Tim into playing highwayman that night."

Aurora crossed her arms sullenly. "I don't wish to hear any more of this."

Diana ignored her and went on relentlessly. "There's something else you should know. You were so upset during the funeral that Father sent you home with your nurse rather than allow you to come to the grave-yard. You didn't see Lord Silverblade's face when they lowered Tim's coffin into the earth. He was weeping openly and without shame. Most men would try to mask their grief, but not Lord Silverblade."

Aurora scoffed, "He was probably afraid for his own life."

Diana just looked at her in exasperation. "Later, by the lych-gate, after everyone else had gone, he stopped me. He told me he wished he had forced Tim to stay in that night, but now it was too late. He'd never see him again, never laugh with him, never carouse with him." Diana said softly, "I've never seen a man so devastated by a friend's death. Nothing I said could console him."

"The marquess is a consummate actor, Diana," Aurora said. "He fooled even you."

Now Diana rose, her placid brow furrowed in anger. "I've just told you what I saw with my own eyes, Aurora. Why would I lie to you?"

"But Father said—"

Diana made a mutter of impatience. "You profess to seek the truth about that night, yet when it's staring you in the face, you refuse to believe it!"

"I would expect Lord Silverblade's friends to defend him."

Diana was silent for a moment. Then she said, "Did you ever stop to think that perhaps Father didn't tell you the truth?"

Aurora's eyes turned colder than ice. "Father wouldn't lie to me."

Diana threw up her hands in vexation, her patience worn out at last. "Believe whomever you please, Aurora. If you want to go on thinking the worst of Lord Silverblade, if you want to let yourself be eaten away by thoughts of revenge, feel free to do so." Now her voice rose. "But kindly spare the rest of us your brooding, sullen face and fits of temper!"

Aurora just sat there gaping, for her usually calm sister had never once raised her voice to her.

Suddenly there came a knock at the solarium door, and when Diana snapped, "What is it?" the major-domo entered and informed them that there was a Lord Witherspoon to see Miss Aurora.

"Lord Witherspoon?" Aurora looked at her sister helplessly. "I know no Lord Witherspoon."

Diana smiled, dissipating her anger. "Lord Witherspoon is the short young gentleman who danced with you at the ball. I'm sure he would be mortally offended if he knew you did not remember him, Aurora."

Suddenly the unpleasant picture of a short young man whose eyes had kept wandering down Aurora's gown all evening sprang to her mind and she groaned.

"Lord Witherspoon . . . Now I do remember." She looked at Diana in appeal. "Must I see him? Can't you tell him I have the plague and you don't know if I shall ever recover?"

Diana laughed. "I'm afraid you must see him, my dear. It's evident that he was smitten with you and has come to call. The least you can do is sit and talk with him for a few moments."

"I'll agree only if you remain as my chaperon."

"I promise not to leave you alone together for one second," Diana replied.

The two sisters strolled out of the solarium arm in arm, both thankful that the angry words between them had been said and done with. They were friends again.

Lord Witherspoon did not disappoint Aurora. As they sat in the drawing room and conversed, the young man's feverish eyes kept drifting down to the low, square-cut bodice of Aurora's gown. So absorbed was he in Aurora's neckline, Lord Witherspoon even failed to respond to Diana when she offered him a glass of sherry.

Aurora steadfastly refused to discuss any topic other than horses and hounds, and within fifteen minutes the young lord was stifling a yawn of boredom and rising to leave. Aurora and Diana escorted him to the door, and stood there waving until Lord Witherspoon's elegant carriage disappeared down the drive. Then the two sisters went inside and collapsed in gales of laughter.

While Diana returned to her embroidery, Aurora decided to go for a walk. She left the house for the small summerhouse at the far edge of the garden.

No sooner did she seat herself than she saw Halley come walking toward her in his graceful stride. He was elegantly attired as always, in a new dark blue coat and pale yellow brocade waistcoat.

As she watched him, Aurora thought she detected something different in his demeanor today, but she couldn't tell what it was.

He swept his hat off as he climbed the steps of the summerhouse.

"Was that the gallant Lord Witherspoon's carriage I just saw hurrying down the drive?" he asked with a dazzling smile.

Aurora nodded glumly. "He came to call upon me."

Halley's brows rose as he seated himself across from her and proceeded to adjust the Mechlin lace at his wrists. Then he looked around as if expecting to find a mirror hanging in the folly, and when he realized there was none, he casually draped his arm across the back of the bench.

"Witherspoon is a potential suitor, I'll be bound."

"I sincerely hope not. I'll die of the plague before I marry Lord Witherspoon," Aurora said.

Halley burst out laughing. "Am I to infer that you don't return the young gentleman's affections?"

"You infer correctly," Aurora replied with an impish grin.

Suddenly Halley got a faraway look in his eyes, and he seemed to be speaking to himself as he murmured, "No, Aurora, you need a very special man to protect you."

"I beg your pardon?"

His hazel eyes looked right through her, alarming Aurora with their intensity. Then he grinned disarmingly. "Come, Aurora. Walk with me."

He rose and started down the folly's steps before she had a chance to question him further. All she could do was hurry to catch up.

They walked in silence together, for Aurora sensed at once that Halley had something serious to discuss with her. He walked with his hands clasped behind his back, and he stared at the ground as though trying to collect his thoughts.

Finally, when they were a good distance from the house, with no one to see or hear them, he stopped and turned to her.

"Aurora, what do you think of me?"

She regarded him in puzzlement. "What do I think of you? I . . . don't understand."

"Come, come, don't dissemble with me. Do you find me comely, repulsive—"

"Oh, no, you are not repulsive." Aurora tried to control her embarrassment by pretending she was having such a discussion with an older brother. "I think you are quite comely."

"Most women do think me handsome."

Aurora made a pretense of stooping to pick a wildflower growing at the side of the path. "Why are you even asking my opinion on such a matter, Halley? Surely Diana's opinion is the one you should be seeking."

He took a step closer to her, making Aurora uneasy. "Not that it matters, but what I am about to propose to you will be so much easier for you to accept if you think me well-favored."

Aurora felt a sudden premonition of foreboding twist deep inside her. She was wary of the predatory look in Halley's eyes, which were glittering with a strange, feverish light.

She stepped away from him, her entire body tense and ready to spring away like a startled fawn. "I . . . don't understand."

"It's quite simple, really." He took a deep breath. "I want you for my mistress."

The wildflower fell from her fingers. "You want me to—"

"Be my mistress. You heard me correctly the first time, Aurora."

She was paralyzed with shock. She couldn't have fled from him if she wanted to.

"You can't mean what you say, Halley!"

"Oh, but I do. I want to be your lover, Aurora, and your protector." While Aurora stood there gaping at him, he took several steps away from her. "I must confess that when you first came to live at Overton Manor, I didn't like you at all. You were always so defiant, so hoydenish and unfeminine. And, of course, there was your innocence. I have always found innocence quite tiresome in a woman once she reaches a certain age."

Now he turned and raked her up and down with a look that was blatantly lustful. "But I sense in you a passionate nature, my dear. It just needs to be . . . awakened properly." He raised one brow and asked sternly, "You haven't been with another man, have you?"

His brazen question outraged her. "That, sir, is none of your affair!"

"I thought not," he said with a knowing smile. "And I'm relieved, because I am not accustomed to taking another man's leavings."

Aurora was finding it as difficult to speak as it was difficult to breathe. "But what about Diana? Are you just going to turn her out?"

"Of course not. I intend to keep the both of you. We shall be a cozy *ménage à trois,* my dear, the only difference being that Diana will not know our *deux* has become a *trois.*"

"Th-that is wicked and depraved! Diana will never agree to such an arrangement."

"Ah, but she will never know, because neither of us is going to tell her."

Aurora's mind raced ahead, desperately seeking any excuse that would dissuade him. "Come, Halley. She is bound to find out. The first night you do not come to her bed, she will suspect something is amiss."

Halley shrugged nonchalantly. "And what if she does? There is nothing she can do about it. I am her protector, and she will obey me. As will you, if you wish to continue living here at Overton Manor."

Aurora had never felt so helpless or trapped in her entire life. She retaliated as best she could. "What if I go to my sister this minute and tell her what you have proposed?"

"Don't threaten me, Aurora. I'd deny such charges. She loves me so much she would believe me. Even if you did manage to convince her you were telling the truth, what could she possible do about it?" His voice grew mocking. "Leave me?"

Aurora regarded him with a sinking heart. She knew he spoke the truth. Diana would never take her sister's word over that of the man she loved. She would betray her own sister before she gave up Halley.

"Don't look so despondent, my love," he said. "You could be giving yourself to a graceless oaf like Witherspoon. I promise to be a most attentive lover, attentive and generous. You'll want for nothing, and everyone will envy you as they do Diana." Then he smiled slowly. "Perhaps I'll even give you Firelight. If you please me, that is."

"But you don't love me!" Aurora wailed in desperation.

"So you must have love . . ." Halley shook his head. "No, I don't love you, but I find you very beautiful, and spirited enough to keep me amused. Diana has been so bland lately. I fancy I need a little pepper in my diet."

Aurora eyed him warily, wondering when he was going to force his attentions on her, but Halley just stood before her, running his short, blunt fingers along the brim of his hat.

She knew now that she couldn't afford to antagonize him, so she appeared to surrender. "I . . . I must have time to consider your proposal."

"Of course. I don't expect you to slip between my sheets right this minute. What kind of man do think I am?"

Aurora knew now, but wisely refrained from replying, and willed her traitorous face to remain expressionless.

"I'll want your decision in two weeks," he said, then bowed to her, set his hat back on his head, and sauntered off down the way he had come, self-assured and confident that she would comply with his desires.

Aurora stared at his retreating figure, while wave after wave of panic washed over her. She felt light-headed, as though she hadn't eaten in a long time, but she took a deep breath and the feeling passed.

She turned and kept walking down the path, her mind racing. What could she do? She knew she could expect no help from her sister. Halley was right about that. If Diana had to choose between her lover and her sister . . .

Where else could she go? She had sought refuge at Overton manor because she had lost her home in Ireland.

She wouldn't even consider accepting Halley's offer. She had seen the way he treated Diana. Oh, he was generous with material comforts, but he never allowed her to express an opinion contrary to his, never allowed her an original thought. Diana was nothing more than a nonentity in his eyes, someone to parrot his opinions and increase his own sense of self-importance.

Aurora shook her head at the irony of it. Halley had grown tired of Diana because she was too spiritless, but he was the one who had made her that way. Now that he had broken Diana, he wanted to break Aurora as well.

Well, she was not going to allow it to happen.

When she finally stopped walking, she found herself beside a brook that chugged and gurgled along. Feeling warm, she knelt down, dipped her cupped hands into the cold water, and splashed it on her face.

Suddenly that gesture reminded her of the night of the ball, and she laughed with relief. She was not entirely alone and friendless after all. There was one person who might sympathize with her plight and help her, but Aurora had to act right away.

When she returned to the house, she rushed right upstairs to her room, sat down with paper, quill, and sandbox, and wrote a letter, the most important letter of her life.

Aurora watched from the head of the stairs as the majordomo took several letters from the carrier, placed them on a silver salver, and took them to his master.

She held her breath and prayed.

Seven days had passed since she had posted her letter, and still no reply. If she received no word within the week, Aurora would have no alternative but to become Halley's mistress.

She returned to her room to wait for the summons she yearned for. By the time her maid came to dress her for supper, Aurora knew with a discouraged heart she had waited in vain.

Several more days passed, and still no letter from London.

Time was running out, as Halley reminded Aurora one morning when he insisted on joining her for her daily ride.

"Have you reached a decision, my lovely Aurora?" he asked as he drew his horse alongside Molly.

She resisted the impulse to shrink away from him in revulsion. "No, I haven't, Halley."

He smiled, a wolfish baring of his teeth. "I am mortally offended. Most women wouldn't hesitate to become my mistress, but I am very selective. Diana accepted the moment I asked her."

"I am not Diana."

Comprehension lit up his handsome features. "Ah, now I understand. You are being reserved to entice me further, to inflame my passions and make my conquest of you all the sweeter." He chuckled. "My, what a clever wench you are, Aurora, beneath that veneer of innocence."

Aurora blushed to the roots of her hair at such frank and lascivious banter. "Molly needs a good run. If you'll excuse me, Halley, I'll—"

Before she could escape, Halley reached out and grasped Molly's bridle. His tone was low and deadly as he said, "I enjoy a little game of cat and mouse as well as the next man, Aurora. But I grow weary of your ineffectual attempts to cheat me out of what I want. You have four more days to come to a decision."

Then he released her horse and rode away.

* * *

Nothing came in the post the following day, or the day after that.

On the third day, Aurora was sitting in her bedchamber when a summons came from Halley.

"He must want my decision today," she muttered despondently.

Resigned to her fate at last, she squared her shoulders and went down to the drawing room.

When she knocked and was admitted, Aurora was startled to see Diana there as well as Halley, who wore a barely concealed scowl of displeasure.

Aurora's heart raced in panic. Halley must have told Diana about his desire for Aurora, and she was amenable to such an arrangement.

Aurora was about to open her mouth to speak, when she noticed Halley pick up a letter from the table by his side. Her hopes soared, and she kept silent.

"I've just received a letter from the Duchess of Kilkenny, Aurora," Halley said, giving her a suspicious look. "She says she enjoyed your company so much at our ball that she wants you to come to stay with her in London for an extended period."

"This comes as a . . . a great surprise to me," Aurora stammered. "I . . . I'm quite flattered."

"She was quite taken with you," Diana said with a delighted smile. "Do you wish to go to her in London? Of course, Halley and I don't want you to feel as though we are forcing you out of the manor."

Aurora tried not to appear too eager. "I do so enjoy living here, but I think London would be exciting. I've never been to London, and as long as the duchess desires my company . . ."

"Then you shall go," Halley said. "I have no wish to offend the Duchess of Kilkenny, or her husband, for that matter. The duke is a powerful man, with many connections."

"When shall I leave?" Aurora asked.

"As soon as your clothes can be packed," Diana replied. Then she looked at Halley. "Can you spare a carriage to take Aurora to London?"

"Of course. How would it look to Kilkenny if I

allowed my ward to travel by stagecoach or even a post chaise?"

Diana beamed. "How exciting! You will adore London. I know it's huge and teeming with people, but there are so many shops to patronize, and Vauxhall for entertainments. The Kilkennys will be perfect hosts."

"I'm sure it will be a novel experience for me," was all Aurora said, though she was so jubilant she wanted to shout from the rooftops.

"Now, let us go upstairs and decide what you shall take with you," Diana said, leading Aurora to the door.

They had almost reached it when Halley called to them. "Diana, why don't you go ahead? There are a few words I must say to Aurora."

Without questioning him, Diana just smiled and left the two of them alone.

Aurora turned to face Halley, her mouth suddenly dry with apprehension. She was surprised to find him smiling. Then, without a word, he walked over to a decanter on the sideboard and poured himself a claret.

He stared deeply into his glass for several seconds as though studying his reflection; then he turned to Aurora and raised it in a toast.

"To a very clever wench." And he downed the drink in one swallow. "You have won the first round, Aurora, with your clever move. But don't think yourself too clever, for I shall win the second. There will come a day when the duchess will tire of your company and send you home. I shall be waiting, and you can be certain that you shan't escape me this time."

Aurora didn't even try to deny what she had done, for it was obvious that Halley knew.

He turned away from her. "You are excused. I believe you have packing to do."

Knees shaking with relief, Aurora ran from the drawing room as fast as she could.

Diana felt as though she were walking on air.

"That invitation was a gift from the gods," she

mumbled happily to herself as she walked back to Aurora's room to supervise the packing.

She didn't stop to question the duchess's motives for inviting Aurora to stay with her in London. It was sufficient that she had been asked, and that Halley had agreed to let her go.

It was not that she feared losing Halley to her own sister, she reassured herself hastily, for her position as his mistress had never been stronger. But she just needed some time alone with Halley to ensure that it remained that way.

When she arrived in Aurora's room, Diana rang for Sarah, and by the time the maid appeared in the doorway, Aurora herself joined them.

She left for London the following day.

Aurora's last memory of Overton Manor was of Diana standing on the steps crying and waving a handkerchief, while Halley stood behind her, his mouth stretched in a grim parody of a smile.

7

KILKENNY House was not at all what Aurora had expected. After driving through the dark, narrow, filthy streets of London, where row upon endless row of houses were squeezed together and nauseating odors arose from the filth thrown into central gutters, she began wondering if she had made a mistake by seeking sanctuary with the duchess. London was a noisy, frightening place that made her wish for the peace and serenity of the countryside.

But when her carriage finally arrived at the Kilkennys' residence, Aurora could have wept with relief. Kilkenny House was a grand town house protected by a high wall and a spiked wrought-iron fence. Built of mellow gray stone, its entrance was a magnificent pillared portico that reminded Aurora of the entrance to Silverblade.

Silverblade . . . She forced all thoughts of that man and his house from her mind as she stepped down from the carriage and made her way up the steps.

The majordomo was already waiting at the door. He made a courtly bow and bade her enter.

"Miss Aurora Falconet to see the Duchess of Kilkenny," Aurora said. Her eyes were drawn upward even as she spoke, for the foyer was a spacious rotunda, and its high domed ceiling was made entirely of glass to catch all available light, even on a drab, gray day such as this.

"Her grace is expecting you, miss," the man said gravely. "If you will follow me . . ."

Aurora fell into step behind him, trying to resist staring at the polished marble floor, paneled walls, and intricate molded plasterwork on the ceilings.

The majordomo threw open two large doors to announce, "Miss Aurora Falconet, your grace," in a booming voice.

Aurora took a deep breath to steady her quavering insides, threw her shoulders back, and strode into a drawing room done in pale yellow and resplendent with Chinese-style lacquered furniture. Her kid slippers sank into a thick, lush carpet that muffled every footstep.

"Aurora!" the duchess cried, rising from a satin-covered chair to greet her guest. "I thought you would never arrive!"

She gathered her silk skirts and swept across the drawing room, only stopping when she reached Aurora's side. Then she grasped her hand warmly and kissed her on the cheek.

Aurora blushed as she remembered her manners. She bobbed the duchess a curtsy and murmured, "Good day to you, your grace. I am forever in debted to you for agreeing to receive me."

The duchess made a clucking sound of disapproval. "If you persist in calling me 'your grace' you may turn right around and go back to Overton Manor."

For one horrifying moment Aurora thought the duchess meant it, and she suddenly turned white.

But when Katherine smiled charmingly and added, "I thought we had agreed to be Katherine and Aurora to each other?" she was so relieved she could have cried.

"If you wish, your . . . Katherine," Aurora said.

Katherine led her over to a chair opposite her own and indicated that Aurora should be seated. "I do. Didn't I tell you the night of the ball that we were destined to become the best of friends?"

Aurora twisted her fingers in her lap. "You did. And I . . . I hope I haven't presumed upon the friendship you so generously offered."

Katherine didn't reply as she tugged at an embroidered bell-pull on the wall. When she was seated, her face was both grave and sympathetic.

"I must admit that I was most surprised to receive your letter. I thought you were happy living with your sister."

"I was, until—"

Aurora was interrupted by the arrival of the major-domo, who was ordered to bring hot chocolate and cakes.

When the man left, Katherine said, "In your letter, you sounded quite desperate to leave Overton Manor. Would you mind telling me why?"

Aurora didn't falter as she said, "Lord Overton wanted me to become his mistress."

To Aurora's surprise, Katherine wasn't shocked at all. She reached over to a small silver dish, offered Aurora a sweetmeat, then selected one herself and popped it into her mouth. When she finished eating, she said, "So, the temptation of having another beautiful Falconet under his roof was too much for poor Halley."

Panic clenched at Aurora's stomach. She had fled to Katherine expecting sanctuary and sympathy, and here she was acting as though it were an everyday occurrence that a man might take two mistresses under one roof!

"Poor Aurora. I can see by the expression on your face that such an arrangement was not agreeable to you."

Aurora's voice was filled with loathing as she replied, "The man is my own sister's lover! How could I be so disloyal to Diana, even if I were attracted to Halley?"

Katherine nodded in approval. "I would have done the same in your position."

Privately Aurora suspected that Diana was well aware of Halley's keen interest in her beautiful younger sister, and was secretly relieved to have Aurora out of the way. Not that Aurora could blame her. She would probably feel the same way if she were in Diana's position. No, her departure from Overton Manor was best for all concerned.

Suddenly she and the duchess were interrupted once again by a maid bearing a huge silver tray set with a silver pot of hot chocolate, several plates of tiny iced cakes, cups, and silver spoons.

When the servant left and Katherine began to pour, she said, "Why don't you enlighten me further?"

So, while she ate and drank hot chocolate, Aurora told the duchess all about Halley's offer and how hopeless her situation was.

"That is why I wrote to you, begging you to invite me to London," Aurora said. "I was desperate. I had no one else to turn to, nowhere else to go. If you hadn't agreed to have me, I would have had no other choice than to become Halley's mistress."

The duchess just shook her head as she sat back in her chair. "A *ménage à trois* has become quite fashionable in our circle, but I for one would never tolerate it. It's one thing for a man to discreetly keep a mistress, but quite another for him to live openly with two woman under the same roof."

Aurora made no comment, just sipped her hot chocolate thoughtfully. She thought to herself that if she loved a man and he loved her, he should have no need of a mistress. But she realized she was an ignorant country miss, not very knowledgeable about sophisticated London society, so she held her tongue.

Katherine smiled, her wide green eyes dancing with conspiracies and schemes. "Well, Aurora, I would be most pleased to aid you in your evasion of Lord Overton. You may stay with me for as long as you like."

"I hope it won't be for very long," Aurora assured her. "I have come to London to seek employment."

The duchess choked on her sip of hot chocolate. "Employment?" she squeaked, aghast.

"Yes. I thought about this very carefully on the way to London, and decided that I wish to become a governess. I'm sure I know enough to teach children their sums and how to read."

Katherine shook her head, marveling at Aurora's

naiveté. "My dear, you are far too beautiful to become a governess. No lady would countenance such temptation under her own roof, to distract her husband and older sons."

Aurora looked crestfallen, but only for a moment. She brightened as she said, "Then I shall become a paid companion. I understand elderly ladies often hire them."

The duchess raised one skeptical brow. "You would wish to spend the bloom of your youth fetching and carrying for some old crone so envious of your youth and beauty that she would work you to death?"

Aurora stared at Katherine in dismay. "I . . . I hadn't thought of that." Tears of discouragement stung her eyes, and her fingers were trembling so badly she had to set down her cup before she spilled its contents all over her gown. "What am I going to do?" she muttered.

Katherine smiled gently and leaned forward to place her hand over Aurora's. "You're going to put all thoughts of employment out of your head at once. They are most unsuitable for a lady of quality in any case."

"B-but I can't impose upon your generosity forever."

Katherine made a mewling sound of sympathy. "Now, now, Aurora, don't look so despondent! All is not lost. Much can happen to such a beautiful young lady in a city like London, even in the summer. There are many eligible young men out there, ripe for marriage."

Aurora thought of Lord Witherspoon, and she abandoned all hope. So that was so be her destiny after all, even in London.

Katherine brightened as she rose, whirled away from the tea table, and tugged at the bell-pull once again.

"First, we shall get you settled and introduce you to the children—we have two charming boys—then we shall plan a campaign that will have all of London at your feet!" she said with a martial gleam in her eye that would have put a general to shame. "But you must promise not to give Overton a second thought."

Aurora agreed. She had to put Halley out of her

mind and concentrate on making the most of her stay in London.

Aurora stared down at the glittering throng of people in the Kilkennys' ballroom and smiled in satisfaction.

Ever since Aurora's arrival two weeks ago, the Kilkenny's had done everything in their power to make her feel welcome. If they were invited to a rout or a ridotto, they secured an invitation for Aurora as well so she could meet their influential friends. They went riding in the park, browsing in the fashionable shops from Charing Cross to Whitechapel, and attending the theater at Drury Lane.

Tonight they were giving a ball in her honor.

As she stood at the head of the stairs, she couldn't help but recall her first ball at Overton Manor. Then she had hardly recognized herself with her hair powdered and her face stiff with white ceruse. Tonight her auburn hair blazed in all its copper-colored glory by candlelight, and her face looked fresh and lovely without the dead-white paint to conceal its natural beauty.

Suddenly something Lord Silverblade had said to her that night about roses being too beautiful to paint popped unbidden into her mind. Once there, his image arrogantly refused to leave. Against her will, Aurora remembered how he had looked that night, so elegant and commanding, his gray eyes warm and sparkling with amusement, his touch gentle and solicitous, yet exciting.

Aurora knew he was still here in London. She had first seen him at Drury Lane, seated several boxes away with Mrs. Littlewood and her husband. When he noticed her, he seemed disconcerted, for he kept glancing her way, much to the lovely Mrs. Littlewood's ill-disguised chagrin. But Aurora kept her attention focused on the actors and the stage and never looked at him again for the rest of the evening.

In the days to come, she caught glimpses of him riding in the park and attending several social functions, but he never spoke to her and Aurora never acknowledged him.

"I refuse to give that murderer another thought,"

she muttered to herself as she gathered her green damask skirts and glided down the stairs.

She was halfway across the ballroom when she saw him deep in conversation with the Misses Adderley, "two of the most notorious gossips in all of London," according to Katherine.

Aurora stopped in her tracks, her hand flying to her throat in alarm. Just at that moment, Lord Silverblade looked up and saw her. Much to Aurora's dismay, he excused himself and started toward her.

She was about to turn right around and sweep out of the ballroom when she remembered that the Kilkennys hadn't invited him to the ball tonight out of deference to her sensibilities. She was further relieved when she realized the man approaching her was not Lord Silverblade after all, but his cousin, Wesley Devenish.

"Why, Miss Falconet," he greeted her in his soft voice, his small eyes widening as much as they dared, "this is a pleasant surprise!" He seemed certain she would not recognize him, for he added, "Wesley Devenish, at your service. We met at your sister's ball."

"Of course I remember you, Mr. Devenish," she said with a curtsy. "What a pleasure it is to see you again."

"But whatever are you doing here at Kilkenny House? I thought you were staying at Overton Manor, deep in the Surrey countryside. So much more pleasant than the city in summer."

As Aurora explained she was visiting the duchess, she wondered how she ever could have mistaken Wesley for Lord Silverblade, even across a crowded ballroom. They were so very different.

"And how have you been finding London?" he asked.

"Most enjoyable. I have met so many interesting people, and seen such magnificent sights," she replied.

He smiled faintly. "Oh, it has its dark side, I assure you, and I prefer it to country living myself. But then, my commercial enterprises keep me here almost the year round."

Aurora smiled. "I recall my sister mentioning that

you are a merchant, with ships that sail all over the world."

He lowered his gaze modestly. "I am that, Miss Falconet, but my cousin Nick is the accomplished one in the family."

Hearing Nicholas praised brought a hot flash of anger to Aurora's cheeks. "And what has your cousin accomplished, pray tell? He runs an estate he has inherited, with a fortune he also inherited. He no doubt is an excellent shot and swordsman. But you, Mr. Devenish, have earned your way in the world. I quite admire you for that."

Wesley Devenish stared at her in disbelief as though he had never received a compliment in his life. "Why . . . why, thank you, Miss Falconet," he stammered. "But I am not sure that I deserve your praise."

There was such sadness and bitterness in the man's voice that Aurora felt a rush of pity for him. He reminded her so much of the foxhound runt in the Silverblade kennels, doomed to a life of being pushed out of the way by those stronger than he.

She longed to say something comforting, to tell him that she understood how he felt, but just at that moment a young man claimed her for the next dance. After excusing herself, Aurora glided away on her partner's arm.

Wesley stood on the sidelines and watched Aurora bow and sway gracefully to the delicate strains of the minuet. Initially he had thought she was different from all the others. At least she didn't laugh at him behind her fan the way Nick's doxy, that dreadful Littlewood woman, did. But Aurora Falconet pitied him. He could read it in her expressive face, though she had tried her best to hide it. And nothing infuriated Wesley more than being the object of pity.

Suddenly the music slowed and the dance ended. Wesley watched as Aurora curtsied to her partner and began looking around the room. He sensed she was looking for him. Perhaps she felt it was her duty to converse with him, since no other women were.

Resentment bubbled up in him afresh. He turned

away and left Kilkenny House before she could waylay
and smother him with more pity.

"No stay in London would be complete without a
visit to Vauxhall Gardens," the duke declared as their
slender wherry effortlessly sliced through the murky
waters of the Thames River and drew closer to the
Vauxhall Stairs.

Katherine added, "If we ever survive the landing."

Aurora silently agreed. While she had enjoyed the
boat ride from Westminster across the Thames, she
could see their arrival at Vauxhall's waterside was
going to be a rather tumultuous event. There was a
terrible confusion of wherries all trying to land at the
same time, and a crowd of people bawling and quar-
reling with one another while the beadles paraded
about trying to keep order.

Finally several burly men came splashing into the
water and pulled the Kilkennys' craft ashore with such
violence that Aurora feared they would capsize. But
they disembarked without incident and soon joined
the merry, high-spirited throng of Londoners heading
toward the entrance gate.

Aurora showed her silver season ticket at the gate,
then followed her host and hostess down a dark passage.

At her elbow, Katherine said, "Now, get ready for a
truly magnificent sight."

Aurora gasped in delight when they finally emerged.
The gardens blazed with the light of a thousand lamps
that dazzled the eye as they glimmered through trees
that scarcely moved. Before her was the Great Walk,
which stretched the entire length of the gardens, and
all around were the numerous pavilions, temples, and
rotundas for which Vauxhall was famous.

"How beautiful!" Aurora murmured, entranced. She
was surrounded by the sounds of voices and laughter
underscored by the faint strains of music in the distance.

The duke, who tended to treat all women as pretty
children, smiled indulgently at her. "There is much
more to see, but since the concert is about to begin, I
think we should find our box and have some supper."

The supper boxes, as Aurora soon discovered, were

charmingly decorated with paintings and situated near the orchestra, so the revelers could enjoy the music while they dined on paper-thin slices of ham and drank claret. Once supper and the concert were over, she and the Kilkennys began strolling around the gardens.

Aurora had been wandering through a grotto for several minutes before she realized the duke and duchess were no longer standing behind her. Somehow, they had become separated in the crowd. She was alone.

Aurora craned her neck and looked right and left, peering at faces that suddenly all looked alike beneath the paper lanterns. Then she smiled with relief when she saw a woman who looked just like Katherine, but when she went up to her, Aurora discovered that it was someone else. Mumbling her apologies, she turned away.

Panicking now, she ran to and fro, desperately seeking her friends. She hurried past the fortune-telling pavilion, down yet another walk, and beneath several arches. Thoroughly confused and somewhat breathless by this time, Aurora found herself facing a walk unlike all the rest.

She hesitated as she peered at the entrance. This walk was nothing more than a dark forbidding tunnel, with no paper lanterns hanging in the branches to illuminate the way. Aurora bit her lip in vexation as she tried to decide whether to plunge in and hope the Kilkennys had gone down this passage, or to turn away and search for them elsewhere.

"I wouldn't go in there, if I were you."

With a startled gasp, Aurora whirled around to find none other than Lord Silverblade at her elbow.

He bowed politely, but his gray eyes were hard and cold as they captured and held hers. "May I ask why you are wandering around Vauxhall Gardens without a chaperon, Miss Falconet?"

Blue eyes as pale as a tropical lagoon met his, and Nicholas inwardly groaned. He had been an idiot to think he could ever forget those heartbreaking eyes, even if they were now regarding him with supreme disdain.

"I am not wandering around without a chaperon, Lord Silverblade," she replied loftily. "I am here with the Kilkennys. We merely became separated, and I am searching for them."

"Well, you won't find them there," he said, nodding toward the tunnel's entrance. "That, Miss Falconet, is Vauxhall's infamous Lovers' Walk. If you have the misfortune to wander in there alone and unprotected, all you'll find are the unwanted attentions of some base ruffian."

"Thank you for the warning," Aurora said stiffly.

"You're welcome, Miss Falconet. There is nothing I enjoy more than rescuing damsels in distress."

As he had the night of Overton's ball, when she had smeared black lead all over her face . . .

The tender memory of that humorous escapade they had shared threatened to undermine Aurora's resolve to hate him, and in a moment of weakness, she almost relented. Then she hardened herself against him, crossing her arms over her chest to put a physical barrier between them and ward him off.

"I appreciate your rescuing me, Lord Silverblade," she said, "but it changes nothing between us. I will never forgive you for what you did to my brother."

Lord Silverblade's dark, flaring brows came together in a scowl. "So, you continue to bear me a grudge, Miss Falconet? You disappoint me. I had hoped that, given some time, you would realize I am telling the truth about what happened that night."

Aurora gave him a long, cold stare before wishing him good evening and turning to leave.

Nicholas couldn't let her go before he had the answer his wounded pride demanded. He stepped in front of her, effectively blocking her escape.

"Answer me one question, Aurora," he said before she could open her mouth to protest. "I've told you the truth about what happened that night. Why won't you believe me?"

"Because you are a rake and a libertine," she said without hesitation. "And a man without honor."

Nicholas recoiled, then took refuge in mockery to conceal how much her words had stung him. "If your words were swords, I fear I should be mortally wounded."

"I wish my words *were* swords, then I would run you through!"

"The rash boast of a child, Miss Falconet, nothing more," was his bland reply, deliberately calculated to insult and aggravate her. "Now, Miss Falconet, I believe I heard you mention you were searching for your companions. As detestable as my company is to you, I am offering my services."

Aurora was spared refusing him when she heard someone call her name frantically. She turned to see Katherine and the duke hurrying toward her.

"There you are!" Katherine exclaimed. "Kilkenny and I were at our wits' end when we discovered you were nowhere to be found." Then she flashed a dazzling smile at Lord Silverblade. "But I can see you are in good company."

"Your graces," Lord Silverblade said with a deep bow. Then, with a cool glance at Aurora, he added, "I came upon Miss Falconet about to search the Lovers' Walk for you."

Comprehension flashed across the duchess's pert features. "Oh, dear . . . are you sure you're all right, Aurora?"

Aurora nodded.

"Kilkenny," Katherine said to her husband, "I've had quite enough of Vauxhall for one evening. Let us go home, shall we?"

To Aurora's relief, the duke agreed, and after taking their leave of Lord Silverblade, they left without a backward glance.

Nicholas just stood there for a moment staring at Aurora's retreating form and growing increasingly furious with himself.

Why should it matter to him that she thought him a rake, a murderer, and a man without honor? She was a little nobody from Ireland, without wealth or social position. All Nicholas had to do was snap his fingers and half of the most beautiful, eligible women in England would be at his beck and call. He didn't need Aurora Falconet or her good graces.

But deep inside, he knew her good graces mattered a great deal. Just being with her mattered a great deal. She was so courageous, so gallant, that Nicholas always felt his own stature grow in her presence. He had missed that since the rift between them, and he missed their shared laughter as well.

"Admit it, Silverblade," he muttered to himself as Aurora disappeared from view, "you're infatuated with an enchanting child who hates you."

Ever since Nicholas had first learned that Aurora was in London, he had gone out of his way to frequent those places where she might be seen. And he had succeeded. Yet, whenever he saw her riding in the park or seated in the Kilkennys' box at the theater, she assiduously avoided catching his eye. She obviously wanted nothing more to do with him.

He had warned her about the dangers of the Lovers' Walk, and still she treated him with contempt.

Why was he going to such great lengths to win the approval of such a cold, unreasonable wench when he had warm, willing Pamela waiting for him in the Lovers' Walk? He had asked himself that question a thousand times and was no closer to finding the answer.

Nicholas swore under his breath just as Ollie appeared by his side.

"There you are, Nick," his friend said, his face flushed with exertion. "Been looking all over for you." Ollie squinted at him. "Ummm, you look like you want to rip someone's heart out. Nothing I did, I hope."

Nicholas shook his head absently. "I just saw Aurora Falconet."

Ollie's eyes brightened in comprehension, for Nicholas had told him about Aurora's discovery concerning Viscount Havering and the rift it had caused between them. "Bad luck, old man."

"I'm worried about her."

"Do you think there's any truth to the rumor that Overton wanted to make her his mistress?"

Nicholas' lip curled in contempt. "I'm sure it's true. Why else would she suddenly bolt from her sister's home, flee to London, and put herself under the Kilkennys' protection?"

He didn't tell Ollie that he had longed to wrap his hands around Overton's throat when he had first heard those rumors. Aurora was his lover's sister, for God's sake! Did the man have no sense of decency?

Well, at least she was safe with the Kilkennys.

"But for how long?" he muttered to himself.

Then Nicholas shrugged and placed one hand on Ollie's back. Aurora Falconet was no concern of his. "Come. Let us not keep the ladies waiting."

The two of them disappeared into the Lovers' Walk.

8

"WAKE UP, sleepyhead!"

Aurora groaned and tried to roll away from the relentless hand shaking her shoulder, to no avail. Finally she opened one bleary eye to find none other than Katherine already dressed to go out and standing by her bedside.

"Katherine," she said, sitting up and rubbing the sleep from her eyes, "what time is it?"

"Almost eight o'clock," the duchess replied, her eyes sparkling mischievously. "Don't look so astonished. I know I seldom rise before ten, but today I have a special surprise for you."

Now Aurora was wide-awake. "What sort of surprise?"

"Oh, I'm not going to spoil it by telling you. You'll see soon enough. Now, drink your hot chocolate and dress as quickly as you can. Be sure to wear a hat, as we'll be outdoors. Kilkenny and I will be waiting for you in the foyer." Then, with a lilting laugh, the duchess flitted out of the room, leaving Aurora burning with curiosity.

Half an hour later, Aurora was hurrying down the main staircase to where the Kilkennys were waiting.

The duke bowed and wished her good morning. "I understand my duchess wishes our trip to be a surprise for you."

"Then my surprise is a place?" Aurora asked as

they walked out the front door and she saw the coach and four waiting.

"A place and an event," the duke replied cryptically.

"An exciting event," Katherine added, obviously relishing keeping Aurora in suspense. "It's even more exciting than visiting Bedlam to watch the insane perform."

"Are we calling upon someone?" Aurora guessed as the duke handed her into the waiting carriage.

"In a sense we will be calling upon several people," Katherine replied.

"We're going to a fair!" Aurora cried jubilantly.

"In a sense," the duke replied, then helped himself to a pinch of snuff.

Katherine settled her skirts about her. "Let us not tease Aurora any longer. She'll just have to see for herself."

Aurora curbed her impatience and looked out the window as the carriage started moving down the drive away from Kilkenny House. Soon, above the clattering of wheels over cobblestones and the clopping of hooves, she could hear the sound of church bells in the distance. But they were strangely muted today, not pealing joyously as was their custom.

"They sound so solemn," Aurora said to herself. "Perhaps someone has died." Later, she would remember those words, but now she didn't give the bells a second thought.

At first the carriage moved along at a fast pace, and the street was nearly empty of people. Gradually, several people became several dozen, and suddenly those several dozen swelled to become hundreds, clogging the street and blocking the way so the carriage was nearly forced to a standstill.

Aurora craned her neck to look out the window. There was nothing but bobbing heads for as far as the eye could see, a rippling wave of humanity. "What is happening? It's as though we're plowing through a sea of people."

"We are," the duke said mildly, scowling as those same people bumped into his carriage, rocking it. "Fortunately, we are in a carriage, and they are on foot."

Aurora sat back. "This fair we're going to must be exciting."

The Kilkennys exchanged amused glances and secret smiles.

"I'm sure you'll find it as exciting as we do," Katherine said. She wrinkled her pert nose in distaste as the odors of the street assailed her, and she sniffed her scented pomander.

Finally, after what seemed like an eternity to the impatient Aurora, the carriage stopped and Katherine leaned forward, her face flushed with anticipation. "Come, Aurora. We're going to sit on the roof for a better view."

"A view of what?" she asked as the driver pushed aside several people to open the door for them.

"You'll see," was all Katherine would say.

After much assistance from the duke and his driver, Aurora was finally seated atop the carriage and able to get a good look at her surroundings.

She had never seen so many people together in one place, even on market day in Ireland. Why, there must have been thousands! The vast majority milled about on foot, elbowing their way through the mob and occasionally throwing a punch or two when someone didn't stand aside quickly enough. Others had the advantage of being on horseback or in carriages, and could plow through with little resistance. From her high vantage point Aurora could see them filling nearby roads like ants and hanging out of windows in the houses lining the street. Still others were perched on a high stone wall directly across from her or standing precariously on ladders propped up against it.

The general mood of the gathering was festive and lighthearted. The air was thick with the sounds of raucous laughter, shouting, and brawling as fistfights broke out here and there. Street vendors were doing a brisk business selling everything from ballads to hot meat pies, and several sideshows attracted much attention.

Thoroughly puzzled now, and thinking this an odd sort of fair, Aurora looked to her right.

"Where are we?" she asked.

Then she saw it, the three posts that must have been all of twelve feet high, held apart by three connecting crossbars across the top. Even before a nearby hawker bawled, "Get the Last Dying Speech of Gentleman Jemmie Taylor, highwayman, before he's turned off for good!" Aurora knew exactly where she was.

"This is our fair," Katherine said with great relish. "It's known as a hanging fair. We're at Tyburn, my dear."

Aurora stared at the scaffold, the infamous "Triple Tree" of Tyburn, and her face turned chalk white. She gulped in fresh air, trying to stave wave after wave of sheer terror washing over her in great shudders. All she could think of was the night she had found her father hanging from the end of a rope, gently swaying back and forth, back and forth.

Aurora looked around wildly, her terror replaced by suffocating panic. She couldn't breathe. She had to get away from this place at once. Yet she knew escape was impossible. A wall of humanity sealed the Kilkennys' carriage in place and barred her way.

She turned to the Kilkennys to beg them to take her away from this place of death, but the words died in her throat when Katherine smiled and said, "We've been so looking forward to this. It's been six weeks since the last hanging day."

Aurora held her tongue. Her host and hostess would obviously not appreciate having their excursion spoiled by their squeamish guest. She averted her eyes from the scaffold. No one said she had to watch.

The duke squinted up at the sky. "Fine day for a hanging. Warm, with not a cloud to be seen."

Unfortunately for Aurora, the Kilkennys were determined to play the proud Londoners bent on enlightening their country guest.

"Do you see those stands over there?" Katherine asked.

Aurora nodded.

"Those are reserved for the wealthy, so they can have an unobstructed view, but we prefer to sit on the roof of our carriage."

Aurora scanned the faces and was ashamed to say

she recognized many of them. Those fine ladies and
gentlemen in the stands may have thought themselves
far superior to the rabble milling about at their feet,
but their faces gleamed expectantly with the same
blood lust as their common brethren.

Then the duke explained to Aurora that the procession proceeded from Newgate Prison down Tyburn
Road, only stopping at St. Sepulcher's Church, where
the condemned were given a bouquet and a blessing
before they continued the march to the gallows.

Aurora smiled politely and feigned interest, for she
did not want to risk offending the Kilkennys. But she
prayed the ordeal would soon be over and they would
go home.

Katherine fanned herself and said, "Thirty felons
will hang today. One of them is Gentleman Jemmie
Taylor, the highwayman. I understand he is so handsome and chivalrous that dozens of ladies have peti-
tioned the crown to grant him a pardon."

"The petitions were denied," the duke said gleefully, "so he'll swing with the rest of them."

"But I've heard rumors there will be a rescue attempt," the duchess said insistently.

Her husband just scoffed at that, and soon the two
of them were engaged in a heated debate.

Aurora, meanwhile, was sitting there quietly, trying
not to think of poor Jemmie Taylor, when a magnificent gray horse prancing through the crowd caught her
eye.

"Stormcloud!"

Then, as if his rider had heard her call his horse's
name, Lord Silverblade looked across the sea of heads
and stared directly at her. He wore a puzzled expression, as though he were surprised to see her at Tyburn;
then he nodded, tipped his hat, and proceeded to
ignore her.

Suddenly the duchess sat up straight and craned her
neck. "They're coming!"

Everyone seemed to turn at once, and a great deaf-
ening roar rose from the crowd as the sheriffs first
appeared, leading the stately procession of horse-drawn

carts. Each prisoner sat beside his own coffin, the hangman's noose already around his neck as a grim reminder of what was to befall him.

Try as she might, Aurora could not tear her eyes away and stared in fascination as the crowd parted to allow the procession to pass before them.

In the first cart stood a handsome young man in his mid-twenties dressed entirely in white, from his silver-laced hat to his white stockings. Walking on either side of his cart and sobbing were eight pretty young woman, also dressed in white.

"Gentleman Jemmie Taylor himself," the duke said.

Aurora leaned forward and said to Katherine, "Why, that man looks as though he's going to a wedding, not his own funeral."

Katherine nodded. "Isn't it odd? Many who are hanged dress so. Perhaps they want to look their best when they go to meet their Maker."

Aurora could only stare dumbfounded as the young highwayman smiled and bowed to the crowd, determined to enjoy the sensation he was causing during his last moments on earth.

Finally it was time. Jemmie Taylor's cart was driven beneath one of the triple trees and Jack Ketch, the hangman, secured the rope. Then the horse was led away and Aurora squeezed her eyes shut.

Suddenly she felt fingers digging into her arm.

"Look!" Katherine cried excitedly, shaking her.

Aurora's eyes flew open in time to see several people suddenly rush up to the hanged man, grasp his kicking legs, and throw their weight against him, pulling him down, stretching the rope.

A collective moan of disappointment welled up from the mob, and Aurora turned away again.

"That was too quick for the likes of him," the duke muttered, his usually placid face savage.

"You can't blame his family and friends for not wanting to see him suffer," Katherine said. Then she turned to Aurora and explained that most of the concerned slowly strangled to death unless someone helped them along by pulling their legs.

Now the duke was practically jumping up and down

in his place. "Look! They're fighting. Jemmie Taylor's friends are fighting the beadles from Surgeons' Hall for his body."

Aurora looked to see what all the excitement was about. Sure enough, several men were attacking another man with fists and cudgels.

"Why are they fighting?" she asked.

"The crown grants a certain number of condemned felons to the surgeons for dissection in their anatomy classes," the duke said.

"Dissection? What does that mean?" Aurora asked.

After the duke explained, Aurora regretted even asking. She feared she was going to embarrass herself by being sick.

"The mob hates the surgeons," Katherine added. "Not only is a man hanged, his body is taken to be cut up, the final indignity in their eyes."

"How . . . how interesting," Aurora stammered.

"They've got 'im!" the duke cried, beating the air with his upraised fist. "They've got Jemmie Taylor's body away from the surgeons. Perhaps they'll have better luck with the next one."

Whether they did or not was lost on Aurora, for after the first brutal display, she kept her eyes on the sky or the mob itself—anywhere but the gallows and the bodies swinging in the warm July breeze. She realized that criminals had to be punished for their crimes, but she couldn't understand why such kind, gracious, intelligent people as the Kilkennys felt the need to witness such a revolting spectacle.

Well, perhaps she was just a country miss ignorant of London ways.

Aurora lost all track of time. The warm sun beat down on her shoulders, making her hot and thirsty, while even her pomander couldn't mask the nauseating odors of sweaty bodies and unwashed clothes rising from the crowd around her. She saw the carts pass without really looking at the prisoners, heard the exuberant roar of the mob again and again until she thought she'd go deaf. Surely it had to be over soon. Surely the mob had had enough for one day.

Finally, the last cart was approaching the Kilkenny carriage.

Aurora's eyes widened in horror. There, standing in the cart, was a girl of no more than eleven, her thin shoulders stooped, her drawn white face blank and impassive with acceptance.

"Oh, dear Lord, Katherine!" Aurora cried. "They're going to hang a child! We must stop them!"

The Kilkennys exchanged astonished looks.

Her face shaded by the rim of her bonnet, Katherine leaned back and regarded Aurora as if she had suddenly lost her wits. "No one can stop them now. The girl was caught stealing from a house, a crime that is punishable by death. True, she is very young, but she is still a criminal in the eyes of the law."

"Let her serve as an example to anyone else who might be tempted to steal," the duke muttered harshly as he opened his snuffbox.

Now, as the cart passed the Kilkennys' carriage, the condemned child looked up at the fine people seated on its roof. When her eyes lighted on Aurora's face, she must have read the sympathy there, and for the first time in her short, hellish life, she realized that someone cared whether she lived or died. As the tears began streaming down her cheeks, she kept her eyes on that beautiful face, committing it to memory, so she would have something lovely to remember as the life was strangled out of her.

Aurora had never felt so helpless. All she wanted to do was take that child and run as fast as she could, away from this place, away from certain death.

Suddenly she knew what she had to do.

Without a word to Katherine or the duke, Aurora scrambled across the carriage roof on her hands and knees, swung her legs into the driver's box, then began climbing down.

"Aurora, what do you think you're doing?" the duchess cried in alarm, reaching for her.

But Aurora evaded their outstretched hands and stepped into the street, where she was swallowed by the mob.

*   *   *

Nicholas had been watching Aurora ever since he arrived at Tyburn.

The public hangings had ceased to amuse him long ago, and he was only here to see if he had won or lost a wager. Ollie had bet him two hundred pounds that Jemmie Taylor, the gentleman highwayman, would be rescued by his cronies and escape the hangman's noose. Obviously, he observed with irony, both Ollie and Jemmie lost.

But long after he had known the outcome of his wager, Nicholas remained where he was. He told himself he stayed because the crowd was too thick for even Stormcloud to brave, but in reality it was because of Aurora.

From the moment she had seen the first cart, she turned deathly pale and wore a stricken expression of denial and betrayal. As the hangings progressed, she would close her eyes and put her hand to her cheek in distress. But she bravely endured.

Then came the last cart, which proved to be her undoing.

Even Nicholas, who had seen much in his twenty-seven years, was moved by the sight of that terrified, pitiful child going to her doom. So when he saw Aurora say something to Katherine, then climb down from the carriage, he knew exactly what she was going to do.

"The little fool!" he muttered, digging his spurs into Stormcloud's ribs.

The gray lunged forward with a squeal, plowing through the people crowded around and scattering them like a flock of honking geese. Some swore and shook their fists at Nicholas, but no one attempted to stop him and all moved back out of the way of the stallion's deadly iron-shod hooves.

Nicholas stood up in the stirrups and craned his neck, looking for Aurora's wide-brimmed straw hat bobbing up in the crowd, which had suddenly closed ranks around the last cart. Aurora was nowhere to be seen.

Then he spotted a bright cap of copper curls.

Aurora's hat had been knocked off, and she was

struggling valiantly toward the cart. But she was having as much success as a spawning salmon fighting its way upstream. She would surge forward, the mob would push her back. The current of human flesh was too strong for her. She was being pushed farther and farther away.

And then disaster struck.

As Nicholas watched helplessly, several rough, heavyset women all dressed in rags converged on Aurora when they realized she was alone, greedily clawing at the fine lace and ribbons that trimmed her gown. He whipped Stormcloud mercilessly, praying he could reach Aurora in time.

He could see her mouth open in a scream as she flailed the women with her fists, valiantly trying to defend herself. But they were too much for her. She was outnumbered three to one. Already they had nearly torn her skirt away and were grasping at the bodice of her gown. They wouldn't stop until she was naked, and then the men would be on her.

Suddenly, to Nicholas' relief, the mob thinned considerably as it followed the last cart to the gallows, giving him room to maneuver. Snorting and wild-eyed, Stormcloud charged forward into the thick of battle, and Nicholas fell upon the women like an avenging angel, slashing at them with his riding crop again and again. They raised their fat, dirty arms over their heads to protect themselves from the merciless blows and screeched curses at him. When their leader leapt at him with the intention of dragging him from his horse, Nicholas slipped his foot out of the stirrup and brutally kicked her away. She fell on the ground and lay still.

Aurora just stood there swaying, a blank, dazed expression on her face. If Nicholas didn't reach her before she collapsed, what remained of the mob would tear both of them to pieces.

"Aurora!" he bellowed in warning, leaning out of the saddle and charging for her.

She heard him and looked up.

One of the women lunged for Aurora, determined to cheat Nicholas out of his victory. But he was faster.

He crooked his left arm, leaned out of the saddle, and caught Aurora neatly around the waist, snatching her up and away. She was as light as a piece of paper and he had no trouble settling her effortlessly in front of him. The other women's talons clawed only air as Stormcloud sprang away as fleet as a deer and broke free of the mob at last. Nicholas heard a wail of outrage behind him, followed by a string of epithets and hurried footsteps, but he didn't stop or look back, just kept on riding as if his life depended on it.

For the first few minutes of their wild race through the streets, Nicholas forgot about the woman sitting across his saddle, clinging to him, her head lolling against his shoulder. He just wanted to get as far away from Tyburn and the bloodthirsty mob as possible.

Finally, when the shouting faded into the distance, he slowed Stormcloud down to a sedate walk and looked down at Aurora shivering uncontrollably in his arms. The skirt of her gown had been completely torn away, leaving only the ruffled lacy petticoat, and she was trying to hold together what was left of the bodice in a fruitless attempt to cover her breasts. Nicholas noticed with dismay that the freckled flesh of her arms and shoulders was crosshatched with several long, ugly scratches.

Nicholas shifted the reins from his left hand to his right, then gently tilted Aurora's chin so he could look down at her. He was relieved to find the harpies hadn't scratched her face with their sharp, filthy nails. But her vacant, unblinking stare frightened him.

"You're safe now," he said soothingly. "No one is going to hurt you."

Aurora said nothing, just stared out into space. Nicholas wondered in panic if she had heard what he said, or even if she recognized him.

He tightened his hold about her and pressed her cheek against his shoulder, then touched his lips to the top of her head in a brief, reassuring kiss. He looked around and smiled in satisfaction as he recognized the street. He was not far from his house.

He would take Aurora there.

*   *   *

Fifteen minutes later they arrived at Nicholas' town house, a spacious brick dwelling in Grosvenor Square.

When a footman came out to hold his master's horse, Nicholas swung down out of the saddle and managed to catch Aurora as she fell, swooning, into his arms. Then he carried her inside.

He was startled to find Wesley waiting for him.

"Dear me!" Wesley said softly, wringing his hands as he stared goggle-eyed at Aurora's limp form. "Whatever happened to Miss Falconet?"

"She was attacked by the mob at Tyburn," Nicholas replied, brushing past him and striding into the drawing room, where he gently laid Aurora down on the settee and took off his own coat to cover her. Then he bellowed for a footman.

Wesley, who had turned as white as parchment at the mention of Tyburn, was blotting the sweat off his upper lip with a handkerchief. "Is she . . . ?" He couldn't bring himself to say the word.

"Dead? No. She just swooned."

"What do you propose to do with her?" Wesley asked.

"Use your head, Wesley! I propose to send for a surgeon to tend to her, of course."

Wesley withered under his cousin's scorn. "Do you think it wise to keep her here?"

Nicholas frowned in consternation. "What am I supposed to do with her, cousin?" he snapped, losing all patience with Old Immortality at last. "Cast her into the street?"

"Please, Nicholas, don't shout at me so. I meant no offense. I was merely suggesting that in view of your reputation . . ."

Nicholas understood at once. "Under the circumstances, I think Miss Falconet's reputation will remain intact, cousin."

Wesley stepped back and put up his hands as if preparing to ward off a blow. "Please don't take offense, cousin. I was merely—"

"Thank you for your concern, Wesley. But I'm sure all your worries will be for naught. Now, if you'll pardon me . . ."

"Of course." Wesley couldn't leave fast enough. "I shall be on my way. Good day to you, cousin, and I pray Miss Falconet will recover from her ordeal."

The moment Wesley scurried out of the drawing room, the footman appeared and Nicholas told him to fetch Dr. Mortimer at once. Then he was to go on to Kilkenny House and inform the duke and duchess that Aurora was safe with Lord Silverblade and for them to come for her at Grosvenor Square as soon as possible.

When he was alone, Nicholas walked over to the sideboard, poured a glass of brandy, then returned to the settee. He stared down at Aurora lying there, her face so pale each freckle stood out like a dark dot, and he felt weak with relief that she had come to no harm.

He set the brandy on a nearby table, then knelt down on one knee and gently stroked her cheek. "Aurora, wake up."

Her eyes flew open and she started. She must have been reliving the attack in her mind, for she sat bolt upright with a scream of terror, the coat falling away as she began swinging her fists at imaginary assailants. Nicholas backed away before a wild blow caught him in the jaw.

"Hush!" he said, grasping her wrists to still them. "You're safe now. Safe. No one is going to hurt you."

For a moment she was too caught up in her private hell to comprehend what he was saying, and she continued to struggle, her slight body writhing and twisting in her attempts to free herself. But Nicholas held her fast and kept repeating her name over and over again in a gentle, soothing voice. Gradually her wide blue eyes lost their dazed, numb look as she became aware of her surroundings.

She stared at him. "N-Nicholas?"

"Yes." He hesitated, watching her warily, wondering if her need of comfort was greater than her hatred of him.

To his relief, it was. Aurora did not try to fight him.

When her shallow breathing deepened and she was calm at last, he handed her the brandy and said, "Drink this.'"

Aurora took it, but her hands were shaking so badly,

Nicholas had to steady them with his own as she brought the glass to her lips. She gasped and choked, but she drank every drop greedily.

"Feel better?"

Aurora nodded as she pulled up the coat to cover herself. Then a look of bewilderment passed over her face. "Why did those women attack me? I've never done them any harm."

"They attacked you because they are very poor and they thought they could steal the fine silk from your gown and sell it for a few shillings." Nicholas chided her gently. "You should have stayed in the Kilkennys' carriage. No one would have harmed you under the duke's protection."

Her wide eyes filled with tears and she sniffled. "I wanted to help that poor child in the cart."

Now Nicholas rose and looked down at her sternly, "You are much too impetuous for your own good, Aurora. There was nothing you could have done for her. She was tried and sentenced. Even if you had managed to escape the wrath of the mob and succeeded in freeing her, you would have been caught and brought up on charges yourself."

He was silent for a moment as he studied her lovely face surrounded by its halo of fiery hair. "Somehow, I don't think you would enjoy life in Newgate Prison, my dear."

She winced at his harsh words, then closed her eyes and leaned back against the settee with a weary sigh. "The poor child . . ."

A foxhound pup that was the runt of the litter . . . a poor waif hanged for the crime of stealing . . . Nicholas shook his head. London was no place for an innocent with such a tender heart. She would see things here that would break her heart again and again, until nothing was left.

Nicholas knew precisely what this exasperating child-woman needed. She needed a husband, or at least a protector with a firm hand.

But before he could tell her this, Dr. Mortimer arrived. He cleansed Aurora's long, deep scratches, applied a soothing salve, then gave her a sleeping draft before Nicholas could tell him that the Kilkennys would be arriving at any moment to take Aurora home, and that she would not be spending the night at Grosvenor Square.

The damage done, all Nicholas could do was carry her up to his bedchamber, then wait for her to awaken.

Hours later, Aurora opened her eyes and found herself lying on her back in the middle of a strange bed. She looked around an elegantly furnished but decidedly masculine bedchamber.

"Where am I?" she muttered, and tried to sit up. Pain like white-hot needles shot through her arms and chest, forcing her to lie back down again, gasping. She held up her arms and was appalled to see several long scratches there. When she looked down, she saw that all there was left of her pretty green damask gown was its bodice, and that was torn almost to shreds, revealing too much of her breasts to be modest.

Suddenly her mind cleared and all the hideous memories came flooding back: the hangings, the girl in the cart, those crude women tearing at her clothes, and Lord Silverblade charging down to pull her to safety. She remembered where she was now. She was in the man's house, resting in his bed.

He had saved her life. Lord Silverblade, the man who had murdered her brother, had saved her life today at considerable risk to his own. She hadn't even thanked him.

Aurora lay there quietly for a long time, watching the pink-and-gold light of sunset fade into the semi-darkness of twilight through a window to the right of the bed. She thought long and hard about many things. Finally she reached a decision.

Rising at last and ignoring the pain, she looked around the bedchamber for something to cover herself with. She noticed Lord Silverblade's coat draped across the back of a chair, the same coat he had covered her with downstairs.

Aurora put it on, then went to find him.

He was in his study, seated at a desk and writing, for she could hear the soft scratching of his quill in the silence. A solitary candle silhouetted his strong, distinguished profile.

"Lord Silverblade, may I speak to you?"

Nicholas looked up to find Aurora hesitating in the doorway. She looked like a child playing at dress-up, for his coat was much too large for her slight frame, hanging down past her knees, while the sleeves reached nearly to her fingertips. Right at that moment, she looked so very young and vulnerable, her face still soft and drowsy with sleep, he felt an irrational desire to protect her and keep her from harm. That thought brought him up sharply. This was the second time she had aroused such feelings in him, and he was not accustomed to it.

He rose and bowed. "Of course, Miss Falconet. Do come in." As Aurora entered the study, he added, "I trust you slept well after your ordeal and are now feeling much better?"

"The scratches sting a bit, but otherwise I feel very well, thank you."

He indicated a chair for her, but Aurora declined with a shake of her head and resolutely remained standing.

"You saved my life." It was almost an accusation.

He smiled wryly. "I told you I enjoy rescuing damsels in distress."

She shook her head. "It was much more than that. I . . . I could have died today. I would have, if it hadn't been for you, Lord Silverblade." She looked up at him, her eyes luminous and as dark as lapis lazuli by flickering candlelight. "Thank you."

"You're most welcome, Miss Falconet." Nicholas glanced out the window, and when he saw night had almost fallen, he added with a trace of annoyance in his voice, "Now, I think we should be getting you back to the Kilkennys, since they apparently are not coming to fetch you."

Aurora moistened her lips. "Before we go, I have something else to say."

When he raised his brows in silent inquiry, she said, "I wish to apologize for misjudging you."

Nicholas stared at her. "I find myself quite speechless, Miss Falconet. I'm afraid I don't understand."

"At Vauxhall, you asked me why I didn't believe you concerning Tim's death."

"And you said it was because I was a rake, a libertine, and a man without honor," he reminded her softly.

Even though her pale cheeks suffused with color, Aurora raised her stubborn chin proudly. "Well, I was wrong, Lord Silverblade, and I apologize. I know now that you could have never killed my brother."

Nicholas felt his heart give a wild, exultant leap of joy, but he schooled his features to remain expressionless. "I see. Do forgive me, but may I ask what it was that caused you to change your opinion of my base character?"

Now she looked away. "You have always been very kind to me, and you saved my life today. Somehow, I cannot reconcile the man I have come to know with a murderer."

He couldn't resist saying, "But your father said—"

"We all have our treasured illusions. My father could not face the fact that his beloved only son was to blame for his own death, so he blamed you instead. And I could not bring myself to admit that my flawless brother could be so . . . so stupid as to bring about his own death."

Nicholas knew what such an admission had cost her in pride and shattered illusions, and he could think of nothing to say that would not sound trite or false. Instead, he slowly approached Aurora and held out his hands to her. "Friends again?"

Aurora smiled tremulously and nodded. Then she placed her hands trustingly in his, and his strong, warm fingers closed over hers, bringing them up to his lips. As Lord Silverblade's warm mouth grazed the backs of her hands in a fleeting kiss, Aurora felt his strength flow into her, bolstering her shattered pride and making her feel whole again. Yet the intimacy of his touch made her pull away and she turned from him shyly.

"Will you kindly escort me back to Kilkenny House?" she said. "The duke and duchess will be worried."

The moment Aurora uttered those words, Silverblade's mood changed, becoming at once sober and reflective. "Indeed they will. Come. Let us be on our way at once."

Soon Lord Silverblade's carriage was pulling up before Kilkenny House. Every window on the ground floor blazed with light.

Aurora, her torn dress concealed by the long cloak Lord Silverblade had slipped about her shoulders before their departure, stared out the window. "It would appear the Kilkennys have callers."

Seated across from her, Lord Silverblade swore under his breath. "Now, that is most unfortunate. I had hoped to escort you back inside unobserved."

Aurora frowned in puzzlement. "Why should we care who sees us?"

He shook his head. "My sweet, innocent Aurora. You, an unwed gentlewoman, have just spent the entire afternoon unchaperoned in the company of a bachelor gentleman. Who, I might add, does not have the most sterling of reputations."

"And if someone were to see us, my reputation would be ruined."

Lord Silverblade nodded. "I fear so."

Aurora clutched the cloak more tightly about her. This was a repeat of what had happened at Overton's ball, but much more serious in nature. "What are we to do?"

"We shall do what we did the night of Overton's ball. We shall enter through the servants' entrance."

Then Lord Silverblade opened the door, stepped down, and turned back to assist Aurora.

No sooner did she disembark than she heard a voice say, "Why, it's Miss Falconet, fresh from her daring rescue from the Tyburn mob."

Aurora looked up to see two women standing there, and her heart sank when she recognized the notorious Adderley sisters.

"Misses Adderley," Aurora murmured in acknowledgment, while Lord Silverblade bowed. Since the sisters were twins and had the annoying habit of dressing alike to purposely confuse people, very few could tell who was who unless they chose to identify themselves, with one usually referring to the other by name.

The one on the right stepped forward and said, "Miss Hope and I saw it all from the stands. In fact, we wondered what had happened to you after Lord Silverblade's dramatic rescue, so we called upon the duchess to see if you were all right." She smiled slyly. "She told us you were upstairs, resting after your ordeal."

Miss Hope smirked. "Why, Miss Faith, it would appear Miss Falconet has discovered the secret of being in two places at once."

Aurora felt Lord Silverblade stiffen beside her as he gripped her elbow and prepared to extricate them from this tense situation.

"There is no need to concern yourself, ladies," he said, guiding Aurora past the two women. "Miss Falconet is safe and sound. Good evening."

Without another word, he and Aurora left the Misses Adderley standing alone to speculate.

Katherine and the duke were waiting in the foyer, and the moment Aurora walked in, the duchess rushed forward and enfolded her in a crushing embrace.

When Aurora winced, the duchess released her and cried, "Dear God, Aurora! Are you unharmed?"

Aurora nodded. "I am fine, Katherine, truly. I have a few scratches, but am none the worse for wear. Lord Silverblade sent for a surgeon to tend me."

The duchess exchanged a nervous, fearful look with her husband, who was taking snuff. "Let us all withdraw to the drawing room," she said.

When they were all assembled and the doors closed for privacy, Katherine turned to Lord Silverblade, her green eyes flashing with anger.

"Whatever possessed you to take Aurora to your house, my lord? Why didn't you bring her directly here?"

"Miss Falconet was in pain, your grace," he replied calmly, "and my house was closer."

"But didn't you stop to consider what it would do to her reputation?" the duke demanded. Aurora had never seen the mild-mannered Kilkenny so furious.

"My first consideration was the lady's physical well-being, your grace."

Katherine said, "We assumed you would bring her here, so when we were finally able to get away from Tyburn, we returned to Kilkenny House. All we found was a footman with a message."

"May I ask why you didn't send a carriage for her, your grace?" Nicholas asked, trying to keep his temper in check.

"Because by that time," the duke began, "our house was crawling with callers. We couldn't leave without arousing suspicion."

Why couldn't they have just sent a carriage for Aurora, Nicholas thought to himself, and smuggled her back into the house with no one being the wiser? No, the Kilkennys had not handled the situation well at all.

Katherine started pacing the room in agitation. "Everyone at Tyburn—everyone—saw you carry her off. All of London is agog. I've lost count of the number of gossips who have called here today, on the pretext of inquiring about Aurora's health."

"And what did your grace tell them?" Lord Silverblade asked, his patience wearing thin.

"That she was upstairs, resting after her ordeal," the duchess replied.

Nicholas groaned inwardly.

"But . . . but the Misses Adderley just saw me arrive with Lord Silverblade," Aurora pointed out. "They knew I was not here, as you claimed."

Katherine turned white, then sank down into a chair with a theatrical groan. "Oh, dear God! All is lost. Those witches will spread tales all over London. Aurora will be ruined. Ruined!"

Aurora looked from Lord Silverblade to Katherine in mute appeal. "Surely the situation can't be as black as you paint it."

The duchess stared up at her pityingly. "Oh, I assure you the situation is quite grave, Aurora. A woman's good name is all she has in this world to protect her. When that is lost . . ."

"Perhaps all is not yet lost," Nicholas said. "Why don't we wait and see if the Misses Adderley do their worst."

"Yes," Katherine said with a sigh. "Perhaps I am worrying for naught. Perhaps nothing will be said."

"And if something is said?" the duke persisted.

He and his wife exchanged looks; then Katherine turned to Nicholas. "If that is the case, drastic measures will have to be taken."

Aurora found herself wondering just what those measures would be, and for the first time, she felt afraid.

9

AURORA felt as if she had contracted the plague.

At the Eastlakes' rout, all of the young men who had once tripped over each other in their haste to dance with Aurora now sought out other partners. Those same young ladies who had once been so friendly now congregated in little groups and stared at her over their fans when they thought she wasn't looking, whispering among themselves.

What Katherine feared the most had come to pass: Aurora's reputation was ruined, thanks to the Misses Adderley and their gossiping tongues.

Finally Aurora could tolerate the isolation no longer. She rose and went to find Katherine, trying to ignore the whispers as she passed and trying not to show how much the lies hurt her. The duchess, deep in conversation with their hostess, Lady Eastlake, excused herself when she saw Aurora approach.

"Katherine," Aurora said, "I'd like to leave now, if you don't mind. No one will say two words to me, and I feel as though everyone is laughing behind my back."

Her friend sighed in resignation, her expression troubled. "Yes, I think it's best, under the circumstances. I'll collect Kilkenny, and we'll leave. We must have a conference to decide what is to be done with you."

They managed to pry the duke away from a group of his political cronies, said good night to their host

147

and hostess, and were just about to leave when none other than Lord Silverblade himself entered the Eastlakes' ballroom.

Much to Aurora's chagrin, no one was ignoring him for his part in her disgrace. Indeed, men came up to him and slapped him on the back as if to congratulate him, while women floated past and fluttered their eyelashes in hopes of attracting the attention of such a handsome scoundrel.

Aurora felt her anger rise at the injustice of it all, and when Lord Silverblade glanced up and held her gaze, she quickly looked away. Then she turned to Katherine and said, "Let us be off, shall we?"

When they reached the foyer, however, Aurora heard a familiar voice behind them say, "One moment, your graces. May I have a word with you?"

The Kilkennys and Aurora stopped and turned to find Lord Silverblade approaching.

He nodded to Aurora, then said to the duke, "May I be so bold as to ask the reason for your hasty departure, your grace?"

"I fear the worst has come to pass," the duke said portentously, nodding in Aurora's direction.

Aurora was gratified to see that this bit of news dismayed Lord Silverblade. He turned to her, those smoky eyes regretful. "I am truly sorry that you have been made to suffer for my lapse of good judgment, Miss Falconet."

"So am I, Lord Silverblade," she replied icily.

"If there is anything I can do to make it up to you . . ."

"You have done quite enough, sir," she replied, and turned away.

She knew she was being most unfair to hold him responsible for her predicament, especially when he seemed genuinely sorry. After all, he had saved her life.

"We are on our way back to Kilkenny House to decide what is to be done," Katherine said. "Good evening, Lord Silverblade."

Even after Lord Silverblade wished the Kilkennys and Aurora a good evening, she could not bring herself to speak to him or spare him a glance. She just followed the duke and duchess out into the cool summer air, her shoulders slumping dejectedly as she wondered what was going to happen to her now.

Nicholas watched the trio depart, then turned and entered the warm, crowded ballroom. But his mind was not on the festivities tonight.

He couldn't stop thinking of Aurora and the way she had looked at him, her wide blue eyes filled with the reproach of one betrayed. She blamed him for her situation, and rightly so. He who knew the rules of society by heart should have been more careful not to break them so cavalierly.

But as he stared at the ballroom filled with people, he found he could not regret what he had done and felt he didn't need to justify his actions to anyone. Unfortunately, petty minds were quick to believe the worst, and an innocent young woman was being made to suffer.

What would happen to Aurora, he wondered, now that her reputation was in tatters? Her only alternative would be to marry someone beneath her, a pox-ridden old man thrilled to get any woman, let alone a young, beautiful one. Or perhaps her sister would allow her to rusticate until the scandal died.

Her sister would, but Overton wouldn't.

Nicholas grew livid when he thought of the fate awaiting Aurora at the hands of Lord Overton. He would not be gentle with her or tolerant of her headstrong nature. He would play cruel mental games until he crushed her magnificent spirit and she became as meek and acquiescent as her sister.

Nicholas' jaw tightened. He would never let that happen to her. Tim would have wanted him to look after his sister, to keep her safe from men like Overton, and Nicholas fully intended to do so. He owed his old friend that much.

He startled himself by admitting that he had very strong feelings for the irrepressible chit. She had insinuated herself into his heart without his even realizing it, and the thought of her disappearing out of his life forever and into the arms of another man unleashed violent feelings of jealousy.

Suddenly Nicholas saw Ollie's portly form weaving its way through the crowds toward him.

He greeted his friend, then said, "And where is the beauteous Bess this evening?"

"She's performing tonight," Ollie replied, reaching beneath his wig to scratch his head. "In fact, if I don't get to Drury Lane to watch her, she'll have my hide."

Nicholas chuckled at that and helped himself to a glass of punch.

Ollie kept shifting his weight from one foot to the other and looked decidedly uncomfortable. Finally he said, "That was a nice bit of riding the other day at Tyburn. Saw you myself from the stands."

"So did half of London, unfortunately."

Ollie cleared his throat and hesitated again.

"Out with it, Ollie," Nicholas said with a touch of annoyance. "If you keep what you have to say inside, you'll burst."

"Umm, is it true what they're saying about you and Miss Falconet?"

Nicholas sipped his drink. "Yes, I did rescue her from the mob, and yes, I did take her to my house to tend to her injuries. But no, I did not ravish her or compromise her in any other way."

"Didn't think you did," Ollie mumbled, plainly embarrassed.

"I confess I am curious. What exactly have people been saying?"

After Ollie told him, Nicholas had to exert himself to keep from flinging his glass across the room. "I'd like to rip out their lying tongues with my bare hands!" he muttered savagely.

He only calmed down after his friend placed a placating hand on his arm and said, "No harm done to you."

"What about Miss Falconet, the innocent party in all this?"

Ollie's hand fell to his side. "You know as well as I that it's not the same for a woman. She was here tonight, and I felt badly for her."

Nicholas didn't need Ollie to tell him what had happened. He had seen it often enough in the past, the looks, the whispers, the ostracism that could drive a woman to tears and banish her back to the country in disgrace.

"Don't look so glum, my friend," Ollie was saying. 'This disaster is not your fault."

"Oh, but it is," Nicholas replied grimly, "and I intend to take full responsibility for it."

And he stalked off without another word, leaving Ollie to ponder just what he meant to do.

Aurora stood at one of her bedroom windows and dabbed at her eyes with her handkerchief.

Ever since Lord Eastlake's disastrous ball a week ago, she hadn't set foot outside Kilkenny House. At least she was safe here, safe from pitying stares and shocked whispers. But even this sanctuary was soon to be denied her.

Just that morning, Katherine had informed her that she and the duke had regretfully decided it would be best for all concerned if Aurora returned to Overton Manor.

Aurora could only stare at the duchess in disbelief. When she finally regained some semblance of her wits, she threw herself down at Katherine's feet and begged, "Please don't send me back! You know what Overton will do to me."

"I'm sorry," Katherine said with genuine regret as she helped Aurora to rise, "but I have no choice. Even the Kilkenny name and our position can't protect you. But if you return to Surrey and stay in the country for a while, this scandal is sure to die down." Katherine smiled reassuringly. "Once everyone forgets, I'm sure you can return to London and be accepted once again."

Aurora couldn't control the bitter tears that coursed down her cheeks. "Who will want me once Overton is through with me? Answer me that, your grace!"

Katherine bristled, suddenly every inch the imperious duchess. "You will not use that tone of voice with me, Aurora!"

"I'm . . . I'm sorry," Aurora said with a sniff. "But I thought you, of all people, were my friend."

Katherine had the grace to look away in embarrassment. "I am afraid there are some things that exceed even the bonds of friendship." Then the duchess walked to the door. She stopped and turned around. "I wrote to your sister and explained what has happened. She and Overton should be arriving sometime today to take you home."

Then she left Aurora to contemplate her fate.

Aurora stared at the packed portmanteaux standing at the foot of her bed and she fought back the fresh tears that threatened to fall. She had no other choice but to return to Overton Manor and accept whatever terms Overton had to offer.

Suddenly there came a knock on the door. When Aurora answered it, a footman said her guests had arrived and he was to carry her bags downstairs. Aurora thanked him and strode from her bedchamber without a backward glance.

The moment Aurora walked into the drawing room, Diana was on her feet with a cry of delight.

"Aurora!" she said, giving her a crushing hug. "How wonderful it is to see you again, even under such horrible circumstances."

Aurora tried to smile and failed. "The duchess has told you . . . everything, then?"

Diana nodded, her blue eyes solemn. "I am so, so sorry this had to happen to you, my dear."

"Most unfortunate," Overton drawled from the vicinity of the marble fireplace. He managed to tear himself away from his reflection in the mirror long enough to turn to her.

Aurora looked at him standing there, his eyes luminous with amusement and triumph, a slight mocking curve to his mouth, and she felt like a wee helpless mouse facing a large cat of particular strength and cunning.

"But as upsetting as this entire affair is, it has its bright side," Overton said.

"I fail to see what that can be," Aurora retorted

He smiled sweetly. "Why, because it brings you back to us, of course. Isn't that right, Diana?"

"Of course, Halley. It's been too quiet with Aurora away."

Overton collected his hat from a nearby table. "Since we have such a long drive back to Surrey, I would suggest that we be on our way. I would imagine Aurora is most anxious to leave London, aren't you, my dear?" Then he bowed to the Kilkennys and thanked them for their hospitality.

Good-byes were said all around, though Aurora's to the Kilkennys were somewhat reserved and strained. Just as she, Diana, and Overton were about to leave, the majordomo announced that Lord Silverblade had arrived and wished to speak to Miss Falconet.

"Whatever can he want of me now?" Aurora muttered to Diana. "Hasn't he done enough already?"

Suddenly Lord Silverblade filled the drawing-room doorway, his cold gray eyes flicking over everyone present, lingering on Overton reprovingly. After wishing everyone good day, he smiled and added, "Don't tell me Miss Falconet is leaving us so soon?"

The duke cleared his throat with a loud "ahem," then said, "We thought it best if she returned to the country."

"And we have come to take her home," Diana added.

Lord Silverblade looked directly at Aurora and she felt her heart skip a beat.

"Then I arrived just in time, he said, pausing dramatically, "to ask for Miss Falconet's hand in marriage."

Everyone froze; then five pairs of eyes stared at Lord Silverblade in stunned silence.

Overton was the first to speak. "Isn't this proposal a bit sudden, Silverblade?" he asked suspiciously.

"Actually, I have been considering it for quite some time," he replied, much to everyone's astonishment, including his own.

"So you want to marry her, do you?" the duke asked, reaching for his snuffbox. "Well, it would be the honorable thing to do, and it would certainly put an end to all this malicious gossip floating about."

Both Diana and the duchess looked too dazed to say anything. However, listening to the men discuss her as if she were nothing more than a brood mare being sold at auction caused Aurora to regain her wits quickly.

"But I do not wish to marry Lord Silverblade!" she protested.

If the man were offended by her blunt refusal, his composed features did not show it. He addressed the company. "If you will all excuse us for a moment, I would like to speak to Miss Falconet alone."

"Of course," the duke said, heading for the door. "Come, Katherine. Take as much time as you need, Silverblade."

Everyone began following him, even Diana, who paused only long enough to squeeze Aurora's hand in mute encouragement. She closed the door after her, leaving Aurora alone with Lord Silverblade.

As the two faced each other squarely, each waiting for the other to speak, Aurora felt her resentment of the man well up afresh.

"Would you please explain yourself, my lord?" she said, fighting to stay calm.

"What is there to explain?" he replied, adjusting the lace at his sleeves. "I have just asked for your hand in marriage."

"But why? You don't love me, and I have never given you cause to believe I would welcome your suit."

His mouth twisted into a mocking smile. "That is certainly true. Our encounters have been anything but smooth. And as to my loving you . . ." He shrugged apologetically. "I will not lie. I cannot say that I have ever loved any woman, but I do admire you, Aurora. And after we are wed, I am sure we'll get along quite famously."

"But why do you wish to marry me when you can have your pick of any woman in London, as everyone persists in assuring me?"

Her sarcastic tone caused a glimmer of amusement to flash in his eyes; then it died as he regarded her thoughtfully. "Please sit down, and I shall explain."

When Aurora was seated on the settee, with Lord Silverblade across from her, his long legs stretched out before him, he said, "It's time I married and fulfilled my duties to my family. And you, Aurora, need the protection of a husband before you embroil yourself in any more scrapes. Don't look so offended.

You know you do. However, I'm afraid my thought-less behavior at Tyburn has quite ruined your chances of ever securing a suitable match."

She stared straight ahead, her back rigid. "You mean that no decent man will have me now because of what people think happened between us that after-noon."

Lord Silverblade didn't have to say a word for her to know it was true.

Aurora rose, a feeling of hopelessness weighing her down, and she went to the window. But as she stared down into the garden, she felt helpless and trapped, like a bird beating its wings futilely against its cage.

She heard Lord Silverblade's footsteps as he rose and crossed the room to stand behind her. He was so close, she could have leaned back against him without any effort.

"You really have no alternative, Aurora," he said, his voice soft and regretful in her ear. "Your home in Ireland is lost to you. The Kilkennys have turned you out because of the scandal. You know as well as I what you will face if you return to Overton Manor. Where else will you go? What will you do? Become a ladies' maid or a whore?"

His brutal, scornful words shocked her and she spun around to face him, brushing his coat with her arm. She was furious at the injustice of it all and her own inability to fight it because of her sex. "And you think marriage to you would be preferable to my becoming Overton's mistress?"

"Wouldn't it?"

Aurora felt powerless and defeated. She turned away again, pressed her face against the cold windowpane and silently wept.

"What's this?" he inquired softly. "Tears from my brave Rory?"

His teasing tone and the use of her pet name coaxed a tremulous smile out of her. "I do not feel especially b-brave at the moment. I am frightened."

"Don't be," Nicholas pleaded as he turned her to face him. "You have my word that there is nothing for you to be afraid of."

Aurora didn't know why she went to him when he held out his arms to her. She was sobbing so hard she couldn't think clearly. But on some primitive level, she realized that with her life spinning out of control, Nicholas was a rock that could anchor her firmly to the ground. As his strong arms clasped her to him, Aurora could feel his strength surrounding her, warming her, giving her back the courage that had been ground out of her by circumstances. Beneath the hard muscles of his chest she could hear his heart beating strong and steady.

Resting his cheek against the crown of her head, the fragrant scent of her hair filling his nostrils, he said, "You will have the protection of my name. No one would dare harm you, and I will see that you want for nothing."

Aurora clung to him and listened as his deep, gentle voice went on to enumerate the many advantages to being the Marchioness of Silverblade. She would be accorded respect as his wife and the mistress of his house and lands. He also added that if at some future date they decided they did not suit after all, they could go their separate ways.

Aurora squeezed her eyes shut against the soft velvet of his coat. In a wee voice she asked, "Shall we have separate bedchambers, my lord?"

Finally he released her and held her at arm's length, the spell broken at last.

"Is that what you really want?"

Aurora kept her gaze leveled on one of his waistcoat's silver engraved buttons. She thought of his hot, fevered kisses the night of Overton's ball and how they had left her weak-kneed and breathless.

"Look at me, Aurora," Lord Silverblade commanded. When she reluctantly raised her eyes to his, he repeated, "Is that what you really want?"

"N-no."

Lord Silverblade's eyes smoldered and darkened, becoming almost black. "Splendid, because I would have to be mad to ever agree to such an empty, shallow marriage, my beautiful Aurora," he said softly as his gaze roamed over her tearstained face. "Besides, I need an heir, and to the best of my knowledge, there is only one way—one very pleasurable way, I might add—to accomplish that feat."

She swiped at her eyes with the back of her hand and darted away from him, as if she feared he would try to force himself upon her right there. "I . . . I must have some time to consider your proposal, my lord."

He was implacable. "What is there to consider? To my mind, it is quite evident what your only choice can be. You're only postponing the inevitable."

"I would still like some time to . . . accustom myself to the idea," she insisted.

"And where will you stay while you come to a decision?"

"Overton manor. Surely Halley won't attempt to seduce me if he knows you have asked for my hand."

"I'm afraid you underestimate my Lord Overton. If he succeeds in seducing you, Aurora, I will withdraw my marriage proposal," he warned her sternly. "I can't risk my heir being another man's bastard."

Aurora's spirits plummeted, and she had to fight back the tears again.

"Why don't I prevail upon the Kilkennys to allow you to stay for just a little while longer?"

"But just this morning, the duchess seemed most eager to be rid of me," Aurora said.

"Since I am to make an honest woman of you, I'm sure they shall have no objection. Perhaps they will let your sister stay as well, to keep you company."

"So, my fate is sealed, then."

"I'm afraid so, Aurora. There is no escaping it."

He stepped forward as if he meant to take her in his arms again, but when Aurora shrank away, he stopped and regarded her with an expression she could not fathom. Then he bowed and said, "I shall tell the others you have graciously consented to become my wife." Then he grinned and added, "Eventually."

Then he left her.

Diana was growing most impatient with her sister. Seven days had passed since Lord Silverblade had asked for her hand, and Aurora still hadn't formally accepted his proposal.

Now, as Diana marched down the corridor to Aurora's room, she promised herself that today was the day her sister was going to commit herself to Lord Silverblade.

She found a dispirited Aurora seated on a chair before the window, staring into space.

"Good morning, Aurora," she sang cheerfully as she swept into the room. "How is my favorite sister today?"

Aurora made some reply, but her voice was so soft and listless that Diana couldn't hear what it was.

Diana pursed her lips in an angry line. "Aurora," she said, standing before her sister with her hands on her hips, "this fit of the sullens has gone far enough. You are sorely trying everyone's patience!"

Aurora looked up, a woebegone expression on her face. "I don't wish to marry Lord Silverblade."

"But why not? He is handsome, wealthy, titled . . . in a word, perfect!"

Diana didn't add that Aurora's marriage to Lord Silverblade would be perfect for her as well. With Aurora married, she would not be underfoot at Overton Manor, tempting Halley with her sparkling eyes and youthful exuberance. Yet she would be living close by, enabling Diana to see her whenever she wished.

Aurora said, "I meant I have no wish to be married to anyone."

"I realize you are very young, Aurora, but surely even you realized that you would eventually marry. Every woman wishes to be married."

Aurora shook her head. "I had always thought I would stay at Falconstown forever, taking care of Father. And when he died, I would remain there, a spinster raising my horses and hounds."

The touching confession left Diana speechless.

Aurora's lower lip trembled. "My world was turned upside down when Father died."

Diana knelt at Aurora's side and grasped her hands tightly. "But you've got to make the best of it, Aurora. Life is unfair and fortune capricious. The best a woman can hope for is marriage to a man who can provide for her and protect her."

"A man like Lord Silverblade."

Diana nodded. "Need I remind you you could do worse. Much worse."

"I realize that," Aurora admitted in resignation, "but there is much about Lord Silverblade that disturbs me."

"Confide in me, Aurora. Perhaps I can ease your fears."

When Aurora hesitated, her cheeks turning a delicate pink, Diana suspected her sister's reservations were of a particularly intimate nature. Her suspicions were soon confirmed when Aurora began talking about Mrs. Littlewood in a soft, halting voice.

Diana listened attentively, then rose. "It is common knowledge—to everyone except Mr. Littlewood, I suspect—that Mrs. Littlewood is Lord Silverblade's mistress. But this should not concern you, Aurora. As his wife, you will be above it. Even if he does keep a mistress after you are married, I am sure he will be discreet about it and never shame you by flaunting her in public."

"I see."

"No, I don't think you do. This is the way men are, and we have no choice but to accept their faults and weaknesses. Besides, you will have your household to manage and your children to raise. That will keep you occupied. If it doesn't, you can always take a lover of your own—after you provide Lord Silverblade with his heir, of course."

Diana could tell by the distasteful expression on Aurora's face that such a life didn't appeal to her. But she would grow to accept it in time. All women learned to accept and adapt eventually.

"Tomorrow night the Kilkennys are giving a ball, as you know," Diana said with a smile. "I think that would be the perfect time to tell Lord Silverblade you will accept his proposal of marriage, don't you?"

Aurora looked away and nodded listlessly, her shoulders slumped in defeat.

Diana leaned over and hugged her. "Once you are married, you will wonder how you could have been so foolish." Then she rose and went to the armoire at the

opposite end of the room. "Now," she said, swinging
open the doors, "which gown do you intend to wear to
the ball tomorrow night?"

She smiled to herself. She had won.

Aurora stood at the ballroom's entrance with the
Kilkennys, smiling and chatting with those very same
people who had ostracized her just a week ago.

To all outward appearances, she was charming and
vivacious, but inside, she was seething at the unfair-
ness of it all. Now that Lord Silverblade wished to
marry the woman he had reputedly dishonored, Aurora could be welcomed back into London society.

Now who should approach her but the Misses Adderley.

Aurora would have liked nothing better than to
claw out their eyes, but she forced herself to smile and
nod politely.

"Miss Faith and I have heard felicitations are in
order," Miss Hope said.

Aurora composed her face into a blank mask. "Why,
whatever do you mean?"

"Now, now, Miss Falconet," Miss Hope said, playfully tapping Aurora's arm with her fan, "don't be
coy with us. Miss Faith and I are always the first to
know."

And the first to spread your vicious gossip, Aurora
thought furiously.

"We understand you have agreed to become the
Marchioness of Silverblade," Miss Faith said.

Her sister leaned forward and murmured to Aurora,
"So wise of you, my dear, under the circumstances."

"What circumstances are those, pray tell?" a deep
masculine voice inquired from behind them.

Aurora looked up to see Nicholas standing there, a
scowl of displeasure between his brows.

Suddenly confronted, the Misses Adderley both
turned an identical shade of beet red and began fanning themselves in unison.

"Why, Lord Silverblade," Miss Hope tittered. "You
quite surprised Miss Faith and me."

He bowed. "Do forgive me for eavesdropping, ladies, but I couldn't help overhearing your conversation. To what circumstances were you referring?"

His inquiry was polite and his expression bland, but Aurora could see the fierce anger smoldering deep in his eyes, and she actually felt sorry for the Misses Adderley.

The sisters exchanged frightened looks. They enjoyed destroying reputations in secret, through innuendo and rumor, and Aurora suspected no one had ever confronted them before. Until now.

One swallowed hard, her Adam's apple bobbing up and down nervously in her skinny neck. "Why . . . why, Miss Hope and I meant nothing by the remark, Lord Silverblade, nothing at all."

Her sister added, "Now, if you'll excuse us . . ."

Nicholas moved quickly to block their escape. He smiled charmingly. "My dear Misses Adderley, I cannot have you, of all people, believing such gossip and vile slander about my intended. I have asked Miss Falconet to become my wife for one reason and one reason only." He looked over at Aurora and gave her an intimate stare that made her blush. "That is because I love her to distraction and wish to spend the rest of my life with her. There are no other circumstances."

"Of . . . of course, Lord Silverblade," one stammered.

"Miss Hope and I never believed those rumors for an instant," the other added.

"That is most gratifying, ladies, most gratifying." Then Nicholas stood aside with a bow and allowed them to scurry past.

The Adderleys dispatched, he turned to Aurora with a mischievous glint in his eye and grinned.

She smiled back. "I think you have put the harpies to rout, my lord."

"I've been wanting to do that for a long, long time." He stepped closer to Aurora and raised one questioning brow. "Did I hear them correctly? Have you agreed to become the Marchioness of Silverblade?"

Aurora's smile died and she looked away. "What choice do I have, under the circumstances, as Miss Hope—or was it Miss Faith?—so eloquently put it?"

He took her hand and kissed it, the light of triumph shining deep in his eyes. "You are a brave and valiant fighter, Aurora, but the mark of a truly great fighter is to know when to capitulate to a superior opponent."

"You have won but one battle, Nicholas," she said, raising her chin defiantly. "I'm sure there will be more to come. In fact, I promise you a lifetime of them."

Nicholas was undaunted. "That sounds quite ominous, my beautiful Aurora. Here I am, thinking I am to acquire a docile, demure, obedient wife, but in reality it appears I am to gain a combatant in the lists of matrimony. How devilishly intriguing."

Suddenly Katherine appeared at their side and informed them that, as guests of honor tonight, they would be expected to lead the first dance. So Aurora let her future husband escort her out onto the dance floor.

The music started and the dancing began.

Nicholas was an excellent dancer, as Aurora knew, and for the first few minutes she lost herself in the sheer pleasure of dancing with him. He exerted his considerable charm to make her feel as though she were the only woman here tonight, and irresistibly desirable. Nicholas flirted outrageously with her, his eyes never leaving her face even when they moved apart, and occasionally he would murmur something witty that made her smile.

Aurora knew what he was doing. He was purposely coaxing her into being at her best tonight and pretending to everyone here that theirs was a love match.

Then, when one of the steps called for her to curtsy to him and turn away, she noticed a familiar figure standing at the edge of the dance floor, watching them.

It was Mrs. Littlewood.

For just a second their eyes met across the ballroom. The look Mrs. Littlewood directed at Aurora was so malevolent that it caused her to miss a step. When Aurora recovered herself, Mrs. Littlewood was gone.

After that, Aurora couldn't concentrate. She smiled and tried to look as though nothing was troubling her, but seeing Mrs. Littlewood has forced her to think of Nicholas' licentious reputation.

Diana's heart-to-heart discussion about the amatory foibles of the masculine sex had done nothing to ease Aurora's misgivings about her future husband. She couldn't help but recall the garden at Silverblade, its voluptuous pagan statuary, and the discarded stocking she had once found there. It had been all so disturbing because it represented a world beyond Aurora's experience.

As she glided past her intended, she tried to put such thoughts out of her mind. They would only frighten her unnecessarily.

The dance drew to a close. Nicholas bowed and offered her his arm. "Thank you, my dear. You dance wonderfully. Now, if you would come with me, there are some people I would like you to meet."

She forced Mrs. Littlewood out of her mind as she went to circulate among the many guests.

Pamela was definitely on Nicholas' mind that evening.

After he had introduced Aurora to Lords Cox and Haze, Nicholas left her with Ollie, who was engaging her in a spirited discussion about horses. Then he sought out Pamela.

He found her outside, in the garden. She was alone.

He thought she looked especially beautiful tonight, the moonlight turning her powdered hair to silver. She had daringly placed a black star-shaped patch just above her left breast, to entice a man's gaze downward. Nicholas smiled to himself as he walked toward her.

"Why are you all alone," he said softly, "when there are so many cavaliers inside to court you?"

"The garden looked so beautiful in the moonlight," she replied, "and the ballroom too crowded."

Nicholas could hear the edge of sadness to her voice, though she tried her best to hide it. Several days ago, when he had informed her of his impending marriage as gently as possible, she seemed to accept it with good grace. But he knew differently.

He resisted the impulse to take her in his arms, for he knew anyone could be watching and he would not disgrace his future wife with more gossip. Nicholas lowered his voice and murmured, "My marriage needn't change our situation."

Hope sprang into her eyes as she tilted her head back to look at him, but she said nothing.

"I will still need you, Pamela. I will still want you. That will never change." He smiled as his gaze rested on that damned enticing patch. "We shall just have to be more . . . discreet."

"But what about your bride, my lord? Surely she will object to sharing you with another woman."

"She will never know, in much the same way that Littlewood will never know your secrets."

That seemed to satisfy Pamela, for she lowered her lashes and gave him a conspiratorial smile.

Nicholas whispered, "Do we understand each other, then?"

"Completely, my lord."

They started back toward the house together, but Nicholas let Pamela precede him. He followed a few minutes later.

Aurora concluded her discussion with Ollie and looked about in search of Nicholas. She scanned the sea of painted faces in the ballroom, but his was not among them. Just as she was about to go out onto the terrace, she passed a secluded alcove and inadvertently overheard the end of a conversation that caused her to stop and listen.

". . . and she seems to be well-bred, not the usual low sort that appeals to Silverblade's, shall we say, debauched tastes."

The words and the accompanying chuckles sent a shiver of apprehension down Aurora's spine.

She peered around the swagged draperies that concealed an alcove and saw two finely dressed ladies and two gentlemen seated there, too absorbed in their private conversation to notice her.

"But then," one of the women said, "perhaps it is her virginal innocence that appeals to him."

Aurora drew back behind the safety of the draperies just as a man sniggered. "She'll lose that soon enough, I'll be bound."

She felt her cheeks burst into flame, and she knew she should have turned and left them alone to their gossiping. But she couldn't. Her legs had suddenly turned into tree trunks and seemed rooted to the ground.

A lewd, suggestive voice added, "But perhaps she will enjoy being stripped and birched while his friends watch."

More ugly, raucous laughter, followed by, "Or will she prefer watching him while he rogers the beautiful Mrs. Littlewood?"

Aurora gasped in outrage, but she was too humiliated to fling back the draperies and confront the gossip mongers, so she willed her wooden legs to move and fled outside onto the terrace.

She stood there leaning heavily against the balustrade and gripping the cool, rough stone with stiff, nerveless fingers. Her breath was coming in deep, ragged gasps as she fought to regain her composure.

She recalled the vile things she had just overheard and felt sick to her stomach. Aurora squeezed her eyes shut and took slow, steady breaths until the feeling passed.

She shook her head in mute denial. Nicholas couldn't be guilty of such perverted, disgusting acts. Those people had been engaging in malicious gossip, nothing more. There wasn't a grain of truth to what they said.

Or was there?

She dismissed that niggling doubt at once. Surely Diana would never have agreed to this marriage if Nicholas were a man of debauched appetites. No, it was all malicious gossip, nothing more.

Aurora took another deep breath to quell the fluttering in her stomach, then turned and went back into the house.

10

AURORA sat across from Nicholas in the dark carriage and stared out the window. It was well past midnight. The narrow streets were empty, save for the occasional watchman making his rounds armed with a lantern and a spear-tipped stave, and the houses stood dark and quiet, their occupants abed. She stifled a yawn, and heard the soft sounds of Nicholas stirring.

"Tired?" he asked.

His features were barely visible in the weak light provided by the lanterns positioned outside the carriage windows, but Aurora was very aware of those bright, penetrating eyes watching her every move.

"A bit," she replied without looking at him.

"Did you enjoy yourself this evening?"

"Yes, I did." She didn't add that she wished the Kilkennys had accompanied them to Lady Crombie's drum, for ever since Aurora had overheard those people discussing Nicholas' amatory leanings in such explicit detail, she felt more nervous than ever about being alone with him. Always the considerate escort, he hadn't left her side for an instant tonight, thus adding to her discomfort.

Now, as she sat wedged into one corner of the carriage and pretended to be absorbed in the buildings slipping past her window, Aurora wondered what Nicholas was going to do next. Since they were unchaperoned for once, she prayed he was going to be enough of a gentleman to take her right back to Kilkenny House, with no unexpected stops along the way.

Suddenly, without warning, he said, "Aurora, is something wrong?"

She jumped. "Wrong? Why, whatever could be wrong?"

He folded his arms. "If I didn't know better, I would swear you are afraid to be alone with me. You seemed quite dismayed when the duchess complained of being out of sorts and the Kilkennys declined to accompany us tonight."

Aurora turned and raised her head bravely. "Is there some reason I should be afraid of you, my lord?" she asked, an implicit challenge in her voice.

He smiled in the darkness, a flash of white teeth. "None whatsoever."

That would have to be reassurance enough.

Aurora was just about to turn back to her window when she heard the driver shout out a curse. The next thing she knew, the carriage came to an abrupt, unexpected stop, pitching Aurora forward so that she collided heavily with Nicholas as he was flung out of his seat as well.

"What the hell . . . ?" Nicholas untangled his limbs from Aurora, rose, and lifted her to her feet. "Are you unharmed?" he asked, his grip firm on her arms as he steadied her.

Aurora nodded shakily as she eased herself back into her seat. "I . . . I think so. Whatever caused the carriage to stop so suddenly?"

"I intend to find out," Nicholas replied, flinging the door open with his right hand while his left rested on the hilt of his sword. "You stay inside until I tell you it's safe to come out."

Aurora swallowed hard as he stepped down and closed the door behind him. Had some highwayman accosted them and caused their carriage to stop? She knew the streets of London were not safe, especially this late at night, but she never dreamed someone would dare accost Lord Silverblade's carriage.

She placed one hand to her heaving breast as if to

quell her wildly beating heart. She heard low, serious
voices, but they lacked urgency and menace, so she
threw caution to the winds and stuck her head out the
carriage window to see what was going on.

What she glimpsed caused Aurora to utter a strangled cry of dismay and sent her flying out of the
carriage, heedless of Nicholas' warning.

No sooner did her feet touch the ground than Nicholas came striding back to restrain her.

"Aurora, please! Get back inside! You don't want
to see this." His strong fingers dug into her arms and
he deliberately blocked her way.

But she managed to peer around him at the carriage
horses standing so quietly and flicking their tails against
their haunches. Only three of the magnificent bays
were still standing. The fourth was on the ground,
lying still in his traces where he had fallen.

Aurora looked up at Nicholas out of beseeching,
anguished eyes, "Is he . . . ?"

"I'm afraid so," Nicholas replied gently. "Hill said
he slowed down the moment the horse staggered. When
he stopped, the animal just collapsed and died. Don't
distress yourself. There's nothing anyone could have
done."

She closed her eyes and shuddered. "Poor thing."

Nicholas scowled and scanned the quiet, deserted
street, and when Aurora looked up at him, she could
tell the dead horse was the furthest thought from his
mind. When she looked around, she understood Nicholas' uneasiness and shivered with apprehension.

Aurora didn't know London well enough to recognize their location or exactly how far away from
Grosvenor Square they were. But she could see it was
a less-populated part of the city. There was a row of
modest houses to her left, but on the right was a
walled-in graveyard and wooded area, the perfect hiding place for highwaymen or other footpads.

Here they were, three travelers, alone and unarmed
save for Hill's musket and Nicholas' sword. With one
horse down, their carriage wasn't about to make any
quick getaways.

She shuddered involuntarily.

Nicholas felt her tremble and smiled down at her, but the warmth of reassurance didn't reach his eyes as he said, "Don't worry, Aurora. No harm will come to you."

Then he set her aside and called up to the driver. "Let's see if we can get the harness off him. "We'll have to leave the carcass in the street until morning, but at least the others will be able to pull the carriage back to Grosvenor Square."

"Right, milord," Hill agreed as he jumped down from his box and strode over to the dead animal lying on its side.

While the men knelt and began unbuckling the harness, Aurora turned away, unable to look at the poor dead horse for another second. However, a sudden movement from the opposite end of the street caused her head to jerk up and her eyes to widen in alarm.

There, loping silently out of the darkness like wolves, was a band of burly, hulking shapes heading straight for the disabled carriage. Feeble light from the half-moon high in the sky danced and glinted off steel, and Aurora realized with mounting horror that they were all carrying drawn swords.

"Nicholas!" she screamed.

Their presence revealed, the men broke into blood-curdling whoops that shattered the stillness of the night as they gathered speed and surged forward.

Before Aurora could blink, Nicholas was at her side, his sworn drawn and ready. "Mohocks, Hill!" he called back to the driver, who was already scrambling back up into his box for the musket he had left there. "Aurora, stay out of the way."

Mohocks! Aurora felt a hot surge of panic and dread as she backed away and flattened herself against the carriage. Even she, a provincial country miss, had heard of the notorious Mohocks, gangs of fierce, bored young bucks who roamed the streets of London at night and waylaid unsuspecting travelers, sticking them with their swords and making cruel, humiliating sport of them.

The pounding of footsteps and shrill cries grew louder as the Mohocks grew closer, ever closer. By moonlight, Aurora could see they were all masked, too cowardly, she thought in disgust, and afraid that someone would recognize them.

Suddenly a flash of powder burst from the driver's box and a shot rang out. One of the oncoming Mohocks screamed and fell to the ground. With a collective bellow of rage, his cohorts attacked.

Two of them rounded the carriage and went after Hill. The other four slowed down and faced Nicholas, each careful to stand just out of reach of his sword's deadly point.

Nicholas knew he was hopelessly outnumbered, but with a little skill and a lot more luck, perhaps he could even the odds enough to scare them off.

"I say we cut off an ear," one them growled.

"I say we strip his lady and each take her," another one countered, flicking a glance at Aurora that made her cringe inside.

A third roared with laughter. "And let his lordship watch!"

The threat to Aurora was too much for Nicholas. He quickly lunged for the nearest man and had the satisfaction of burying the point of his sword in the Mohock's arm. He quickly pulled back and danced out of reach as the man grunted and swore, his sword falling from his useless arm. This direct attack infuriated his cronies.

"Now, that's not very sporting of you," one of the men scolded as he and another moved to Nicholas' right, while another veered to his left, seeking to get behind Nicholas' guard and trap him.

As Aurora stood helplessly, she heard the scuffle in the driver's box, followed by muffled blows and a groan. She didn't need to look to know that the two Mohocks had overpowered poor Hill. In another second they would be joining the others to taunt and attack Nicholas. Five men against one . . .

Aurora had never felt so helpless in her entire life. She yearned to fling herself at the nearest brigand and

fight him with her bare hands, but she knew that
would only distract Nicholas and place him in further
danger. She scanned the dark, shuttered windows in
the houses across the way. Didn't anyone hear what
was going on? Wasn't anyone brave enough to come
to their aid? But all was silent.

Suddenly, without warning, she felt herself grabbed
from behind. Aurora struggled, but she was hugged by
a pair of relentless muscular arms while a second man
laughed and began tearing at the strings of her cloak.

"Let me go!" she cried, kicking and twisting to free
herself, but to no avail.

The man who held her only laughed and tightened his
crushing hold.

Nicholas, who had managed to wound another as-
sailant in the fray, heard Aurora cry out and allowed
himself the luxury of a brief glance in her direction. It
was all the distraction his opponents needed. They
swarmed all over him like starving wolves attacking a
wounded stag.

Pain like a white-hot poker shot through his thigh,
and then his sword was knocked out of his hand.
Before Nicholas could dive and retrieve it, a hamlike
fist connected with the side of his head, causing dozens of tiny stars to explode behind his eyes. He gasped
as nameless faces swam and blurred before him; then
another fist pounded into his midsection, robbing him
of precious breath even as the exquisite pain made
him double over in agony.

The last thing he heard before the blackness claimed
him was Aurora screaming his name. . . .

Aurora screamed when she saw the men converge
on Nicholas, and she screamed again when she saw
him fall to his knees. Then a red haze of fury filled her
eyes. She didn't even feel one of her assailants tear at
the bodice of her gown with greedy fingers. They had
killed Nicholas and were going to rape her. There was
no escape.

Suddenly the front door to one of the houses flew
open and a skinny little man wearing nothing but a
nightshirt and cap came rushing out, carrying a lantern

and brandishing a musket. He was followed by a much younger man, fully dressed and carrying two pistols. The shadow of a rather large woman filled the lighted doorway.

"You've had your sport for tonight," the man with the musket bellowed. "Now be off with the lot of you before we start shooting!"

Aurora felt herself released so quickly she staggered and would have fallen if she hadn't grabbed on to the carriage wheel for support.

"Don't shoot," the Mohocks' leader grumbled, taking the opportunity to kick Nicholas one last time before lowering his sword. "We were just having a bit of sport."

Two of them retrieved their fallen compatriot and then they were gone, fading silently back into the shadows from whence they had come.

"Nicholas!" Aurora murmured, tears streaming down her face as her fingers fumbled with her cloak to cover herself.

"You all right, miss?" the little man asked, peering at her out of dark, owlish eyes as he came over to assist her.

She nodded, then lurched forward, her eyes never leaving Nicholas' supine form.

"Is he . . . ?" she asked the other man as she knelt beside Nicholas. He looked unnaturally pale by lantern light.

The younger man shook his head. "He's still alive, but they roughed him up some. Looks like they got him in the thigh."

As Aurora cradled Nicholas' head in her lap, a shadow loomed over her, and she looked up to see the fat woman standing there shaking her fist at the departing Mohocks.

"Damned virgin-breakers!" she muttered savagely. "Honest folk aren't safe in their own beds with the likes of them around. You should have shot every last one of them, Clarence."

"Now, now Jenny . . ." the man in the nightshirt said. "We've already got a dead horse lyin' in the

middle of the street. That's going to take some explaining to the watch as it is.''

Aurora smoothed some hair back out of Nicholas'
face. The skin of one of his cheekbones was broken
and red where they had hit him, and a thin dark line
of blood trickled from the corner of his mouth. His
face felt so cold to her touch.

The next fifteen minutes were a blur to Aurora. She
was vaguely aware of the fat woman returning to stanch
Nicholas' wound and bind it with linen strips. Then
there were other people coming and going. Hill regained consciousness and discussed the situation with
the watchman who appeared out of nowhere, too late
to do any good.

A horse appeared out of nowhere and was hitched
to the Silverblade carriage; then several men put Nicholas inside. Aurora joined him and finally they were
on their way.

Aurora collapsed into the nearest chair, leaned her
weary head against its high back, and let out a sigh of
relief. The surgeon had finished his grisly work and
departed after leaving Aurora detailed instructions
for his patient's care. The bloodstained linens and
bandages had been discreetly whisked away. Nicholas'
house was quiet. She closed her eyes and slept.

When Aurora next awoke, it was late morning.

She looked at Nicholas lying on his back in bed, his
head turned toward her, and she could have wept.
An ugly black bruise had risen on his cheekbone and
his left eye was swollen shut. Nicholas' lower lip was
split, but at least he hadn't lost any teeth in the fracas,
and the surgeon had assured her that the several cracked
ribs would mend. Every time Aurora thought of what
those men had done to him . . .

She extended her hand and gently brushed aside a
lock of dark hair that had fallen across his brow. He
stirred and murmured something unintelligible, but
did not waken.

Nicholas had fought for her; now Aurora would
fight for his life. She would nurse him day and night

and never leave his side. She would marry him even if she didn't love him and he didn't love her. She owed him that much, and Aurora always paid her debts.

The growling of her stomach reminded Aurora that she was starving, so she rose and went downstairs to get some food. She wondered fleetingly what the Kilkennys had thought when they received her message about the attack and her reasons for staying the night with Nicholas. Actually, she didn't care. After all, she and Nicholas would soon be wed and beyond the reach of gossips.

She had just started down the main staircase when she heard a distraught feminine voice say, "I must see Lord Silverblade at once!"

Aurora looked down into the foyer just in time to see none other than Mrs. Littlewood fling back the voluminous hood of her black cloak to reveal her identity to the footman who had answered the door.

"I'm sorry, Mrs. Littlewood," Aurora called down from the landing, "but Lord Silverblade is not receiving callers."

Mrs. Littlewood looked up, saw it was Aurora, and proceeded to remove her cloak with defiant deliberation and thrust it at the footman. "Lord Silverblade is in his bedchamber?" she demanded of him.

When the footman replied in the affirmative, Mrs. Littlewood swept through the foyer and started up the stairs.

How I hate that woman! Aurora thought.

She firmly stood her ground. "Lord Silverblade has been injured by Mohocks, Mrs. Littlewood, and the surgeon said he is not to have callers. I'll thank you to—"

"Really, you are a most tiresome child, Miss Falconet!" the woman snapped impatiently as she sailed past.

Short of physically restraining her, Aurora was powerless to stop her and it enraged her. She may have been able to handle horses and pistols with practiced ease, but when it came to besting another woman in a duel of words, she was sorely lacking.

She could do nothing but follow Mrs. Littlewood into Nicholas' room and watch helplessly as she gave a dramatic cry of anguish and draped herself over her lover's supine form.

"Oh, my poor darling," Pamela crooned, as tears coursed down her face. Finally she managed to pull herself away and face Aurora. "I'll need clean linen and a basin of cool water if I'm to nurse him. Now, be quick about it!"

How dare she order me about like some chambermaid! Aurora thought.

While she would have cheerfully assaulted the obnoxious woman with her fists, she restrained herself. There were better weapons to be had.

Aurora forced herself to stand her ground and speak calmly. "Does your husband know where you are, Mrs. Littlewood?"

Mrs. Littlewood hadn't expected Aurora to attack from that quarter, and something like trepidation filled her eyes. But she recovered herself quickly. "Of course he does. Silverblade and Littlewood are very good friends. The moment my husband heard what happened, he sent me here to pay our respects."

"News travels fast. I'm sure you won't object to my sending him a note thanking him for his concern."

Mrs. Littlewood glared at her in frank dislike. "That will not be necessary, Miss Falconet," she said in frosty tones. "I have done what my husband asked me to do, and now I must be on my way."

Then, with her head held high, Mrs. Littlewood swept out of the bedchamber, pausing only long enough to look down her thin nose at Aurora and say, "You may soon be his wife, but you'll never have his love," before disappearing down the hall.

As Aurora listened to the hasty footsteps fade, she hugged herself, overcome by a heady sensation of power. She had vanquished Mrs. Littlewood on her own territory, using a woman's wiles, and the feeling was glorious.

But her elation was short-lived. She had won this battle, but she suspected the beautiful Pamela had others in mind.

* * *

Nicholas opened his eyes. He felt weak and drained, and his thigh ached unbearably, like a sore tooth. He found himself clad in an unfamiliar nightshirt, a garment he usually never wore. Then he looked around and saw Aurora sitting in a high-backed wing chair that had been pulled closer to his bedside. Her eyes were closed and she was sleeping soundly, her head drooping against her shoulder.

Suddenly she stirred, and her eyes opened. She caught him staring and smiled.

"You're awake. How are you feeling?" she asked gently.

Nicholas raised a hand to rub his jaw and was startled to find several days' growth of rough, scratchy stubble there. "I feel as though I've been trampled by the mob at Tyburn."

"I'm not surprised. You've been very sick. We were attacked by Mohocks. They wounded you and beat you."

Mohocks . . . Nicholas closed his eyes as it all came rushing back to him. "How long have I been unconscious?" he asked.

"With the fever, five days all told."

He remembered now the feeling that he was being consumed by hellfire, with only Aurora's angelic face floating above his to reassure him he was not. Nicholas looked at her, and for the first time noticed the deep shadows beneath her eyes, and he cursed himself for a fool. He suspected he had gotten more sleep than she had.

"And you've been here the whole time, watching over me?" he asked her again.

"Of course," she replied, startled he should even ask. "You were wounded trying to protect me. The least I could do was nurse you."

"Night and day?" he asked devilishly. "What of your reputation?"

"Since that has already been ruined," she replied tartly, "I saw no need to be overly concerned about it. The Kilkennys know I am here and had no objections."

"I see." He groped for her hand again and just held it this time, finding her touch oddly comforting. "Thank you, Aurora," he murmured, before exhaustion overtook him and he drifted off to sleep again.

By the time another week had passed, Nicholas had had enough of his enforced convalescence, though he admitted with a sly grin that he enjoyed Aurora's nursing. She was at his beck and call to fluff his pillows, change his bandages, feed him beef tea, and satisfy his every need.

Well, almost his every need, he amended.

But he was restless now, eager to be up and about.

He threw back the covers, swung his long legs over the edge of the bed, and sat up. For a moment the room wavered and swam before his eyes, and he had to hold his head to steady it. When the feeling passed, he rose shakily and took a tentative step. To his relief, his wounded leg supported his weight, though it felt stiff and sore. But he still ached all over and felt as weak as a newborn calf.

Still, he managed to make it to the center of the room before the door opened and Aurora swept in carrying a tray.

She stopped, aghast. "Nicholas!" Then she set down the tray and advanced upon him with a belligerent gleam in her eye. "Get back to bed this instant! The surgeon said you must remain in bed for at least another day."

He just stood there swaying slightly as he fought for his balance. "You sound exactly like Old Biddy, the nurse I had as a child," he grumbled. "She was forever bullying me. Well, I never obeyed her then and I'll be damned if I'm going to obey you now."

"We'll just see about that."

Yet the touch of Aurora's hand on his arm seemed to restore his strength. She looked especially fresh and lovely on this sunny August morning, the fiery copper of her hair demurely concealed beneath a white mobcap. The attar of roses she wore banished the stale odor of the sickroom most pleasantly.

"You needn't treat me like some doddering old invalid," he said as she began leading him back to the bed.

"You're as weak as a kitten," she insisted.

"Am I, now?" Well, he would just show her . . .

Nicholas hunched his shoulders and leaned heavily against her, shuffling his feet like an old man of eighty. He allowed Aurora to assist him into bed; then without warning he grasped her wrist and pulled. Aurora shrieked and tumbled down beside him in a flurry of silk skirts and petticoats. Then Nicholas quickly threw one leg across hers, pinning her down before she could roll away and escape.

"Nicholas, let go of me this instant!" Aurora hissed, writhing beneath him as she struggled to free herself and sit up.

Nicholas held her down effortlessly. "So, I am as weak as a kitten, am I, Miss Falconet? I'm afraid you've misjudged me once again."

Aurora's eyes widened in alarm when she realized the danger she was in, and her breath was coming in short, shallow gasps. "If you lay a hand on me, I'll scream this house down!"

He propped himself up on one elbow and looked down at her in amusement. "Scream away. My servants shan't come to your aid. They're in my employ, remember?"

When she tried to knock his arm away, he merely caught her wrist and pinned her arm above her head. "Save your strength for other things, my dear."

She stopped struggling at last. What was the use? There was no escape. Aurora closed her eyes and waited for the inevitable. She felt Nicholas release her wrist, but his bare, muscular leg still lay heavy across her knees. Her eyes flew open when the mobcap was snatched off her head and the curls came tumbling down in wild abandon.

He sifted his fingers through her hair while his eyes roved slowly over her face. "Your hair is like fire, but your eyes are like ice," he murmured, his breath warm against her cheek. "Which are you, my beauty, fire or ice?"

No man had ever said such sweet, seductive words to her before, and it took all of her strength to resist him. But Nicholas had an unfair advantage. He was a practiced seducer who knew how to woo a woman with honeyed phrases and make her body betray even an iron will.

Now he drew closer, nuzzling her ear as he whispered, "Heal me, Aurora."

Aurora shuddered helplessly as his questing lips traced the outline of her ear, then nipped at the earlobe.

"Let me go, Nicholas. Please."

"Not yet." His mouth trailed down her neck, sending little shocks of pleasure skittering across her skin, until she shivered and gasped.

His light, teasing caresses so distracted her that she was only dimly aware of his nimble fingers undoing the bodice of her gown. When she suddenly realized her breasts were bare to his ravenous gaze, Aurora's face turned scarlet with shame.

"You mustn't," she whimpered, clutching the material together and hastily trying to cover herself.

Nicholas captured her hand and brought the open palm eagerly to his lips, all the while drinking his fill of her loveliness. Her breasts were small and hard rather than full and soft, like Pamela's, but the nipples were large and rosy, straining for his touch. Nicholas felt himself grow rigid with desire beneath his nightshirt.

His voice was thick and raspy as he said, "How beautiful you are!"

Aurora looked up at him beseechingly out of tear-filled eyes. "No man has ever—"

"Then let me be the first to give you a woman's special pleasure," Nicholas whispered.

He took her soft sigh for surrender. Nicholas lightly grazed one breast, then the other, savoring its silken texture and firmness, his eyes never leaving Aurora's face. Then he smiled in satisfaction as he saw her expression of fear gradually change to one of surprise, then wonder.

When Nicholas began caressing the taut nipples with

his fingers, Aurora's eyes closed and her lips parted as she caught her breath in surprise. Seeing her drowning in the sensual world of passion he was creating caused the sweat to rise on Nicholas' brow and left him feeling weaker than before.

He continued to fondle her until she relaxed completely, her breathing deepening. When her eyes flew open in mute appeal, he knew what she wanted, even though she might not be sure herself. Lowering his head, Nicholas flicked his tongue along one straining peak, then the other, again and again, until Aurora's sights turned to groans and she begged him to stop.

Her passionate response was making him so lightheaded he thought he would faint, but he couldn't stop. Not now.

The moment he drew a sweet nipple into his mouth and began suckling her, Aurora stiffened and arched toward him with a wordless animal cry.

"I'll stop now, if you wish," he said with a teasing smile, knowing full well what her response would be.

"No!" she cried desperately, clutching her fingers in his hair to hold him in place.

"No, what? You must tell me what you want, my fiery Aurora."

She hesitated, then surrendered. "I . . . I don't want you to stop."

Was this passionate, sensual creature the same Aurora who had wished for separate bedchambers once they were wed?

"Splendid, because I have no intention of stopping."

Nicholas lifted his leg to release her, confident she was too far gone to want to escape him now. He caught his breath as a spasm of pain clutched at his leg. But he chose to ignore it and lifted Aurora's skirts instead with his free hand.

His fingers moved lightly up her inner thigh, teasing and exciting her warm, smooth flesh. Aurora groaned again, and her thighs relaxed, parting of their own volition, inviting him to continue his sweet onslaught. Suddenly, much to Nicholas' chagrin, his questing fingers encountered unexpected resistance.

He lifted his head. "You're wearing drawers!"

Aurora stared down at him in puzzlement. "Of course I'm wearing drawers."

He had only enough strength to murmur, "Most women don't, my sweet," just before he collapsed.

The moment Aurora felt herself buried under a deadweight, she knew it was not part of her seduction to be crushed beneath him. Something was dreadfully wrong.

"Nicholas!" she cried, trying desperately to wriggle out from underneath him. She succeeded in rolling him onto his back, where he lay, eyes closed and face as white as the bed linens.

"The surgeon told you to stay in bed another day!" Aurora admonished his unconscious form as she hastened to return herself to some semblance of decency. "Why couldn't you have listened, you impossible man!"

Then she fled from the room, calling for someone—anyone—to ride for the surgeon at once.

The surgeon arrived quickly, examined Nicholas, and prescribed more bed rest. Several days later, Nicholas was fit enough to return to Surrey.

He and Aurora were to be married in three weeks.

"You know very well that Nicholas does whatever he wants, when he wants, Grandmother. He listens to no man—or woman, for that matter."

"You needn't remind me, Wesley," Lady Vivien said bitterly as she seated herself again in a rustle of stiff taffeta.

Wesley wrinkled his nose in distaste as one of the dogs chose to lie at his feet. "At least he won't be marrying one of his doxies. That in itself should console you."

"It doesn't!" the old lady snapped. Then she added distastefully, "Is it a love match?"

Wesley's brows rose nearly to his hairline. "Nicholas in love? Good Lord, no! My reckless cousin compromised the lady and felt honor-bound to make restitution, that is all."

While the marchioness listened, Wesley told her all about the dramatic rescue from the Tyburn mob and what had ensued.

"Do you know if Mary approves of her son's marriage?"

"As far as I know, my aunt hasn't even met the girl, let alone learned that her son intends to marry her."

"Splendid. That gives me some time." As if in answer to her grandson's speculative look, the marchioness added, "Something must be done to frighten off the Falconet chit, Wesley."

He looked at her with wry amusement. "What do you propose to do, Grandmother? Weigh her down with stones and drop her in the Thames? Make a handsome settlement on her to ensure her disappearance?"

"Don't be absurd!" Lady Vivien snapped. "I merely want to speak to the child. Perhaps I can make her see the folly of marrying my grandson. Is she staying at Silverblade?"

"And risk a scandal? No, she's at Overton Manor, staying with her sister until the wedding."

Lady Vivien nodded. "Bring her to me, Wesley, at two o'clock this afternoon. Miss Falconet and I are going to have a little tête-à-tête, one she will never forget."

Aurora sat in the folly, sipping cold ginger beer and trying not to think of Nicholas.

It was impossible. Every time she closed her eyes and concentrated on the soothing humming of bees in the nearby garden, she couldn't help recalling his ardent caresses in his bedchamber and how she had so wantonly responded to his skilled touch as though she had no mind of her own.

"Dreaming of your intended bridegroom, sweet Aurora?" said a scornful voice from the foot of the folly steps.

She started guiltily and opened her eyes to find Halley standing there.

With slow, sure steps, he began climbing the stairs. "Or perhaps you're dreaming of becoming a marchioness. That's quite an accomplishment for a baronet's daughter, I must say. Or perhaps you're dreaming of the Silverblade fortune at your disposal, and those thousands of fertile acres to rule like a queen."

Aurora resisted the impulse to shrink away as Halley entered the folly and stood looking down at her with something like disappointment in his eyes. Ever since her arrival back at Overton Manor yesterday to stay with Diana before her wedding, she had managed to avoid being alone with Overton.

"I am marrying Lord Silverblade because I have no other choice," she replied flatly, "and you know it."

"Oh, but there are always choices, Aurora, if we are brave enough to make them."

Her cheeks colored. "Somehow I find being his wife preferable to sharing you with my sister, Lord Overton."

A slow, unpleasant smile lit his features. "You say that now, but wait, Aurora. Wait until you have been married to him awhile."

She thought of what she had overheard the night of the ball. "Wh—what do you mean?"

Overton smiled again. "I'll leave that to your imagination, my dear." Then he said, "I've come to tell you that Wesley Devenish is here to see you. I believe he wants to take you to call upon his grandmother. The old termagant wants to look you over, I suspect."

Aurora thanked him and went running out of the folly, eager to get away from Lord Overton as quickly as possible.

"Thank you for agreeing to see my grandmother, Aurora," Wesley Devenish said as he handed her down from his carriage.

"The pleasure is all mine, Wesley," she replied.

During the ride from Overton Manor to the Silverblade dower house, Aurora and Wesley had become friendly enough to call each other by their Christian names, since they would soon be cousins by marriage.

Once she was out of the carriage, Aurora studied the dower house with interest. Privately, she thought the Queen Anne-style house of cream-colored stone too large for just one person, but she kept her opinion to herself.

"I hope you will still feel that way after you have seen Grandmother," Wesley said.

The note of warning in his voice put Aurora on her guard. "Am I to infer that she will not be pleased to see me?"

Wesley smiled down at her benignly as he rang the bell. "Let us just say that Grandmother had another candidate in mind for Cousin Nick's wife."

Aurora's optimism faded. "Oh, I see."

"Grandmother can be quite intimidating," he went on. "But I'm sure you're more than a match for her, Aurora."

"Thank you for warning me," Aurora said, just as a footman came to the door to admit them and showed them to the drawing room.

Aurora was startled to find the door opened by a blackamoor boy dressed as a miniature sultan, complete with plumed turban and an inquisitive monkey on his shoulder.

"This is Juma, my grandmother's page," Wesley told her.

Aurora felt dark brown eyes regard her with curiosity. "Juma . . ." she murmured politely. "I am Miss Falconet, here to see the dowager Marchioness of Silverblade."

The boy, who couldn't have been more than eight years old, bowed gravely and bade them enter.

The moment Aurora stepped into the room, she was confronted by three fat spaniels sniffing at her skirts. With a cry of delight she knelt and extended her hand to pet the nearest one.

"I wouldn't do that if I were you," said a daunting voice. "They dislike strangers and are apt to bite."

Aurora jerked her hand away and rose, searching for the source of that voice. The marchioness was sitting in the center of the settee like a queen holding court. When she impatiently waved her hand for Aurora and Wesley to enter, the dogs went to lie at her feet and Juma took his position on a stool to her right.

As she crossed the room, she was conscious of the old lady's eyes taking in every detail of her appearance, from her tip-tilted straw hat to the sack gown of printed Indian cotton she wore.

When Aurora reached the settee, she curtsied and said, "Good afternoon, ma'am. It is a pleasure to see you again."

"Miss Falconet, sit down. Juma and Wesley, leave us."

When the two women were alone, the marchioness glared at Aurora. "Let us forgo meaningless chatter, Miss Falconet, and be frank. I dislike you, and I dislike the idea of your marrying my grandson even more."

Aurora marshaled her defenses and raised her chin a proud notch. "But you don't even know me well enough to dislike me, ma'am."

She smiled, stretching the wrinkled flesh across her jaw. "Oh, but I do, my dear. I know you are nothing more than a baronet's daughter, a conniving chit without breeding, social position, or a dowry, who has somehow managed to snare my unsuspecting grandson into marrying you."

Aurora recoiled from the vehemence of the woman's accusations, then recovered herself. She had been taught to respect her elders, but this vituperative old lady was clearly not worthy of that respect.

"You falsely accuse me, ma'am."

The marchioness's eyes narrowed slyly. "Oh, do I, now?"

"Yes, you do!" Aurora retorted angrily. "It is true that I am a baronet's daughter without social position or a dowry, but I did not snare your grandson into marriage. He was the one who compromised me. He was the one who ruined my good name, and offered marriage as a way of saving my honor."

"Honor? Pah!" the old lady spat. "You and that trollop of a sister of yours don't know the meaning of the word."

Aurora sprang to her feet, white-hot fury pulsing through her veins. Without a word, she whirled on her heel and headed for the door.

"Come back here!" the marchioness screeched, hauling herself to her feet. "You'll stay seated until I dismiss you, you impudent chit."

Aurora turned to face her. "I will not stand here and listen to you malign me and my sister."

The marchioness advanced on her, moving quickly for one so advanced in years. Her bony claw shot out and clasped Aurora's wrist in a surprisingly strong grip, and cold gray eyes held hers.

"Listen to me, Miss Falconet, and mark my words well. I would advise you not to marry my grandson, if you know what is good for you. If you choose to disregard that advice, you will live to regret it."

Aurora felt the blood pounding in her ears. She licked her lips, which had suddenly gone dry. "I wonder what Nicholas would say if he knew you were threatening me, ma'am?"

The malevolent look fell from the old lady's face like a mask, to be replaced by a look of pure innocence. She smiled sweetly. "Me, an old lady whom no one listens to? Why, my dear Miss Falconet—granddaughter—surely you have misunderstood what I just said to you. I merely invited you to call to welcome you into our family with open arms."

Aurora shivered in the warm room. All she wanted to do was flee from this madwoman and her threats. But she forced herself to bend down and extend her hand to the three dogs that had followed their mistress and were gathered patiently around her skirts.

"I told you they bite," the marchioness said with some asperity.

One of them came forward, licked Aurora's fingers, and allowed her to pat his head.

Aurora looked up at the marchioness. "I think their mistress is the only one who bites, ma'am."

She left without another word.

The moment Aurora set foot in the foyer of Overton Manor, she found Diana waiting for her, a dazed expression on her face.

"Diana, is anything wrong?" she asked.

Diana shook her head. "Come to your bedchamber at once. You won't believe your eyes."

The moment Aurora stepped into her room, she felt as though she had walked into a draper's shop. There were robes *à la française,* sack gowns, morning gowns, and gowns with Watteau pleats, dozens of them spread across the bed, draped over the backs of chairs, hanging in the open armoire. They were made of the finest brocades, silks, damasks, and cut velvets Aurora had ever seen, all in autumn colors of gold, green, yellow, and deep bronze.

She fingered an exquisite evening gown of flowered French silk, then turned her attention to a wrapping gown.

"I . . . I don't understand," she stammered in bewilderment. "What did all these gowns come from?"

Diana smiled. "They were delivered while you were calling on the marchioness." She handed Aurora a letter. "This should explain everything."

Aurora broke the seal and read the letter. All it said was "To my beautiful bride. Nicholas."

"All of these clothes are from Nicholas?" Aurora asked in awe. "They must have cost a fortune!"

Diana nodded. "These printed Indian cottons are very expensive." Then she added, "I must confess I am partly responsible. When your betrothal was announced, Nicholas asked me for your measurements and swore me to secrecy. He chose these for you himself and had them made as a surprise."

Aurora was too stunned to speak.

Diana went over to a chair and came back holding nankeen breeches, a lawn shirt, waistcoat, and coat of fine cinnamon-colored velvet.

"He had his tailor make these for you as well," she said with a smile.

Aurora ran her hand over the rough nankeen of the riding breeches. "These are men's riding clothes."

"Look again," Diana said. "They're too small for a man. They're for you."

Aurora was so moved, tears stung her eyes. So he understood after all. While others were scandalized by her hoydenish behavior, Nicholas didn't mind if she rode about the countryside dressed as a man.

"Well, I'll leave you to contemplate your riches," Diana said and left.

Aurora waited a moment to make sure Diana had gone, then stripped off her gown and tried on her riding clothes.

When she was dressed, she went to the mirror and smiled in delight. Nicholas' tailor had worked miracles. The breeches fit her boyish hips to perfection, and the coat her slender shoulders.

But her visit to the old marchioness dampened her pleasure in her new wardrobe. As she adjusted the ruffles at one wrist, she wondered if she should tell Nicholas about his grandmother's threats. Then she decided against it. After all, what could a harmless old lady possibly do to her? All Aurora would do is upset Nicholas unnecessarily.

Her thoughts were interrupted by a maid who stared at her in shock before she found her tongue and told Aurora that the Marquess of Silverblade was waiting to see her in the drawing room.

Without bothering to change, Aurora went downstairs to thank Nicholas for his generosity.

She found him staring out the window, his hands clasped loosely behind his back. The afternoon light falling on his face played up the pallor of his skin and the deep hollows left from his illness, but he was quickly regaining his strength and looking more fit with each passing day.

He turned and smiled, his eyes lighting up at the sight of her. He bowed. "You look quite elegant, young sir."

Aurora made a leg and sketched him a courtly bow in return. "It's all in the tailoring, my lord."

Nicholas came to her and kissed her hand. "Of all the lovely gowns I bought for my bride," he said with a rueful shake of his head, "she loves the breeches best."

She looked away and thanked him shyly.

"There are several items lacking, I'm afraid."

Aurora racked her brain. "Not that I could see, my lord. I have a new gown for every occasion."

Nicholas' smile was mischievous as he leaned over and whispered, "I neglected to order any . . . drawers."

Aurora turned away so he wouldn't see her blushing in embarrassment. She recalled that afternoon he had pulled her down on the bed and begun caressing her so shamelessly. If her drawers hadn't stopped him just in time, she would not be a virgin on her wedding day.

Behind her, he said, "As fetching as you look in your riding attire, I would ask you to change into something more suitable, my dear. I'm taking you to meet my mother."

His mother . . . The recluse who wore a black silk mask and saw no one.

Aurora whirled around. "Your mother?"

Nicholas smiled dryly. "Since we are to be married, I thought it best she meet her future daughter-in-law sometime before the event, don't you?"

"Of . . . of course," Aurora said

As she started to leave, Nicholas stopped her. "Oh, one more thing . . ."

Aurora turned, looking at him expectantly. He reached for her left hand and held it while he fumbled in his waistcoat pocket.

"What betrothal would be complete," he said softly, singling out the third finger, "without a ring."

Before Aurora realized what had happened, she was staring down at the most beautiful ring she had ever seen, a plain large oval sapphire set in an ornate gold setting.

"It's . . . it's beautiful!" she stammered, holding it up to the light, where it sparkled and winked like blue fire.

"I tried to find a stone that matched the color of your eyes, but I failed. This sapphire came the closest. It especially reminds me of your eyes when they darken with defiance, as they so often do when we are together." Then Nicholas drew her free hand to his lips and kissed it. "Now our troth is sealed."

His portentous words made Aurora imagine she heard a prison door clang shut, and the ring seemed to weigh her hand down like a heavy iron shackle. It proclaimed to the world that she belonged to him and was now one of his many possessions, like the great estate of Silverblade and his stallion Stormcloud.

She knew he was expecting her to say something, so she managed to smile and murmur, "You are too generous, Nicholas."

"It is no less than my bride-to-be deserves."

"I'm not sure of that."

"Well, I am."

Feeling suddenly uncomfortable, Aurora turned away from him. "If I am to meet your mother, I really should change into something more appropriate. If you'll excuse me . . ."

"Of course."

She hurried away before Nicholas could say another word.

11

AURORA hesitated before the closed double doors and moistened her dry lips with the tip of her tongue, then smoothed the skirt of her new flowered silk gown with a nervous hand.

"Do I look presentable?" she asked Nicholas, who stood patiently by her side.

He smiled down at her. "Not only do you look presentable, you look beautiful, my dear. That dress is a particular favorite of mine. I'm pleased you chose to wear it to meet my mother."

His confident pronouncements uplifted her flagging courage. Aurora took a deep breath, squared her shoulders, and nodded at Nicholas.

"She will adore you, you know," he said as he knocked three times.

Aurora looked doubtful. "A hoyden who races about the countryside dressed in breeches?"

He grinned back. "Hoydens in breeches make the best wives."

Their banter was cut short by the sound of measured footsteps approaching the doors, and Aurora had just enough time to compose herself before one of them swung open to reveal a tall, thin woman with a somber, guarded expression.

"Good afternoon, Rose," Nicholas said without smiling, and Aurora sensed some long-standing antagonism between master and servant. "I believe my mother is expecting us."

For one second Aurora feared this woman was going to confront Nicholas and refuse them admittance. Then she stepped back and said, "The marchioness is expecting you, your lordship."

"Splendid," he replied, ushering Aurora before him. "That is all, Rose. You may leave us now."

"Yes, your lordship." She left them, though Aurora had a feeling it was with great reluctance.

But she could not spare another thought for a mutinous servant. Nicholas had slipped her arm through his and was leading her through one of the most beautiful sitting rooms Aurora had ever seen. It was quite spacious, with ornate plasterwork on the ceiling and the walls were painted in restful tones of pale blue and ivory. The graceful, elegant furniture was upholstered in rich silks and damasks, and the carpets were so thick and soft they muffled every footstep. Everywhere one looked, there was something to delight the eye—a painting of a gentle bucolic scene, an arrangement of flowers, the spinet standing against one wall.

Lady Mary had created a beautiful world for herself right here in her own apartments, a world where she had everything she wanted and would never have to leave. Yet for all its gentle elegance, Aurora found the room to be a cold, unwelcome place. Laughter was a stranger here.

Glancing about, she also noticed reflective surfaces had been kept to a minimum. No mirrors graced the walls, all candlesticks were made of porcelain rather than silver, and even the polished tabletops were concealed beneath damask cloths.

Aurora forced herself to look directly at the marchioness, who was seated on a settee at the far end of the room as they made their way toward her. She feared if she looked away, her future mother-in-law would interpret the gesture as one of revulsion, and hate her for it.

"Good afternoon, Mother," Nicholas said, his deep masculine voice out of place in this delicate feminine bastion. He released Aurora's arm, approached the marchioness, and bowed over her outstretched hand. "Thank you for agreeing to receive us."

Aurora was aware of a pair of lifeless gray eyes regarding her from out of the eye holes in that black silk mask. Aurora smiled tentatively, but the other woman looked away, turning her attention to her son.

"Please be brief, Nicholas," she said in a listless voice. "I am too tired to receive callers today, but Rose said you insisted."

A fleeting expression of anguish flitted across Nicholas' face; then it was gone so quickly that Aurora thought she must have imagined it. "I only called to introduce you to my betrothed, Mother. Otherwise I wouldn't have disturbed you."

Then he turned to Aurora and extended his hand, her signal to approach the settee for the introduction. Aurora moved forward spontaneously and placed her hand in his, trying to keep from showing her shock and chagrin at his mother's lack of interest.

Nicholas had just informed his own mother that he was getting married, and she was acting as though she didn't care one whit!

Aurora stood face-to-face with her reclusive future mother-in-law. Lady Mary was tall for a woman, and all skin and bones, with hair that had once been as dark as Nicholas', but which was now completely white. Her dress was of a style popular nearly a decade ago, and Aurora suspected she hadn't purchased any new gowns since her husband's death.

"Mother, I would like to present Miss Aurora Falconet," Nicholas said. "Aurora, this is Lady Mary Devenish, the Marchioness of Silverblade. My mother," he added, almost as an afterthought.

Again Aurora felt those lifeless gray eyes on her as she curtsied deeply. "I am honored to meet you, my lady."

The marchioness's head drooped. Aurora couldn't tell whether the woman was tired, bored, or acknowledging the introduction with the briefest of nods. Then she looked up sharply and said, "Aurora . . . What a lovely name."

Aurora smiled, encouraged by the comment. "Thank you, my lady."

She waited for an additional sign of welcome—a clasping of hands, a quick hug, a sparkle of enthusiasm in that soft, rasping voice behind the mask—but none was forthcoming. There were no endless questions about Aurora's family and background that any mother would ask of the woman her son was marrying. It was obvious Nicholas could marry a goat as far as his mother was concerned.

Suddenly Aurora was furious with this cold, unfeeling woman, so absorbed in her own pain she couldn't even feign interest in her son's betrothed or their upcoming wedding. Aurora wanted to reach out, grasp her by the shoulders, and shake some sense into her.

Instead, she smiled sweetly and quickly seated herself beside Lady Mary on the settee, ignoring Nicholas' startled look. "I'm honored that your son chose me to be his wife, Lady Mary," she said, clasping the other woman's hand in her own. "I promise that I shall be a good wife to him, and you will be proud to call me your daughter."

"I . . . I am sure I will," the marchioness stammered, disconcerted by Aurora's directness.

Aurora risked a glance at Nicholas, who was still standing, and was relieved to see the corners of his mouth twitch in a suppressed smile. Then he said, "Both Aurora and I would be honored if you would attend the wedding."

Suddenly Lady Mary's eyes filled with fear and panic. She snatched her hand out of Aurora's grasp, rose, and walked over to the window.

"It's impossible," she said flatly to Nicholas. "You know I never leave my rooms except to stroll in the garden. I cannot attend your wedding. You mustn't even ask such a thing of me."

He stiffened, trying to control his bitter disappointment. "I was hoping you could make an exception in this case, madam. After all, I am your only son," he added dryly, "and I don't get married every day. Surely you could—"

"I will not attend your wedding!" she cried, whirling on him. Then she placed a shaking hand against her heart. "Leave me now and send Rose to me at once. I am feeling poorly and must rest."

Nicholas feigned indifference by bowing and saying, "As you wish, madam. Good day."

But as Aurora rose and went to his side, she could see the deep hurt he was trying so valiantly to mask. She curtsied, wished the woman good day, and left with Nicholas.

When the double doors closed behind them, Aurora said tentatively, "I . . . I'm sorry."

"For what?" he snapped without looking at her or breaking stride.

"That your mother will not be attending the wedding. I know it would have meant a great deal to you, and—"

"You presume to know too much, Aurora," he said, suddenly stopping and grasping her arm. Nicholas glared down at her through narrowed eyes of steel. "I knew all along my mother would never agree to leave her rooms, especially for something as trifling as my wedding. I merely asked her as a courtesy, nothing more."

"I see," Aurora said.

She understood all too well. Nicholas had been hurt by his mother's refusal, but was too proud to admit it, especially to Aurora. So he feigned unconcern and concealed it by lashing out at her in anger.

He released her and resumed walking, more slowly this time, and the anger seemed to leave him.

"Once you are mistress of Silverblade," he went on, "you'll become accustomed to Mother's odd behavior. She keeps to her rooms. Occasionally she'll see Wesley or my grandmother for a short period of time. But for the most part, the household runs around her, as though she didn't exist."

"How sad."

Nicholas gave her a strange look. "It's the way she wants it, Aurora." Then he smiled. "At least you will not be cursed with an interfering mother-in-law, the way my mother was."

Aurora thought of her visit to the dowager Marchioness of Silverblade, and she could well believe it.

"And your grandmother?" she asked. "Will she interfere?"

Nicholas drew her arm through his. "Let her try, and she'll have to deal with me."

While they were walking down the main staircase, Nicholas asked Aurora if she would like to take a stroll down to the kennels to look in on her favorite foxhound pup before returning to Overton Manor. She agreed enthusiastically.

As they stepped outside and rounded the house, Aurora suddenly realized that in a short three weeks' time she would be Aurora Devenish, Marchioness of Silverblade, and this vast estate would be hers. There would be a household to run, social obligations to fulfill, and the tenants' welfare to see to. She would be bound forever to the man now walking by her side, sharing his bed and eventually bearing his children.

Suddenly the sheer enormity of what she had agreed to hit her like a bolt of lightning, and she felt herself drowning in a sea of self-doubt. What if she failed? What if she and Nicholas didn't suit after all? What would become of her then?

Off in the distance, she heard Nicholas say something to her. "I . . . I beg your pardon?"

He smiled indulgently. "I just asked you if you meant what you told my mother."

"And that was . . . ?"

His lips twitched and his eyes sparkled with mirth. "You've forgotten already? For shame, Aurora. Correct me if I'm wrong, but didn't you tell my mother that you were proud I had chosen you for my wife?"

Aurora shrugged. "What else could I tell her, my lord? That you compromised me and I had no other choice but to accept your proposal?"

Nicholas burst out laughing, causing one of the gardeners trimming a hedge to glance at them, then return to his task.

Nicholas shook his head. "You won't yield an inch, will you?"

Aurora smiled impishly. "If I did, you would become even more insufferable than you already are."

"Is that what I am, insufferable?"

"Insufferable, arrogant, overbearing, domineering . . ."

He appeared more amused than insulted, for his shoulders shook with laughter. "I have a high opinion of you as well, Miss Falconet. I find you exasperating, willful, headstrong, and defiant. Defiant most of all."

Aurora nodded in cheerful agreement, then echoed, "Defiant most of all."

Suddenly she noticed the obscene statue through the trees, and her lighthearted mood evaporated like fog in bright sunshine. Once again Nicholas tried to steer her away from it, but this time she resisted.

"What is this?" she asked, withdrawing her arm. "I've never seen this before."

Before Nicholas could protest, she left his side and started walking toward this other garden.

Nicholas cursed himself for every kind of fool when he caught up to Aurora. She was flushed with embarrassment from her chest to her hairline, and her soft lips were curled in revulsion. Then she turned her back on it as though she couldn't bear the sight of it for one more second.

She said, "That is the most lewd, obscene statue I have ever seen."

The look of accusation in her eyes, the note of censure in her voice, made Nicholas feel like a prurient little boy rather than a grown man of rather sophisticated pleasures. He didn't like being made to feel that way by anyone, least of all an innocent, unwordly chit like Aurora. For the first time in many a year, he felt uncomfortable and ashamed of himself. And he resented it.

Well, he told himself ruthlessly, it was time his innocent wife-to-be acquired a lesson in worldliness.

"You think it lewd, my dear?" he drawled, stifling a yawn of boredom. "I regard it as a work of art, an excellent example of classical sculpture. It depicts Priapus, the Greek god of procreation, and I acquired it in Rome several years ago while traveling the Continent. I had it set here to scandalize the local bumpkins and amuse my friends."

"And has it succeeded?"

"Too well," he blandly replied.

She looked at him. "Nicholas, will you do me a great favor?"

"If it is within my power."

She swallowed hard, and he could tell she hated asking him for anything. "Would you please remove this statue? I find it offensive."

Normally Nicholas wouldn't have refused her anything when she looked at him with such appeal. But Aurora had made him feel shame, an alien emotion. He felt the overwhelming compulsion to retaliate in kind, to make her feel foolish and unworldly.

"I am sorry to hear you say that, Aurora, for I have grown quite attached to the old fellow," he said, realizing he sounded pompous, even to his own ears. "It's as much a part of Silverblade as the main house or the Chinese summerhouse. You'll soon grow accustomed to his presence, and if you don't, you can easily avoid looking at him by walking around the garden."

"So you will not remove the statue," she said stiffly.

"No," he said gently, but with great finality. Then he crooked his arm and thrust home his parting shot. "Perhaps you will feel more at home with the foxhound pups."

Suddenly Aurora felt awkward and stupid. Nicholas had just intimated that this garden was reserved for the sophisticated pleasures of adults, while she was still a child gamboling with puppies.

Rebellion burned hot and fierce in her breast. She ignored his arm and impulsively blurted out, "If this statue is not removed, I shall not marry you."

One look at his tight, implacable face told her she had pushed him too far this time. His nostrils flared as his breathing quickened, and a pulse beating in his neck betrayed the full extent of explosive anger kept in check.

His arm dropped to his side and he regarded her out of hard, stone-cold eyes. "Threats this late in the game, my dear?" He shrugged. "As you wish. I'm sure Lord Overton will be overjoyed with your news."

Aurora had fully expected him to capitulate. Up until now, Nicholas had seemed willing to do anything for her, to indulge her every whim. He had bought her a new wardrobe, the sapphire betrothal ring, and was doing everything within his power to make her feel comfortable with this forced marriage of theirs. Now he had done a complete reversal and was threatening to send her back to Overton, and all because of a statue.

Aurora felt faint and swayed on her feet. "You . . . you wouldn't . . ."

"It is you who are threatening to jilt me, Aurora," he reminded her brutally. "Under the circumstances, I have no other alternative."

"Why must you be so unreasonable?" she wailed. "All I'm asking you to do is remove that stupid statue!"

"And I don't wish to remove it!"

Now Aurora understood all too well. She rounded on him, eyes flashing blue fire. "And since you are the great Lord Silverblade," she jeered, "your wants and desires are all that matter. You arrogant, insufferable monster!"

"Monster?" he said coolly. "Arrogant, insufferable *master* would be more appropriate. Your master, Aurora. And the sooner you learn to accept that fact, the happier we both shall be."

Aurora's palm itched to slap his sneering face, but Nicholas' curt, "Don't you dare!" stopped her from doing something she was sure to regret bitterly.

They confronted each other like warring fighting cocks, each waiting for the other to make the first move.

Finally Nicholas said, "Well? Who is it to be? The arrogant, insufferable monster, or Lord Overton?"

Aurora bit her lip to fight back humiliating tears of defeat. "You know I have no wish to return to Lord Overton," she said quietly.

He nodded without smiling. "A wise choice, my dear. Now, let us see the pups," he said with surprising gentleness as he offered his arm to Aurora, who thought it best to take it, however reluctantly.

Later, when Nicholas was seated across from her in the carriage, escorting her back to Overton Manor, he observed a shudder passing across Aurora's slender shoulders. It took all the strength he possessed to keep from going to her and pulling her into his arms. He hadn't meant to be so harsh with her this afternoon, but she had provoked him as she was so adept at doing when he least expected it. Provocative . . . that was exactly the word to describe Aurora right at that moment. Her head was resting back against the squabs, elongating her slender neck and thrusting her small ivory breasts up and almost over the edge of the bodice. Nicholas forced his gaze up to her face. Aurora's beguiling blue eyes were staring out the window, her lids half-closed in serene contemplation.

Nicholas wondered what she was thinking. Somehow he suspected it was something other than green fields scattered with black-and-white spotted cows. He yearned to ask her, for he suddenly wanted to be a party to her thoughts. But he knew she wouldn't confide them to him. Hurt feelings and resentment, the remnants of their heated exchange, still hung between them, separating them as though a high stone wall now stood between them.

He shifted in his seat and folded his arms over his broad chest. If he were any judge of women, he knew Aurora would soon forget about their little altercation. Women who were quick to anger were often just as quick to forgive and forget.

As if to prove his own theory, he smiled and resumed his good-natured teasing of her, trying to draw her out of her black mood. Before they arrived at Overton Manor, Aurora was laughing and bantering with him again, the incident apparently forgotten.

On the morning of her wedding day, Aurora awoke bathed in cold sweat, her heart slamming against her ribs in sheer terror.

She sat up in bed and hugged herself, shivering and gasping, while whispering, "It was only a bad dream," over and over again to reassure herself.

When she was calm again, she reclined against the pillows and wondered how she was ever going to find the strength to marry Nicholas and endure her wedding night.

She took a deep breath and willed herself to remain dry-eyed, for she knew if she started crying now, she'd never be able to stop. Then she gathered all the courage she possessed and rang for Sarah to help her dress.

When Nicholas saw Aurora enter the ballroom on Lord Overton's arm, he thought she looked like an ethereal vision in her wedding dress of white and silver. She also looked terrified.

As Aurora walked down the narrow aisle between the thirty close relatives and friends that had been invited to the intimate ceremony, Nicholas noticed she moved slowly, as one drugged with opium, her face stiff and unsmiling. He tried to catch her attention and ease her nervousness with a conspiratorial wink, but Aurora stared at some point beyond him, her eyes unblinking and glassy.

Well, he told himself ruefully, at least she wasn't going to bolt and leave him standing red-faced before the minister and guests.

The moment Aurora was by his side, Nicholas reached for her hand, squeezed her icy fingers, and whispered, "Brave lad," so only she could hear. His encouraging words had the desired effect. Aurora's shoulders shook with silent laughter, and the inner fire rekindled itself in her eyes so they sparkled and glowed once again.

They exchanged their vows clearly and confidently, though Nicholas noticed with some amusement Aurora's hesitation before the word "obey." Then the minister pronounced them man and wife, and Nicholas brushed his lips across his wife's mouth in a chaste kiss to seal their bargain.

Afterward, Nicholas patiently endured all the back-slapping and handshaking from his groomsmen and guests, but in actuality, all he wanted to do was get Aurora away from these people and back to the quiet and privacy of Silverblade. As Aurora stood by his side, trying her best to impersonate a happy bride,

Nicholas could tell she was having a difficult time of it. Her face was as white as her gown, and her smiles were too forced and too bright. She looked as though she would burst into tears if anyone said the wrong thing.

"Be brave for just a few moments longer," he murmured. "We shall leave after the toasts have been said."

Aurora nodded briefly in reply and looked vastly relieved.

After all the guests raised their glasses to the newlywed couple and Nicholas toasted his marchioness, he and Aurora slipped out of the ballroom into a waiting carriage and departed for Silverblade.

Nicholas sat back against the butter-soft leather squabs and regarded Aurora with tender concern. From the moment they had entered the carriage, she hadn't said a word to him. She just wedged herself into the farthest corner and kept staring longingly out the window like one of Lady Vivien's caged canaries.

Vexed as he was that Aurora was ignoring her husband so blatantly, Nicholas had expected as much. After all, he had practically forced her into this marriage.

"You can't avoid talking to me forever, you know," he said gently.

She started, and when she stared at him, Nicholas was reminded of the look of fear in a doe's eyes just before he shot it.

"I . . . I beg your pardon," Aurora said, twisting the heavy gold wedding band as if she would tug it off. "I was preoccupied with my own thoughts."

"I'm sorry the ceremony wasn't the wedding of your dreams," he said.

Aurora scowled at him. "What do you mean?"

Nicholas gave her a cajoling smile. "Don't all young ladies dream of a lavish wedding in a cathedral, with twelve attendants and hundreds of guests, followed by a banquet and ball?"

She sighed and averted her face. "Since I never

thought to be married, my lord, I never thought to dream about my own wedding one way or another."

"Come now. Surely you knew you would marry one day."

But Aurora denied it, and assured him she had intended to remain a spinster, looking after her father in his old age, then staying on at Falconstown after he died.

Thinking of her father caused bright tears to fill her eyes, though she quickly dabbed them away with her handkerchief.

"I wish your father could have been here to give you away," Nicholas said, "and Tim to be my grooms-man."

She smiled tremulously at that. "I wish they could have been here as well."

Nicholas leaned across her voluminous brocade skirts and took her hand in both of his. "Rory," he began, his voice soft and serious, "I know ours is not a lovematch. There is nothing either of us can do to change it now. We must make the best of what fortune has dealt us." He looked deeply into her eyes. "Do you understand?"

Even though she nodded slowly in assent, Nicholas could tell that his attempts to reassure her had failed. The haunted, fearful look in her eyes remained, and he couldn't for the life of him figure out why.

But as the carriage passed through the gates of Silverblade and into the park, Nicholas saw Aurora start and glance about wildly. Then he suddenly realized what she was so afraid of and why. He could have laughed out loud at his own stupidity.

He knew just how to make her feel at ease.

Leaning back in his seat, he said, "Aurora, I would like to propose a wager."

That caught her interest. "A wager? What sort of wager?"

"I believe you once boasted to me that you were as good a shot as any man."

"I am," she replied without a trace of conceit.

"Splendid. I have the perfect opportunity for you to make good your boast, and for very high stakes."

"Whom will I be shooting against?"

"Me."

Now she was becoming suspicious of his motives. "And the stakes?"

Nicholas propped his elbow on the windowsill, rested his forehead in his hand, and paused for a second before saying, "You, my dear."

Aurora's lips moved, but nothing came out. Finally she uttered a strangled, "Me? I . . . I don't understand."

"It's simple, really. If you win our little wager, madam, you may refuse me admittance to your bed for as long as you please. A year . . . forever." Now he smiled, his voice as smooth as silk. "But if I should win, you shall grace my bed whenever I wish it, starting with our wedding night." Nicholas raised his brows in a mocking question. "A sporting wager, don't you think?"

"Is it, my lord?" Aurora challenged. "Or are the odds tipped in your favor? I know you to be a formidable opponent."

He shrugged. "Yet you claim to be as good a shot as any man. Any gentleman I know would not be so reluctant to prove his own prowess, no matter how skilled his opponent."

He was deliberately goading her, for Nicholas knew Aurora considered herself to be as honorable as any man.

"And if I don't agree to your wager?" she demanded.

"Then you shall spend our wedding night with your husband, as all new brides do." He paused to brush away an imaginary speck of lint from his breeches. "But at least I am offering you an opportunity to postpone your marital obligations until you are amenable."

"I will accept the terms of your wager," she said without hesitation.

"I thought you might; that is why I took the liberty of having your pistols packed along with your feminine fripperies." He raised a questioning brow. "Unless, of course, you prefer swords."

Aurora smiled. "Pistols will do."

Nicholas grinned. "A sensible choice." He leaned forward and extended his hand to seal their bargain.

They shook hands just as the carriage pulled up before the entrance to Silverblade.

Half an hour later, after all the servants had met the new marchioness and Aurora changed out of her wedding dress and into breeches and a shirt, she and Nicholas met in an open field past the gardens for their shooting match.

Once their pistols were primed, Nicholas said, "The best of four?"

Aurora nodded. "And if there is a tie, the fifth shot decides."

"Agreed," Nicholas said. "Ladies first, madam."

Aurora emptied her mind of all superfluous thoughts and concentrated her attention on the target set up at the opposite end of the field. If she allowed herself to think of losing, she knew she would.

She raised her pistol and fired. When the smoke cleared and she stepped back, Nicholas took his turn, and they both waited for the gamekeeper's pronouncement.

"First to his lordship!" came the call from the opposite end of the field.

Aurora disregarded her husband's cocky smirk and took her best shot, but it was not good enough. Nicholas won the second round as well.

Aurora waited for him to make some disparaging comment to unsettle her further, but to her astonishment, he said nothing, just concentrated on reloading his pistols.

Much to her delight, Aurora won the third round and felt her confidence returning with a rush. The last round was the deciding one, and she could not afford to lose her concentration. There was just too much at stake.

After both she and Nicholas took their turns and were waiting for the call, Aurora felt her stomach flutter with nervousness.

"Fourth round to her ladyship!"

Nicholas frowned and mused, "If I had known you

were this good, madam, I would have insisted on
swords."

"Thank you for the compliment, but we still have
the deciding round," she replied, and reloaded.

When they were ready, Aurora aimed and fired.
Nicholas did likewise. Then both watched the gamekeeper stride over to the target and examine it. He
turned. Aurora held her breath.

"Final round to—"

She squeezed her eyes shut and uttered a prayer.

"—his lordship!"

Her eyes flew open in disbelief. The match was over
and she had lost.

Nicholas didn't say a word or even look at her. He
went striding across the field to the target, pulled it
down, and came walking back, all the while studying it
with rapt concentration.

"You may have lost, but not by much, if that's any
consolation," he said. "See for yourself."

Aurora stared at the target. Nicholas' shot was only
a hairbreadth nearer the center than hers. However,
the knowledge that she had lost by such a slim margin
only made her feel more desolate. She would share his
bed on their wedding night after all.

She ignored the hard lump of disappointment lodged
in her throat and raised her head proudly to take her
defeat like a man.

"Congratulations, my lord," she said. "Well done."

Nicholas' eyes widened in surprise. He had expected
her to burst into hysterics, rattle off a long list of
excuses for losing, then try to wheedle him into releasing her from their wager. But she didn't. She accepted
defeat with more grace and valor than half the gentlemen he knew.

He bowed. "And you, madam, are a most worthy
opponent."

Aurora acknowledged the compliment with a brief
nod, and seemed pleased, but Nicholas could see the
dread growing in her eyes as she thought of what
losing the wager entailed.

Seeking to distract her, he said, "Come with me.
There is something I wish to show you."

Aurora walked beside him in silence until she saw they were approaching the stables, and her interest was aroused. She wanted nothing more than to mount a horse and ride like the wind, leaving all her troubles behind her.

"There is an additional benefit to being married to me," Nicholas was saying as they entered the quadrangle. "You may ride any of the horses in my stable."

"Even Stormcloud?" Aurora asked, suddenly excited at the prospect of having the spirited gray at her disposal.

"Even Stormcloud. But after you see the horse I've just bought, I think you'll forget about him very quickly."

"Oh, I doubt that," Aurora said as they made their way to the paddocks behind the main buildings.

But when she saw Nicholas' latest acquisition prancing about the paddock as though seeking to escape, all thoughts of Stormcloud fled from her mind.

She walked up to the fence like one in a trance. "Firelight."

At the sound of his name, the chestnut stallion stopped and raised his magnificent head, his liquid brown eyes fastening on Aurora. Then he whickered a rumbling greeting deep in his chest and came to her, popping his head over the high fence so she could stroke his face.

"Sweet baby," Aurora crooned.

Then she turned to Nicholas, watching her with a strange expression on his face. "Why are these white and silver ribbons threaded through his mane?" she wanted to know.

Nicholas smiled sardonically. "Since my ostlers would have a devil of a time trying to wrap him up in tissue paper, I settled for ribbons in his mane."

"Wrap him up? I . . . I don't understand."

"Isn't it the custom to wrap wedding gifts?" Nicholas asked. When Aurora nodded, he added softly, "Since Firelight is one of my wedding gifts to you . . ."

Aurora's hand stopped in mid-stroke, and she gaped at Nicholas out of astounded eyes. "For me? Firelight belongs to me now?"

He nodded.

Then, to his chagrin, her face crumpled and she burst into tears.

Suddenly annoyed with her for rejecting his gift, he said in tight, clipped tones, "Do forgive me. I bought him from Overton—and at an outlandish price, I might add—under the delusion that you would be pleased."

"But I . . . I am," she protested, hiding her face against the horse's cheek. "It is the most wonderful gift I have ever received."

Suddenly she flung her slight weight into Nicholas' arms, startling him, and wrapped her arms around his waist.

"Thank you," she whispered into his chest. "No one has ever given me such a magnificent gift."

He smiled to himself. How like her to prize a witless, half-mad horse over her sapphire betrothal ring. He surprised himself even more by understanding why she did.

"You're most welcome."

Suddenly the feel of her pliant body pressed against his was eliciting quite a different response from Nicholas. He became acutely aware of her breasts crushed against his ribs, and her hips molding themselves to his own most provocatively. He fought to control himself as he gently disengaged her. He would not claim his prize until nightfall, and that was a long way off.

"Would you like to go riding?" he asked her. "There's much of the estate you haven't seen yet."

Aurora's ice-blue eyes lit up at the prospect. "I would love to." Then she grinned. "Perhaps we could race Firelight against Stormcloud to see who is the faster."

Nicholas looked skeptical. "Since they're both stallions, I'm sure they would rather fight than race."

Aurora shook her head. "If I tell them to mind their manners, I'm sure we'll have no trouble with them."

She cupped her hand to her mouth and leaned over to whisper something into Firelight's ear. Much to Nicholas' astonishment, the stallion suddenly grew still as if he were listening, and his brown eyes softened in understanding. Then he blew softly through his nostrils in assent.

Aurora grinned. "He understands now. He'll be as docile as a baby. You'll see."

Nicholas signaled for the horses to be saddled, and watched with a bemused expression as Aurora whispered her commands to Stormcloud as well. Then he and his exultant wife began their ride.

True to Aurora's word, the two stallions were as docile as a pair of lambs.

All Nicholas could do was stare at Aurora and ask, "What will you whisper in my ear tonight to tame me?"

Nicholas glanced at the clock on the mantel. It was his wedding night.

He took one last look around to make sure the setting was perfect. The draperies had been drawn across the windows to shut out the night and make the room snug and intimate, while a small fire glowed in the grate to ward off the unseasonable chill in the air. Candles in two silver candelabra provided deep seductive shadows, and a decanter of claret was there to ease his reluctant bride into a mellow, accepting mood. The bed's damask curtains were parted, the covers turned down in anticipation, and the sheets delicately perfumed with aromatic dried herbs and flowers.

As Nicholas draped the black velvet banyan over his sleek, naked body, he cocked an inquiring brow at the closed door that separated his suite of rooms from Aurora's. Much to his chagrin, he found himself feeling apprehensive about her. Would her fear of him finally override her sense of honor? He wanted her, but he didn't want to hurt her and provide her with a lifetime of resentment.

"You're acting like a virginal bridegroom," he muttered to himself in disgust. "You've slept with women before. You know how to make this the most memorable night of her life, whether she wants it to be or not."

Despite a confidence born of considerable experience, he felt his hand trembling ever so slightly when

he raised it to knock on her door. Would he find her
cowering in some corner, ready to scream the walls
down if he dared approach her? His mouth widened in
a smile. Somehow, that picture did not fit the spirited,
combative Aurora he knew. She was all fire, not ice.

He knocked once and the door swung open immediately, leading him to believe she had been waiting for
his summons.

Aurora—his wife now—stood framed by the doorjamb. She stood there so straight and stiff, with her
jaw set in determination, that Nicholas was reminded
of a painting he had once seen in Rome depicting a
group of Christians waiting to be devoured by lions.
Doomed martyrs. That's what Aurora looked like, a
virginal martyr about to be sacrificed on the altar of
his lust.

He wanted to take her in his arms and soothe her as
one would comfort a child, but he resisted with all his
might. He knew if he treated her like a child tonight,
Aurora would likely remain one throughout their marriage, never taking responsibilities for her own actions. He wanted her to fully experience the joys of
her womanhood tonight.

Nicholas extended his hand to her and gazed deeply
into her eyes. "You look beautiful," he said, his voice
a throaty purr.

She was wearing a long white gown so gossamer that
it must have been spun from moonbeams. As it rippled to
the floor, it outlined Aurora's small, high breasts and
clung to her slender hips and long, coltish legs.

Aurora stammered out her thanks, and placed
her hand in his. As his fingers closed around hers,
she flinched, but didn't pull away.

"Come," he said gently, drawing her into the room.
"Let's sit before the fire and have some claret."

Suddenly she was distracted by the mural on the
ceiling.

"What is that?" she asked, craning her head back
for a better look.

"*The Rape of the Sabines*," Nicholas replied, trying
to ignore the way Aurora jumped at the mention of
the word "rape." He went over to the decanter and

began pouring the wine. "That's why my bedchamber is called the Sabine Room. And despite what you are thinking, it does not serve as inspiration."

She covered her embarrassment by quickly asking, "How do you ever get any sleep with that overhead?"

"Oh, one gets used to it," he replied, handing her a glass. "In fact, I even have names for all the actors in this particular drama."

That wheedled a small smile out of her.

"The stout greedy fellow carrying two women is named Maurice," he told her, "and the skinny one attempting to pry that reluctant damsel from the Corinthian column is called Harvey."

Aurora's slender shoulders began shaking with laughter and she entered into the spirit of the game. "And the ugly, dim-witted fellow beneath the cherub?"

"Overton, of course."

She gave him a look of pure skepticism. "Now you're jesting with me."

"True. But I think it's appropriate, don't you, since my lord Overton is preoccupied with his looks?"

She giggled. "If he knew, he'd be so mortified he'd call you out."

"I daresay it would be pistols for two, coffee for one."

The lighthearted badinage eased the tension between them and relaxed her, for she sipped her claret, glided over to the fireplace, and seated herself in the wingback chair.

No sooner did Nicholas drape his arm across the back than Aurora drained her glass in two gulps and held it out to him. "May I have another? The claret is uncommonly good."

Nicholas knew what she was trying to do, of course, but he had no intention of making love to a drunken woman. Aurora must be in complete control of her faculties, for he intended this night to be memorable for her as well. So when he refilled her glass, he brought it back to her with the stern admonition to drink this one slowly.

Silence fell between them.

Nicholas was content to wait, for he proposed to

gentle her like a high-strung horse, not break her spirit. But he found himself entranced by the serene picture Aurora presented as she sat there staring moodily into the glowing coals of the fireplace. Her red-gold hair glinted in the light, shooting sparks of molten copper as if it had life of its own. Nicholas reached down and gently stroked it, savoring its soft, smooth texture. She stirred, but she didn't start or pull away, so he gently ran the backs of his fingers down her cheek in a tentative caress, feeling his own desire for her building.

It was time.

He rounded the chair and stood before her, smiling down at her as he extended his hand. "Come to me."

Aurora froze inside. The moment she had been dreading for weeks had come upon her. Her terrified gaze darted about the room, searching for the instruments of perversion she had heard about.

"What are you looking for, Aurora?" Nicholas said coldly, his patience quickly evaporating at her constant mistrust of him. "A means to escape me? I can assure you there is none."

The wine had loosened her inhibitions so she blurted out, "I was looking for the birch rods."

Nicholas' bark of laughter seemed to explode through the room. "Birch rods! Why would I keep birch rods in my bed . . . ?" His voice trailed off and his gray eyes narrowed into slits as the reason for her unreasonable fear of him suddenly became obvious.

He knelt before her and took her cold, stiff hands in his. "Aurora, who told you I was going to hurt you in that way?"

She swallowed hard, looked down, and forced the words out. "The . . . the night of the ball, I overheard some people talking about you."

"Will you tell me what they said?"

Aurora's face grew hot with mortification as she related exactly what had been said, and she was quite unprepared for the vehemence of Nicholas' reaction.

He swung to his feet with a violent oath and braced himself against the mantel, his whole body quaking with the effort to control his rage. "If I knew who they were, I would call them out!"

Hot tears of relief slid down Aurora's cheeks. "You mean you don't . . . ? You aren't . . . ?"

With a groan of remorse, Nicholas whirled around and pulled her into his arms, holding her tightly against his heart. "My sweet, foolish, innocent Aurora, I may be a notorious rake, but I do not beat women and I don't force myself upon them. And I certainly don't invite spectators into my bedchamber!" he added indignantly.

Aurora buried her face in the soft velvet of his banyan to hide her scarlet cheeks.

Above her, she heard him murmur, "Did I hurt you the two times I kissed you?"

She shook her head.

"Have I ever hurt you in any way?"

"N-no."

"Then you must know that I will not hurt you tonight. You have my solemn oath as a gentleman."

Aurora sighed. How could she have ever believed such vile slanders about the man who had done so much for her?

"Please forgive me, Nicholas," she whispered. "I've been such a fool. I should have known all along that those people were indulging in gossip, nothing more."

He tilted her chin so he could look at her, his expression tender and solicitous. "I can understand why you believed them. Lord knows, I deserve it. But I wish you had trusted me enough to tell me why you were so frightened."

"I do trust you, with all my heart. Now."

"Then let me prove to you that I'm not such a monster after all."

Aurora stood there facing him, her hands resting lightly on his shoulders, and she searched the depths of his gray eyes, now almost black in the shadowed room. There was no coldness there, no reserve, just warmth, and a gentleness she had never imagined he possessed.

She reached up and placed a tentative hand on his smooth, hard cheek, startled and overwhelmed when he responded by trembling at her touch. Then she stood on tiptoe, tilted her head back and just brushed his lips lightly with her own in mute encouragement.

When Nicholas returned her kiss, it was as though his hard, smooth mouth were dueling with her, moving with maddening slowness one moment, followed by a sensuous onslaught that took Aurora's breath away. She closed her eyes and emptied her mind of all doubts and misgivings, surrendering herself to him completely.

Nicholas seemed to sense this, for he stepped back a pace and slipped Aurora's hand beneath the heavy velvet of his banyan. Her eyes widened momentarily as her fingertips grazed wiry hairs, then hard, corded chest muscle, but she did not pull away. Flattered and emboldened by Nicholas' gasp of delight, Aurora unfastened the garment, slid her other hand beneath it, and gently pushed it off his shoulders so it fell to the floor.

He was naked.

To Aurora's astonishment, she wasn't embarrassed, perhaps because she had already seen him half-naked that morning by the summerhouse. All she could think of was how sleek and beautiful he was, so strong and graceful and untamed, his skin luminous in the candlelight. She ran her hands lightly across his shoulders and down his chest, stopping at the scar across his left breast.

"How did you get this?" she whispered.

"A duel with swords when I was about your age."

Her fingers continued their explorations across his ribs and down to his narrow waist, stopping at another scar.

"And this?" she asked.

"A duel with pistols a year later. I needed practice."

Aurora would have continued her leisurely exploration of his body, but when she caught a glimpse of his fully aroused manhood, she suddenly became shy. To cover her reluctance, she reached up and behind his neck, her nimble fingers working swiftly to untie the black ribbon there.

The unexpected gesture must have pleased him, for

he grinned and shook his head, sending his dark, glossy hair falling nearly to his shoulders like a lion's mane.

"Now let me see you," he said, his long fingers reaching for the thin satin ribbons that held the lacy bodice of her nightgown together. His eyes danced and sparkled with mischief and humor. "Unless, of course, you're wearing drawers to thwart me again."

Aurora started giggling so hard, she didn't have the strength to object when he eased the nightgown from her body, swept her into his arms, and carried her over to their marriage bed.

At first he just held her against his shoulder, stroking her bare arm and whispering endearments against her hair to soothe her and allay her fears. When Aurora relaxed and slid her arm around his waist, he began kissing her, slowly, luxuriantly, his hot mouth branding her forehead, her eyes, her mouth, before trailing down the slender column of her throat.

Aurora's head lolled back as she focused her undivided attention on all of the delightful, exciting things Nicholas was doing to her body. She bit her lower lip to keep from groaning as he began licking her breasts, making her feel as though she were being devoured by flames.

"Let me give you a woman's special pleasure," he had said to her that afternoon in London, and just the memory of what was to come next made Aurora shiver in anticipation.

When he drew one taut nipple into his mouth, then the other, back and forth, sucking harder each time, Aurora knew she was lost. She couldn't help herself. All vestiges of maidenly modesty fell away and she shocked herself by panting and moaning like a harlot.

Her uninhibited response didn't shock Nicholas, however. On the contrary, it aroused him further.

His caresses deepened and he began exploring her, letting his fingers wander down Aurora's flat belly until they rested against her womanhood. Aurora started at the intimacy of his touch, but as Nicholas continued the maddening stroking, her thighs parted of their own volition in mute invitation.

As Aurora became enslaved to her own passions she heard a voice not unlike her own urging him to touch her there, harder, and when he did, her response was a low animal moan of pleasure that seemed to delight him more than mere words. She became a wild, wanton creature in his hands, awakened to her own sensuality.

Finally, when Aurora thought she'd go mad, Nicholas poised himself above her for their union, murmuring, "I'll hurt you only this once, my Rory. Never again."

But Aurora was so hungry to be possessed by him that she barely felt the resistance and sharp pain as he eased himself into her. Then all she knew was heady, tingling pleasure, rising, subsiding, building again, until it exploded within her, destroying the old Aurora forever and forging a new one in her place.

Just before Aurora drifted off to sleep, she whispered in his ear, "I'm glad I lost the wager."

She felt a rumble of laughter well up from deep in his chest. "So am I, darling Rory, so am I."

For the next several days it seemed to Aurora that she and Nicholas never left his bed.

"You still have much to learn, my hoyden wife," he would say to her, and commence with yet another pleasurable lesson.

Under Nicholas' expert tutelage, Aurora learned how to bestow pleasure on a man as well, to test her own power as a woman. She learned how to use her fingers, lips, and tongue to enslave her arrogant husband until he writhed beneath her helplessly and begged her to end his torment. It was a side of Nicholas she had never suspected existed.

Neither maid nor valet dared interrupt them. At mealtimes, trays were discreetly left in the sitting room, to be consumed at will or not at all.

By the time they emerged into the world, Aurora felt as though she had been Nicholas' mistress for years.

12

AURORA stood before the open armoire and tried to decide which one of her many beautiful gowns she was going to wear today. But her attention kept wandering to the closed door that separated her suite from her husband's. It took all the strength of will she possessed to keep from crossing the room, opening that door, and enticing him into bed.

She chuckled to herself as she rang for her maid to help her dress. As Nicholas had pointed out this morning, they had spent the first week of their marriage in bed and had to face the world sometime. He had an estate to run, and she the household. Besides, he had whispered against her hair before she reluctantly rose to return to her own bedchamber, nightfall would come soon enough.

Aurora poured herself a cup of hot chocolate and walked over to the tall window overlooking the rolling front lawn and the park beyond. She shook her head and laughed at herself. She had been so foolish—so childish—to fear her physical union with Nicholas. No woman could have asked for such a gentle, considerate bridegroom.

Yet as she sipped her chocolate, fresh doubts began to creep across her thoughts like the clouds stealing across the clear blue sky. True, when she and Nicholas were in bed together, locked in each other's fervent embrace, Aurora felt as though she had known him all her life. But by the harsh light of day she wondered if he would become a different person, someone difficult to know.

The knock on her door reminded Aurora that the real world was about to intrude with its demands and responsibilities. She set her cup down and crossed the room to admit her maid.

After luncheon, Nicholas had an appointment with his estate agent, so Aurora was left to her own devices. She decided it was time to call upon her mother-in-law.

Aurora knocked on the double doors leading to Lady Mary's rooms and waited.

Since the afternoon of that disastrous introduction, Aurora had made up her mind that she was going to do everything in her power to win over the withdrawn, reclusive woman. Even if she couldn't persuade her to leave her rooms and take her rightful place with the family, Aurora was determined to elicit some sort of response from her.

Now the door swung open to reveal the dour Rose.

"Yes, madam?" Rose said in an unenthusiastic voice.

Aurora smiled brightly. "Good afternoon, Rose. I would like to see Lady Mary."

"I'm afraid that is quite impossible, madam," the maid replied, trying to bar the way with her slight form. "Her ladyship is having one of her megrims and doesn't wish to be disturbed."

"I am very disappointed to hear that," Aurora said. "Tell her that I shall call upon her tomorrow to see how she is faring."

"Her ladyship might still be ill. Her megrims often come upon her swiftly and last for several days."

Aurora looked the maid squarely in the eye and said, "In that case, I shall call the day after tomorrow, and every day after that until she is feeling well enough to receive me."

Rose's dark eyes glittered with annoyance, but she bowed her head deferentially. "I shall relay your message to her ladyship."

"Thank you, Rose. See that you do." With that, Aurora turned and left her.

True to her word, Aurora called upon Lady Mary the following day and was turned away once again with the same excuse. Undaunted, she returned the day after that, as she had threatened.

This time, Rose admitted her, though grudgingly.

Aurora smiled as she glided through the sitting room toward the masked figure seated on the settee.

"Good afternoon, Lady Mary," she greeted her when they came face-to-face. She wanted nothing more than to take the other woman's hands in her own, but she decided it was too soon. "I was so sorry to hear you've been indisposed for several days. You are feeling better, I trust?" Then Aurora seated herself without invitation.

She ignored the baleful expression in the gray eyes regarding her through the mask's slits, and smiled.

"Thank you, Aurora," Lady Mary replied. "I am feeling much better this afternoon."

Aurora waited. Silence, nothing more.

Have it your way, she thought grimly.

Aurora said, "Since you were unable to attend the wedding, Lady Mary, I thought you would enjoy hearing all about it." Before Lady Mary could decline, Aurora plunged on. "Nicholas obtained a special license and we were married at Overton Manor. It was rather small, with only thirty guests, and . . ."

She chattered on and on as though her tongue rolled on wheels, describing in great detail the floral decorations in the ballroom, what the guests wore, and the various wedding gifts they had received. As she spoke, she watched Lady Mary surreptitiously, and noticed with a sinking heart that the expression of absolute boredom glazed her eyes for the entire time.

Finally, discouraged beyond reason, Aurora capitulated. "I think I have quite overstayed my welcome." She rose and curtsied. "Good day to you, Lady Mary. I am sorry for tiring you."

She left feeling as though she had spent the last hour banging her head against a stone wall.

Several hours later, Nicholas left his mother's rooms feeling as though he had been struck by lightning.

If he had been astonished to receive a summons

asking him to call on her, he was positively incredulous when he heard what she wanted of him. It was the first time since her beloved husband's death that Lady Mary had asked anything of her son, the first time she had displayed any interest in the world beyond her suite and garden.

Nicholas shook his head as if to clear it, then raked his fingers through his hair. He wondered what had caused this change in her, even one so minor. Could his mother be feeling guilty over the fact that she had refused to attend her own son's wedding? A bitter smile tugged at the corners of his mouth. Guilt was an alien emotion to her.

Well, whatever the reason, he was thankful for small favors.

He went to find Aurora, suddenly eager to share his good news with her.

She was in the salon, playing the spinet. Trying to play the spinet, Nicholas amended with a silent chuckle.

As he watched Aurora and listened to her fingers halt and stumble over several chords in succession, Nicholas found himself thinking of Pamela, and how he had spent hours listening raptly to her playing. She excelled at the spinet the way she excelled at all the feminine arts, her long, elegant fingers coaxing the most beautiful, complex sounds imaginable out of the instrument.

Suddenly Aurora looked up, caught him staring, and blushed hotly. "Now you know another of my many shortcomings, my lord," she said with a sigh. "The music I make would set a dog to howling."

She looked so crestfallen, Nicholas couldn't help smiling. "Ah, but you have many other . . ." He deliberately lowered his gaze to her square neckline, where the tops of her breasts rose and fell provocatively. ". . . attributes, my lady."

Aurora blushed again and lowered her gaze. Nicholas could tell she was still not used to such intimate bantering, even from her own husband.

He sought to put her at ease.

"Something very interesting happened to me just a few moments ago," he said, standing beside the spinet.

Aurora's brows rose. "What was that?"

"My mother summoned me to her chambers today."

"And that surprised you?"

His smile was sardonic as he explained that his mother never, ever summoned him to her chambers. "She also made a request of me."

"What sort of request?"

"She asked me to have a miniature painted of you," he said, his voice soft with wonder. "It's to be her wedding gift to me." Then he reached into his pocket and removed a tiny parcel wrapped in paper. "And she asked me to give this to you."

He watched Aurora's eyes widen as she took the package from him and began to unwrap the paper. She gasped as her efforts revealed a small, finely wrought cameo brooch set in gold.

"How exquisite!" she said, studying it from all angles.

"It's Mother's wedding gift to you," he said. "It may not look grand, but I'll have you know that brooch was one of the first gifts my father ever gave her. My mother is excessively sentimental. I'm surprised she is so willing to part with one of her treasures."

"That makes it an even more special gift. I wouldn't trade it for all the diamonds in the world," Aurora replied softly, and when she looked up at Nicholas, he noticed her eyes were unnaturally bright.

He reached out to tilt her chin toward him and studied her face. "Thank you for being so kind to my mother," he whispered, before lowering his head and kissing her.

The moment Aurora's soft, warm lips molded themselves to his mouth, Nicholas felt the first stirrings of desire deep in his loins despite his best efforts to control himself. But Aurora was so lovely, so intoxicating. The attar of roses she always wore filled his nostrils with its sweet perfume, and her mouth tasted like rare ambrosia to his plundering tongue. She did not pull away with protests of being discovered by a servant, but leaned toward him, seeking him, wanting him shamelessly.

Nicholas was pleased to comply. He slipped his fingers beneath the fabric of her bodice, reveling in the texture of her breast, skin as silken as a rose petal, the nipple pebble-hard and aching for his touch. Aurora stiffened and moaned against his mouth, but did not try to evade his bold advances.

He tore himself away, and noticed with some satisfaction that Aurora looked chagrined.

"I think we should retire to my bedchamber, madam," he said in a voice husky with passion, "before I take you right here on the spinet seat."

His wife grinned up at him as she placed her hand in his. "Deuced uncomfortable that would be, my lord."

"Deuced uncomfortable indeed," he agreed with a laugh.

The following morning, Aurora went to call on Lady Mary once again.

"My lady is having another bout of the megrims," the solemn Rose informed her, "but she will see you if you agree to speak to her through closed bed curtains."

"Of course," Aurora said, startled by the unusual request.

She followed the maid through the sitting room to the bedchamber beyond. Much to Aurora's astonishment, this room was as austere as the sitting room beyond was sumptuous. The walls were painted plain white and it was as sparsely furnished as a nun's cell, with only a bed, washstand, tallboy, and armoire. There was no dressing table laden with feminine fripperies so dear to the lady of fashion, and of course, no mirrors to reveal a ruined face.

There was, however, a large portrait of a man Aurora assumed to be Nicholas' late father hung on the wall directly opposite Lady Mary's bed. The likeness of her beloved husband would be the first image she saw upon rising, and the last at night as she drifted off to sleep.

The heavy blue damask draperies surrounding the bed were drawn, and Aurora assumed that Lady Mary was not wearing her mask this morning. Rose drew up a plain wooden chair, then departed, and Aurora sat down.

"Good morning, Lady Mary," she said cheerfully, addressing the curtains near the head of the bed. "I'm sorry to hear you are not feeling well today."

"Good morning, Aurora," came the reply. Without the mask to muffle her speech, Lady Mary had a pleasant voice, low and distinctive. "Thank you for your concern."

"I just wanted to thank you for the lovely wedding gift. I'm wearing it now."

There was a pause. "Its value is chiefly sentimental," Lady Mary said apologetically, "but you're Nicholas' wife now and I wanted you to have it."

"I shall always treasure it because it meant so much to you."

Her response must have pleased Lady Mary, because Aurora thought she detected a smile in the woman's voice when she said, "It pleases me to know you appreciate the significance of my gift."

"Nicholas told me its history."

She stared at the portrait. How like his father Nicholas was, tall, commanding, with those same piercing gray eyes captured so eloquently by the artist.

"And what of your history, Aurora?" Lady Mary asked. "Where do you come from and how did my son meet you?"

Aurora was so excited she wanted to pull back the draperies and hug her mother-in-law, but she restrained her impetuosity just in time. Although the woman's sudden willingness to open up to her was encouraging, Aurora realized that she mustn't push her too hard or fast, or the Lady Mary would draw back into her shell.

So Aurora sat back and began talking about herself, being careful, however, not to upset Lady Mary by relating such tragedies as Tim's death or the death of her father. But she told the truth about her meeting with Nicholas and the real reason for their marriage.

"So yours was not a love match, as was mine," Lady Mary said, her voice heavy with disappointment.

"I'm afraid not, my lady," Aurora said, then added hastily, "but we are getting on splendidly nonetheless. As Nicholas is so fond of saying, 'We suit.' "

A long, wistful sigh came from behind the drapery. "Suiting is not the same as loving. My William and I had a love match like none other."

Suddenly Aurora heard the distinct sound of sniffling, followed by a muffled sob. "Lady Mary, are you all right?"

"I'm . . . I'm sorry, my dear. Those painful memories just overwhelm me at times. Please leave at once and send Rose to me."

"Let me help you," Aurora pleaded, her hand raised to pull back the drapery.

"No! I told you to leave me!"

The woman sounded on the verge of panic, so Aurora said soothingly, "As you wish. Good day to you, Lady Mary. I'll send Rose to you on my way out."

After luncheon, Aurora changed into a smart riding habit of dark blue camlet and went down to the stables to select a suitable mount. Since she would be calling upon Diana at Overton Manor, Aurora decided that Halley's ostlers would not be too eager to see Firelight, so she selected another mount instead.

As she rode through the park, Aurora felt a twinge of guilt for not calling upon her sister sooner, for she had been married almost two weeks and not once had she communicated with Diana in any way.

She smiled to herself as she trotted through the main gate and nodded to the porter. Surely Diana would understand that she had little time for anything these days.

When she arrived at Overton Manor and was told to wait in the foyer, Aurora felt a feeling of foreboding settle into her bones. She sensed something was dreadfully wrong. When Halley himself came striding toward her, she was certain of it.

"Well, my dear Aurora," he said with an unpleasant smirk as his bold gaze raked her up and down, "I see that being Silverblade's marchioness agrees with you. You have the look of a woman who hasn't been let out of a man's bed for weeks."

Aurora felt her cheeks redden at his crude remark. "I am here to see Diana," she said coldly.

Halley bowed with a mocking flourish, then adjusted the sleeves of his blue damask jacket. "But of course. She's up in her bedchamber, though not for long."

"What do you mean?"

His brown eyes sparkled. "I wouldn't want to spoil her surprise. I'll let her tell you."

Then he bowed again, turned, and sauntered off, stopping only to glance at his reflection in a nearby mirror.

Puzzled, Aurora gathered her skirts and went rushing up the stairs. When she reached Diana's sitting room, she knocked, but there was no answer.

"Diana?" she called out, opening the door and stepping inside.

Aurora stopped and stared. There, in the middle of the sitting room, were several portmanteaux piled high atop one another.

"Diana?" Aurora called apprehensively, walking into the room.

Suddenly the door to the bedchamber beyond swung open and Diana emerged, a green velvet gown draped across her arms. When she saw Aurora standing there, she stopped, started, then burst into tears.

"Diana, what is the matter?" Aurora demanded, rushing over to her sister.

Diana, sobbing now, flung the gown on the floor and threw herself into Aurora's arms.

"What's wrong?" Aurora murmured, cradling her sister against her shoulder as if she were a baby.

For a moment Diana didn't even attempt to respond, just cried her heart out. Finally she pulled herself away and said, "Halley has thrown me out. He . . . he doesn't want me anymore."

She sobbed afresh. Aurora stood there stunned, unable to comprehend what she had just been told. Gradually Diana's words seeped into her numb brain. Halley was dissolving their union after seven years. He didn't want Diana for his mistress any longer.

"There, there," Aurora crooned, stroking her sister's shuddering back, "calm yourself and tell me what happened."

Diana took several gulps of air, and her sobs dissolved into hiccups. She drew away and faced Aurora squarely, blotting the tears away with a handkerchief. She looked desolate and wounded. When she spoke,

the words were forced and slow, as though it pained
her to say them.

"This morning Halley informed me that he was tired
of me, that I no longer pleased him, that I . . ." Diana
closed her eyes. ". . . bored him."

"But, Diana, you love him!"

Diana's eyes flew open. "Evidently he no longer
loves me. He told me to have my bags packed and
leave by this afternoon."

Aurora shook her head. "He can't do that to you,
not after all these years, not after all you've meant to
each other."

"Oh, but he can," Diana reminded her with an
ironic smile. "I am not his wife, remember, I am
merely his mistress. I have no legal recourse, no say in
the matter."

"It's not right."

Diana's voice was heavy with bitterness as she picked
the velvet gown up off the floor, smoothed and folded it.
"Father warned me that I was making a mistake. He told
me this would happen, but I didn't believe him. Other
men discarded their mistresses so callously, not my
Halley. He was cut from uncommon cloth. He would
keep me with him forever. What a damned fool I was!"

Aurora thought of Halley's intention of having a
cozy *ménage à trois* with the Falconet sisters, and she
fervently prayed he hadn't mentioned it to Diana before discarding her. Still, Aurora couldn't help but feel
responsible for her sister's plight.

She cleared her throat and said, "Perhaps there is
another woman in his life."

"That's the first thing I asked him, and he denied it."

Aurora breathed an inward sigh of relief. That would
have been too mortifying for Diana. She didn't know
what else to say except, "What are you going to do
now, Diana? Where will you go?"

"I'm going to London."

"To stay with the Kilkennys?"

Diana's smile was wry. "With my reputation? No,
I'm afraid that would be presuming on Katherine's
friendship far too much. I plan to stay with Lady
Fanshaw until I can find another protector."

"Another protector?" Aurora said sharply. "Surely one was enough."

"Spoken with a married woman's lofty disdain for her less-fortunate sisters," Diana said.

"I'm . . . I'm sorry." Aurora rushed to apologize. "I didn't mean that the way it sounded. I speak without thinking, as you well know."

Diana smiled. "No offense taken. But that is the way of the world, Aurora. I have lived with Halley without the benefit of clergy for seven years. No 'respectable' man would want me for a wife now. The best I can hope for is another protector, and a generous one."

Suddenly Aurora brightened. "Diana, why don't you come to live at Silverblade? I'm sure Nicholas wouldn't mind. Then you wouldn't have to—"

"Sell myself to the highest bidder?"

Aurora turned pink with anger. "That's not what I meant and you know it, Diana Falconet! You offered me a home when I needed one, and I'm just trying to return the favor."

Fresh tears glistened on Diana's long lashes and she smiled tremulously. "I know you mean well, Aurora, but you and Nicholas are newly married. I'm afraid my presence there would be intrusive."

"Please reconsider. I'm sure Nicholas would welcome you."

"There is nothing to reconsider, Aurora. I appreciate your generous offer, but I think my fortune lies in London."

Aurora stood there watching Diana pack, and she was suddenly overcome by an aching sadness clutching at her heart. First she had lost Tim, then her father. Now she was about to lose Diana as well at a time when she most needed the wise counsel of an older sister. She would truly be alone.

"There!" Diana said, straightening as the last portmanteau was packed and closed. She looked around her sitting room for the last time. "I shall miss this place. I was growing quite fond of Overton Manor."

Amanda broke down. "Oh, Diana . . ."

"Hush, Aurora, don't cry. I'm through shedding

any more tears over Halley." She smiled bravely. "I'm about to embark on a new adventure and hopefully start a new life. We Falconets are a resilient lot and can recover from any adversity."

"You promise to write to me and visit?" Aurora demanded.

Diana nodded. "I promise." Then she looked at Aurora. "You are very lucky, you know. You're married to a wonderful man and have the protection of his name. You'll never have to live in fear of being cast aside, Aurora."

Suddenly there came a knock on the door, and when Diana said, "Enter," the majordomo appeared to tell her the footmen were here for her bags and the carriage was waiting.

Aurora and Diana went downstairs together and said their good-byes outside. Then Diana got inside the carriage and Aurora mounted her mare to return to Silverblade.

The carriage started down the drive. Aurora hesitated, scanning the windows, hoping to see Halley standing in one of them for one last glimpse of the woman he had once loved.

All the windows stood empty like pairs of expressionless eyes.

Uttering a stream of curses upon Halley's unfeeling head, Aurora turned her mare's head, kicked her sharply in the ribs, and sent her galloping back to Silverblade.

When she arrived and Nicholas saw her ravaged, tearstained face, he immediately enfolded her in his arms and demanded to know what had happened. He was sympathetic when Aurora explained, but he also reminded her that Diana had known the risks she was taking when she agreed to become Halley's mistress.

A week later, Aurora received her first letter from Diana telling her that she was enjoying her stay with Lady Fanshaw and was the toast of London.

But Aurora found her concerns for her sister fading under domestic problems of her own.

Aurora stared at the miniature and smiled. Lady

Mary's wedding gift to her son was finally completed, and the results were outstanding.

"Am I really this beautiful?" Aurora asked herself in wonder as she examined the tiny portrait in the early-afternoon light.

"You may be comely enough, but you're singularly lacking in manners!" came a daunting voice from the salon doorway.

Aurora whirled around to find the dowager marchioness standing there, followed by Juma.

"Lady Vivien," Aurora greeted her coolly.

The old harridan swept into the room in a rustle of pale pink taffeta and seated herself on the settee without so much as a by-your-leave, while her page stood guard behind her.

"Married three weeks already and you haven't had the common courtesy to invite me to call upon you," she said with a patronizing sniff.

Aurora set the miniature down on a nearby table and seated herself in the wing-back chair across from the old lady. "After our last meeting, my lady, I assumed you had no desire to call upon me."

"Impudent chit. I may not hold you in high esteem, but you are still married to my grandson, so I will tolerate you as a member of this family."

"You are too kind."

The faded gray eyes blazed, but Lady Vivien made no comment on Aurora's faintly ironic tone. Instead she said, "How is marriage to my grandson?"

Aurora smiled sweetly. "Do forgive my atrocious manners. Would you like some refreshment, Lady Vivien? Some tea perhaps, or a cordial?"

The old lady glared at her. "Some elderberry wine would refresh me."

Aurora looked at the page and said, "Juma, some elderberry wine for your mistress. I'm sure you know where the keeping room is. And you may stay behind for some of Cook's raisin cakes."

The boy looked at Lady Vivien, and when she nodded imperceptibly, he left the salon to do Aurora's bidding.

When she and Lady Vivien were alone, Aurora

said, "Not that it's any of your concern, madam, but Nicholas and I are quite happy with each other."

"Are you, now?"

"Yes."

Lady Vivien rose and went to one of the windows, unmindful of the fact that the thin October light was deepening every wrinkle in her face. "But I wonder for how long?"

"For an eternity, I would imagine."

"Or until your guilelessness begins to bore him and he takes up with the Littlewood woman again." The old lady's smile was as malicious as it was dazzling. "It's only a matter of time before he does, you know. Nicholas is rather notorious for his inconstancy with the ladies. As loath as I am to admit it, my grandson is a rake and a libertine. Oh, he could be reformed, of course, by the right woman, but you, my dear, are not woman enough for that Herculean task."

She is trying to rattle me, Aurora thought, just like Mrs. Littlewood.

She forced herself to smile serenely when what she really wanted to do was scream at the old harridan. "We shall just see about that, madam."

Lady Vivien seated herself again. "Oh, I'm sure the first few weeks of your marriage will be blissful, for you are a novelty for Nicholas. Then he'll grow restless, and want to entertain his libertine friends again. You'll protest, because after all, what respectable woman would want those people cavorting about her house and grounds in such a scandalous manner?"

She leaned forward. "And your beloved husband will insist. That's when you'll learn how very little power you have over him, my dear, and how little regard he has for your feelings." Lady Vivien sat back with a wide smile of satisfaction now that she had done her worst.

"Amusing conjecture, madam, nothing more," Aurora said, studying her fingernails nonchalantly.

The dowager marchioness was silent, but Aurora noticed the crafty look that fleetingly passed across her face.

She was spared further conversation when a maid

entered the salon with a tray bearing a glass of elderberry wine, which the dowager marchioness sipped
with great relish.

When she had drained the glass, she said to Aurora,
"And what do you intend to do about that garden?"

Aurora raised her brows. "That garden?"

"My grandson's so-called Garden of Eros, guarded
by that obscene abomination." She gave Aurora another sly look. "Any respectable wife would have had
it torn down by now. It's an affront to the sensibilities."

Aurora shrugged. "I really haven't had time to concern myself with it, Lady Vivien."

The old lady wagged her finger. "Well, I suggest
you do. A house takes its moral tone from its mistress,
you know. Take your sister, for example . . ."

Finally goaded beyond endurance, Aurora jumped
to her feet, her eyes blazing. "I will not have you
speaking that way of my sister, Lady Vivien!"

"She should have known. Halley's father kept his
mistress for twelve years before throwing her over for
a titled gentlewoman. Like father, like son."

"I think you had better leave, Lady Vivien," Aurora said between clenched teeth.

The old lady looked aghast. "Why, I never have
been subjected to such an insult in my entire life!" she
sputtered. "Thrown out of my own grandson's home
like a beggar . . ." She hauled herself to her feet.
"Wait until I tell Nicholas what you have done. He'll
be furious with you."

She left in an indignant rustle of taffeta, muttering
to herself.

When she was alone, Aurora collapsed into the
chair, shaking with relief. But Lady Vivien's malicious
presence seemed to linger like a bad smell in the
salon, oppressing Aurora. She rose quickly and went
outside. She needed fresh air and sunlight to cleanse
away the taint of innuendo the old lady had left behind.

But once outside, even the chilly autumn air and the
pervasive smell of wood smoke couldn't cheer her.
Lady Vivien's call had unsettled Aurora more than she
cared to admit.

She pulled her wool shawl closer about her shoulders. Was there some truth to what Lady Vivien had said? Would Nicholas grow bored with her and rekindle his relationship with Mrs. Littlewood?

When she thought of Nicholas making love to another woman the way he made love to her every night, she felt her cheeks grow hot with a raging jealousy the likes of which she had never experienced.

Irrational tears stung her eyes and she staggered blindly down the garden path. By the time she had wiped them away, Aurora discovered she was standing before Priapus and the entrance to the Garden of Eros. She had asked Nicholas to remove it, and he had refused. Dared she risk asking him again?

Perhaps Lady Vivien was right: Nicholas did not intend for marriage to interfere with his pleasures.

Revulsion rising in her throat, Aurora turned and headed for the solace of the kennels.

Nicholas found her there a short time later, sitting on the grass and playing with the foxhound runt she had dubbed Humphrey.

He watched her in silence for a moment as she teasingly pushed the pup away every time he tried to bound on her skirts, and finally scooping him into her arms and hugging him so tightly that Humphrey squirmed out of her grasp and landed in her lap with a squeal.

"Aurora," Nicholas said, "I've been looking all over for you."

Her head jerked around, and Nicholas was startled to see something like fear flash in the depths of her eyes for just an instant. It vanished so quickly, he thought he had imagined it.

"I was just playing with Humphrey," she said.

The pup came up to Nicholas and began sniffing at his boots, so he knelt on one knee and tickled him on the belly. "I think you were right about him, Aurora. He seems to be putting some meat on his bones."

"He's been holding his own with the others," she said.

She sounded so distant that Nicholas looked at her sharply. "Aurora, is something wrong?"

"Wrong? Why do you say that?"

"You seem preoccupied and dispirited."

The look of tender concern on Nicholas' face made Aurora want to fling herself into his arms and beg him to refute his grandmother's dire prophecies, but she held herself in check. Nicholas might be her husband, but his moods could be mercurial and she never knew just what his reaction would be to any given situation. She knew she could never bear it if Lady Vivien were right.

She shrugged and looked away. "I was just thinking about Diana. I miss her very much, and I worry about her."

Nicholas smiled gently. "She is your sister and you care about her."

Aurora began plucking up blades of grass and muttering, "Women are nothing but pawns."

Nicholas signaled for the kennelmaster to come for Humphrey, handed the puppy over, then stood beside his pensive, remote wife.

"Why do you say that?" he asked, fighting the urge to caress the nape of her neck with its downy auburn hairs.

Aurora sighed and stared out at the horizon of treetops now turning vivid golds, scarlets, and browns. "We women have no voice in how we shall live our lives. All Diana wanted was to live the rest of her life with Halley. All I wanted was—" She caught herself in time and fell silent.

"—to be a spinster at Falconstown for the rest of your days," Nicholas finished for her.

"And I would have been able to, if I were a man," Aurora said defiantly.

Nicholas sensed her distancing herself from him and returning to the rebellious child she had been before their marriage. The abrupt change took him aback and frightened him just a little.

"Has your life here been so insufferable, Rory?" he asked, carefully controlling his voice so it betrayed no emotion. "Have I been such a cruel, demanding husband?"

Aurora looked at him. Despite Nicholas' best efforts to control himself, Aurora could tell he was baffled with her. His gray eyes were as cold as steel, and he was rigid with the effort of trying to control his anger.

Fearing a confrontation with him, Aurora rose. "N-no, Nicholas. My life here has been anything but insufferable, and you are the most considerate of husbands."

He rose to stand by her side and tilt her chin, forcing her to face him. "Then why are you acting as though you would rather be anywhere else?"

"Thinking of Diana made me melancholy for a time," she said lamely. "Please forgive me."

He smiled, then brushed a kiss across her lips. "There is nothing to forgive."

As they started back to the house together, Nicholas said, "I've been selfish to keep you all to myself. I think I shall invite some friends to stay with us for a few days."

Aurora's heart sank. "Which friends?"

"Oh, Lords Oliver, Cox, and Haze, and their ladies. We're old friends. You met them briefly at our wedding."

Nicholas' libertine friends, the ones who conducted "Pageants of Venus" and disported themselves in the Garden of Eros.

Aurora felt her mouth go dry with apprehension. "Do you think it wise, Nicholas? I have only been the mistress here for three weeks. I don't feel confident about having guests just yet."

Nicholas slid his arm about her waist and held her close. "Nonsense, Aurora. You've been managing Silverblade as though you were born to it. I'm sure you'll be a perfect hostess."

Lady Vivien's words echoed through Aurora's mind. "Please Nicholas. I . . . I'd rather not entertain just yet."

Once again he dismissed her reluctance with a patient smile. "You needn't worry. My friends are a witty, easygoing lot and will pull you out of your despondency in no time. Besides," he insisted, "they are my friends and I wish for them to know you better."

Aurora could see he was not going to allow her to refuse. All she could do was make the best of it and pray that what she feared would not come to pass.

Several days later, on a Friday evening, Aurora, Nicholas, and his friends were seated in the salon watching Bess perform a scene from her new play.

Aurora glanced nervously at her guests. She had to admit she found it difficult to reconcile these people with their scandalous reputations. Ollie looked more like a mischievous cherub than a rake, and Lords Cox and Haze were as elegant and urbane as Nicholas, with no traces of dissipation written on their young, handsome faces. Their beautiful ladies were warm, friendly, and most decorous. While they bantered good-naturedly with one another, not a ribald remark was passed among them. They were the very models of propriety.

Now Aurora noticed one of the footmen coming to light the candles. Twilight was fast fading. Soon the moon would rise, illuminating the statuary and sculpting shadows in the Garden of Eros. Would her guests soon withdraw, even though the nights had grown colder? Would Nicholas allow them to disport themselves as they had before? Would he want her to join him?

Suddenly the sound of applause rippling around her snapped Aurora out of her reverie. When she saw Bess give her an odd look, she realized everyone else in the room was applauding while their hostess was not. Blushing furiously at her *faux pas*, Aurora smiled apologetically and quickly joined in, but one look at Nicholas' black scowl leveled at her told her she was too late.

Then Nicholas rose with a grin and went up to Bess. "Thank you, Bess," he said. "A splendid performance." When she acknowledged his compliment with a graceful curtsy, he turned and said to Lady Peg, "The entertainment will be complete if you agree to play for us this evening."

When Lady Peg nodded amidst a flurry of applause and went over to the spinet, Nicholas lingered behind and murmured to Aurora, "I would like to have a word with you, madam. Alone."

Before Aurora could protest, Nicholas grasped her elbow in one hand, a candle in the other, and marched her out of the salon.

As Aurora tried to match her stride to his, she knew her rude behavior toward his friends had angered him. Nicholas stared straight ahead, his grasp on her elbow light but firm, and he said not a word as he ushered her down the hall and into his study.

Once inside, he set the candle on his desk, then went back and slammed the door, the ensuing gust causing the flame to flicker wildly and sputter. When he turned to face Aurora, his eyes were glittering savagely, his mouth drawn in a taut line of displeasure.

"Now, Aurora," he began with exaggerated patience, "will you kindly tell me why you are being so rude to my friends?"

"I am not being rude!" she retorted defensively.

"Oh no?" His sardonic voice mocked her and he crossed his arms on his broad chest. "Ever since our guests arrived, you've either been as skittish as Firelight or as animated as a corpse. I invited my friends here to become acquainted with my beautiful, vivacious wife, and all they've seen so far is a shallow husk of a woman."

Before she could reply, he smiled suddenly, a light, teasing note in his voice as he said, "Would you have me proven a liar and braggart, Rory, a maker of idle boasts?"

"You've boasted of me to your friends, my lord?" Aurora asked incredulously.

He nodded, his stern gray eyes suddenly softening with tenderness. "You find that so surprising? But yes. I've told them all what a charming, witty, vivacious hoyden I married." Then his smile died. "But one would never know it by the way you're acting tonight. Will you kindly tell your mystified husband the reason for your puzzling metamorphosis?"

When she hesitated, Nicholas shook his head ruefully. "You still don't trust me completely, do you, Aurora? You still feel compelled to keep secrets from me."

The undercurrent of pain in his voice made her feel overcome with remorse. She didn't want to hurt him, not when they were getting along so well.

Her eyes downcast, Aurora murmured, "It was something your grandmother said to me . . ."

Nicholas rolled his eyes and sighed dramatically. "I might have known. What vicious lies did the old harridan spread about me this time?"

In a halting, embarrassed voice, Aurora told him all about Lady Vivien's visit, leaving out nothing. Every once in a while she would risk a glance at Nicholas to gauge his reaction, and she realized with a sinking heart that he was still angry with her.

So she was startled when Nicholas smiled gently and came toward her, taking her hands in his warm, firm grasp. "I wish you had confided in me about my grandmother's visit, Aurora. I could have set your groundless fears to rest."

Aurora felt her cheeks grow hot. "She . . . she lied to me, then?"

Nicholas nodded solemnly. "About many things. She may be my grandmother, but she is a meddling old harridan who sought to take advantage of your innocence and trusting nature, my dear. She preyed upon your fears in the hopes of driving us apart and gaining an ally in this household."

Then Nicholas told her why he had banished Lady Vivien to the dower house in the first place.

"My father was a fine man—God rest his soul—but he allowed his mother to dominate him. When she tried to exert her influence over me, I rebelled and refused to succumb. She has always resented me because I will not allow her to dominate me as she dominated my father. Life with my grandmother in residence here at Silverblade became so unbearable that I finally had no alternative but to send her away, for my own sanity's sake."

Aurora shook her head. "And to think I almost believed her spiteful lies about you."

Nicholas took her hand and held it against his heart. "You have a kind heart, Rory, and you are trusting." Then he looked down at her. "I will admit that my guests have disported themselves in the Garden of Eros, but never in October, for the ground is far too cold! But that ended the moment I married you." His voice grew low and as soft as a physical caress. "You are my wife now, Aurora. I would never allow my friends to shame you or your position as Lady Silverblade in any way. They know that."

Aurora sighed. "Thank you, Nicholas. I do apologize for not trusting you."

He smiled indulgently. "This is all so new to you, Rory, and to me as well. We are still strangers to each other. We both have much to learn."

Aurora raised her chin defiantly. "But at least I have learned my lesson concerning your grandmother. She will never make a fool of me again."

She looked so determined and courageous that Nicholas' heart went out to her. He laughed. "Shall we return to our guests, madam?"

Aurora returned his smile as she placed her hand through his arm. "I shall show them just how charming, witty, and vivacious I really can be."

They went to join their guests.

13

AURORA halted Firelight on the crest of a hill to give the lathered stallion a breather after their long, hard ride around the vast grounds of the estate. The sun had risen several hours ago, but stagnant pools of ground fog still lingered like waiting wraiths in the ash groves and deeper valleys below.

She leaned forward and slapped Firelight's neck. "We should be getting back, boy. Our guests will be rising soon, and Nicholas will be wondering where I have gone."

Since he had come to bed long past midnight, he was sleeping so soundly, Aurora had been able to slip out of bed for her morning ride without disturbing him.

When Firelight began pawing the ground, impatient to be galloping off again, Aurora touched her heel to his side and sent him cantering down the slope. No sooner did she reach the base of the hill than she noticed another horseman riding across the field toward her.

As the rider grew closer, Aurora could see it was Ollie. His chubby cheeks were buffed to a rosy glow by the crisp morning air, and without his wig to conceal his closely cropped golden curls, he looked for all the world like an angelic cherub from one of Nicholas' Italian paintings. Despite the fact that his protruding belly strained the buttons of his waistcoat, Ollie sat his horse firmly, with grace and natural ease.

Now, as he rode up to her, his shocked dark eyes roved over Aurora's masculine attire. "Well, I'll be damned! I thought you were one of the grooms. I was just about to ask you if you had seen Lady Silverblade, and lo and behold, you are she."

Aurora laughed as she raised one hand to push back a stray curl and wished him good morning. "I often dress this way when I go riding. It's one of the privileges of being a marchioness."

He chuckled, drawing his gray gelding alongside Firelight. "People will think you merely eccentric rather than mad."

They rode in companionable silence for a few moments; then Aurora said, "I hadn't expected anyone to be up and about this early on such a frosty morning."

Ollie stared straight ahead as he said, "Do you mean after our exhausting revels in the Garden of Eros?"

Aurora shot him a glance of alarm and blurted out, "But Nicholas assured me—"

"I was merely being facetious, Aurora," he said gently. "We were up gambling for half the night."

Aurora was so embarrassed, she wished the ground would split open and swallow her.

He added, "One of the reasons I roused myself out of a warm, comfortable bed this morning was so I could have a word with you in private, without my friend Nick interrupting."

Aurora plucked at Firelight's mane. "What did you wish to speak to me about?"

"Sundry matters, such as the Garden of Eros and what is reputed to go on there on balmy summer nights, Nick's reputation . . . As his friend, I wish to enlighten you about certain misconceptions."

Now Aurora was intrigued. "Misconceptions?"

Ollie smiled and nodded. "Misconceptions and downright lies." His eyes twinkled with mischief. "Did you know, for example, that we are reputed to conduct Roman orgies under the watchful eye of old Priapus? That we abduct virgins from nearby villages and sacrifice their innocence to"—he wiggled his brows comically—"our unbridled lusts?"

Aurora giggled in spite of herself, for Ollie had that effect on her.

He chuckled. "Not that my Lord Cox wouldn't like to, mind you, for I think he would like to be renowned as a man of depraved tastes." Ollie grew serious once again. "That's all they ever were, Aurora. Misconceptions and lies. Fodder for narrow, petty minds, nothing more. I'm surprised Nicholas hasn't told you."

Aurora was confused. "But . . . but his reputation . . ."

Ollie sighed in exasperation. "Let me tell you a few things about my friend Nick, since has not seen fit to enlighten you himself." Ollie ran his hand through his hair, tousling his curls.

"It all began seven years ago, after your brother was killed during that stupid, senseless prank.

"Tim was like a brother to Nicholas, and when he died, poor Nick was beside himself. We all despaired of his sanity. Then, shortly after, both of his parents contracted smallpox. His father died of it, and his mother became a recluse, hiding from the world behind that damned black mask of hers, as you know."

Ollie stopped for a moment and looked at her imploringly. "Try to imagine how he felt, a young man of twenty, to lose the two people closest to him—three, if you count his mother—all in the space of several months.

"Nick was always a bit wild, but after this, he decided that if all that he loved was going to be taken away from him, he'd enjoy life to the fullest. The pursuit of pleasure became a religion to him, and that's when the rumors first started. But he didn't care. I think it amused him to try to live up to his notorious reputation. Then, several years ago, he decided to tour the Continent."

While Aurora listened, Ollie described some of Nicholas' wild escapades in France, Spain, and Italy that made her blush.

"He found the statue of Priapus in Rome," Ollie said, glancing at the object in question as they slowly rode by it, "and he brought it back to England more to shock his grandmother and the local gentry than anything else. Oh, the uproar that the statue caused! The local parson even used it as the subject for a Sunday sermon—thinly veiled, of course, so as not to offend his wealthiest parishioners, the Silverblade family. Soon the statue became reputed to have, umm, magical powers."

Aurora's brows rose skeptically. "Magical powers?"

Ollie nodded, his plump cheeks pinkening. "The power to endow a man with great, umm, amatory prowess if he slept under the benevolent eye of Priapus."

Aurora couldn't help but laugh at first; then her smile died and her face lit up in sudden comprehension. "And that is why Nicholas' guests began taking to the garden at night."

"Ah, I knew from the very first moment I met you that you were an uncommonly intelligent woman!" Now Ollie's round face suddenly grew contemplative. "I've always thought it odd that a good reputation is a fragile thing, easily destroyed, but a bad reputation is as solid as a mountain and just as difficult to destroy, even when a man has changed."

"And you think Nicholas has changed?" Aurora asked.

"Oh, we've been friends from the cradle and I know he's changed." Ollie shrugged. "I won't pretend Nick is a saint. Many of the rumors about him were true in the old days, but not today. Yet his reputation dogs him like a foxhound on the scent. I would hate to see such rumors come between you, for Nick obviously cares about you a great deal."

Aurora shook her head. "You are mistaken there, Ollie. Nicholas married me for convenience and to save my honor, nothing more."

"I beg to differ with you Aurora. I've seen the way old Nick looks at you when he thinks no one is watching." Then he chuckled. "He never looked that way at Pamela Littlewood or any of his other mistr . . . Um, sorry. No, my friend Nick has fallen in love, whether he wants to admit it to himself or not."

"In love? With me?" Aurora shook her head, refusing to believe it. "No, Ollie, you're wrong about that."

Ollie inclined his head respectfully. "Far be it from me to contradict a lady, but I know Nick and I've known more than a few of Nick's women. And I say he's in love with you." His voice was filled with a mixture of amusement and astonishment. "Imagine . . . Silverblade in love with his own wife."

Aurora was so disconcerted by Ollie's revelations that when they reached the stableyard, instead of dismounting along with him, she said, "I think my horse needs another run to work off his high spirits. If you'll excuse me . . ."

Before Ollie could protest, she wheeled Firelight around and went cantering off. She didn't pull up her horse until she was well away from all signs of human habitation. Stretched out before her were the gentle rolling hills of Silverblade, to the right a wooded copse aflame with autumn's colors of red and gold. Above her a hawk floated in lazy circles against a backdrop of clouds as he scanned the earth for a hapless rabbit or unsuspecting partridge.

As Aurora settled back in the saddle, she mulled over what Ollie had said. She was willing to concede that Nicholas might have changed, that he was trying to live down his scandalous reputation. After all, he had done the honorable thing by marrying her, and he no longer allowed his guests to avail themselves of the Garden of Eros out of deference to her position as his wife. He might respect her, but love her?

Aurora absently scratched Firelight's neck as they walked across a field.

"No," she said aloud, "I'm afraid I don't believe that Nicholas loves me."

If her husband really loved her, he wouldn't be so imperious with her all the time. As it was, he never let her forget he was the master of the house and always had to have his own way.

And what of her feelings for him?

Aurora closed her eyes and trembled. When Nicholas was holding her in his arms, making passionate love and whispering such sweet, tender endearments to her, she actually imagined she felt something like love for him. But when he acted as though her feelings meant nothing to him, any bonds of affection forged during the night quickly disappeared in the revealing light of day. He became the Marquess of Silverblade, haughty and sardonic, imperious and quick to anger, one who made her unsure of herself and her position in his heart, if indeed she even had one.

When Firelight shook his head and began prancing impatiently, Aurora realized she had been daydreaming too long. Glancing up at the sky, she noticed the sun had climbed even higher. Guessing it to be around ten o'clock, she turned Firelight and headed back to the house.

Once inside, Aurora glanced down at the long table in the hall and was surprised to see a letter addressed to her waiting on the silver salver. Her excitement grew when she saw it was from Diana, and she hurriedly broke the seal and began reading.

The first paragraph expressed Diana's hope that Aurora and Nicholas were enjoying good health, and contained chatty snippets of gossip about London life. But it was the second paragraph that caught and held Aurora's attention.

"I have met the most interesting man," Diana went on to say. "His name is Lord Jason Barron, Marquess of Penhall, and he resides in Cornwall. He is something of an eccentric, and he seldom comes up to London, preferring the bucolic charm of West Country life as he does. Although he is not at all handsome (in fact, some might consider him ugly), I find him charming, attentive, and intriguing, and I think these feelings are reciprocated. He calls upon me nearly every day and seems quite smitten with me. Would you say, my dear sister, that he sounds like a promising catch?"

"Indeed I would," Aurora murmured to herself, tapping the letter against her palm.

As she strode through the hall, her footsteps echoing loudly, Aurora felt as though a heavy burden were being lifted from her shoulders. She had never stopped blaming herself for spoiling Diana's situation with Overton, but after receiving this promising letter, she felt her guilt assuaged somewhat.

She frowned as she started down a corridor. Of course, the ideal situation would be for this Marquess of Penhall to offer marriage to Diana, but . . .

Aurora was walking past the ballroom when she heard the unmistakable clangor of steel ringing against steel. Intrigued, she stopped and peered inside.

There, in the center of the huge room, Nicholas and Lord Cox faced each other in grim determination, swords in hand, while the rest of the guests stood aside, quietly observing.

Aurora watched spellbound as Nicholas suddenly lunged at his opponent, only to have Lord Cox leap back and successfully parry his thrust. Then Lord Cox took the offensive, rushing Nicholas, forcing him to retreat this time.

Aurora found herself filled with grudging admiration. Nicholas was a superb swordsman, his light, lithe body seemingly in tune with his weapon as he parried and feinted. He was extremely quick and agile, his mind sharp enough to race ahead and accurately guess what his opponent was going to do next.

When Aurora saw Nicholas suddenly drop back, as if tiring, she wanted to shout and warn Lord Cox that it was all a trick. But it was too late. Lord Cox lunged, only to find Nicholas' buttoned sword point against his neck. He stopped stock-still and didn't move until Nicholas lowered his weapon with a laugh.

"Is there any man you can't beat?" Cox muttered with a mixture of admiration and consternation as he ran his sleeve across his forehead, shiny with sweat.

"I'm sure there is," Nicholas replied with a grin after catching his breath. "I just haven't met him yet."

"Perhaps that is because he is a woman, my lord," Aurora said boldly, the heels of her boots tapping loudly as she crossed the ballroom.

Nicholas mopped his wet face with a towel and turned to his guests, who were all staring at Aurora as though she had gone mad. "Well, my friends, I do believe my wife has just issued a challenge to me."

"I would like to fight you, my lord," she said, "but some other time, when you're not so worn out. After all," she added with a mocking grin, "I wouldn't want to take unfair advantage of your exhausted state."

Nicholas' eyes narrowed dangerously at her baiting. "Let's just see about that, shall we?"

Aurora went upstairs to fetch her father's sword, and when she returned, Ollie said, "We men have wagered that Nick will win, while the ladies are counting on you to take the game."

Aurora bowed to the women present in appreciation of their confidence in her abilities, then turned to Nicholas, who was regarding her with keen amusement in his eyes.

"Terms, my lord?" she asked, affixing the button to her weapon's sharp point.

"A touch anywhere on the body," he replied.

Aurora agreed with a brief nod as she whipped her sword through the air, letting it sing, testing it. Then she was ready. She and Nicholas faced each other.

"*En garde*, Lady Silverblade," he said.

"*En garde*, Lord Silverblade," she replied.

They raised their swords in salute, then stepped back and waited for Bess's signal.

Nicholas circled Aurora warily, just observing her for the moment, trying to determine her strengths and weaknesses. He had to admit he had agreed to the match only because he wanted to teach her the folly of a woman challenging a man to a duel with either swords or pistols. But as he watched her superb fencing form, he realized with some astonishment that this slip of a girl was going to tax him to the limits of his skill and make him earn his ultimate victory.

Suddenly she lunged for him. Blades clanged as he parried her thrust nicely, and responded with one of his own, which she deflected almost contemptuously, then danced out of reach.

As the fighting went on, Nicholas tried different maneuvers designed to trick her into letting down her guard, but Aurora must have had an exceptional instructor, for she did not fall into the traps Nicholas set for her.

Aurora felt her confidence soaring. At first she sensed Nicholas was holding back out of deference to her sex. But as she became more aggressive, showing him she meant to win this fight, he began defending himself in earnest. He was a skilled swordsman, crafty and quick, yet thanks to her father's training, Aurora was able to hold him off.

Aurora found herself facing the ballroom entrance when a sudden movement in the doorway momentarily distracted her. Standing there was none other than Pamela Littlewood.

The momentary break in her concentration was Aurora's undoing. She tore her gaze away from her rival and turned her attention back to Nicholas, but it was like trying to gather leaves in a storm. She felt her foil knocked right out of her hand, followed by the point of Nicholas' weapon against her chest.

The game was over.

"It would appear I have captured your heart, madam," Nicholas said, his eyes glittering with victory.

"It would appear so, my lord," she replied in surrender to the accompaniment of groans of disappointment from the ladies present.

Nicholas drew his foil away to salute her. "A fine game, Rory. As with pistols, you are a most worthy opponent."

Aurora thanked him with an inclination of her head, but her attention was focused on Mrs. Littlewood, who was gliding toward them, a warm smile on her face.

"Congratulations, Nicholas," she said without so much as glancing at Aurora. "What a splendid display of swordsmanship."

Before she could hear Nicholas' response, Aurora walked away under the pretext of retrieving her foil. She was all too aware that sweat dripped from her face and stained her shirt in dark circles under the arms. To add to her mortification, Aurora detected the pungent odor of horse still clinging to her clothes from her morning ride. All she wanted to do was get out of the ballroom as quickly as possible and hide where no one would find her.

As she picked up her foil and gratefully accepted a towel from Ollie, Aurora felt her resentment grow. The audacity of the woman to stroll into her former lover's house as though she owned it!

Aurora finished wiping off her face and glanced at Nicholas to gauge his reaction. Much to her chagrin, he was smiling down at Pamela as though he saw nothing wrong in welcoming his former mistress into his wife's home. His other guests, however, appreciated the awkwardness of the situation, for they all looked decidedly embarrassed.

"If you will all excuse me . . ." Aurora said, addressing everyone present.

Then she strode out of the ballroom before her anger got the better of her and she did something she was sure to regret.

No sooner had Aurora's footsteps died away than Nicholas grasped Pamela's arm, excused himself, and ushered her out of the ballroom and into the library.

He closed the door behind him and lounged against it as he turned to face her. "What in the hell are you doing here, Pamela?"

The iciness of his voice caused Pamela's expression of delight to change to one of bewilderment. "I . . . I thought you would be pleased to see me, Nicholas."

"I am pleased to see you, my dear," he replied, not making a move toward her, "but not here. I am a married man now, and your presence here is an insult to my wife."

She looked as though he had just slapped her. "But I thought you said your marriage would make no difference to our relationship?"

Pamela looked so forlorn and helpless standing there in her becoming gown of pale yellow silk, her eyes dewy with unshed tears, that Nicholas relented and went to her.

"And I meant it," he said, taking her into his arms. Her body was lush and so yielding, not hard and resilient like Aurora's. "But we must be discreet."

Now he put her away from him. "As a neighbor, you may call here with Littlewood at any time, but you must not call alone. I will find some way to be with you. Perhaps we can meet discreetly in London . . ."

"When?" Pamela asked eagerly, her lovely face alight with anticipation.

"Once my marriage is more . . . settled."

Pamela seemed on the verge of saying something, then changed her mind. She smiled seductively to hide her disappointment, causing Nicholas to catch his breath. "I shall count the days, my lord. And the nights most of all."

Before he could stop her, Pamela stood on tiptoes and kissed him. As her small pointed tongue invaded his mouth with such practiced skill, he felt his senses spring to life of their own volition, and he responded to her out of habit rather than desire. Nicholas grasped her arms and crushed her to him so that he could feel her soft breasts straining against his chest. He returned her kiss with such passion that it was a breathless Pamela who drew away first.

She gave him a coquettish smile as she glided toward the door. "I wouldn't wish to insult your wife by remaining any longer, Nicholas, so until we meet again . . ."

Then she winked at him brazenly and left.

Nicholas just stared at the closed door for what seemed like an eternity; then he turned and threw himself down into the nearest chair. Pamela's scent clung to his shirt. It was cloying, not soft like the attar of roses Aurora wore. The taste of Pamela's mouth lingering on his annoyed him for the first time in his memory. Without thinking, he drew the back of his hand across his lips. When he realized what he had done, he felt ashamed.

He rose, stalked over to the brandy decanter, and splashed a generous measure into a glass. Then he went to a window and watched as Pamela's carriage moved slowly down the drive.

Beautiful, seductive Pamela, his eager mistress for two years, had lost interest for him. And all because of a slip of a red-headed hoyden who had insinuated herself into his life with her insolence and spirit.

Nicholas downed his brandy in two gulps, making his empty stomach contract in protest. What was happening to him that a beautiful, desirable woman like Pamela Littlewood no longer attracted him? He smiled self-deprecatingly. Perhaps Aurora had whispered some Gypsy spell into his ear after all during their long, leisurely nights of torrid lovemaking.

Suddenly Nicholas wished he had never promised Pamela their union would continue. His only excuse was that when he had made that rash vow in the Kilkennys' garden, he had never dreamed there would ever come a day when he would want to break it.

He swore under his breath and paced around the room. He knew Pamela loved him, though she had never dared admit it to his face for fear of losing him. Love was not part of their arrangement. Now he had given her false hopes, and he had to find a way to let her down gently. But in the meantime, he had some explaining to do to Aurora.

He had seen her grimace of dislike when Pamela walked into the ballroom, and this time, anger, not tears had filled her eyes. She had been so furious she had hurried from the ballroom before Nicholas noticed she was gone. Nicholas shook his head. Mistresses and wives . . . they were like oil and water.

He whirled on his heel and went to find her.

Aurora reclined in her bath, but her thoughts were not on the rapidly cooling water. In frustration she slapped it with a resounding smack, creating swells that splashed over the side of the tub and onto the floor.

Now she wished she hadn't slunk away from Pamela Littlewood like some whipped dog. She should have confronted her, demanding that she leave at once and never return.

Aurora sighed. Such behavior was childish and rude, and Nicholas would never tolerate it. Perhaps she should have taken her husband's arm possessively and graciously welcomed Mrs. Littlewood to Silverblade, feigning a confidence she was far from feeling.

Tears of frustration and confusion filled her eyes.

She never knew what to do in such situations, never sure of what Nicholas' reaction would be.

Suddenly there came a knock on the door, and when Aurora bade the person to enter, Nicholas himself strode in. When he saw she was in her bath, his eyes lit up and a smile played about his mouth.

Even at the risk of angering Nicholas, Aurora couldn't control herself any longer. She blurted out, "What is that woman doing here?"

He stood beside the tub and looked down at her. "She came to pay a morning call."

"I trust she will not be making a habit of it?"

Nicholas' eyes danced with devilment. "Jealous?"

Aurora's cheeks burned and she sponged her shoulders vigorously so he wouldn't see how truly furious she was. Jealous, indeed!

"I am not jealous!" she snapped, trying to keep her lower lip from trembling and betraying her.

Nicholas knelt on one knee and rested his forearm negligently across his upraised thigh. His face was just inches from Aurora's. "I told you when I married you that I would protect and honor you," he said gently. "I do not intend to embarrass you by parading my former mistresses through Silverblade."

Former mistresses . . . Aurora risked a hopeful glance at him and saw her own reflection mirrored deep in his eyes. Did this mean he had finally broken off with Mrs. Littlewood forever?

Nicholas reached out to twirl an errant copper curl around his forefinger. "I sent her away," he said, his voice throaty and intimate. "I told her never to call again unless she were accompanied by her husband."

Aurora's heart sank and her gaze slid away from his. She wanted to ask Nicholas how he could even look Mr. Littlewood in the eye under the circumstances, but she decided to be prudent and not mention it.

As if reading her thoughts, Nicholas placed his fingertips beneath her chin and turned her to face him. "I know you would prefer never to socialize with the Littlewoods at all, but they are neighbors of ours. My father and Pamela's husband were very close friends. It would not be right to cut them off completely."

That mollified Aurora somewhat. She suspected Mrs. Littlewood wouldn't dare try to ensnare Nicholas again with her husband present.

"I understand," she said.

Nicholas' smile was lazy and tantalizing as he drew closer and closer to her. His fingers traced the line of her jaw before stealing around to the nape of her neck so he could hold her fast. "I knew you would," he murmured just before he leaned over the rim of the tub and his smooth, warm lips captured hers in a stirring, lingering kiss.

As Aurora closed her eyes and abandoned herself to the sweetness of his mouth, she thought she detected the faint cloying scent of a woman's perfume mingling with his own clean masculine scent. But when Nicholas reached under the water to fondle her breast, such suspicions vanished in the wake of the pleasure he was arousing so expertly. Her lips parted and she whimpered against his mouth, yearning for more.

"Slippery," she heard him murmur above her, and she could tell that he was grinning wickedly. Her eyes flew open only long enough to see his gray eyes darkening with mounting desire.

When his hand began traveling relentlessly downward, Aurora fell back against the edge of the tub with a groan. "My lord," she gasped as his fingers found their mark, "we shouldn't . . . We have guests awaiting us downstairs."

Nicholas' own breathing was becoming just as ragged. "They are fully capable of amusing themselves."

Then he stopped abruptly and swung to his feet with careless grace, pulling Aurora with him until she stood shivering in the tub, more from interrupted delight than the slight chill in the room. Damp tendrils of dark auburn hair clung to her neck and shoulders, and her glowing ivory skin was as glossy and wet as a mermaid's.

"Ah, *The Birth of Venus*," Nicholas murmured appreciatively as he stood back to study her. When Aurora gave him a puzzled look, he added, "It's the name of a painting I once saw in Italy. One day, you shall see it, and then you will know why you reminded me of it as you stood in your tub."

Then he left her to fetch a thick towel warming on a rack by the fire and he wrapped Aurora in its thirsty folds. Just as she was starting to dry herself, Nicholas swung her into his arms, towel and all, and carried her into her adjoining bedroom.

As he dropped Aurora on the bed and followed her down, he grinned. "Let our guests amuse themselves awhile longer."

Aurora smiled and welcomed him with open arms.

Later, as she lay curled on her side, her body sated and dry from the raging fires of their lovemaking, Aurora studied the man lying beside her, his chest rising and falling in the slow, contented rhythm of deep sleep.

Dear God, how I love him, she said to herself without thinking.

Aurora caught herself. Love Nicholas? How absurd! She didn't love him. He had compromised her, practically forced her to marry him, refused to remove that obscene statue . . . And, she reluctantly admitted, he had saved both her life and honor.

Aurora rolled on her back and stared at the bed's canopy. She strengthened her resolve and forced all thoughts of love out of her mind. She couldn't allow herself to fall in love with Nicholas, because he would only break her heart. He didn't love her, despite what Ollie claimed. Not once, in all their nights together, had her husband ever told her he loved her.

Aurora closed her eyes. She would not make the first move and risk his rejection and mockery. She would not leave her heart unguarded and defenseless for Nicholas to plunder at will, especially when he guarded his own so well.

When Nicholas rose, they dressed and rejoined their guests.

Nicholas was true to his word. In the ensuing weeks Mrs. Littlewood never once came to call, and Aurora was gradually beginning to feel more secure as the mistress of Silverblade.

As the month of October rolled to a close, Aurora realized with increasing dismay that she was falling in love with her own husband despite her best intentions to resist his powerful attraction. No matter where she was, she constantly listened for his footsteps like a hound awaiting its master. Her eyes had a will of their own as they followed him whenever he left the room, and she felt oddly bereft until he reappeared. Just to hear him speak in his deep, melodic voice sent her heart racing uncontrollably, yet she also enjoyed the companionable silences as long as Nicholas was nearby when she happened to glance up.

Still, every night, as Nicholas loved her so exquisitely and completely with his body, she yearned for him to say he loved her with his whole heart. And every time he didn't, Aurora would stare out into the darkened room, her yearning unfulfilled.

Yet she could not bring herself to confess that she loved him. If he did not share her feelings, such an admission could only serve to humiliate her and cause him to withdraw from her. Her pride kept her from putting such power in his hands.

Then on one bright morning in early November, Aurora awoke late with a splitting headache and a scratchy feeling deep in her throat. Ignoring the temptation to stay in bed and sleep all day, she roused herself and rang for her maid to help her dress.

She barely touched her hot chocolate, for it hurt her throat to swallow; then she went in search of Nicholas. She found him in his study, going over the estate accounts.

He rose and smiled when she entered the room. "Ah, there is my sleepyhead wife now."

"I'm afraid I didn't even hear you rise this morning," she said apologetically as she kissed him on the cheek.

"You were sleeping so soundly I couldn't find it in my heart to awaken you," he said.

"I wish you had. I'm going to be late for my appointment with Vicar Wentworth if I don't hurry."

Nicholas raised his brows. "And why do you wish to see the good vicar?"

"He wishes to see me," Aurora corrected him. "I suspect it's about raising funds for a new roof for the church."

Nicholas chuckled at that. "Wentworth has a silver tongue, so don't let him talk you into mortgaging Silverblade for it."

"I won't," she promised, then turned to go. But Nicholas called her back and handed her a letter.

"It's from your sister," he said. "It arrived this morning."

Aurora eagerly took the letter, broke the seal, and quickly devoured every word written in Diana's dainty hand.

"I trust all is well?" Nicholas asked.

"Diana has found a new protector," she replied without looking up at her husband. "She says she has decided to accompany this Lord Penhall back to Cornwall."

Nicholas sat back in his chair and frowned reflectively. "Are you pleased for her?"

Aurora's brows shot up in surprise. "Of course. Oh, I wish he were going to marry her," she admitted reluctantly, "but I know Diana will do what's in her own best interests. She always has."

Suddenly Nicholas' eyes narrowed suspiciously. "Aurora, are you feeling well? Your voice sounds hoarse and your eyes are lackluster."

She smiled. "I feel fine, Nicholas. Truly. Now, if you'll excuse me, I shall be on my way."

Once she was seated in the carriage and on her way to the village of Abinger, Aurora had to lean back against the squabs and close her eyes, for she suddenly felt drained and listless. To her relief, the feeling soon passed and she was able to enjoy the view of fields from the carriage window.

Just as her carriage was passing the entrance to Overton Manor, Aurora was surprised to see none other than Halley come riding down the drive and signal to her driver to stop.

Aurora was on the verge of telling her driver to

continue, for she still felt great animosity toward Lord Overton after his callous treatment of Diana. But she realized the advantage of remaining friendly neighbors, so she gritted her teeth and tried to be civil to the man as he rode abreast of her window.

"Good morning, Aurora," he said, flashing a grin as he doffed his cocked hat with its jaunty plume.

"Lord Overton," she murmured coolly, without smiling.

"How fortunate that you should pass by at this particular moment," he said. "I was just on my way over to Silverblade to tell you my good news." He waited for her to make a polite inquiry, and when she stubbornly remained silent, he added maliciously, "I wanted you to be the first to know that I am betrothed."

Aurora glared at him and resisted the impulse to tell him about Diana's Lord Penhall. "How wonderful for you."

"The lady's name is Lettice Carver," he said, adding, "Lady Lettice Carver. Her father is the Viscount Rothingham, and—"

Aurora could tolerate no more. She called for her driver to proceed and the rest of Overton's conversation was lost in the rattle of carriage wheels as they sped away.

Aurora was seething with such indignation that her head began pounding like a drum. After Diana had sacrificed seven years of her life to the vain, petulant Lord Overton, he was marrying someone else, a titled gentlewoman, as he had so smugly pointed out, the daughter of a viscount.

Hadn't Lady Vivien once warned her this would happen, that Overton would behave just like his father before him and discard his long-standing mistress to marry a gentlewoman? It galled Aurora to think the old lady was right.

As she sat there quietly fuming, Aurora realized she was shaking all over, but she attributed it to her agitated state. By the time she reached the vicarage, she was sweating profusely, but again she dismissed it and concentrated on listening to what the vicar had to say.

It wasn't until she was back in the carriage that she

realized something was dreadfully wrong. Great chills racked her body, yet when she put her hand to her forehead, her skin burned as though it were on fire. Then her hand fell listlessly to her side as the strength drained out of her limbs.

"What is happening to me?" she murmured, dazed. She was so weak, she didn't have the strength to hold up her head, and it rocked back listlessly, sending her hat tumbling off.

After what seemed an eternity, the carriage pulled up in front of Silverblade's pillared portico and rolled to a halt. When a footman opened the door for her, Aurora found she couldn't move.

"Get . . . Lord Silverblade," she managed to croak, sending the startled lad racing up the steps to fetch his master.

Aurora floated, weightless, on the edge of consciousness. Her head ached with a blinding pain, as though an iron band were being slowly tightened around it. She was vaguely aware of Nicholas bounding down the stairs and flinging the carriage door open while calling her name in a worried voice. He was so close, yet he sounded so far away. She felt hands grabbing her, anchoring her to earth, and she caught a glimpse of Nicholas' worried, alarmed face just before the darkness descended.

Nicholas gripped the carved bedpost until his knuckles turned white.

"What is wrong with her?" he asked the doctor who had just finished examining Aurora.

The surgeon's face was grave as he left the bedside. "She has contracted a particularly virulent fever, your lordship. I've seen several cases in the village, and among the tenant farmers. Has your wife been calling on your tenants lately?"

"Of course," Nicholas replied. "She takes a great personal interest in them and called upon several of them just last week."

The surgeon nodded. "She probably unwittingly entered a house where one of the children was sick."

Impotent rage blazed through Nicholas. "They should

have warned her," he muttered fiercely. When he found out which of his tenants was responsible . . . He pushed such thoughts of vengeance out of his mind. His wife was his first concern now.

Nicholas looked at Aurora lying there, still unconscious, and he felt so helpless. He took a deep breath and forced himself to ask the one question he dreaded asking: "Will she die?"

The surgeon hesitated, as though debating whether to tell him the truth or spare him. Finally he said, "I will be honest with you, your lordship. Several villagers have died of this fever. But perhaps with diligent nursing, the fever will break and her ladyship will be one of the fortunate ones. She is young, healthy, and strong, so that should tip the scales in her favor."

Nicholas snapped, "Tell me what to expect, and what I must do to make her well again."

When the surgeon told him and left, Nicholas took charge at once. He informed the staff that their mistress was gravely ill and readied himself to fight for Aurora's life.

Aurora was dying. Neither the Silverblade fortune nor Nicholas' sheer force of will could save her.

Seated by his wife's bedside, Nicholas uttered a deep moan of weariness and despair. He hadn't moved in three days except to change the cold compresses on Aurora's fevered brow and to force a cup of water past her parched lips and between her chattering teeth so she could drink. He had slept only fitfully himself, and had eaten just enough to keep from fainting from hunger.

He rubbed his eyes and glanced at the window. It was morning again, and still Aurora's fever hadn't broken. She had been drifting in and out of a delirium all this time, muttering incoherent sentences and sometimes thrashing about wildly.

Nicholas reached for her limp hand, now lying so still atop the coverlet, and clasped it, hoping to convey his own strength to her and give her the will to fight. He was alarmed to find her hand still hot and damp.

Still, he pressed it to his cheek. "You must fight, my brave, fearless Rory," he urged her.

All during her illness, he had spoken to her as if she could hear him. He didn't know if it did her any good, for she didn't give any indication that she heard him, but it made him feel useful and eased his feelings of helplessness.

"You must live, my darling," he said, bathing her face again, "because if you don't, I don't know how I shall go on living without you."

Nicholas uttered the words almost without thinking, then realized he meant every word. This defiant, exasperating slip of a girl had succeeded in doing what countless other beautiful, accomplished women had never been able to do: capture his heart and earn his love.

She stirred, her body stiffening as the chills gripped her again. Aurora's lips moved, but she spoke only urgent, incoherent whispers that Nicholas couldn't understand. Her breathing was labored and shallow, every gasp ending in a soft rattle that chilled Nicholas to the marrow.

But at least she was still alive. That alone gave him hope.

Suddenly there came a soft knock on the door. Thinking it was one of the maids with a fresh basin of cold water, Nicholas rose to let her in.

When he opened the door, his mouth dropped in astonishment to see his mother standing there.

"Mother, what are you doing here?"

She regarded him somberly through the slits in her mask. "I was worried about Aurora. How is she?"

"The fever is still rising," he replied in a hollow voice.

"Nicholas, you look exhausted. Why don't you let me nurse her while you get some sleep?"

He shook his head emphatically. "Thank you for offering, Mother, but no. I will not leave her."

Lady Mary was silent for a moment. Then she said, "So you do love her after all."

Nicholas' harsh bark of laughter was mocking and filled with self-loathing. "Was it obvious to everyone except me? Oh, yes, Mother, I love her. I think I loved her from the first day I saw her. Now, if you'll excuse me, I must return to my wife."

His mother wisely left him alone.

Nicholas sat on the edge of the bed and gently brushed tendrils of wet hair away from Aurora's ashen face. "I love you, Aurora," he said aloud, as though testing the sound of such a declaration. "Do you hear me? I said I love you with all my heart."

When Nicholas thought of life without her, terror rose up in his throat and he almost screamed. He would never see her pale blue eyes light up with mischief and darken with passion, never hear her lighthearted laughter ring through the halls. There would be no one to tease him or defy him or outrageously challenge him to a duel. She would never ride Firelight so recklessly again or see Humphrey justify her faith in him on the foxhound's first hunt. Life loomed before Nicholas like a dark, empty corridor with no light at the end to make the journey worthwhile.

For a moment he lost his mind. He grasped Aurora by the shoulders, shaking her, begging her not to die. Then sanity returned, and he gently put her from him, embarrassed by his own weakness and his deep need for her.

He returned to his chair to wait and watch. Soon exhaustion overtook him. Nicholas' head fell forward onto his chest and he dozed.

Suddenly a noise sent his eyes flying open. He found Aurora seated bolt upright in bed, staring at him, her eyes wide but unseeing, her mouth slack.

"Tim?" she cried in her delirium, as large beads of sweat rose on her brow and her breathing quickened.

Nicholas was at her side in an instant. "No, Aurora, it's Nicholas."

"Got to find Tim," she whimpered, crying. "He's waiting."

Without another word, she fell back against the pillows and lay as still as death.

The first thing Aurora noticed when her eyes flickered open was Nicholas. He was half-seated on the edge of a chair, half-resting on the edge of her bed, only the crown of his dark head visible above his crossed arms. He was sleeping, his shoulders rising and falling rhythmically, so Aurora didn't disturb him.

As she lay there, she tried to recall what had happened to her, but her memory was blank. She knew she had been very ill. She felt weak and helpless, and the unpleasant acrid odor of her own sweat was strong in her nostrils, making her wince in distaste. Her hair probably hadn't been brushed in days, so she imagined her copper mane was dull and lifeless, a rat's nest of snarls and tangles.

Aurora looked at Nicholas tenderly. She remembered now. Throughout her illness, he had been there, urging, imploring, and cajoling her not to give up, and even threatening her if she did. His voice, and his voice alone, had been her lifeline.

She couldn't resist. She raised her hand with superhuman effort and stroked his ebony hair, savoring the soft, silken texture of it.

He started at her touch and his head flew up, his swollen red-rimmed eyes filled with anguish. He stared at her and blinked several times as though he couldn't believe she was real.

"Aurora?"

She had only enough strength to smile tremulously.

His hand went to her forehead. "Cool . . ." he muttered idiotically. "The crisis has passed . . . the fever has broken." Then with a great shuddering sigh he closed his eyes, grasped her hand, and brought it to his lips.

Aurora felt his mouth tremble beneath her palm, and as she watched, tears filled the corners of Nicholas' eyes and began streaming down his unshaven cheeks. She had never seen a man cry before, especially a man like Nicholas, and it quite touched her heart.

"Dear God . . ." The words were a choked sob, his voice shaking with deep emotion. "I don't know what I would have done if you had died, Aurora. I love you so much."

Then he released her, hid his face in his hands, and

wept unashamedly as he must have the day of Tim Falconet's funeral.

I love you so much. Her proud, arrogant husband had just confessed that he loved her. Aurora felt tears of happiness fill her eyes.

"And I love you, Nicholas," she whispered, reaching for his hand. "More than life itself."

Aurora sat at her sitting-room window watching the fierce November wind shake the last of the brown, dried leaves from the trees in the park beyond. She sighed. The gray, overcast day matched her mood. It had taken her two weeks to fully recuperate from her illness, and not once in all that time had Nicholas reaffirmed his love for her. She was beginning to think she had imagined his impassioned declaration at her bedside.

Oh, he had been attentive enough, seeing to it that she lacked for nothing, from special delicacies to tempt her appetite to thoughtful little presents that amused her.

But he never again said those words Aurora longed to hear.

Suddenly there came a knock at her door, and when she called out, Nicholas walked in. Aurora's heart gave a queer little lurch in her breast at the sight of him. The charcoal-gray velvet coat he wore accentuated his superb physique and saturnine good looks. He looked so virile, so desirable, the epitome of unselfconscious masculinity as he crossed the room with almost feline grace.

"Are you ready to receive your guests?" he asked, smiling down at her.

Aurora started. "Guests?"

He nodded. "Grandmother and Wesley are waiting to see you now that you are well enough to receive them." His eyes sparkled with mirth as he added, "Old Immortality avoided this house like the plague while you were ill, but he did send his regards through Grandmother quite often."

Aurora couldn't resist giggling. "I'm relieved I didn't

die. At least I spared him having to make a trip to the Continent!"

Nicholas laughed out loud. "I see you are fully recovered, madam," he said, then went to admit their guests.

Lady Vivien entered first, her head raised regally as though Aurora should be so honored to receive her. She carried a wrapped parcel, which she thrust at Aurora with a lukewarm, "So pleased to see you up and about, my dear," before easing herself down onto the settee.

"Thank you, Lady Vivien," Aurora said.

Then Wesley came forward in his short, mincing stride, but seemed reluctant to approach Aurora. "Do forgive me," he muttered, taking out his handkerchief and dabbing at the moisture on his upper lip.

Nicholas had to take the proffered package from him and hand it to Aurora.

As Wesley seated himself next to his grandmother, he said, "We were all so worried about you, Cousin Aurora."

Aurora was just about to reply when she felt Nicholas' hand on her shoulder. He said, "Had anything happened to her, I would have been beside myself. You see, I do love my wife very much."

Lady Vivien and Wesley appeared as startled by Nicholas' revelation as Aurora herself, then made appropriate comments to cover themselves. But Aurora wasn't listening. Her heart was filled to overflowing with love for Nicholas, and she could barely contain her joy. What had started as a marriage of convenience had grown into a love match.

Not only had he said he loved her, he had declared his love publicly, before his grandmother and cousin.

Later, after Aurora opened her gifts and her guests finally left her and her husband alone, she looked up at Nicholas inquiringly.

As always, he seemed to know just what she was thinking, and smiled. "Do you think I didn't mean what I said to you?" he murmured, running the backs of his fingers down her cheek in a tender caress.

Aurora looked away, suddenly shy and ashamed of

herself for doubting him. "But after that one time, you never said—"

"Sometimes it's difficult for me to put my feelings into words, Aurora," he explained, kneeling beside her chair and looking up at her. "We Devenish men are taught to keep our emotions inside of us, to always be strong." He sighed as he looked over at her trembling hands. "There are so many things I wish to say to you, dearest heart."

The tears of relief and happiness he had shed at her bedside had told her more about Nicholas' true feelings than mere words ever could.

She reached out, cradling his beloved face in her hands, savoring the softness of his skin and the hard, unyielding muscle and bone beneath it. "Then say them to me, my love. In bed."

He caught his breath at the seductiveness and excitement in her voice and his eyes smoldered in anticipation. "You're sure you're strong enough, Aurora? You're sure it's not too soon?"

Aurora stared deeply into his eyes, the color of quicksilver and smoke in the thin wintry light. "You have been so patient, my love, and so have I. But now I have a fever of quite a different nature and only you can appease it. Love me, Nicholas. Now. Please."

He rose and extended a trembling hand to her. "Come, my love. There is much I have to say to you that should have been said a long time ago."

She placed her hand in his and felt his fingers tighten possessively as he helped her to her feet and led her into the bedchamber. There he undressed her slowly and carefully, as if even the gentle tug of a ribbon could somehow injure her. But once they were lying naked in each other's arms, Aurora gave herself to him with such wild abandon that Nicholas realized with delight and wonder that his wife had returned to him at last.

14

IT was a perfect day for a fox hunt, Aurora decided as she slowed Firelight down to a sedate walk after the hounds had lost the scent again. The November morning was clear and cloudless, the air tangy with wood smoke and crackling with just enough chill to make even the most docile of mounts as spirited as young colts.

"Not that you're not spirited enough," she crooned to her horse as she slapped his neck.

Ahead of her, the bewildered foxhounds were still milling and sniffing about, trying to pick up the elusive fox's scent for the sixth time that morning. Behind her, the rest of the straggling riders were just beginning to catch up.

Aurora noticed the field had thinned considerably from the original group of fifty men and women that had gathered in Abinger for the hunt. A quick tally told her that nearly thirty had fallen by the wayside, the victims of high hedges, wide ditches, or uncooperative mounts. Of the ones who had come this far, perhaps only ten would have the skill and endurance to see the hunt all the way through to the kill. Aurora fully intended to be one of them.

She scanned the horses, looking for any sign of Stormcloud and Nicholas. She wanted to impress him with the fact that she was leading the field. She wanted him to be proud of her today. But her anticipation quickly turned to disappointment. There was not a dappled gray horse among those present. Nicholas was nowhere to be seen.

Suddenly Aurora's heart stopped in panic. What if Stormcloud had taken a bad fall and Nicholas was injured? She herself had been concentrating so hard on the punishing hunt that she hadn't really been paying attention to her husband's whereabouts in the field. In the beginning, Nicholas had been right behind her, but now . . .

She turned Firelight's head and addressed the other riders in a worried voice. "Has anyone seen Lord Silverblade? Has he taken a fall?"

The riders turned to one another, mumbled something among themselves, then shook their heads slowly. No one had seen Nicholas.

Suddenly Lord Overton came riding up to Aurora. While all the other men were red-faced and puffing, their boots and breeches spattered with dried mud, he looked as fresh as he had at the beginning of the hunt.

Aurora was about to turn away and cut him, but his words brought her up short. "I saw your husband a few miles back. He was helping Mrs. Littlewood to her feet. Her horse had refused one of the jumps and she went flying over instead. I would imagine he's taken her back to Silverblade to tend her . . . injuries."

The damage done, he smiled slyly, then became civil once again. "I understand your sister has found herself a new protector."

Even though it was true that Diana was living in Cornwall with Lord Penhall, Aurora didn't think it any concern of Lord Overton's and she bluntly told him so in a cold, daunting voice.

He merely grinned and said, "Be sure to tell her that I'm soon to be wed," before doffing his hat and riding away.

But Diana was the last thing on Aurora's mind. She felt herself overcome by a sick feeling of disappointment and dread. All morning she had risked life and limb to impress Nicholas with her horsemanship, and all this time, he had been with Pamela Littlewood.

She turned away so the others wouldn't notice the

way her lower lip trembled with the effort of suppressing tears.

"Why couldn't he have let someone else escort Pamela back to the house?" Aurora said crossly to herself.

But she had no time to dwell on it, for one of the hounds picked up the fox's scent and announced his findings to the others with a clear, bell-like cry of excitement. When the huntsman's horn sounded, Aurora was off with the others, all thoughts of Nicholas forgotten.

An hour later, when the hunt was finally over and the fox gone to earth, Aurora could think of nothing else except Nicholas and Mrs. Littlewood. Even the hearty congratulations of her fellow huntsmen on her splendid ride meant little to her now.

As the huntsmen trudged across the fields, talking with each other eagerly of the soft leather chairs and hot mulled cider that awaited them at Silverblade, Aurora hung back to be alone with her thoughts.

Ever since Nicholas had declared his love for her, their marriage had been perfect. The rake had been replaced by the most loving and attentive of husbands, making Aurora feel secure and confident. She had thought Nicholas' love was unshakable. Now she wasn't so sure.

The riders topped a hill, and Aurora could see Silverblade spread out below her. She felt her throat suddenly go dry with apprehension, and fresh doubts assailed her. She knew it was customary for gentlemen like Nicholas to discreetly keep mistresses without their wives ever knowing. Perhaps her husband intended to renew his affair with Mrs. Littlewood without his wife ever knowing.

Aurora's mouth tightened in a determined line. Well, she had no intention of being one of those complaisant wives who turned a blind eye to their husband's infidelities. She loved Nicholas too much. When she thought of him lying naked with Pamela in his arms, pleasuring her to the point of delirium as he did with his wife, Aurora felt a jolt of primitive jealousy shoot through her.

Touching her heel to Firelight's side, she urged him into a slow canter. Refreshed after his long walk, the stallion readily complied.

When Aurora arrived back at the house, she searched everywhere for Nicholas and Pamela, but to no avail. They were not in the salon with the other guests, still in their riding clothes as they sipped mulled cider and recounted various long-ago trials and triumphs in the hunting field. They were not in the solarium, appreciating the view, or the library, innocently flipping through the large selection of books and periodicals.

With a sinking heart, Aurora went upstairs to Nicholas' suite of rooms.

Just as she was passing Nicholas' sitting room, the sound of muffled laughter from within brought her up short. She listened, her ear pressed against the door. Nothing. Holding her breath, she slowly turned the knob and opened the door just a crack.

She wished she hadn't.

There, seated all snug and cozy in a leather wing-back chair before a crackling fire, was Pamela Littlewood, a rug thrown across her lap to warm her. She held a glass of wine and was smiling up at the man standing with his arm draped across the back of her chair. It was Nicholas, inclining his head toward her and smiling at something she had just said.

Summoning all the strength she possessed, Aurora closed the door noiselessly and glided away. When she turned a corner, she could contain herself no longer. Her knees were shaking so badly she had to lean against the wall or collapse.

She stood there with her eyes closed, her mind racing. What should she do? She could storm right back and confront Nicholas, but she dismissed that at once as being too childish. She had to deal with him as a mature, sophisticated woman would.

Aurora racked her brain, wondering what she should do. Suddenly the answer came to her in a flash.

She whirled on her heel and flounced off.

Nicholas watched Aurora flit about the ballroom

like some exotic butterfly. She had been ignoring him all day, ever since she returned from the hunt, and he wondered what he had done to annoy her so. The only time he could recall Aurora ever being this cold toward him was when she had suspected him of being responsible for her brother's death.

His heart constricted in pride as he watched her, for she was easily the most beautiful woman here tonight. Disdaining pastels because of her vibrant red hair, Aurora was wearing a brocade gown of deep green and the emerald necklace Nicholas had given her after her convalescence. She had filled out since her illness, and now her pale ivory skin glowed with robust good health and enthusiasm.

Suddenly Nicholas scowled as he watched Aurora being led out onto the dance floor on the arm of Sir Andrew Lade's handsome son. She had refused to dance with her own husband just minutes ago on the pretext of attending to her duties as hostess, yet here she was dancing with a total stranger.

After the Lade boy came Fox, Haze, and Ollie. In fact, every gentleman present was the recipient of a smile, a melting look, a hand on the arm. Every man except Nicholas.

And others were beginning to notice.

Suddenly Nicholas felt a hand pluck at the sleeve of his coat, and he turned to see his grandmother standing there, glaring up at him.

"Grandmother . . ." he murmured in dismay. "You are enjoying yourself this evening, I trust?"

The old lady snorted in derision, causing the purple aigrette plumes in her silver hair to shake. "I was, until your wife started behaving so disgracefully."

"Need I remind you that my wife has a name, Grandmother?" he said. "It's Aurora, in case you've forgotten."

"She seems to have forgotten she is your wife, the way she's flirting shamelessly with every man in sight!" The dowager marchioness squinted up at him, determined to cause trouble. "You and your marchioness having marital difficulties already, Nicholas? I warned you nothing good would come of marrying such a common chit."

Nicholas clenched his teeth, refusing to let the old witch bait him. "Aurora and I are not having marital difficulties, Grandmother. She is young yet, and deserves to enjoy herself at her first hunt ball."

Lady Vivien sniffed derisively. "Is that what you call her disgraceful behavior, enjoying herself? If I were you, I would—"

"But you are not me, Grandmother," Nicholas said, fighting to keep his temper in check, "and I will thank you to keep your meddling nose out of my affairs."

He strode off, leaving Lady Vivien sputtering about how no one ever listened to her now that she was old.

Nicholas noticed Aurora blatantly flirting with yet another handsome gentleman over by the French doors, and he could tolerate it no longer. He crossed the room and approached them.

"If you will excuse me, sir," he said, bowing to the gentleman, "I would like a word with my wife."

Aurora began to protest with a sharp, "But, Nicholas, I—"

"Aurora," he said firmly as he grasped her elbow, "I need to speak to you alone. Immediately."

She must have recognized the dangerous edge to his voice, for she murmured, "Of course," made her excuses to the other gentleman, and allowed Nicholas to steer her out of the ballroom and into the empty study.

Aurora regarded Nicholas as he closed the door behind him. Judging by the black scowl that marred his brow, he was furious with her. So her plan to pay him back in kind for his dallying with Pamela had met with success. Yet why did she feel dispirited instead of triumphant about her victory?

"You wished to speak to me, my lord?" she inquired innocently as he turned and came toward her with his customary catlike grace.

"I merely wish to know, Aurora, why you've chosen to ignore me all evening, while flirting with every other man present."

Aurora was not fooled by his deceptively conversational tone and polite manner. His eyes betrayed him. They were all cold steel and fury. But she would not cower before his anger or dissolve into helpless tears this time. Her hurt was so great it demanded to be shared.

She made her eyes round and guileless. "Was I flirting, my lord?"

Nicholas exploded. "Don't play the innocent with me, Aurora! You know you were, and I want to know why!"

"I see, Nicholas," she said softly, running her fingertips along the top of a nearby chair. "What's good for the gander is not good for the goose in this instance."

"What are you talking about?" he snapped.

She bit her lower lip to keep the unwanted tears stinging her eyes from falling. Try as she might, Aurora couldn't keep up the brittle, unfeeling facade any longer, the pretense of not caring how much he had hurt her. She felt that pain and it came pouring out in a rush.

"I led the hunt today," she said. "I wanted you to be proud of me. Yet when I looked for you, you weren't there." Her voice shook with accusation. "Someone told me that Mrs. Littlewood had taken a fall, and you escorted her back to the house."

She made him feel so guilty that Nicholas lashed out in his need to defend his actions. "Pamela sprained her wrist in that fall, and she was badly shaken. I happened to be nearby when it happened, so I took it upon myself to escort her back to Silverblade. She couldn't go alone." He glared at Aurora. "You, of all people, should know how serious a fall in the hunting field can be."

"And once you had escorted her back to Silverblade, you couldn't have rejoined the hunt? You had to remain with her in your sitting room for the rest of the morning?"

Nicholas' steadfast gaze wavered when he realized Aurora must have seen them together. "Pamela was on the verge of losing control of herself," he said lamely. "She begged me to stay with her."

"I see." Aurora took a deep breath to settle her

quivering insides. "And your mistress takes preference over your wife." Before Nicholas could reply, she rashly blurted out, "Did you make love to her, my lord?"

Her accusation stung him like a lash, and for a moment all he could do was stare at her, aghast that she could even think such a thing of him.

"No!" he snapped, his fury mounting. "I did not sleep with Pamela while you were riding to the hounds." He saw the relief flood Aurora's face, and she looked on the verge of flinging herself into his arms, but she had wounded him with her false accusation, and he was not ready to forgive her so quickly.

"It's gratifying to know, madam," he began, his voice cold and sarcastic, "that you trust me so much, that you are a woman not given to petty jealousies and petty vengeances."

To his satisfaction, Aurora's face turned scarlet with embarrassment as his words hit home.

"I . . . I'm sorry, Nicholas," she said softly, taking a tentative step toward him.

It took all the strength he could muster to prevent himself from extending his arms to her and forgiving her at once. Instead he said, "I'm afraid I am not ready to accept your apology, Aurora. I admit I should have returned to the hunt, but you could have trusted me." He bowed to her. "I think we both need time to heal our wounds."

Then he turned and left her.

Nicholas had to find Pamela.

He realized now that he should have broken off with her the moment he had become betrothed to Aurora. It would have been clean and quick. But by trying to be kind and breaking with her gradually, he had only succeeded in hurting his wife and creating a barrier of mistrust between them.

He scanned the ballroom, but Pamela was not by her husband's side or dancing. Nicholas decided to try the chambers upstairs. Perhaps she had gone to lie down.

Once he found her, he would tell her that it was over between them. There would be no trysts in London or anywhere else. She would be devastated, he knew, but it was the best he could do.

Back in the study, Aurora stared at the closed door. "Damn you, Nicholas Devenish!" she swore, then dropped down into the nearest chair and burst into tears.

Aurora knew she was right. Nicholas should have returned to the hunt after escorting Pamela back to Silverblade. Yet he had twisted everything around so that Aurora looked like a jealous, vengeful wife, not the injured party.

She dabbed at her eyes with a handkerchief. If she were right, why did she feel so miserable about it? She knew the answer at once. She hated being angry with Nicholas about anything. She wanted to bask in the warmth of his love, not wither in an icy blast of his black temper.

Aurora began thinking about what Nicholas had said, and gradually her sniffling stopped. He had wounded her by going with Pamela, but she was not entirely blameless. She hadn't trusted him, after all, and trust was a vital part of any marriage.

The surprise and hurt in Nicholas' eyes when she had accused him of sleeping with Pamela had been almost too much for Aurora to bear.

She knew what she had to do. She would go to Nicholas at once and apologize. Perhaps this time he would accept her apology and all the bad feelings between them would be forgotten.

Rising, Aurora went in search of her husband.

She looked in the ballroom, but Nicholas wasn't there. Neither was he in the salon, nor the library. Finally Aurora asked one of the passing footmen if he had seen Lord Silverblade, and he told her that he had seen the master going upstairs.

Upstairs, where all the bedchambers were . . .

Aurora shook her head to clear it of suspicion as she started up the stairs. She told herself over and over that she trusted Nicholas, that she must not allow her aversion to Pamela Littlewood to cloud her thinking.

But that fragile trust evaporated as she rounded a

corner just in time to see Nicholas and Pamela locked in a heated embrace.

Aurora uttered a strangled sob, whirled on her heel, and fled.

She was, Aurora decided bitterly, as accomplished an actress as Bess. She had played the role of the charming hostess well tonight, smiling and chatting through the rest of the ball, seeing their guests to the door as they left, standing by Nicholas' side as though they were still happily married.

But when the front door closed on the last guest, she could endure the farce no longer. Aurora slipped upstairs before Nicholas could say a word, and for the first time in her marriage, she locked her door against him. She would not share his bed tonight. She could not, after knowing he had been with Pamela.

No sooner had Aurora dressed for bed than there came a knock on the door adjacent to Nicholas' sitting room.

"Aurora?" he called.

Heart hammering wildly against her ribs, she went to the door but made no move to unlock it. "Go away, Nicholas. I'm tired and wish to sleep."

In the ensuing silence she could envision him scowling as he pondered the full import of her words. Aurora saw the doorknob slowly turn as he tested it.

"Aurora, open this door!" he bellowed.

Trembling with fear now, she almost relented. Then she thought of Nicholas' body molded to Pamela's, his mouth crushed against hers in an intimate kiss, and his betrayal strengthened her resolve. Aurora's hand fell away.

"Go away, Nicholas!"

"Aurora, I wish to speak to you." The words were clipped, anger barely under control. "Now, open this door before I break it down!"

When Aurora didn't answer, there came the resounding crash of a fist pounding against wood, then another. Aurora flinched, sprang back, and hugged herself, praying that the door would hold against Nicholas' determined onslaught.

Then he stopped. All was quiet.

Aurora breathed a sigh of relief. He had given up and gone away. He was not going to demand his conjugal rights tonight.

Suddenly Aurora heard a more fearsome sound, the soft insidious scraping of a key turning in the lock. Then the knob turned and the door swung open to reveal Nicholas.

He just stood there for a moment, framed in the doorway, both hands braced against the jamb as if to contain his horrible anger. Nicholas' face wore a dark, menacing look of rage, and his eyes glittered like silver in the sun as his implacable gaze beheld his defiant wife.

He stepped into the room and taunted her by holding up a key. "Did you really think you could keep me out if I wanted to get in?"

Aurora said nothing.

Nicholas tossed the key into the air and caught it neatly in one hand, his eyes never leaving her face. "You must have locked your door against me for only one reason. You don't wish to share my bed tonight, do you?"

She swallowed hard and shook her head.

"May I ask why?"

"You know why."

He cocked one brow quizzically. "Don't tell me you're still furious with me for not returning to the hunt? Good God, Aurora! Are you going to hold that against me forever?"

She turned and walked away from him. "After you left the study, I thought long and hard about what you had said, and decided that I had been as much at fault as you, Nicholas. You were right. I should have trusted you."

Aurora turned to face him. "I went looking for you, to apologize again, and do you know what I saw?" Before he could answer, she said, "I saw you and Pamela embracing in the upstairs hall." She added bitterly, "So much for trust."

She looked so vulnerable in her misery, so appealing, that Nicholas' heart was filled with regret for what he had done to her.

"Aurora," he said gently, going to her and reaching for her. When she shrank away from him and just stared with those great, accusing eyes like sapphires set in ivory, Nicholas realized the full extent of her torment.

His arms fell to his sides and he made no further move to touch her. "I must explain something to you, and I hope you'll understand."

Then he stepped away and rubbed his forehead to collect his thoughts. "When we were first betrothed, I will admit that I had planned to go on seeing Pamela." Behind him, he heard Aurora's sharp intake of breath, but he ignored it and continued. "After all, you and I were marrying for convenience, not love." Now he turned and smiled. "But that was before I found myself falling in love with you, my darling Rory. When that happened, the mere thought of Pamela's embraces left me cold."

"Then why were you together tonight?" she demanded in an anguished voice.

"What you saw was Pamela embracing me, Aurora. I was not embracing her. I was walking down the corridor when she suddenly came out of one of the rooms and flung herself into my arms. She caught me by surprise. I quickly disengaged myself from her and told her there could never be anything more between us than friendship. Unfortunately, you didn't see that."

Judging from the expression on Aurora's face, she wanted to believe him. Then, as if to test him, she asked, "Why didn't you tell her sooner, before the hunt? Why didn't you tell her the day she came to call at Silverblade and found us dueling?"

So she wasn't going to relent until he had satisfactorily explained. Nicholas reminded himself that she was still very young and very hurt.

He said, "Because I was trying to be kind to her. A gentleman cannot cruelly discard someone who once meant something to him. I had hoped Pamela would see how happy and content I was with you, and that she would bow out of my life gracefully and make no more demands. Regretfully, she didn't. She kept badgering me to renew our affair."

He reached out and gently ran the back of his hand along Aurora's curved jaw. "But I was the world's biggest fool, Rory. By being so concerned with Pamela's feelings, I hurt you. And for that I am truly and deeply sorry."

She stepped away and turned her back to him, frowning and staring at the floor. For one horrible moment Nicholas feared he had wounded her past forgiveness this time. But then she turned around and faced him squarely.

"You are a kind, generous man, Nicholas Devenish, to be so concerned about your former mistress's feelings," Aurora said softly, her voice trembling. "I hope you will forgive me for my childish jealousy."

Then she flung herself into his arms, knowing she would never find peace anywhere else but in his loving embrace.

Arms she had feared would never hold her again pressed her against him with fierce possessiveness. Aurora heard him murmur, "My dearest, darling Rory," over and over before his lips sought hers in a deep, passionate kiss that banished all doubts and healed all wounds.

When they finally parted, breathless, Nicholas looked down at her with melting tenderness and said, "Will you promise me something, Aurora?"

"Anything, Nicholas."

"Promise me that you will always share your doubts and fears with me before they become grave misunderstandings that threaten our love."

"I promise, Nicholas, if you will do the same."

He gave her his solemn promise. Then he handed her the key to the adjoining door and placed his fate in her hands. "Do you still wish to lock your door against me, madam?"

Aurora took the key, gave Nicholas a thoughtful look, then strode over to the door. For one agonizing moment he feared she was going to ask him to leave. But instead she closed the door, locked it, and leaned back against it with a slow, lascivious smile of unabashed lust.

"Now you are my prisoner, my lord, and I shall decide when to set you free."

Nicholas caught his breath as his wife glided toward him, more exciting than any mistress in her desire for him.

"But first you must make love to me," she said in a husky voice as she began undoing his banyan with agonizing, deliberate slowness, tormenting him. "And if you please me, I shall never set you free, you lucky man."

"I shall do my best to prove myself worthy, my lady," he replied, impatiently tugging at her wrapping gown.

When they were both naked and hungry for each other, he did just that.

Several weeks later, Wesley was standing in the salon, occasionally glancing out the window at the cold gray December landscape. The gardens were brown and lifeless, stripped of all fall's vibrant color, and the trees beyond nothing but tall black skeletons, their limbs rattling together like bones in the wind.

He shuddered at the image that popped unbidden into his mind. With Christmas just three weeks away, this was no time to think of skeletons and death.

Wesley placed his forefinger against his nose in an attitude of contemplation. He wondered why Cousin Nick had summoned him down to Silverblade on a matter of great urgency. Suddenly the sound of approaching footsteps echoing down the hall told him he would soon find out.

"Wesley," Nicholas said with a bright smile of welcome as he swaggered into the salon. "Thank you for agreeing to come down to Silverblade in such wretched weather."

"Your message was so intriguing, how could I resist?" Wesley said with an affable smile, but his insides were churning with resentment. Nick's "message" had been more like a royal command.

"Come to my study," Nick said. "We can talk in private there."

Once they were comfortably seated, Nick leaned back in his leather chair and came right to the point. "Wes, I know this must be deuced awkward for you, and it's awkward for me as well. But I'd like to help you, if you'll let me. I know this has been a particularly bad year for your shipping company, but perhaps a sizable investment on my part could help until you're on your feet again."

Wes rose and went to the window, being careful to keep his back toward Nicholas so his cousin couldn't see the rage darkening his usually placid features and momentarily robbing him of coherent speech.

After a moment had passed, he forced himself to say, "I . . . I appreciate your thoughtfulness." He managed to sound genial, when all he wanted to do was send his fist crashing into Nicholas' handsome face, no matter what the consequences.

"Families should help each other," Nicholas said. "And if there is anything I can do to help you out of this predicament, all you have to do is ask."

Wes turned slowly. "Thank you for your generous offer, cousin, but it is quite unnecessary. It is true that this has been a particularly unlucky year for my company, but I expect my fortunes will improve a hundredfold next year."

Nick frowned. "I would hate to see you lose your company because of foolish pride, Wes."

"I can assure you that I'm in no danger of losing my company."

And even if I were, he added silently to himself, you are the last person in the world I would go to for help.

As Nicholas studied him intently, Wes knew he didn't believe him. But he just smiled and said, "Well, my offer still stands. If you ever need anything . . ."

"You shall be the first one I ask," Wes said smoothly. Then he turned to leave. "If you'll excuse me, I think I shall call on Aunt Mary while I'm here."

"Of course."

Wes bowed and hurried out of the study in his

short, mincing stride, sick with anger and suppressed rage. As he fled down the empty corridor, he was so furious he felt as though he were going to explode.

How dare Nicholas humiliate him so! Under the guise of offering help, his cousin had plainly told him he thought him incapable of succeeding at anything on his own. Wes seethed with indignation even as he mocked himself. Poor, incompetent Wesley Devenish. All he had to do was place his company in his cousin's capable hands, and of course Nicholas would make a success of it. Didn't everything Nicholas touched turn to gold?

Wesley took out a handkerchief and dabbed at the corners of his mouth. He fought to calm himself. This grievous insult would not go unpunished. He would see to that. Then he went in search of Lady Mary.

In another part of the house, Aurora was pacing her sitting room and sighing in consternation. What could she give Nicholas for Christmas? The man had everything. Well, not everything, she amended. He did not have the heir he wanted. Aurora smiled to herself as she stared out at the gray, turbulent sky. Now, that would be the perfect Christmas gift, but there were no signs of that happening as of yet.

Perhaps Lady Mary would have some ideas for her. Aurora went to call upon her mother-in-law.

As she walked down the long corridor, Aurora thought of how much Lady Mary had changed since her son's marriage. Aurora had been patient and persistent, always seeking to draw out the reclusive woman by constantly seeking her advice about everything from disciplining the servants to organizing last month's hunt ball. At first Lady Mary had been reluctant and standoffish. Now she welcomed Aurora's calls and the two were almost as close as mother and daughter.

Even the solemn, overly protective Rose had warmed to the new young mistress of the house. When Aurora knocked on Lady Mary's door and Rose answered, the maid greeted her with something like a warm smile and a cheerful, "Good morning, Lady Aurora. Have you come to call on her ladyship?"

"Yes, Rose, if she will receive me."

"She will always receive you."

Lady Mary, seated on the settee, rose as Aurora entered the room and walked toward her, arms outstretched. "How are you, my dear?" she asked, taking Aurora's hands since her mask prevented her from giving her daughter-in-law a welcoming peck on the cheek.

"Actually, I am in a quandary," Aurora replied as she and Lady Mary walked to the settee and Rose was dismissed.

"Oh?" Lady Mary said as they were seated.

"Christmas will be here in three weeks, and I can't decide on a gift for Nicholas," she said. "Can you offer me any suggestions?" Seeing a telltale sparkle leap into Lady Mary's eyes, Aurora added hastily, "Aside from a son, of course."

Lady Mary shrugged philosophically. "All in good time, my dear." Then she sighed. "When a person is so wealthy he wants for nothing, you have two choices. You can either give him something impossibly extravagant or something that money cannot buy."

Suddenly Aurora had an idea.

She placed her hand on Lady Mary's arm. "Will you be my Christmas gift to Nicholas?" she asked, her voice rising with excitement.

Lady Mary backed away. "Me? I don't understand."

Aurora could hardly contain herself. "Your son hasn't seen your face for seven years. I think the greatest gift anyone could give Nicholas is to have you join him and the rest of the family for Christmas dinner this year."

Lady Mary's shocked eyes filled the slits of her mask. She brushed Aurora's hand off her arm and rose to her feet. "I . . . I can't. You ask the impossible of me."

"Where would be the harm in spending a few hours with your family on Christmas Day?"

"I couldn't bear it! Christmas dinner was always so special to my dear William. The memories . . ." She shuddered and hugged herself. "I couldn't endure it without him. I just couldn't!"

"Yes, you could!" Aurora said, rising and going to her. "There would be no one else there except Nicholas, myself, Lady Vivien, and Wesley. If you didn't wish the servants to see you, I'm sure we could make some arrangement to accommodate you."

"No, I'm sorry, Aurora, but I just can't do it."

"Please, Lady Mary. Just think of what it would mean to Nicholas, to be a family again on Christmas."

Lady Mary's entire body trembled in fear. "They would all shudder in revulsion and look away in disgust if they saw my face the way it is now. Pockmarked. Horribly disfigured. Ugly."

"Not if you concealed it with paint. Both men and women who have smallpox scars do."

"No! I will not!" Her voice rose in agitation. "And I don't wish to discuss it further, Aurora."

"But, Lady Mary—"

"I said I don't wish to discuss it!" she screeched.

Aurora fought to control her temper. "I never realized it until this moment, Lady Mary. But you are nothing more than a vain, spoiled, selfish woman who enjoys wallowing in self-pity."

The woman spun around, her gray eyes flashing through the slits in the mask. "How dare you say such things to me!"

"I dare say them because they are the truth," Aurora retorted. "You don't care about Nicholas' feelings. You never have, otherwise you would have come to our wedding. All you care about are your own. I think you enjoy hiding away, making people feel sorry for you. It gives you some sort of power over them."

A strangled sound of rage emanated from behind the mask and for one moment Aurora thought her mother-in-law was going to attack her. But all Lady Mary did was snarl, "Get out! Leave my rooms at once and don't ever come back."

"With pleasure." Aurora held herself erect and swept from the room.

The moment she was out in the corridor and Lady Mary's door locked behind her, Aurora instantly regretted her impetuous tongue. "Dear God, what have I done?"

She never should have spoken so candidly. In the space of a few seconds, she had destroyed the fragile bond of friendship and trust it had taken her months to achieve.

Aurora hesitated, then turned back. She stopped herself just in time. As young and inexperienced as she was, she knew instinctively she would only make matters worse if she tried to apologize. Besides, she knew she was right. Let Lady Mary apologize to her.

Aurora squared her shoulders resolutely and walked away.

No sooner had she reached the end of the corridor than she saw Wesley coming from the opposite direction, his tall, gangly frame bobbing up and down with every step.

"Why, good morning, Wesley," Aurora greeted him with a wide smile. "What brings you out to Silverblade on such a grim, cold day?"

His small feral eyes lit up as he bowed over her hand. "I just came to call on Grandmother, and decided to call upon Aunt Mary while I was here."

Aurora grimaced. "I'm afraid you won't find Lady Mary in the most receptive of moods, Wesley."

He sighed. "Oh, dear. I was so hoping to see her today."

"Well, we are always pleased to share your company. At least have a cup of tea with me while you are here."

"I would like that very much, Cousin Aurora. You are always too kind to me."

When they were seated in the salon and Aurora rang for tea, she said, "You and Grandmother Devenish are coming for Christmas dinner, are you not?"

Wesley's fleshy lips parted in a smile. "Of course. We'll be here for the annual Christmas Eve revels for the tenants as well."

Aurora had recalled Lady Mary telling her that from the time of the first Marquess of Silverblade, each successor had always opened his doors to his tenants and their families every Christmas Eve for dinner and a ball. But Christmas Day was a quiet time, always reserved just for the family.

Aurora sighed. She wanted her first Christmas with Nicholas to be perfect, but it wasn't going to be unless she could give him the perfect gift.

Wesley's eyes narrowed further. "Why, dear cousin, you look so very sad. Not trouble with Nick, I pray?"

Aurora flashed him a radiant smile as she seated herself across from him and smoothed the velvet skirt of her sack gown. "Nicholas and I are the happiest couple on earth, Wesley. No, I was just trying to decide what I'm going to give him for Christmas."

Wesley put his finger to the side of his large red-veined nose and studied her for a moment. Then he said, in his slow, deliberate way of speaking. "Perhaps I can be of assistance. I just received a shipment of fine, rare snuff bottles from China. I'm sure Nick would like to add one to his collection."

Aurora had seen her husband's collection of snuff-boxes, and she was certain not one of them was a snuff *bottle*.

"How unusual," she murmured, considering it carefully.

"Most unusual," Wesley agreed. "And rare. No other gentleman in London would have one exactly like it."

"Are they expensive?"

"Very. But since you are my cousin and have always been so kind to me, I would be willing to accept any reasonable offer."

Aurora brightened at once. If she could not give Nicholas an heir or his mother's presence at the Christmas dinner, a rare snuff bottle might be the answer. An impossibly extravagant gift for a man who had everything.

"That sounds wonderful, Wesley," she agreed. "Will you bring them round and let me select one?"

"I regret most of them are already spoken for, but I have one I can guarantee Nick will like."

Aurora sought to hide her disappointment behind a smile. "I'm sure whatever you select will be fine."

Then tea arrived, and they spent a pleasant hour discussing London.

One week later, Wesley called again with the snuff bottle.

Aurora ushered him into the library and locked the door behind them to make sure Nicholas wouldn't suddenly walk in and spoil his wife's surprise. Then she turned to Wesley and said, "May I see it?"

"Of course," he replied, and reached into his waistcoat pocket.

The snuff bottle was wrapped in a square of black velvet, which Wesley unfolded for Aurora's inspection. Her eyes grew round as she took the small round bottle and turned it over in her hand.

"What is it made of?" she asked.

"A precious stone called jade. The Chinese value it highly. It's decorated with a carved dragon."

"It's beautiful," Aurora murmured.

"Nick is a man of impeccable taste and difficult to please. I'm certain he would be honored to add such a unique gift to his collection."

"I'm sure he will," Aurora agreed.

After Wesley agreed to sell the snuff bottle for the price of Aurora's dress allowance for one month, he departed, leaving her to admire Nicholas' gift. Aurora was so excited, she wanted to give it to him right away, but she restrained herself.

Christmas would come soon enough.

"Congratulations, Cousin Aurora," Wesley said as he escorted his grandmother into the dining room for Christmas dinner. "The tenants' ball last night was magnificent."

Aurora flushed with pleasure at his high praise. "Thank you, Wesley. Everyone seemed to enjoy it."

Nicholas beamed down at her proudly. "In previous years, the ball ended at midnight, but last night, no one wanted to leave!"

Aurora stifled a yawn as she entered the dining room on her husband's arm. It had been nearly three o'clock in the morning before the last tenant had left

Silverblade, and Aurora was still feeling the effects of the all-night revels.

Lady Vivien, resplendent in pale green satin that made her complexion look sallow, glared at Aurora as they approached the table. "I would have chased them all out at midnight," she grumbled. "The tenants are there to serve us, not the other way around."

"Now, Grandmother," Nicholas said, "a few extra hours didn't make any difference."

The old lady shook her head as Wesley held her chair for her. "Gives them ideas above their station, if you ask me. But then, no one cares about my opinions anymore."

Nicholas ignored her gibe and said, "Shall we open our gifts before dinner?"

Everyone agreed as they seated themselves and began opening the boxes that had been set atop the dinner plates at each person's place.

Aurora gasped in astonishment when she opened Nicholas' gift to her. There, lying on a bed of white satin, was the most magnificent sapphire necklace she had ever seen.

"Nicholas!" she gasped. "It . . . it's beautiful!"

"Beautiful jewels for a beautiful woman," he murmured, reaching out to clasp her hand. "The stones are all oval-cut to match the one in your betrothal ring."

Suddenly Aurora wished with all her heart that she had gotten him something more lavish than the snuff bottle. It seemed so insignificant when compared with his magnificent gift.

But when Nicholas saw what she had given him and his face lit up with pleasure, she knew she had chosen well.

He knew what it was at once. "A Chinese snuff bottle made of jade. What a truly unique gift, Rory. I will be the envy of every gentleman in London."

"A unique gift for a unique man," she said with a radiant smile.

While Lady Vivien politely thanked Nicholas for the modest onyx eardrops he had given her, Aurora noticed the old lady glancing at the sapphire necklace with grim disapproval, as if Aurora weren't worthy of so lavish a gift, even from her own husband. Wesley, however, seemed genuinely appreciative of the pair of silver candlesticks, and that mollified Aurora.

"Shall we dine?" Nicholas asked.

When everyone murmured assent, Nicholas signaled to the majordomo to begin serving the meal, so he didn't notice the dining-room doors suddenly swing open. But Aurora did.

Her eyes bulged in disbelief and she struggled to her feet. "Lady Mary!"

The room was so hushed, Aurora fancied she could hear three heads swing toward the feminine figure approaching the table somewhat hesitantly. Everyone else sat motionless for what seemed like an eternity.

Aurora could only stare, speechless and dumbfounded, for the black silk mask was gone. Since she had taken Aurora's advice and painted her pitted complexion with white ceruse, anyone would have been hard-pressed to find any aftereffects of the smallpox. She was a beautiful woman, with delicate bone structure and those large, luminous gray eyes, so like her son's.

"Merry Christmas, everyone," Lady Mary said with a nervous, tentative smile. "I thought I would join you this year. I hope you don't mind."

"Mind?" Nicholas staggered to his feet, an expression of such joy on his face that Aurora was moved to tears. He walked over to his mother, enfolded her in his arms, and hugged her. Then he took her hand and escorted her to the table.

Aurora stepped away from the table. "Under the circumstances, Lady Mary, I think you should occupy the place of honor at your son's right."

She smiled. "Thank you, Aurora." Then she looked up at her son. "Aurora persuaded me to join you for Christmas dinner. I believe I am Aurora's Christmas gift to you, Nicholas."

Nicholas' head turned, and he regarded his wife with such a look of love and gratitude that everyone present was moved. When he spoke, his voice shook with deep emotion. "This is the finest Christmas gift anyone has ever given me. Thank you, Aurora."

Lady Vivien, unable to let anyone else be the center of attention for very long, muttered, "Well, Mary, it's gratifying to see you've finally come to your senses, as I've advised all along."

Like her son, Lady Mary would not give the spiteful old lady an inch. "Oh, if it hadn't been for Aurora, Vivien, I would still be hiding away from the world. She made me realize that my behavior has been very selfish and it's time I took my place in the family."

Lady Vivien just glared at Aurora in sharp-eyed silence.

Wesley rose, ever anxious to placate. "Whatever the reason, it's wonderful to have you back among us, Aunt Mary." He kissed her on the cheek.

Then Nicholas drank toasts to his mother and his loving wife, and the lavish Christmas dinner began.

That night, Aurora stood before one of the frost-flecked bedchamber windows, dreamily staring out at the snow that was beginning to fall so gently and silently, blanketing the lawns like white dust. Even the crackle and hiss of logs burning in the fireplace couldn't disturb her tranquil thoughts or shake her deep-seated contentment.

When her adored husband came to stand behind her and slipped his arms about her waist, drawing her closer, she leaned back against his solid form with a satisfied sigh. She felt him rest his hard cheek against the top of her head.

"What a wonderful Christmas this has been," she murmured, closing her eyes.

"This has been the most memorable Christmas of my life," Nicholas declared, his warm breath tickling her ear, "and I have you to thank." Then he chuckled softly, his wide chest rumbling with the sound of mirth. "I think I have married a Gypsy witch. Not only have you tamed the most notorious rake in London, you have transformed my reclusive mother into a member of this family again. I don't know how you do it, Rory."

"Gypsy magic."

Nicholas laughed again and buried his face in her fragrant silken hair, his voice mellow and husky as he said, "I believe it. Tell me, what sort of spell will you weave around me next?"

Aurora turned in the loving circle of his arms and boldly grinned at him. "Why don't you undress me and find out?"

Nicholas caught his breath at the seductive sparkle in her eyes, luxurious midnight blue in the semidarkness of the room. He raised his left hand to caress her satin cheek with his thumb, and gasped with a combination of surprise and pleasure when Aurora suddenly turned her head and gently nipped at his hand.

"My lady is a vixen with sharp teeth," he growled, pulling her into his arms. "I can see that I shall have to tame her wanton ways."

"You can try, my lord," Aurora whispered, slipping her dainty hands beneath the soft velvet of his banyan and letting her fingertips play across his muscular chest and up to his shoulders.

Suddenly the last log in the fireplace burned out with a sharp hiss and sent a shower of red and yellow sparks dancing up the chimney.

Aurora shivered. "It's growing cold in here, my love."

"I have a remedy for that."

Nicholas stepped back apace and within seconds his wife's velvet dressing gown was lying in a crumpled heap around her well-turned ankles. He took a second to feast his eyes upon her perfect ivory body before making short shrift of his own garment, trembling as the chill in the room rushed to engulf him. Then he swung her into his arms and carried her over to the bed.

Soon the cold sheets were warmed by the heat of their passion as they loved each other well into the night. By the time morning came, Aurora's wee smile of contentment told Nicholas that she was sufficiently tamed indeed.

15

AURORA flung open the windows and breathed deeply, savoring the rich, loamy scents of the earth awakening after its long winter sleep.

"Spring at last," she said to herself, leaning her elbows on the windowsill and staring out at the landscape.

After a seemingly endless cold, drab winter, the trees had lost their gaunt, skeletal look and were filling out with lush green leaves. Below Aurora's window, the gardeners were busy turning earth and weeding around the first colorful blossoms of spring. Breezes were warm and fragrant, and birdsong plentiful and cheerful.

Aurora moved away from the window and smiled to herself. Almost a year had passed since that fateful day she had come upon Nicholas and Pamela Littlewood in the Chinese summerhouse. Never had she dreamed that nearly one year later she would be so happy and so content with her life.

Oh, her life wasn't as perfect as it could be. She still showed no signs of breeding a longed-for heir, and Diana's protector showed no signs of wanting to marry her. But neither Pamela Littlewood nor any other woman posed a threat to Aurora's happiness any longer. Nicholas adored her, and she basked in his love like a flower in the sun.

Sometimes the intensity of her love for Nicholas

frightened her. He was her life. Aurora loved him so completely, with every fiber of her being, she knew she would readily give her own life for his without a moment's hesitation. She knew that if the day ever came when he didn't want her, she would cease to have a reason to go on living.

"Now, now, Aurora," she muttered to herself, "you mustn't indulge in such morbid thoughts on a beautiful May day, especially when you're having guests for luncheon."

Suddenly there came a knock on the door, and when Aurora answered it, one of the footmen told her that Lord Silverblade's guests from London had just arrived.

Aurora took one last glance at herself in the mirror, then went downstairs to greet her guests.

Just as she was passing Nicholas' study on her way to the salon, Aurora noticed the door had been left ajar and she could hear raised voices coming from within the room.

"Grandmother," she heard Nicholas say in his tight, controlled voice, "this is none of your concern!"

"You're wrong there, my boy," Lady Vivien replied, her raspy voice shrill and combative. "The future of the Silverblade line is my concern. You've been married for nine months, and your wife should have shown some signs of presenting you with an heir by now. You have been sleeping with the chit all these months, now, haven't you?"

"Grandmother!" Nicholas roared dangerously, his patience worn out at last.

But the old lady was unabashed. "Then the fault lies with your wife. She's failed you, Nicholas. She's barren. There will be no heir for Silverblade. Now, if you had only consulted me before you married—"

Aurora didn't stand around to hear her husband's reply. White-faced and trembling, she almost ran down the hall, away from Lady Vivien's grating, implacable voice, all the more hateful because it verbalized the very doubts Aurora was having about herself.

But the words haunted her, even though she tried to

drive them from her mind. "She's failed you, Nicholas. She's barren. There will be no heir for Silverblade."

Before entering the salon and confronting Ollie and the others, Aurora paused to compose herself. She couldn't let anyone see how much Lady Vivien's cruel, careless words had upset her.

But despite her best intentions, Aurora found it impossible to think of anything else. Though she tried her best to present a calm, carefree facade to her guests, Lady Vivien's words niggled at the back of her mind and caused her own self-doubts to blossom.

By the time they all sat down to luncheon, Aurora was finding it difficult to hide her despondent mood, even among such lighthearted company. When the meal was over, she pleaded a headache, excused herself, and went to her bedchamber.

Several minutes later she heard a knock on the door, and when she bade the person enter, she wasn't surprised to see Nicholas standing there, an expression of puzzlement on his handsome face.

"Are you all right?" he asked as he entered the room.

Aurora shrugged and turned away from him, not quite knowing how to put her own misgivings into words. She found herself being grasped by the shoulders and turned around to face him.

"Aurora, what is the matter?"

She sighed deeply. "Everything."

"Everything?" he teased her playfully. "I thought you were happy with me."

"I . . . I am. But I overheard you and your grandmother talking in the study, and she is right. I've failed you. I'm barren and will never be able to give you the heir you want, Nicholas."

He held her at arm's length, his mien serious, his eyes as cold as gunmetal. "Didn't I once warn you not to take anything that meddling old fool says to heart?"

"Yes, but this time she spoke the truth!" Aurora wailed. "Having an heir means a great deal to you. You've told me so yourself."

He nodded somberly and moved away from her. "I won't deny that it's not important. If I don't have an heir, Wes will inherit everything, and I shudder to think what will happen if he does."

Nicholas then went on to explain how Wes had not run his own shipping company very well, resulting in huge losses and fluctuating fortunes year after year.

Aurora looked morose. "I can understand why you wouldn't want a similar fate to befall Silverblade."

"Exactly." Nicholas studied her intently for a moment. "Having an heir is crucial to Silverblade's survival, Aurora. But not at the expense of your happiness, my darling." His voice was a soothing caress. "Never that."

She scanned his beloved face, searching for any sign that he was lying just to spare her feelings, but all she saw was honesty and truth. He meant every word he said.

"Oh, Nicholas," she murmured, resting her head against his shoulder, "I've been such a fool."

He reached for her and held her as if he'd never let her go. "You mean the world to me, my love. Your happiness is all that matters to me. I hope you realize that."

She nodded silently.

Nicholas was silent for a moment, then smiled down at her. "I've just had a thought."

"And what is that?"

"Why don't we go to London for a few months? I think a change of scene will do us good."

Aurora felt her spirits lift at the prospect of being away from the thoughtless, caustic tongue of Lady Vivien. "That would be splendid."

Nicholas touched her mouth in a light, quick kiss. "Have your maid begin packing as soon as our guests leave."

"With pleasure," Aurora agreed with a radiant smile.

Nicholas rose and extended his hand to her. "Now, let us return to our guests."

Several days later, Lord and Lady Silverblade left for London.

Nicholas entered the crowded room at White's and scanned the tables to see if there were any places

available where he could sit in on a game. He breathed
deeply and fancied he could smell the heady combination of exhilaration and desperation in the air as fortunes were casually won or lost on the turn of a card.

Finally he noticed a chair empty opposite Ollie and
Haze at the whist table, so he made his way over. As
always, the superstitious Ollie was wearing his coat
inside out for luck. To conceal his expressive face and
avoid revealing his hand, he also wore an outlandish
straw hat bedecked with flowers and ribbons dangling
from its wide brim.

"Ollie," Nicholas said with a teasing smile, "is that
you beneath that exquisite work of millinery?"

His friend raised his head. "You recognized me."

Nicholas chuckled. "How could I help it?" Then he
turned to the others. "Gentlemen, do you mind if I
join you?"

Ollie groaned in dismay. "It would appear my winning streak will soon come to an end," he muttered
morosely.

"Then why not withdraw before Silverblade sits down
to play?" Lord Haze advised.

"Because I live in the misguided hope that I shall
one day beat him," Ollie replied.

Everyone at the table laughed at that and nodded in
agreement, for Nicholas' expertise at cards and his
formidable luck was well-known.

As Nicholas seated himself, the man on his right,
Lord Marchmain, glanced over and said, "Haven't
seen you here in months, Silverblade. Thought you
gave up cards for good."

The man to Nicholas' left, Lord Feverstone, added
in a teasing tone, "Haven't you heard, Marchmain?
Our Lord Silverblade is so enamored of his beautiful
bride that he never leaves her side, even for a bit of
gaming."

Marchmain, who had married a shrew for her fortune and was living to regret it, muttered, "Can't say
that I blame him. If I had a beautiful wife at home, I'd
never leave her side either!"

Nicholas grinned as Haze dealt him a hand. "And

I'd be at her side tonight if she weren't so exhausted from shopping all day."

All the men around the table chuckled and nodded knowingly.

"Well, gentlemen," Haze said, "shall we play?"

As Ollie had predicted, his winning streak abruptly came to an end with Nicholas' arrival. But he gamely refused to admit defeat even when Haze and Feverstone threw down their cards in disgust and withdrew.

But as the stakes reached 50,000 pounds, even Ollie was forced to bow out, leaving only Nicholas and Marchmain to battle it out.

When Nicholas raised his opponent another 10,000, Marchmain studied his cards, turned white, and shook his head in disgust. "Too rich for my blood, Silverblade. The game is yours."

Nicholas grinned and spread his cards on the green baize table.

Exclamations of admiration rippled through those assembled to watch, and Marchmain uttered a sigh of relief. "Better to lose fifty thousand of my wife's money rather than sixty."

While Marchmain wrote out a promissory note in an unsteady hand, Nicholas graciously accepted the congratulations of the other gentlemen assembled there tonight. As he rose, pocketed the note, and started to leave, he noticed the Earl of Blatchford weaving his way purposefully between the tables and staggering drunkenly toward him.

"Shil-Shilverblade," Blatchford muttered, grasping Nicholas by the arm to steady himself as he swayed on his feet.

"Yes, Blatchford?" Nicholas inquired coolly, for he had never liked the man.

"Y-you made me lose, damn you!"

Nicholas, unable to make any sense of the earl's slurred, garbled speech, scowled in annoyance. "What are you talking about, Blatchford? I've never caused you to lose anything. We've never even played cards together."

The man's jaw went slack as his slow wits assimilated that information. "Not talking about cards, damn you. Talking about the wager."

"What wager?" Nicholas snapped in impatience.

Suddenly everyone in the room ceased whatever he was doing and stared in silence at the two men. Nicholas, however, was too busy with Blatchford to notice that an uncomfortable hush had descended on the room.

"You know . . . the wager." Blatchford seemed annoyed that Nicholas was ignorant of the matter and proceeded to enlighten him. "I bet 5,000 pounds that your heir would be born nine months after your wedding day. And I lost." He tried to focus his blurry eyes and failed. "How. . . . how could you do this to me?"

"How interesting," Nicholas said with an icy calm he was far from feeling. "Tell me more about this wager, Blatchford."

But poor Blatchford was too far gone to speak coherently, so Nicholas turned toward all those assembled.

"Will someone bring me the betting book?" he said.

Within seconds the large book that recorded all wagers made in the club was brought forth and set before Nicholas. He opened it and began thumbing through the pages, hoping that his hand wouldn't betray him by shaking.

Soon he found what he was looking for.

Shortly after Nicholas' wedding day, several gentlemen he knew only by name or reputation had placed bets on the date his first child would be born. The dates ranged from seven months to two years.

He snapped the book shut, turned to his sheepish colleagues, and smiled sardonically. "I am flattered, gentlemen. Although poor Blatchford is out of the running, I shall redouble my efforts to see that one of the participants wins handsomely. And to whoever wins, I myself shall donate ten thousand pounds."

Everyone seemed relieved that the formidable Lord Silverblade was taking the wager in good-natured stride, for the tension evaporated and conversation started up again.

But neither Ollie nor Haze was deceived by Nicholas' brave display. They went to his side at once.

"I'm assuming neither of you knew about this?" Nicholas muttered savagely through his forced smile.

"Of course not," Haze snapped, looking as furious as Nicholas. "We are your friends. We would never be party to such a wicked piece of work, and we'd certainly have told you about it had we known."

Ollie scratched beneath his wig. "Who in God's name would have instituted such a foolish wager?"

"I don't know," Nicholas said, "but I would like you to find out for me."

Ollie nodded. "We'll make discreet inquiries."

"Splendid," Nicholas said between clenched teeth. "And when you do . . ." His fingers tightened around the handle of his dress sword, the implication plain.

He looked first at Haze, then at Ollie. "And if one of you so much as breathes a word of this wager to Aurora . . ." He let the consequences of such a slip hang unspoken in the air.

"No gentleman here tonight would dare," Ollie said, and Haze nodded in agreement.

Satisfied, Nicholas went striding purposefully out of White's before his friends could make him feel even worse by uttering another word of sympathy.

Nicholas leaned back against the cushions of the sedan chair and closed his eyes, trying to reassure himself that what had happened in White's was nothing more than a bad dream.

He had never been so humiliated in his entire life, and he found the experience unpleasant and painful. Oh, he was accustomed to being whispered about, but it was always done in a spirit of shocked outrage or reluctant admiration. He had never given anyone cause to laugh at him.

But that was sure to change if he didn't sire an heir soon.

Now, because of the wager, many gentlemen in London would be scrutinizing Aurora for any signs of impending maternity, and if there were none, they would snicker behind their hands and disparage Nicholas' virility.

How ironic, they would say, that a man with a

reputation with the ladies could not even impregnate his own wife. Or, like his grandmother, they would blame Aurora and brand her barren.

Lord and Lady Silverblade would be held up to public scrutiny and ridicule.

Nicholas rubbed his forehead thoughtfully and swore heartily under his breath. He knew he should put it out of his mind and not give the wager a second thought, but never before had his masculine pride been wounded in such a way, and it lingered in his mind like a festering sore.

Then a devastating thought occurred to him. What if the fault lay with him and not Aurora? What if he couldn't father children? After all, he had made love to scores of women on several continents over the years and he had not sired any bastards to his knowledge. Up until this moment he had attributed it to his careful lovemaking, but now he was beginning to wonder if there was something wrong with his seed.

He recalled a story his father had once told him about a certain Squire Allworthy. For years everyone had assumed the good squire's wife was barren because the couple had no children. Yet, after Allworthy died and his wife remarried soon thereafter, she astounded the neighborhood by presenting her new husband with handsome twin sons nine months after their wedding day. So Nicholas knew all too well that Aurora's childless state might not be her fault.

When the sedan chair finally reached his house, Nicholas paid the men, then stood there staring up at Aurora's room. No candle shone in the window, so he knew she had gone to bed.

With a weary sigh he slowly climbed the steps, let himself in, and went directly to his own bedchamber. This was one night Aurora would have to sleep alone.

Aurora sensed something was amiss.

Her eyes flew open and she looked around. She could tell the sun was shining behind the closed curtains, so it was already morning. Then she looked at the other side of the bed where Nicholas usually slept curled around her with one arm thrown possessively across her waist.

He was not there. In fact, there was no sign that his side had ever been slept in.

Aurora sat up, rubbed the sleep out of her eyes, rose, and put on her wrapping gown. Then she went to Nicholas' room and softly knocked. When there was no answer, she turned the knob and went inside.

Nicholas lay sprawled in the middle of his bed, the covers pulled up to his waist, his forearm flung across his eyes. He was snoring.

Dismay and doubt filled Aurora as she watched him. Why was he sleeping in his own bed? Why hadn't he come to her last night as he always did?

She glided noiselessly on bare feet into the room and seated herself on the edge of the bed. She extended her hand and gently shook his shoulder. "Nicholas? Wake up."

He groaned in protest, and rolled away to avoid her persistent shaking, but Aurora was merciless. She called his name again, and this time he responded by opening his eyes and staring at her as though she were a perfect stranger.

Taken aback at the look in his eyes, Aurora drew her hand away. "Nicholas, what's wrong? You didn't come to bed last night, and I was worried about you."

He rubbed his hand across his unshaven jaw and shook his head as if to clear away the last vestiges of sleep. Then he said, "I came home very late from White's last night and you were sound asleep when I looked in. I didn't want to wake you, so I decided to sleep in my own bed."

Aurora smiled and ran her fingertips down the rippling muscles of his upper arm, delighting at the way he shivered at her touch. Her voice was an enticing purr as she said, "I'm touched by your concern, Nicholas, but you know I don't mind being awakened by you at any time of the night. Or the morning," she added hopefully.

Usually her blatant invitation was all Nicholas needed to pull her down on top of him and drive her delirious with his lovemaking, but this morning all he did was give her a wan smile and a chaste peck on the cheek.

Rebuffed, Aurora felt a chill of foreboding forming in the pit of her stomach. "Nicholas, don't you want to make love with me?"

"I lost heavily at the tables last night," he explained ruefully, not daring to meet her questioning gaze, "and my ardor with it, I'm afraid."

Aurora was quite mystified at the connection, but she realized there was still much about men she didn't understand, so she calmly accepted Nicholas' explanation with a brief, "I see." After a moment's silence she added, "It is not a permanent condition, I trust?"

Nicholas grinned at that. "No, dear Rory, I trust not."

She sighed in relief.

Nicholas stifled a yawn. "But I stayed out quite late last night, and—"

"You want to sleep." Aurora rose and tried to hide her bitter disappointment. "I quite understand."

"You are a paragon among women, my darling."

She smiled at the compliment, then left him to his sleep, confident that he would return to his old self tomorrow, and all would be well between them.

But as the days passed, Aurora realized with growing panic that something was troubling Nicholas.

On the surface, he was the same man she had married. Whenever they appeared in public at Vauxhall or Drury Lane, Nicholas was kind and attentive, teasing and laughing with her and their friends. In private he always sought her company, sitting with her and quietly conversing.

Yet there were times Aurora caught him staring moodily into space, his brow furrowed, his expression brooding and troubled. Then he would catch himself and the moodiness would vanish so abruptly that Aurora wondered if she had imagined it.

Even when he made love to her, he no longer quite abandoned himself to their mutual passion as he had in the past. He held back, distancing himself from her emotionally, if not physically.

Aurora could sense him gradually retreating behind

an invisible wall and shutting her out. She was losing him, and she didn't even know why.

But she promised herself she was going to find out, and soon.

Nicholas stood at his study window staring at the long row of houses on the opposite side of the square. He may have been looking at houses, but his thoughts were back at White's on the fateful night he had learned of the wager and was forced to confront his own inadequacies as a man.

He sighed and rubbed his eyes as if to erase the memory of that night, but it was no use. The memory plagued him like an aching tooth.

Suddenly there came a knock on the door, and when he bade the person enter, Aurora swept in and resolutely closed the door behind her.

This morning she looked ravishing in a form-fitting riding habit of dark green camlet, but when Nicholas took one look at the combative gleam in her eye, he could tell his spirited wife had more than riding on her mind. His spirited wife was preparing herself for a confrontation.

He set a mask of bland affability in place, beamed down at her, and kissed her on the cheek. "Good morning, Rory. I believe I promised we'd go riding in the park. If you'll wait one moment—"

"I'm not here to discuss our morning ride, Nicholas," she said without smiling. "I want to know what's been troubling you for the last several weeks."

He raised his brows and tried to look perplexed. "Why, nothing."

"Don't lie to me, Nicholas!" she cried, her pale blue eyes darkening to sapphire with anger and exasperation. "You've been moody and preoccupied, and I would like to know why."

For one moment he almost relented. Aurora looked like a tower of strength, her bright coppery hair surrounding her head in a beckoning beacon, her smoldering eyes twin pools of understanding, so that all Nicholas wanted to do was fall at her feet and cling to her as helplessly as a baby while he confessed his deepest doubts and fears about himself.

But he couldn't bring himself to accept the comfort he knew she would give so freely and unconditionally. He was a proud, obstinate man who would rather die than admit his weaknesses to a woman, even one he loved as much as Aurora.

He took refuge in anger. "I told you there is nothing troubling me!" he shouted, clenching his hands into fists at his sides.

Aurora flinched from his raised voice as if he had struck her across the face, but she didn't dissolve into helpless tears as she might have in the past. It would have been easier for Nicholas to deal with her if she had. Instead, she stood her ground and glared at him, looking both fearless and afraid.

"How can you deny it?" She raised her voice defiantly until it matched his own and reverberated throughout the quiet room. "You've changed, Nicholas. You've become a different man. I hardly know you anymore."

"Nonsense. You're imagining it. I'm the same man I always was."

"Oh no, Nicholas. The man I married was always forthright and honest with me. The man you've become is secretive."

Aurora approached him, her expression hopeful and beseeching. "You've built a wall between us, Nicholas. You've shut me out of your life." She shrugged helplessly. "Have I done something to anger you? Please tell me what it is and I shall never do it again. Or"—her voice trembled imperceptibly—"is it that you no longer love me, that you don't desire me?"

He steeled himself to resist the heart-wrenching appeal in her voice, though all he wanted to do was gather her into his arms and hold her for dear life.

"You have done nothing to anger me, and I still love you," he said flatly, turning away so he wouldn't be swayed by her incomparable beauty and vulnerability.

"Spoken with such warmth! Such sincerity!" she snapped bitterly.

He whirled on her now. "You are my wife, Aurora, not my keeper! And I'll thank you not to pry into my private affairs!"

That was the final insult.

Aurora was trembling from head to toe. "Private affairs, my lord? I was under the impression that husbands and wives who love each other share what is troubling them. I can see that I was wrong."

With a stifled sob, Aurora fled from the study, slamming the door behind her.

When he was finally alone, Nicholas smashed his fist down against the desk and swore heartily. Why was he so furious with himself? Hadn't he just gotten what he wanted? He had wanted Aurora to leave him alone and she had. Yet why did he still feel so miserable?

Aurora sat in the sedan chair and dabbed at her eyes with her handkerchief. It was dry. She was not surprised. She had no tears left to shed.

After she had bolted from Nicholas' study, she locked herself in her bedchamber, flung herself on the bed, and cried. But through the shuddering sobs that racked her slight frame, she had listened for the sound of Nicholas' footsteps outside her door. At any moment he would come to her and tell her he was sorry for treating her so shabbily. He would draw her into his arms and ask for her forgiveness. Then he would finally confide in her.

She listened and waited, but he never came.

When she finally realized he would not be coming, she wept until she could weep no more. Then she rose, went downstairs, and had the footman summon a sedan chair.

Now the chair was coming to a stop at the address she had given the carriers. Aurora opened the door and disembarked. She told the men to wait, then climbed the stairs to the red-brick town house and rang the bell.

A footman admitted her and showed her to the drawing room. She had not long to wait.

"Aurora, what a pleasant surprise," Ollie said as he entered the drawing room. He looked around in puzzlement. "Where is Nick? He didn't come with you?"

"No, I came alone," she replied. Seeing Ollie's look of discomfort, she added, "Perhaps I shouldn't have, since you are a bachelor gentleman, but you're the only person I can turn to, the only person I trust."

She burst into fresh tears, startling both herself and the placid Ollie.

"Oh, dear!" Ollie said, flustered. "Um, would you like to sit down? Would you like some . . . some tea? A . . . a glass of brandy perhaps? Yes, that's it. Brandy." He rushed over to the decanter and began pouring with an unsteady hand. "You must forgive me, Aurora," he rattled on. "I never know what to do when a woman cries. I always feel so helpless."

She smiled in spite of herself. By the time Ollie handed her the glass of brandy, Aurora had brought herself under control.

"I have to talk to you about Nicholas," she said.

"Nick? What about him?"

"Something's troubling him, Ollie, and he won't tell me what it is." Aurora looked at him with a hopeful smile. "I thought perhaps you could."

Ollie fiddled with the lace at his cuff. "Something troubling Nick? Sorry, Aurora, but I can't help you. If he's distressed about something, he hasn't confided in me."

"But you are his closest friend. I thought surely—"

"I'm sorry, Aurora." Ollie rose and went to refill his glass, purposely keeping his back toward her so she wouldn't see his face.

Aurora rose and went to him. "You're not a very accomplished liar, Ollie. Your face reveals the truth even when you don't want to."

He whirled on her, trying to frighten her with a fierce look. But he didn't have the face or temperament for it, and only managed to look like a sputtering, indignant cherub.

"Lady Silverblade, you insult me!"

"Then shall it be pistols for two, or are you going to tell me the truth?"

Ollie's dark eyes widened. "I've never been challenged to a duel by a woman before."

"Stop dissembling, Ollie. I want the truth."

"Damn it, Aurora!" he cried, backed into a corner

at last and not knowing how to get out of it without betraying Nick. "I told you that I can't help you!"

She watched several emotions war with each other across his face. Suddenly Aurora understood all too well.

"Ollie," she said softly, "did Nicholas make you promise not to tell me what is distressing him?"

"No such promise was ever made because there was never any necessity for such a promise!"

Aurora relented. If she pushed Ollie too hard, he would resist all the harder. He had been Nicholas' friend of long standing before she could make any claim upon him. She knew where he stood.

"Forgive me, Ollie. Nick obviously hasn't confided in you. But I am telling you now that he is very troubled, and I would like your help in finding out what it is."

Disarmed, Ollie said, "He won't tell you what is wrong?"

Aurora shook her head and began pacing about the room as she told Ollie all about her husband's moodiness and irritability. She stopped in front of one of the long, tall windows and stared mindlessly into the street. Her voice broke as she said, "He's shut himself away from me, Ollie. We used to be so close. Now we are virtual strangers who happen to live in the same house."

"I'm . . . I'm sorry to hear that Aurora. Doesn't sound like Nick at all. I know he loves you," he added encouragingly.

Suddenly Aurora turned, a stricken look of sudden comprehension upon her face. "Ollie, do you suppose he's involved with another woman? Has my husband taken a mistress?"

He was at her side in three strides. "Aurora, don't be foolish! You're the only woman for Nick. Told me so himself on many an occasion."

His words failed to reassure her. She shrugged helplessly, and her voice had a defeated, hollow ring to it as she said, "I can think of no other reason for his callous behavior toward me."

Ollie lost his reserve long enough to grasp her by the shoulders and give them a little shake. "Whatever is gnawing at Nick isn't another woman. Pamela is out of his life for good. She's part of the past. I've heard it said she's dangling after some duke now. Nick's forgotten her, and she's after bigger fish than a mere marquess. Believe me, Aurora, you have nothing to fear from Pamela Littlewood."

"You're not saying that just to spare my feelings, are you?"

Ollie released her with a smile and a shake of his head.

Aurora drooped with relief and sighed. Then she straightened shoulders that had become stooped from bearing so much. "Do forgive me. I've taken up enough of your time, Ollie."

He grinned engagingly. "Not to mention ruining my reputation by calling at my house alone."

"You'll survive, my friend," Aurora said, returning the smile.

After Ollie retrieved her cloak and draped it about her shoulders, Aurora grew serious once again. "Ollie," she pleaded, "if Nicholas should happen to confide in you, would you please tell me? If only I knew what was troubling him, I know I could help mend this rift between us."

"I shall do whatever I can to help."

Impulsively Aurora stood on tiptoes and kissed him on the cheek. "Thank you, Ollie. You are a true friend. Don't bother to show me out. I know the way."

Then she wished him good day and left.

Ollie stood at the window and watched Aurora's sedan chair disappear down the street. Then he strode over to the claret decanter, filled his glass up to the rim, and downed it in two swallows. He refilled it and seated himself in his favorite chair. When he closed his eyes, all he could see was Aurora's sad little face looking up at him with such abject misery. When she had kissed him, he felt like Judas.

"Damn you to hell, Nicholas Devenish," he said aloud. "You're breaking that poor girl's heart, and you've made me a party to it."

Suddenly Ollie's placid face twisted with uncharacteristic savagery. He flung his glass with all his might against the opposite wall. The tinkling sound of shattering glass and the sight of ruby-red wine splattering the pale yellow walls perversely pleased him

He rose and called for his chair. Perhaps if he lost enough money at White's he wouldn't feel so guilty about having lied to Aurora.

Nicholas was in a foul black mood tonight. Not even the music, the laughter, the high spirits of the two hundred people crowding his ballroom could do anything to ease his pain.

He searched the crowd for his wife. Wife? He chuckled bitterly at that. She was nothing more than a woman who happened to live with him. They hadn't been physically or emotionally intimate for the last month.

No one would know it to look at her. Aurora mingled with her guests like the accomplished hostess she had become, smiling, laughing, conversing with practiced ease. But every once in a while she would catch Nicholas staring at her. Then the pretense would slip. Her smile would die and all the joy would drain out of her face before she hastily looked away.

Nearly two months had passed since that fateful night at White's. Never had Nicholas dreamed one wager could so turn his life into a nightmare.

Even his closest friend, Ollie, who usually stood by him with unflinching loyalty no matter how outrageous Nicholas' behavior, had deserted him on this issue. He insisted that Nicholas' misery was self-inflicted, a matter of pride more than anything else. A day didn't go by without Ollie entreating him to confide in Aurora and reassure her it was the wager, not anything she had done, that was causing her husband to be so sullen and moody.

For the first time in their long friendship, Ollie was furious with Nicholas. "Can't you see what you're doing to that poor, blameless child, you stubborn fool?" Ollie would rail at him with uncharacteristic anger.

Nicholas could see, all too well. But he couldn't stop himself.

He wondered where it would all end. He was soon to find out.

"Lady Silverblade, you look lovelier every time I see you."

Aurora smiled and thanked the Duchess of Kilkenny, grateful for any excuse to stop thinking of Nicholas, staring at her morosely from across the ballroom.

She did feel beautiful tonight in her distinctive gown of copper-colored damask that played up the red-gold glints in her hair. But then, she thought bitterly, what else did she have to do with her time other than spend it at the mantua maker's, ordering more gowns than she could possibly wear in a year?

"Very daring of you, I must say," Katherine went on. "Every other woman here is a pale summer flower, while you are a robust autumn leaf."

"I am the hostess," Aurora reminded her with a smile. "I can be outrageous."

Katherine looked pleased. "I'll have you know you are becoming quite the fashion leader in London, my dear. You have come a long way from the impetuous waif who scandalized London last year."

Aurora almost blurted out that she would gladly trade the dubious honor to have her husband back, but she caught herself just in time. She had a facade to maintain.

Aurora spent the next several minutes chatting with Katherine, who wanted to know why Diana hadn't come up to London for the season with Lord Penhall. She was in the midst of explaining that her sister had decided to remain in Cornwall because her protector was having his house completely refurbished, when she sensed a presence at her elbow.

Excusing herself to Katherine, Aurora turned to find a young man no older than herself waiting to speak to her.

"Yes?" she inquired politely.

"Aurora, don't you remember me?"

She stared at him in puzzlement, for he spoke with a lilting Irish accent she hadn't heard in a while. He was a tall, pleasant-looking youth, with eager brown eyes and a strong, wide smile.

Aurora frowned. "I fear I don't recognize you, sir, though there is something vaguely familiar about you."

He flashed her another wide, hopeful smile. "I'm Conor. Conor Grantley."

She recognized the name of one of her childhood playmates at once.

"Conor!" she cried, giving the lad an impetuous hug. "How wonderful it is to see you again! Whatever are you doing in London?" Before he could reply, Aurora turned to Katherine. "Katherine, this is a very dear friend, Conor Grantley. His father owns one of the estates bordering Falconstown. Conor, I'd like to present Katherine Crossways, the Duchess of Kilkenny."

It was obvious that Conor wasn't accustomed to being presented to duchesses, for he flushed and stammered, "I am honored, your grace," as he bowed.

"The honor is mine, Mr. Grantley," she replied with a regal smile. "Now, if you both will excuse me, I see my husband summoning me from across the room."

When they were alone, Aurora held him at arm's length and shook her head in disbelief. "No wonder I didn't recognize you, Conor. You've become such a fine gentleman since I saw you last."

His eyes twinkled with pleasure. "And you have grown even more beautiful. I would hardly recognize the hoyden who used to race her pony across the moors with my brothers and me."

Aurora's smile was bittersweet. "Those were pleasant times. But we are not children any longer. I am a married woman now, and a marchioness into the bargain."

"So I understand."

Aurora ignored the look of longing that suddenly sprang into Conor's eyes. She said, "And Falconstown? Has it prospered under Lord Fitzhugh?"

A shadow fell across Conor's face. He glanced nervously around the room. "Is there somewhere we can speak freely, without being interrupted?"

"Outside," Aurora replied. "In the garden."

She led Conor through the French doors and out

into the balmy, moonlit night, unaware that they were being watched.

Nicholas didn't hear what his companion was saying. All his attention had been focused on Aurora the moment he saw her hug her rustic young admirer so enthusiastically. Nicholas wondered who he was. Judging by the poor cut of his clothes, the rustic was a gentleman down on his luck.

Nicholas excused himself, then sauntered across the ballroom with nonchalant grace. He stepped through the French doors, which had been left open on this warm July night. He looked around for any sign of his wife.

It didn't take him long to find her.

She was in another man's arms, kissing him boldly.

A red mist of rage clouded Nicholas' vision. He moved so fast, they didn't even see him coming. Nicholas grasped the other man by the shoulder and pulled him off his wife.

"Nicholas, I can explain . . ." Aurora began, her eyes wide with terror in the moonlight.

Her voice was drowned out by the sickening crack of Nicholas' fist being rammed into the other man's face. His adversary crumpled to the ground with a grunt and lay still

Aurora's hand flew to her mouth and she gasped. "You've killed him!"

"He's merely unconscious. When he awakens, I shall demand satisfaction. He'll die honorably, which is more than he deserves."

"Nicholas, he's only a boy!"

"If he's old enough to try to steal my wife, he's old enough to die like a man." Before Aurora could say another word, he grasped her wrist and started dragging her away.

"Nicholas, you're hurting me . . ."

He ignored her protests and strode with single-minded determination around the back of the house, toward the servants' entrance. They managed to enter the house unseen, and didn't stop until they reached the first unoccupied room he could find.

Nicholas flung her inside so hard that Aurora stumbled and would have fallen if she hadn't grasped a nearby chair just in time. She turned to face him, her heart pounding wildly against her ribs as he locked the door.

"Now, madam," he said, his voice silky with menace, "I want an explanation from you, and it had better be a good one."

Aurora gripped the back of the chair for courage. "Why should I? I can tell by that look on your face that you've already judged and condemned me."

"I find my wife alone in the garden, kissing a strange man . . . What am I supposed to think?"

"I was not kissing him!" Aurora cried hotly. "He was kissing me. There is a difference, as you once insisted to me."

"You weren't exactly discouraging him, my dear."

His disbelieving, sarcastic tone infuriated Aurora. "Oh, I see. When Mrs. Littlewood kissed you, that was acceptable. But when a man kisses me, I am accused of encouraging him and being the guilty party."

Her words fell on deaf ears. "I'm still waiting for an explanation, Aurora."

She moistened her dry lips with the tip of her tongue. "His name in Conor Grantley. He was one of our neighbors in Ireland. I've known him since I was a child. He lured me out into the garden by leading me to believe he was going to tell me something about Falconstown. Before I knew what was happening, he grabbed me and began kissing me. You pulled him off before I had a chance to push him away and slap his face."

Nicholas strode over to her, his face dark and twisted. Aurora shrank away from him, but he reached out and grasped her wrists again, his fingers not only restraining her but also digging painfully into her flesh.

"If you have any ideas of taking this Grantley lad for your lover, Aurora, I would urge you to reconsider. Because if I ever catch you in another man's arms, I'll make you rue the day you were born."

Aurora stood there staring at Nicholas in shock. She shook her head, unwilling to believe what she had just heard from his own lips.

"You don't trust me," she said numbly, trying to dislodge herself. "You really don't trust me. You think I'm going to be unfaithful to you by taking a lover."

He released her and flung her away as though she had suddenly become loathsome to him. "I just want to ensure that my firstborn child is mine, not someone else's."

His unfair, hurtful words made something inside Aurora snap. As white-hot fury bubbled up from somewhere deep inside, she heard herself impetuously retort, "Since you haven't touched me in weeks, my lord, your firstborn child is certain to be someone else's."

He slapped her. It was a light slap that barely stung Aurora's cheek, but the very thought that Nicholas would ever raise his hand to her hurt more than the blow itself.

When Nicholas realized what he had done, a look of self-loathing flashed across his features and he was contrite in an instant. "Aurora, I'm sorry," he said, reaching for her. "I don't know why I did that. My black temper got the better of me. I didn't mean . . ."

Thinking he was about to strike her again, she quickly backed out of reach, cradling her stinging cheek against her palm. Her eyes were wide with fear and panic. "Don't touch me! Don't ever touch me again!"

He stopped in his tracks and his hands fell to his sides. "Aurora, I—"

"Just leave me alone."

His face tightened into a resolute mask. "Fine. We both need time to be alone. I'm sending you back to Silverblade tomorrow morning. If either of us decides we don't wish to be married any longer, I'm sure we'll find some way to remedy the situation."

Aurora was so stunned she gaped at him in disbelief. When she regained her powers of speech, she stammered, "N-Nicholas, what are you saying? You can't mean that!"

"Oh, but I most assuredly do, madam."

Then he made a mocking bow and left her.

When his footsteps died away, Aurora buried her face in her hands and cried.

She was still crying when Wesley found her some ten minutes later.

He just stood there shifting nervously in place as he gaped at her. "Aurora? Whatever is the matter?"

She wiped away her tears and took a deep breath to compose herself. "Nothing, Wesley. Nothing at all."

He approached her chair. "Come now, Aurora. women don't just cry for no reason at all. I can tell that something has upset you."

Wesley looked so sympathetic and understanding that Aurora found herself saying, "Nicholas and I have had a serious argument."

"Oh, dear me. It pains me to hear that. I know Nick has a wicked temper, but I'm sure it's not as serious as you fear."

Aurora smiled dejectedly. "Oh, but it is. He's sending me back to Silverblade tomorrow morning, but he's staying in London."

"He's sending you back to Silverblade? Alone?"

Aurora nodded. "In disgrace."

His thick lips curved up in a reassuring smile. "Don't despair. Once Nick has had time to think matters through, I'm sure he'll rush right home to make amends."

She rose now and took several deep breaths to compose herself. "Somehow, I doubt that. Now, if you'll excuse me, I must return to my guests before I am missed."

Aurora gathered her skirts and held her head high, trying not to think of tomorrow.

16

AURORA leaned back against the leather squabs and closed her eyes, which felt as raw as peeled potatoes. Not even the gentle rocking motion of the carriage could soothe her tumultuous feelings.

All last night, as she slept alone in her wide, empty bed, she had prayed Nicholas would reconsider sending her away. But when she had gone down to breakfast this morning, one look at his drawn, unforgiving face told her he had not. They ate in silence like two strangers, the tension stretching between them like a taut rope. When Aurora was finished, she returned to her bedchamber and dressed in a somber black dress and black cloak, suitable mourning for a dead marriage.

An hour later, the carriage was ready and waiting. Aurora hesitated in the foyer, hoping against hope that Nicholas would at least come down to see her off. After waiting in vain for fifteen minutes, she left without a backward glance.

But as her carriage sped past the outskirts of the city, Aurora couldn't stop thinking of Nicholas. When she remembered his cold, stormy eyes, the razor sharpness of his wit, the ease with which he could make her laugh, her desolation was almost too much to bear.

She pressed her fist against her mouth as if to bottle up her anguish. "Oh, Nicholas, what did I do to make you hate me so? Will you ever love me again?"

She started weeping uncontrollably, grateful that

her maid was ill and couldn't accompany her today. Aurora didn't want anyone to witness her misery and her shame. She wanted to be alone.

Soon Aurora lost all track of time. How long had it been since they left London? Minutes? Hours? Days? She didn't know and she didn't care. Nothing mattered now that she had lost Nicholas forever.

Suddenly a loud crack split the air, followed by several more in rapid succession. Aurora started in alarm. Why, someone was shooting at them! She slid over to the window as the carriage slowed, her heart pounding wildly, Nicholas momentarily forgotten. What she saw made the blood run cold in her veins.

Two masked men on horseback had forced the carriage to a stop and were aiming their pistols right at her.

"Out!" one of them growled, while his companion dismounted and jerked the door open. This one offered his hand to Aurora, but she disdainfully refused it.

"Ain't she the grand lady!" the man on foot sneered to his friend on horseback.

"Won't be for long," the other replied. Oddly colored eyes as tawny as a cat's glittered coldly through the slits in his black crepe domino.

Aurora managed to disembark without stumbling and making a fool of herself. Now that she was out of the carriage, she could see two additional highwaymen by the lead horse along this wooded, deserted stretch of road. Up in the box, Tom the driver and a second man were slumped forward, quiet and still.

"You've killed them!" she cried, bolting forward to go to their aid.

"Now, now, yer ladyship," the man on foot said, grasping her arms from behind and jerking her back to restrain her, "there ain't nothin' you can do fer them now."

"Bastards! Murdering bastards!"

The men on horseback only laughed, while the one holding her gave her arms a painful squeeze and muttered, "You insult me old mother again, an' I'll give you a little bastard of your own to worry about!"

The other men laughed even louder and added coarse threats of their own.

"Show the bitch what it's like to be rogered by a real man!"

"I never 'ad a real lady before."

"Well, now's your chance."

"I 'ave it! Let's each 'ave a go at 'er, one at a time in the bushes."

Terror rose like bile in Aurora's throat as she realized these four highwaymen could savagely rape, then murder her, and she would be powerless to stop them. No one would come to her aid along this deserted stretch of road. She fought down the mindless panic threatening to sweep away all rationality, and forced herself to remain calm and detached. She sensed these men fed on fear, so she willed herself to be strong and brave.

The man on horseback nearest her appeared to be the gang's leader, for he said, "Much as I'd like to roger the bitch myself, we've got work to do before somebody happens along and catches us."

The other men reluctantly mumbled their assent.

Aurora turned to look up at the leader squarely. "What are you going to do with me?"

"You'll find out all in good time," he replied.

Then he nodded to his henchmen. Aurora felt her arms pulled behind her back and her wrists bound securely with rope that cut into her tender flesh. Then a black hood was pulled over her head, depriving her of sight and making her as helpless as a newborn kitten.

"Back in the carriage," her captor snapped, guiding her back up the steps.

When Aurora became disoriented and hesitated in the doorway, the man put his hands on her shoulders and pushed her down, hard. She fell to her knees with a gasp of pain, but she wouldn't give them the satisfaction of crying or begging for mercy.

"Lie on the floor," he barked, "and don't get up until I says so. Any one of us sees your head in the window and we'll blow it off. Got it?"

"I understand perfectly," Aurora replied.

Her captor chuckled lasciviously. "That's 'ow I likes to see a bitch, on 'er knees."

He cupped her bottom with odious familiarity and when Aurora flinched from his touch, he cursed, put one hand between her shoulder blades, and shoved her again. Aurora toppled forward helplessly. She twisted just in time to avoid smashing her face against the carriage floor, but fell heavily on her right arm. Excruciating pain seared her shoulder, but she managed to keep from screaming by biting her lower lip.

When her captor realized she was not going to whimper, he swore again and closed the door. "She's a tough bitch for a lady," he muttered.

"We'll see how tough she is later," the leader commented, his voice trailing off as he rode away from the door. He must have made another comment to his men, for they all laughed again.

Aurora tasted warm, salty blood as she wriggled into a more comfortable position on her side. It was a small price to pay for defying those heartless murderers.

Without the use of her eyes, she had only her hearing to rely on. She fully intended to make the best use of it.

She listened as hard as she could. At first, all she could hear was the wild beating of her heart and her own ragged breathing. Gradually, as the panic subsided, she heard other things as well.

She heard scraping and shuffling in the driver's box, followed by grunts of exertion and more foul curses. Aurora assumed the highwaymen were disposing of the men they had killed, perhaps heaving them into a ditch or burying them in the woods. Poor Tom. She hadn't even known the other man's name.

Then came the slap of leather against horsehide and high-pitched neighs of protest. The carriage moved forward with a jerk and the clopping of hooves. They were on their way.

Aurora was nauseous and sore from being pitched back and forth across the carriage floor.

She had stopped trying to differentiate various sounds hours ago, because all she ever heard was the pounding of hooves and the rattle of the carriage wheels. At least it gave her time to think about her plight.

Since the highwaymen had spared her life, they were doubtless going to hold her for ransom. Aurora stared balefully into the blackness beyond her eyes. Would Nicholas pay a ransom for a wife he no longer wanted?

She felt ashamed of herself for doubting him. He was an honorable man. Even if he no longer loved her, he wouldn't allow her to be murdered.

But who were these men? Aurora wondered. How did they know she would be traveling with such a light escort? And where were they taking her?

She closed her eyes and emptied her mind of all conscious thought. They had said she would learn her fate in good time. All in good time. . . .

Sometime later, Aurora's eyes flew open when she realized the carriage had come to a stop. She held her breath, ears alert and straining for any scrap of sound that would identify her surroundings.

" 'Ere we are, yer ladyship."

Aurora recognized the odious voice of her chief tormentor and the sound of the carriage door opening. He grasped her around the ankles and began dragging her out of the carriage as though she were a side of beef, making crude comments as her skirt and petticoats rode up to expose her shapely legs. When he set her on her feet, Aurora was so befuddled and shaken she almost collapsed.

Her captor chuckled as he steadied her, taking advantage of her helpless state to run his hands across her breasts, squeezing them roughly. "Let me be of assistance, yer ladyship," he said in a prissy, mocking voice.

Three different voices laughed maliciously. So they were still together.

Now the leader spoke. "Well, Lady Silverblade, it's time to remove this."

He snatched off the black hood.

The sudden bright light hurt Aurora's eyes, causing her to squint. She forced them open, eager to see her surroundings. All she caught was a fleeting glimpse of a cavernous room piled high with crates and bales before the back of her head seemed to split open.

Her last conscious thought was that someone had slipped the black hood over her head again, consigning her to the world of darkness once again.

Aurora opened her eyes and instantly regretted it. The blinding pain brought tears to her eyes and wrenched a low moan from deep inside her. Her head ached as though she had drunk a vat of claret, and her mouth felt dry and fuzzy, but at least her arm was no longer as stiff and sore. She lay back and closed her eyes, but the pain in her head gnawed at her like a hound worrying a bone.

But at least she was alive.

Aurora's eyes flew open and she ignored the pain this time. Miraculously, those brigands hadn't murdered her. Relief washed over her in wave after wave as she mumbled a hasty prayer of thanks to God. She looked down. They had untied her hands, though her wrists were red and raw from her bonds. Then she sat up and gingerly fumbled along the back of her head until she found a tender lump the size of a robin's egg.

So that's what had happened when they let her out of the carriage. They had struck her unconscious.

She ignored the throbbing and looked around, suddenly curious as to where they had brought her. From the gentle swaying of the tiny room and a porthole displaying the blue sky, Aurora knew at once she was in the cabin of a ship.

She swung her legs over the side of the bunk and waited for the nausea to grip her. Nothing happened. Emboldened, she rose shakily to her feet and tottered over to the door like a baby taking its first steps.

The door was locked from the outside.

"Did you really expect it to be open?" she muttered to herself.

Aurora next went to the porthole and peered out.

Hope coursed through her anew when she spied a brawny sailor swabbing the deck. Fingers trembling with excitement, she unlatched the porthole and opened it.

"Kind sir!" she called. When the sailor looked up, she smiled and said, "I wish to speak to your captain. There's been some mistake."

Much to Aurora's chagrin, the man ignored her.

"Are you deaf?" she snapped, her patience worn thin at last. "I said I want to speak to your captain immediately!"

He turned his back on her and continued swabbing the deck with long, sure strokes.

Aurora swore under her breath, slammed the porthole shut, and began pacing the tiny cabin, the pain in her head receding as her anger grew.

She was on the verge of trying to pound the door down when she heard the unmistakable sound of a key scraping in a lock. Someone was coming to rescue her and set her free.

Aurora started forward as the door swung open. "Thank God you've come," she blurted out. "I . . ." She stopped dead in her tracks as the hot tawny eyes of the ringleader burned into hers.

"You!" she spat, hastily backing away from him.

Aurora's stomach clenched in fear as she stared at her kidnapper. He was a tall man, powerfully built, with a hard, cruel face devoid of mercy or pity. Against his weathered, sun-bronzed skin, those oddly colored eyes glittered deep gold.

This was no highwayman. This was a cutthroat pirate.

"I trust your chambers are to your liking, Lady Silverblade," he said. At least he spoke well, not coarsely like the others.

"Would it matter if they weren't?" she snapped.

"Of course not."

"Why have you kidnapped me?" Aurora demanded with false bravado. "What am I doing on this ship and where are you taking me?"

He raised shaggy dark brows in mock surprise. "I

need hardly remind you, Lady Silverblade, that you are in no position to make demands of anyone."

"If it's money you want, my husband will pay handsomely for my release and return. I give you my word that no questions will be asked."

The pirate threw back his head and laughed.

"And what, may I ask, is so amusing?" Aurora asked in her haughtiest voice.

"You are, Lady Silverblade. Your husband will pay handsomely for your return? I rather doubt it."

"What are you saying? Of course he will!"

He grinned, revealing sharp, wolfish teeth. "Why should he, when he is the one who hired me and my men to dispose of you?"

"Nicholas? Hire you?" she scoffed in disbelief. "You are a most unconvincing liar, Mr. Whoever-you-are."

The pirate's smile died and his bronzed skin darkened angrily. "Jeer all you like, my fine Lady Silverblade, but listen well. Your beloved husband hired me to intercept your carriage on its way back to Silverblade and to take you on a sea voyage—a very brief sea voyage."

"That's a lie! Nicholas would never be a party to kidnapping and"—she swallowed hard—"murder."

The man shrugged. "You evidently don't know your husband as well as you think. He is as ruthless as I am. He would do anything to rid himself of an unwanted, childless wife."

An unwanted, childless wife . . .

Suddenly the walls of the tiny cabin seemed to close in on Aurora. She tried to breathe and couldn't. She watched helplessly as the pirate spun away from her, then vanished completely into a widening black void.

She was being smothered . . . and then she awoke gasping and sputtering, to find her face and the front of her dress sopping wet. She knew at once that she had fainted and that her captor had thrown water in her face to revive her.

He was standing beside her bunk and staring down at her with a crooked, contemptuous leer, his hands on his lean hips.

Aurora watched out of heartsick glazed eyes as he reached into his waistcoat pocket. He took out something and forcibly pressed it into her hand, smiling in amusement when she flinched as his fingers touched hers briefly.

Then her captor laughed, turned on his heel, and strode out of the cabin without another word. He started whistling a jaunty tune as he locked the door securely behind him and left Aurora to ponder what he had just told her.

She didn't even need to look down to identify what he had given her. The carved jade felt so cool in the palm of her hand. She squeezed her eyes shut, forcing helpless tears to run down her temples.

There was only one person who could have given that brigand Nicholas' jade snuff bottle. And that was Nicholas himself.

The sun was setting in all its fiery glory, but Aurora didn't notice.

She had spent the entire day lying listlessly in her bunk staring at the ceiling out of shocked, lifeless eyes and trying to convince herself that Nicholas had no part in this diabolical scheme. But when she looked at the snuff bottle, she realized she was only deluding herself.

Then she would recall his final words to her: "If one of us decides that we don't wish to be married to the other, I'm sure we can find something to remedy the situation."

His remedy? Hire a gang of unscrupulous pirates to abduct her and throw her overboard when they reached the open sea.

She wondered fleetingly how he was going to explain her mysterious disappearance to her family and friends. Perhaps he would claim she ran off with one of her admirers or met with foul play en route to Silverblade. Tom the driver and his companion would never tell. Nicholas was a wealthy, powerful man with many influential friends. Everyone would believe whatever tale he chose to tell. After all, a wife was nothing more than another possession.

Aurora knew why he had done it. He needed an heir and she couldn't provide one. Now he would be free to marry someone else, someone who could give him what he needed. Perhaps he would find a way to be with Mrs. Littlewood at long last.

Suddenly the thought of that woman taking her place rekindled Aurora's spirit, her overwhelming need and will to live. She rose and looked out the porthole, her startled eyes staring in disbelief.

There, on the horizon, was land.

Aurora's hand flew to her mouth to stifle her hopeful cry. The ship hadn't yet reached open sea. There was a chance—albeit a slim one—that she could dive over the side and swim to freedom. But she had to think of a way to get out of the cabin first. That would be crucial to any escape attempt.

Aurora bided her time, her brain working furiously. She stared out the porthole, watching the orange glow of sunset gradually fade into purple-and-gold twilight. Soon her cabin was so dark she could barely discern its meager furnishings.

Just when she began wondering if her captors were going to leave her sitting in the dark, Aurora heard the door creak open. She tucked her skirts beneath her and cowered on her bunk, trying her best to look demoralized and dispirited.

Her ruse must have been successful, for the man accompanying the leader grinned and said, " 'Er ladyship doesn't look so fine and grand now, does she?"

Aurora recognized the voice as belonging to the man who had cupped her bottom and shoved her into the carriage. She kept her face turned to the wall lest he see the hatred she felt for him mirrored in her eyes.

The leader replied, "That's because she's resigned to her fate," as he lit a candle.

" 'Ere's yer supper, yer ladyship," the other man said, his shoulders shaking with suppressed laughter as he set a plate down on the small table. "Don't see why we be botherin' feedin' you. Yer only gonna be fish bait yerself tomorrow."

Both men roared with lewd, suggestive laughter, sending shivers down Aurora's spine.

"I say we throw the bitch overboard now," the other man said, "but not until me'n the crew 'ave a bit of sport with 'er."

"Not within plain sight of land," the leader said. "Once we weigh anchor and reach the open sea, you can do what you like with her before we throw her overboard."

His companion smacked his lips in relish. "Wait until yer see whats I have planned for you, darlin'. You'll like it real fine. When I'm through with ye, you'll be beggin' to be thrown overboard!"

Aurora bawled and forced tears to stream down her face to hide her elation. These two fools didn't realize it, but they had just given her a precious gift—the gift of time.

"Aw, now see what you've gone and done?" the leader said with false sympathy. "You've made her ladyship cry."

The two men laughed again and Aurora cowered and trembled convincingly.

Finally tiring of making sport of her, the leader said, "There's your supper and a candle so you don't have to eat it in the dark. Don't abuse my kindness by trying to burn down my ship, or you'll die by a less-pleasant method than drowning."

When Aurora was alone, her lip curled into a sneer. "So I'm to be fish bait, am I? Not as long as I have breath in my body, you filthy bastards."

Her stomach heaved when she sniffed the greasy stew congealing on her plate. She took the plate over to her bunk and scraped off the foul concoction, then covered it with the pillow. Even if she dived to a watery grave, she would not be sleeping in this bunk tonight.

Then she stared out the porthole and waited. Much to her delight, she saw a full moon come rising out of the east, a beacon that would lead the way once the time came.

She listened. As the moon gradually rose higher, the ship grew quiet. Aurora took a deep breath to steady her quaking insides. It was time. She stripped down to her bodice and drawers, then concealed her half-dressed state with her voluminous black cloak.

She went to the locked door and began pounding on it. Within seconds the key turned in the lock and the door swung open to reveal a young-looking sailor Aurora hadn't seen before.

Much to her dismay, he seemed as hard and cruel as the others, but she faced him squarely and bestowed on him her brightest smile. "My quarters are so cramped and I long for a breath of fresh air. May I be allowed to walk the deck? Just for a few minutes? Please?" she added in a wheedling voice, while she fluttered her eyelashes helplessly.

His eyes narrowed in mistrust. "I dunno, miss. The cap'n, he said—"

"Oh, please. You seem so different from the others. I can tell you're a good, kind man. What harm could it do? Where could I possibly go? You could watch me every second. I promise I'll be no trouble, no trouble at all."

From down below, she heard raucous laughter and the faint sound of sea chanties being sung out of tune by drunken voices. Before her, the sailor scowled, unable to make up his mind. If only she had something to bribe him with . . .

She happened to glance down at her hand and noticed in some surprise that the sapphire betrothal ring Nicholas had given her was still on her finger. This was no time to be sentimental. Aurora resolutely tugged it off and held it out to the sailor.

"I'll give you this ring if you just let me walk around the deck for a little while. The stone is called a sapphire, and it's very rare and valuable. If you sell it, you can make yourself a tidy little fortune. No one else on this ship would know. And just for letting me out for a little walk."

His eyes grew huge with greed and he grinned. "Aw right, miss," he agreed, taking the ring. "I'll let you out for a bit o' fresh air. Don't see the harm in it, seein' as how you'll be dyin' tomorrow. But the minute the cap'n comes on deck, it's back inside you go."

Aurora's smile was radiant as she forced herself to place a grateful hand on his brawny, hairy arm. "Thank you from the bottom of my heart. You are too kind."

The sailor stood aside to let her pass, and Aurora stepped out on deck. She breathed deeply of the salt sea air, finding it cool and refreshing after the stuffiness of her cabin. At least the pain in her head had dwindled. Then she looked around to get her bearings and devise a plan.

The ship was anchored several miles offshore. Aurora could see a craggy coastline in the ghostly silver light of the moon, hear the faint crash of breakers against the rocks in the distance. She didn't know whether it was the coast of England or some other country, but she didn't care. She drew a tremulous breath. The land looked so far away. Could she possibly swim such a distance?

She clamped her teeth together to keep them from chattering with stone-cold fear. She was going to die tomorrow in any case, so at least she would die valiantly, attempting to escape. It was a chance she had to take.

Aurora looked around again. The sailor who had freed her was the only one on deck. The rest of the men were below, singing and drinking. Her heart quickened. She had to move fast.

She strolled across the deck toward the front of the ship. Her watchdog, figuring she couldn't possibly escape, stayed behind to examine the ring more closely by the light of a lantern. It was exactly what Aurora needed.

She loosened her cloak and placed her hands on the railing, then quickly sprang up with the agility of a cat pouncing. Behind her she heard the sailor's warning cry and heavy booted footsteps racing across the deck to stop her. Down below loomed the water, black and bottomless.

Aurora balanced herself precariously on the railing for one split second. Then she stretched out her arms and dived just as Conor had taught her all those summers ago in Ireland. She heard the sailor curse as he snatched for her and missed, then shouted, "Man overboard! Man overboard!"

Aurora plummeted down, down, down. Just before she sliced the gently rolling surface of the sea, she felt her cloak fall away. Then the water closed over her head, engulfing her.

It was cold, dark, and oh so seductively quiet. As she continued to plummet through the blackness, Aurora almost succumbed to the peace and tranquillity of the sea. Drowning was reputed to be an easy death if one didn't struggle, but her survival instinct was stronger. She stopped her headlong dive and started struggling to the surface. Even in the dark water, the massive hull of the ship was even darker. Though the salt water stung her eyes, Aurora forced them open and searched for the spot where she planned to surface.

Finally, her lungs bursting, she came up alongside the bow of the ship. Gasping hard for breath, Aurora shook the water out of her eyes and clung to the ship's slippery surface with stiff fingers, careful not to be seen. She listened. She could hear shouting, cursing, and hurried footsteps, but she couldn't discern what was being said.

She waited for the sound of a lifeboat being lowered into the water to search for her, but there was nothing, not even a telltale splash. Since her cloak was floating on the water and no one had seen her bob to the surface, perhaps they assumed Aurora had drowned, preferring to take her own life to being thrown overboard tomorrow. She prayed fervently that that was the case.

Aurora's breathing steadied, returning to normal. She looked up at the ship's prow and noticed an unusual double figurehead of two women illuminated by the moonlight. She squinted to read the ship's name engraved on a brass plaque, but the letters ran together in an unintelligible line.

Suddenly she shivered uncontrollably. She knew she would have to make for shore before she expired of the cold. She would just have to risk someone seeing her when next she surfaced for air.

She uttered a quick prayer, took a deep breath, and slipped back into the vast dark sea.

A lone horseman came galloping along the narrow track that followed the winding coastline.

Suddenly he reined in his mount and glanced furtively over his shoulder. All he saw was barren countryside and he grinned in satisfaction. His luck had held. He had eluded them again.

"Good work, old fellow," he murmured to his mount as he slapped the horse's lathered neck. "You deserve a rest. You can walk the rest of the way, and when we arrive, there will be an extra measure of oats waiting."

The horse nodded as if he understood, and adjusted his gait accordingly

His rider reached into his waistcoat pocket, took out a small leather pouch, and gleefully tossed it into the air. The pouch was heavy and jingled when the horseman caught it in one hand.

He grinned again as he tucked away his prize and relaxed his guard. He was out of danger now. He could afford to appreciate this fine moonlit night, with the rough countryside to his right and the shimmering sea to his left.

As his horse made its way along the cliff trail, the rider looked out to sea. In the distance, illuminated by moonlight, was a ship, its billowing sails filled with the night's breeze.

"Smugglers, I'll be bound," he muttered. "Doesn't look like a revenue cutter to me. Well, who are we to judge how a man makes his living, eh, old fellow?"

Suddenly something caught his eye on the beach below. He halted his horse and stared. At first he thought it was an unusual rock formation and was about to ignore it and ride away. Then he noticed an outstretched arm and realized it was a body.

"Poor devil," he muttered with a shudder. "He must have drowned. Don't see no evidence of the wreckers at work tonight."

For the second time he was about to turn his horse and ride away, then stopped. He owed it to himself to investigate. After all, the poor devil could be wearing a gold ring.

The horseman grinned. "Wouldn't do to let someone else profit, now, would it, especially since I seen it first?"

He turned his horse toward a narrow track that wound down the hillside to the beach below. Within minutes he was cantering across the smooth silver sands to where the body lay. He halted his horse and looked down, his face the very picture of surprise.

It was a woman. In the moonlight she looked like an exquisite marble statue he had once seen in Lady Belcourt's garden. She was lying on her back, probably in the exact spot where the cruel sea had left her, with one arm outstretched as if in supplication for her life. Wet sand and seaweed clung to her. The waves and rocks had pounded and torn her clothing into tatters, leaving her nearly naked and vulnerable.

"What a murderin' shame," he said aloud as his gaze roved over her slender, finely made form, lingering on one perfect exposed breast.

But pity didn't deter him. No one could help her now. He swung down from his horse and knelt beside her lifeless form. He reached for her left hand in the hopes of finding a betrothal or wedding ring there and smiled when he saw a heavy gold band there.

Suddenly his smile faded and he scowled as his fingers touched her resilient flesh. Her body was cold, but it was not quite the cold of death. The horseman knew the difference. This skin was still warm deep below. He whipped off his cocked hat and placed his ear against her chest.

Her heartbeat was feeble, but she was alive. Just barely.

He rose to his feet, debating what to do. If he left her here, she would surely die of cold and exposure and the scavenger birds would pick at her until there was nothing left but bleached bones. But he wasn't sure how Ursula would react if he foisted this lovely mermaid on her. It was either the woman's life or Ursula's blind jealousy.

Without giving Ursula a second thought, he untied his heavy cloak and whipped it off. Then he knelt again and gently wrapped the woman in its warm, life-saving folds.

"I hope I don't live to regret this, fair lady," he muttered to the unconscious form.

He had no difficulty lifting her into his arms, for she weighed no more than a mastiff. Then he slung her across the pommel of his saddle and swung right up behind her.

"Sula, do forgive me," he said before touching his heel to his horse's side and riding away from the shore.

17

THE light in heaven was dazzling.

Aurora opened her eyes, fully expecting to find her parents and Tim waiting to welcome her to the hereafter. Instead, she saw a plain small chamber with spotless whitewashed walls and filled to overflowing with bright sunlight. The room contained just a few pieces of simple furniture and the wide-planked wood floors were bare of carpeting but clean. Aurora herself was lying in a firm narrow bed without a canopy, a warm coverlet pulled up to her chin. As she peered beneath the covers just to reassure herself that her body was all in one piece, she noticed her undergarments had been replaced by a night rail of faded blue cotton that had been washed so many times it was as soft as the finest silk.

She was not dead, she was very much alive—sore and exhausted, but alive. Helpless tears of gratitude welled up in her eyes and she uttered a quick prayer of thanks.

She tried to recall what had happened to her after she had struck out for shore, but the images were so vague and fuzzy in her mind. All she remembered was swimming and swimming until her body went numb from the cold seawater and she couldn't swim anymore. Her last conscious thought was of being swept along a strong current and scraped against some jagged rocks while waves crashed over her, choking her and beating her senseless.

Aurora looked around at her humble surroundings again. Obviously someone had found her and brought her to shelter.

Suddenly the door opened slowly and silently and a young girl in a mobcap and immaculate white apron came tiptoeing in carrying a tray.

Her blue eyes grew round with surprise. "Goodness me, miss. You're awake at last."

Aurora managed a feeble smile. "How long have I been sleeping?"

"I heard Mistress Hunt tell Ruth that Master Jack found you on the beach the night before last, so that would make it almost two whole days you been sleepin'."

The efficient maid bustled in, set the tray down on a rickety table, and began fluffing Aurora's pillows so she could sit up in bed. "Are you well enough to have some hot chocolate and rolls? Just out of the oven, they are, crusty and delicious. I can vouch for that."

Aurora's empty stomach growled in response and she laughed. "I'm so famished I could eat an ox."

As the maid poured the chocolate into a thick crockery cup, she said, "My name is Caroline Tregellis, but everyone calls me Caro."

Aurora almost blurted out her real name, but restrained herself just in time. She didn't know where she was or who this Mistress Hunt and Master Jack were. They could be her enemies, and to reveal her true identity might place her in grave danger. Nicholas had taught her well by his example. She would trust no one.

"My name is Diana," she said, thinking quickly. "Diana Timothy." Surely the combination of her sister's and brother's names would be easy enough to remember. She would just have to be very careful to answer to her new name whenever someone addressed her.

"It's a pleasure to make your acquaintance," Caro said, bobbing her a curtsy and handing her the steaming cup. "And I'm right pleased you're going to be well."

Aurora took several sips of the beverage, then said, "Caro, what is this place?"

"The Jolly Wife Inn."

"And where might that be?"

"Why near the village of Porthallow, of course. In Cornwall."

Cornwall, where Diana lived. Aurora's hopes soared to the ceiling. She could seek protection with her sister. Once she explained to Diana that Nicholas had tried to murder her, she would be safe. Or would she?

Suddenly Aurora was assailed by fresh doubts. She remembered all too well that it was she who had inadvertently come between Diana and Overton. What if she sought refuge with Diana a second time and found herself the object of Lord Penhall's desires? She couldn't risk spoiling Diana's chance for happiness again, no matter what the cost to herself.

What if Diana didn't want to risk having her sister around to tempt her current protector? She could simply refuse to believe Aurora's story and send her back to Nicholas. Aurora did not think her husband would fail a second time in his efforts to rid himself of his childless wife.

Aurora strengthened her resolve. She would trust no one, not even her own sister. Her life depended on it.

After finishing her chocolate, Aurora proceeded to devour three rolls spread with butter and warm honey while Caro busied herself tidying up the room.

When Aurora was finished, the maid said, "Now that you've eaten and gotten your strength back, you'll be fit to face Mistress Hunt."

Aurora grimaced. "I don't think I want to face Mistress Hunt. You make her sound like a mean old witch."

Caro giggled. "Goodness me! I didn't mean to. She's not that old, really, and she's a very handsome woman. She's a widow. Her husband named this inn after her, so that tells you something about her, and when he died, she took to running it herself. She's a hard woman to please and she puts on airs above her station, but she's fair and she treats her maids decent. Listen to me, running off at the mouth. Mistress Hunt won't stand for gossiping chambermaids, so I'd best be careful or I'll find myself out of work."

"I'm sure I'll find her to be a lovely woman," Aurora said. "She must be kindness itself to give refuge to a stranger."

Caro shrugged. "I think your being here was more Master Jack's doing than Mistress Hunt's." Then she got a faraway look in her eyes and murmured dreamily, "I wouldn't mind being rescued by Master Jack and having him carry me off on that fine black horse of his." Suddenly Caro remembered herself and blushed. "Goodness me, I've said quite enough. I'll tell the mistress you're awake."

Before Aurora could ask her about this mysterious Master Jack, Caro bustled out of the room and closed the door behind her.

Several minutes later, there came a knock at the door, and when Aurora bade her caller enter, a tall, dignified woman she guessed to be in her late thirties swept into the room. Judging by her authoritative demeanor, this must be Mrs. Hunt, her benefactress.

"I'm delighted to see you awake at last, Miss Timothy," she said in a refined voice that Aurora suspected was more the result of practice than breeding. "You gave us all quite a scare." She approached the bed and nodded. "I am Mrs. Ursula Hunt, the innkeeper of the Jolly Wife."

Aurora noticed the woman's hands were not chapped and red, but smooth and well-cared-for, the nails clean and unbroken. She doubted that Mrs. Hunt scrubbed floors or emptied chamber pots in her inn.

"How do you do, Mrs. Hunt?" she said. "I will forever be in your debt for saving my life."

"No one in need is ever turned away from the Jolly Wife," she said.

"You are too kind."

Now Mrs. Hunt pulled up a straight-backed chair beside Aurora's bed and sat down. Her eyes, a deep shade of green that contrasted strikingly with her white skin and black hair, darkened further with curiosity.

"Are you well enough to tell me what happened to you, Miss Timothy?" she began, her voice soft with sympathy. "How did you come to be lying on the beach in the dead of night? Were you swept overboard from a passing ship? And if that is the case, why didn't they search for you?"

Aurora placed trembling fingers to her forehead. "I beg your pardon, Mrs. Hunt, but it is all still so very painful to me. I can't discuss it just yet. Do give me a little more time to rest, and then I shall reveal all to you."

Mrs. Hunt rose and smiled down at her. "Of course. I didn't mean to disturb you so soon after your ordeal, Miss Timothy. Why don't I return after you've had a chance to regain your strength and we can talk then?"

Aurora managed a shaky smile. "Thank you, Mrs. Hunt. You are very kind and understanding."

"Just rest, Miss Timothy. We'll talk later."

With that, she left.

When she was alone again, Aurora was overwhelmed by panic. She couldn't possibly tell Mrs. Hunt her true identity and that her husband, a peer of the realm, had tried to dispose of her. No one would believe her. There had to be another way.

By the time she heard someone knock once again, Aurora had concocted a plan and had rehearsed just what she would say.

Expecting Mrs. Hunt to walk through the door, Aurora gasped when she saw a man instead.

She pulled the coverlet up to her chin and glared at him indignantly. "Sir, I beg your pardon! I believe you have entered the wrong room. I'll thank you to leave at once."

The man gave her a slow, lazy smile, baring even white teeth and causing a dimple to appear in his right cheek. He sauntered into the room as if he owned it and bowed low.

"If you are Miss Diana Timothy, then I am in the right room," he drawled, his voice as lazy as his smile. "I am Jack Pierce, at your service."

As she studied her rescuer, Aurora had the uneasy feeling that she had met him somewhere before. Yet she knew she would have remembered him if she had, for he was a striking young man in his mid-twenties. Then it came to her in a flash: Jack Pierce reminded her of Tim.

It wasn't a physical resemblance, for Tim had been a blue-eyed redhead like Aurora, while Pierce was swarthy and no doubt sported a crop of thick black hair beneath his periwig. Rather, it was the similar devil-may-care twinkle in his eye, his affable charm, and his commanding way of entering a room. From what Aurora remembered of her brother, there was a presence about him that attracted other people to him like flies to honey, and she sensed this same quality in Jack Pierce. No wonder Caro daydreamed about this dashing specimen of the male sex.

"So you are the man who saved my life. Sir, I owe you a debt of gratitude I can never hope to repay."

Eyes as soft as brown velvet twinkled mischievously. "I am always honored to come to the aid of a lady in distress, especially one as lovely as yourself, Miss Timothy."

Another man who enjoyed rescuing a lady in distress. . . . Aurora took a deep breath to keep the tears from springing to her eyes and forced all thoughts of Nicholas from her mind.

"Gallant as well as handsome," was her bantering reply. Then she added, "Tell me, Mr. Pierce, how did you happen to find me?"

He crossed the room to rest one elegant booted foot against the fireplace fender in a gesture that once again reminded Aurora of Nicholas. "I just happened to be riding by the beach when I noticed a body lying there. At first I thought someone had drowned, so I almost kept right on riding."

Aurora shuddered. "How fortunate for me that you changed your mind."

He grinned. "Very fortunate indeed. I went down to investigate, and discovered you were alive. So I wrapped you in my cloak to warm you, slung you over my saddle, and carried you back here to the Jolly Wife. Ursula—Mrs. Hunt—tended your hurts herself."

Suddenly, as if on cue, Mrs. Hunt herself appeared in the doorway. "There you are," she said to Jack, giving Aurora a puzzlingly reproachful glance. "Poor Miss Timothy needs her rest. You shouldn't be in here bothering her."

"Oh, Mr. Pierce wasn't bothering me, Mrs. Hunt," Aurora protested. "He was just telling me how he rescued me."

Jack Pierce's smile died and he looked most annoyed with Mrs. Hunt. "Miss Timothy seems well rested to me, Ursula. I was just about to ask her how she happened to find herself in the ocean."

Once again Mrs. Hunt seated herself on the chair beside Aurora's bed. "I too would be interested in hearing your tale, Miss Timothy."

Aurora sighed and picked at the coverlet. She was about to give the performance of her life, playing a part that even Bess the actress would envy.

"I have been reluctant to tell you my tale, Mrs. Hunt, because I fear for my life."

Mrs. Hunt and Jack Pierce exchanged brief looks.

"There!" Aurora wailed dramatically, throwing up her hands. "I can see you don't believe me."

"Tell us your tale and let us be the judge," Mrs. Hunt said, her manner guarded and suspicious.

Aurora took a deep shuddering breath to give herself the courage to tell her tale just as she had rehearsed it. "I am a married woman. I was fleeing to my sister's home in Ireland to escape my cruel husband when I was kidnapped by brigands. Last night, before they could kill me, I managed to jump off their ship and swim for shore." She sniffed loudly and her voice quavered on a watery note. "That is how I came to be on the shore."

Mrs. Hunt looked at Jack Pierce again, her eyes filled with skepticism. Then she looked back at Aurora. "Who would want to kill you?"

"My husband."

"How do you know it was your husband that wanted you dead?"

"The leader told me. He also showed me an item of my husband's, a snuffbox I recognized as belonging to him. It was a unique snuffbox. The only way that man could have gotten it was if my husband gave it to him."

"I believe her," Jack said stoutly. "The night I found her, I saw a ship sailing away. No one but brigands would throw a woman overboard to drown."

"Please don't send me back to my husband," Aurora pleaded, folding her hands and extending them. "He will surely kill me if you do."

Mrs. Hunt rose and smiled reassuringly. "Have no fear, Mrs. Timothy. Ursula Hunt isn't about to turn you out. You can stay here until you are well enough." But not a moment longer, was her unspoken warning.

"Thank you," Aurora murmured, her eyes misting over with fresh tears. "You are both too kind."

Mrs. Hunt started for the door, and when she realized that Jack was dallying behind, she turned and said pointedly, "Coming, Jack?" She obviously didn't like the idea of the man remaining alone with another woman.

"I'm right behind you," he replied with a dimpled smile at Aurora, and they both left.

When she was alone, Aurora leaned back against her pillows in relief. They believed her tale. Although what she had told them was close to the truth, she knew she would still have to be very careful not to contradict herself, because lies had an insidious way of trapping the person who told them. She would have to be on guard at all times lest she give herself away.

She rolled over on her side and slept.

Several days later she had physically recuperated from her ordeal and was allowed to leave her bed.

Aurora sat on the top of the sharply sloping hill, the skirts of her borrowed homespun gown spread on the grass about her. Below, the inn yard of the Jolly Wife bustled with activity and noise, for one coach had just driven up, while several carriages were preparing to leave. The air was thick with the sounds of hooves ringing on cobblestones, neighing horses, and the shouts of the ostlers as they changed the coach's team. But despite all the activity, Aurora felt bereft and alone.

She squinted in the strong sunlight and stared out at the sea, shimmering in the distance like her lost sapphire ring. She still resisted believing that Nicholas had tried to have her killed. She still loved him, even now, in spite of all she had suffered. Yet while her heart steadfastly refused to believe him guilty, her head told her otherwise.

She could not ignore the irrefutable evidence of the Chinese snuff bottle. Wesley had assured her it was rare and one-of-a-kind, and if perchance it had been stolen, Aurora would have known about it. No, the only way her abductors could have obtained it was if Nicholas himself had given it to them.

Still, Aurora fought against her own suspicions. "No! Nicholas couldn't be so cruel. I know him! He would have at least spared me the knowledge that he had ordered my death."

Yet in the past few weeks he had treated her with such indifference and scorching disdain, she wondered if she really knew him at all.

"May I join you?"

The lilting masculine voice jolted Aurora out of her reverie. She looked up to find Jack Pierce idly standing there, his slight weight resting on one leg as he regarded her with a disarming smile.

"Please do."

He dropped down beside her, then leaned back and negligently propped himself up on one elbow. He wore no coat or waistcoat this morning, just a white lawn shirt carelessly left open to the waist and tucked into black breeches that hugged his narrow hips and thighs like a glove.

Aurora glanced at him surreptitiously. Where his shirt was open, she could see his bronzed, muscular chest sprinkled with black, curling hairs, but she felt no heady rush of desire the way she did when she gazed upon Nicholas' body. She suspected Jack would be disappointed if he knew she was impervious to his considerable virility, for it had not taken Aurora long to deduce that he considered himself irresistible to all women. One had only to watch him reduce poor Caro to blushes and stammers with a flattering remark or a playful cuff under the chin to know that.

Still, his blatant masculinity and closeness did not make Aurora uneasy. Thinking of him as a brother robbed him of an aura of seductiveness.

When the silence between them had gone on too

long, Aurora said, "The Jolly Wife looks like a most prosperous inn."

Jack shrugged. "Prosperity comes and goes, depending on how many carriages stop this way. Ursula has known some lean times, but then, so has everyone else in this part of the country. The Cornish are hearty, independent folk. They find ways to survive."

Aurora glanced over at him. Ever since her arrival at the inn, she had wondered just what Jack Pierce did to earn his keep. He wasn't an ostler and he didn't tend the coffee room. But perhaps he performed other "services" for Ursula for his room and board. In any case, Aurora thought it prudent to keep her suspicions to herself.

"So you were born here in Cornwall?" she said, trying to prompt him to speak about himself.

Jack shook his head. "I was born in Devon, near Exeter. My father was a tenant farmer, but I had no taste for such a hard, unrewarding life. Since I always was a handsome, charming lad," he added with another quick grin and a broad wink, "I went into service. I became a footman for the widowed Lady Belcourt."

The laughter left his voice when he said the woman's name, and his face hardened into a savage mask that sent a shiver of fear running down Aurora's arms.

"Why aren't you still in her employ?" she asked.

Jack looked at her, his expression veiled and guarded now, all traces of mirth gone. Finally he shrugged. "What's the harm in telling you? It's common knowledge. The good lady took a fancy to me and kicked me upstairs. Right into her bedchamber." He glanced at Aurora to see what her reaction would be. When she didn't look shocked, he continued.

"She dressed me like a gentleman and taught me how to behave like one. She wanted to introduce me to all her fine friends, you see, so I had to learn how to behave properly in such refined company. Yes, the good lady certainly gave this poor farmer's son a taste for the finer things in life."

Suddenly his mouth tightened into a thin harsh line. "Then she kicked me out like I was a dog."

Aurora was appalled. "How . . . how cruel!"

"Yes, indeed. There were no more silks and satins for Jack Pierce, and no references."

Aurora knew all too well that without a reference from his last employer, Jack Pierce would never find another position as footman.

Jack shrugged again. "That was more than two years ago. It's over and done with as far as I'm concerned."

Over and done with, like her marriage to Nicholas.

Now Jack's generous, expansive mood returned. "Anything else you want to know about me, feel free to ask."

"What about your family?"

"They're all dead now," he said flatly, without much regret. "So I'm all alone in the world, except for Ursula. What about you?"

Aurora stared out to sea and blinked hard to fight back the tears. "Except for my sister, my family is gone. And the man I married tried to have me killed."

Jack was silent for what seemed like an eternity. Finally he said softly, "But you don't believe it, do you?"

Aurora stiffened and inhaled sharply. Then she looked at him in dismay. "You didn't believe my story, did you?"

"Not the part about your cruel husband. If it's one thing Jack Pierce knows, it's women. I can read 'em like a book, and I can tell when a woman is pining away for her man." He smiled flirtatiously, causing his dimple to appear. "And you, my fair Diana, are pining away for this husband of yours, the lucky man."

It was on the tip of Aurora's tongue to deny it, but she couldn't. She had never felt so bereft and alone, and she needed to trust someone. Jack had saved her life and he seemed sympathetic beneath all his swagger and bluster.

With a groan of anguish Aurora said, "Deep in my heart, I know he's incapable of harming me, yet the evidence against him is so damning. Should I take a chance and return to him? Oh, Jack, I've asked myself that a thousand times. Yet if I do, I may be giving him a second opportunity to murder me." She shuddered.

"And he would not fail this time. He is a very thorough man."

Jack stared out at the horizon, his brow furrowed in thought. Then he said, "Could someone else have wanted your death, someone close to your husband perhaps?"

Suddenly Aurora's eyes widened and her heart began slamming against her ribs in excitement. "Now that you mention it, his grandmother once threatened me if I married her grandson. Perhaps it was she who arranged to have me kidnapped."

But the more she thought about it, the more Aurora realized she couldn't pin the blame on Lady Vivien, no matter how much she would have liked to. Soon after Aurora and Nicholas had arrived in London, they received word the old harridan had become gravely ill, drifting in and out of consciousness, though she was expected to recover. So she hadn't even been in London when Aurora was kidnapped. Even if Lady Vivien had hired someone else to steal the snuff bottle from Nicholas, there was no way she could have learned about Aurora's departure in time to have her kidnapped.

Aurora sighed. "No, I'm afraid she couldn't have done it," she said, and explained why. "I'm afraid my husband is the most logical suspect."

Then she looked at Jack beseechingly. "What should I do? What would you do in my situation?"

Without hesitation he replied, "I wouldn't risk going back to him, that's for sure, even if he is your husband."

That surprised Aurora. "You wouldn't? Why not? You said yourself I've been pining away for him."

He shook his head and grinned lazily. "That may be true, but even though you are a member of the weaker sex, you can't be softhearted when it comes to your life, Diana. If you're wrong about this man . . ." Jack jerked his forefinger across his throat as though someone were slitting it with a knife.

Aurora shuddered and felt sick to her stomach.

"It's a hard, cruel world we live in, Diana Timothy," Jack said, his eyes somber. "I suspect you've led a sheltered life and never learned that. Well, I have, the hard way. And I'm warning you not to trust your heart when your life is at stake."

Suddenly Jack grasped her hand and held it so tightly Aurora couldn't pull away. "We're all alone in the world. We're born alone and we die alone. Somewhere in between, maybe we find someone to comfort us for a little while, if we're lucky. But it never lasts, and we're alone again. Always remember that. It never lasts."

Then he rose, bowed, and went swaggering down the hill.

Aurora sat at the window and stared out across the fields, feeling as bleak and desolate as the countryside wrapped in a thick fog from the sea.

Three weeks had passed since Jack had saved her, and her welcome at the Jolly Wife was wearing thin. Aurora knew this because she had overheard a conversation between Jack and Ursula just that morning as she was walking past the coffee room.

"She can't stay here forever, Jack," Ursula said in a peevish tone. "These are lean times. I'm losing money on her room because I can't let it out to paying guests. And I'll never see a shilling for the food she eats."

"Never knew you to be so mean-spirited, Sula," Jack replied, his voice filled with mild surprise. "I always thought you were a warm and generous woman."

"There's a limit to my generosity, Jack. I've got workers to pay."

"If it's a matter of a bed for Diana to sleep in, she can always share mine."

Aurora had blushed at that, even though she detected a teasing note in Jack's voice.

Then there was silence.

When Ursula spoke, she sounded spiteful and furious. "Is that why you want her here, because you fancy her? You want her for your mistress instead of me?"

"So that's why you're so eager to be rid of her—you're jealous! My Sula is jealous!"

"Do I have reason to be? Tell me the truth, Jack Pierce, or so help me, I'll—"

"You'll what? Turn me in? Is that what you want, to see me swinging from a rope or dangling from the gibbet?" When Sula made no reply, the timbre of Jack's voice changed, becoming soft and beguiling. "No, my dear sweet Sula, you wouldn't do that to your dashing Black Fox, now, would you?"

Again, silence, followed by an urgent gasp. Aurora could imagine what they were doing and she blushed again.

"No, Jack," Sula said, panting, with a catch in her voice, "you know I'd never turn you in. Never. You're my man, Jack." Desperation quickened her speech. "I love you. If you ever left me, I'd—"

"Hush, Sula. You know I'm never going to leave you as long as I have breath in my body."

"Diana is so young . . . so beautiful" was her wistful comment, and Aurora's heart went out to the older woman past her prime.

"True, but so are you, and you are my lady, Ursula."

Silence again.

Finally Ursula surrendered. "Diana can stay as long as she likes."

Aurora slipped back upstairs and returned to her room.

She walked away from the window and twisted her fingers together nervously as she thought about what she had learned today. She had long suspected that Jack and Ursula were lovers, despite the fifteen-year difference in their ages, so that revelation came as no surprise. She shouldn't have been surprised to learn that Jack was involved in something illegal as well.

Aura suspected him of being a smuggler. That would certainly explain why he was riding alone on the beach that night.

She shrugged. It was no concern of hers. She had heard that half the population of Cornwall was engaged in smuggling or wrecking, the common folk and gentry alike, so why should she condemn Jack Pierce? She liked the rogue, and she owed him her life.

She also felt guilty for imposing on Ursula's hospitality.

Suddenly Aurora knew what she had to do. She went downstairs to find Ursula.

She found her in her closet of a study, seated behind a battered old desk, her account book spread out before her. A frown of worry scored her brow.

"Ursula, I must speak with you about a matter of great importance," Aurora said.

If Ursula considered Aurora a rival for Jack's affections, she didn't show it. She smiled benignly. "Yes, Diana, what is it?"

"I realize I have been abusing your hospitality, and I would like to make amends by working for my room and board." Aurora raised her head proudly. "I wish to be a chambermaid, like Caro and Ruth."

Ursula's broad shoulders began shaking with suppressed mirth, and the corners of her mouth twitched as she fought to keep from laughing out loud.

When she regained some semblance of self-control, she said, "I'm afraid that is out of the question, Diana."

"May I ask why? I am strong. I could do the work."

Ursula sat back in her chair and regarded Aurora strangely. Her voice was filled with resentment as she said, "Anyone with eyes in his head can tell you're a lady of quality. Oh, don't deny it. People like me can recognize our betters a mile off."

"Perhaps what you say is true. But that doesn't mean that I can't learn."

Ursula's thick black brows rose nearly to her hairline. "Have you ever emptied chamber pots, Mrs. Timothy, or scrubbed floors until your soft white hands were chapped and callused? Or lugged buckets of hot water up three flights of stairs until someone's bath was filled just to their liking?" When Aurora said nothing, she nodded. "I thought not. But Ruth and Caro do, every day, without complaint."

"I want to do something to earn my room and board, Mrs. Hunt," she insisted stubbornly.

"Jack is earning it for you."

"I won't accept charity!"

"Proud, are we now? Well, take it from me that pride doesn't put a roof over your head or clothes on your back. But I suspect you always took those things for granted until now."

Aurora could think of nothing to say because Ursula spoke the truth.

"Take what Jack Pierce offers and be thankful for it."

Then she returned to her books, wordlessly dismissing Aurora as though she were a servant.

It was well past midnight and Aurora still couldn't sleep. Nicholas haunted her. Every time she closed her eyes, she saw his stern, handsome face, the face she once would have died for. Now she was plagued by doubts, torn by indecision.

Restless, she left her bed, dressed, and headed for the stables. She and horses had always been kindred spirits. Perhaps one of them would give her the answers she sought, the peace her soul craved.

Aurora found the barn dark and redolent of the rich, warm scent of hay and horseflesh. She breathed deeply as she set her candlestick down in a safe place, feeling calm and relaxed among the animals shifting and stamping in their stalls. They were as restless as she was tonight, as if they sensed something was about to happen.

For the next fifteen minutes Aurora went from stall to stall, stroking curious faces and talking in a low, soothing voice. Her expert eye told her none of the animals kept here were of Firelight's caliber, and she was disappointed. She had been looking forward to a long ride on a vigorous horse tomorrow.

Suddenly she heard the unmistakable sound of hoofbeats in the stableyard. Aurora froze. Who was riding in at this late hour? She blew out her candle, crouched low behind one of the stalls, and peered out into the darkness.

Minutes later the stable door swung open, revealing the silhouette of a lone man leading a horse. Aurora heard the sound of tinder being struck; then the stable was bathed in light as the man lit a lantern.

It was Jack, all dressed in black and carrying two pistols in a crossbelt that ran over one shoulder, down across his chest, and rested against his hip. He was leading a sleek, fast-looking black horse that looked as though it had been ridden hard.

As Aurora watched in growing curiosity, Jack led his mount to a stall and began removing his tack. When he finished, he stroked the animal's face fondly.

"Good work tonight, old fellow. They'll never catch up with us now."

Then he went over to a tall stool and began emptying his pockets onto it. Aurora caught the bright flash of gold by lamplight, heard the faint clink of metal striking metal.

Then she knew. Before she could catch herself, she gasped in astonishment.

Jack heard her. He whirled around, one pistol drawn, the cunning, desperate look of a cornered fox on his handsome face.

"Come out before I blow your head off," he snarled.

Aurora stood up and faced him.

"What in the hell are you doing here, Diana?" Judging by his black scowl, he was not pleased to see her. "Why aren't you in bed, where you belong?"

"I couldn't sleep," she replied. She looked at Jack's booty spread about the stool seat. "You're a highwayman, aren't you." It was a statement rather than a question.

His dark eyes turned as hard as obsidian and held no softness, no mercy, reminding Aurora of the men who had abducted her. "It's a shame you had to discover my secret, Diana. I was becoming rather fond of you."

Aurora felt a small skein of fear begin to unravel in the pit of her stomach. "I won't tell anyone, Jack, I swear it. You saved my life. Your secret is safe with me."

The swaggering, devil-may-care ladies' man had vanished. In his place was a merciless criminal, indifferent to all else but his own survival.

"I can't risk it, Diana."

She raised her head defiantly. "What are you going to do to me? Throw me back into the sea where you found me?"

"I could do that. After all, your husband thinks you're dead already. No one would be the wiser."

Aurora took a tentative step forward. "I can't believe you would do that to me, Jack. You're not a murderer."

His eyes remained brittle and hard. "Believe what you like. Didn't I tell you that you can't let your heart rule your head when your life is at stake? Well, mine is at stake right now."

"I said I wouldn't tell a soul. You have my word."

He snorted in derision. "I know all about fine ladies and their word of honor. Lady Belcourt swore up and down she would never cast me aside, and look what happened."

"But I am not Lady Belcourt."

Aurora tried to keep from shaking as her thoughts raced ahead, frantically seeking a way out of this volatile situation. Suddenly a solution so wild, so improbable, presented itself to her that she almost discarded it at once as being too absurd to be considered. But when she saw Jack cock his pistol, she knew she had to do something before he shot her where she stood.

"I will prove to you that I can be trusted," she said desperately.

He eyed her insolently, his dark eyes lingering on her small, high breasts, then traveling down to her boyish hips. Jack grinned. "A tumble between the sheets in exchange for your life? As much as I'm tempted, I think not. I already have a mistress who pleases me."

Aurora's face flushed, but she held his gaze. "I wasn't offering myself to you as a mistress." The next words tumbled out in a rush. "I want to ride with you, Jack. I want to be a highwayman."

His eyes bulged in astonishment. Then he guffawed, causing the horses to stamp the floor in alarm. "You? Ride with me? Women don't ride the high toby. They stay home and wait for their men to return and bed them."

"Not I, Jack Pierce! I'll have you know I can ride and shoot better than most men, yourself included."

The challenge in her voice abruptly cut off Jack's laughter. "Can you, now?"

Aurora stepped closer, making her tone eager and

persuasive, for her life depended on it. "Let me prove myself, Jack. That's all I ask."

"And if you fail?"

"I won't. But if I do . . ." She faltered, then shrugged fatalistically. "You may do with me what you will."

When he still seemed reluctant, she pressed her point home. "If we rode together, one of us could keep our pistols trained on the drivers while the other could relieve the passengers of their valuables. With an accomplice and two more pistols, you could increase your take."

She could see the idea appealed to him, but, being a man, he wasn't about to capitulate right away.

"What if I trust you and you go to the law as soon as my back is turned?" he demanded.

"And risk arrest myself? I'm not a fool, Jack Pierce. I was clever enough to escape from that ship, wasn't I? We'd be in this together. I don't fancy dangling from a rope any more than you do."

"That's what you'd be risking if you rode with me."

Aurora shrugged. "What does it matter? My sister would only return me to my husband, so I'm alone in the world, just like you. I have no friends except you and Ursula. I have to make my own way the only way I know how."

He looked her over again impersonally, as one would judge a piece of horseflesh. "You're a comely parcel of goods, Diana. You could always make your way by finding yourself a man to take care of you."

"Not if I'm dead. Besides, I'd rather die than become a whore, Jack."

Dark eyes burned into hers. "I'll wager you would, Diana," he mused.

"So, will you let me ride with you?" Aurora held her breath, for her life was hanging on Jack's reply.

He lowered his pistol. "I'll have to think about it after I see if you can ride and shoot as you brag. In the meantime, I'm going to sleep with you tonight just to make sure you don't do anything foolish." When he saw Aurora's terrified look, he grinned. "Sorry to disappoint you, but I won't be sharing your bed. I mean to sleep on the floor."

Then he escorted Aurora back to the inn.

In London, Nicholas sat in his study and toyed with
the jade snuff bottle Aurora had given him for
Christmas.

As he traced the carved dragon with his forefinger,
he thought it quite ironic that even though he had sent
Aurora away, she was still here with him, day and
night, a rebellious, irrepressible spirit that even his
anger couldn't dim.

Nicholas leaned back in his wing-backed chair and
groaned aloud. When he had so callously sent her
back to Silverblade, he had thought he wanted to be
rid of her, to have time and privacy to think. He never
dreamed he would miss her so desperately and yearn
for her return. The three weeks she had been gone
seemed like three lifetimes.

He had been terribly cruel and unfair to her. He
realized that now. He had unjustly accused her of
flirting with other men when he himself had withheld
his love from her, leaving her doubtful and confused.

And it was all because of that humiliating wager.

Nicholas rose and paced around the room like a
caged tiger, his thoughts racing. The wager had been a
blow to his considerable masculine pride. Instead of
confiding in Aurora, he had shut her out and kept his
humiliation to himself, letting it fester and grow until
he became so miserable he lashed out at her.

He remembered the last time he had seen her, when
they ate breakfast together before she was to leave. At
the beginning of the meal, she had watched him with
hope in her eyes. But as the meal progressed, the
hope kept fading, growing dimmer and dimmer like
the setting sun. By the end of the meal, it had died.
She rose from the table and left without a backward
glance, listless and broken at last. He hadn't even
gone to the foyer to see her off, though he knew she
had waited there for him, still patient and trusting
right up until the very end.

"Dear God, Aurora," he muttered, "what have I
done to you?"

There was only one thing he could do. He had to

ride to Silverblade and beg her forgiveness on his knees if he had to. Perhaps if he swallowed his pride and explained about the wager, she would understand why he had behaved as he had. He prayed he would not be too late.

Nicholas glanced at the clock on the mantel. Two o'clock in the morning. It would be sheer madness to travel at night, but Nicholas' need to be with Aurora, to hold her in his arms again, to love her as she deserved to be loved, almost overrode common sense. But he restrained himself. It would be daylight in a few hours. He would go to her then.

The moment the carriage pulled up before the entrance to Silverblade, Nicholas flung the door open and stepped out. He took the steps two at a time and set his hat and gloves on the hall table before the majordomo could even blink in surprise.

"Good afternoon," he said. "Where is Lady Silverblade?"

"Good afternoon, your lordship. She is in the salon, playing cards with Lady Vivien."

"The Lady Vivien has finally recovered from her illness, I take it?"

"Yes, your lordship."

A smile tugged at the corners of Nicholas' mouth. Aurora playing cards with his grandmother? This he would have to see for himself.

But when Nicholas strode into the salon, it was not Aurora who was seated across from Lady Vivien, but his mother. He stopped in his tracks and stared at the two women in bewilderment.

Lady Mary smiled broadly. "Why, Nicholas, what an unexpected pleasure to see you here."

"Have the pleasures of London paled so quickly?" Lady Vivien asked while studying her cards.

"I can see that illness has not blunted your sharp tongue, Grandmother," he said. "You're looking well."

She coughed, then sniffed irritably. "You sound almost disappointed." When Nicholas made no comment, she added sarcastically, "I was quite overwhelmed by all the attention you paid to me during my illness."

Nicholas continued to ignore her deliberate baiting and stepped forward to give his mother a perfunctory kiss on the cheek. "Forgive me if I seem surprised, but Simms said that Aurora was here."

Lady Mary regarded him oddly. "Why would he say that when he knows Aurora isn't here? She was in London, with you."

Nicholas straightened as an alarm bell started ringing in his head. "She must be here. I sent her back to Silverblade three weeks ago."

Lady Mary turned ashen beneath her paint. "Nicholas, Aurora never arrived. She is not here."

"Is this some kind of jest, Mother?" Nicholas demanded, his voice rising. "Has Aurora told you she doesn't wish to see me?"

Lady Mary rose now, her astonishment plain. "This is no jest. I am telling you that I have been alone here for the past three weeks. Aurora never arrived!"

"Then where in the hell is she?" Nicholas bellowed, running his hand through his hair in agitation.

Lady Vivien looked up from her cards to regard him out of sly eyes, a self-satisfied smirk on her mouth. "I know where she is. She's run off with one of her admirers. I told you the chit was common, Nicholas, but no one ever listens to an old lady."

"Vivien, hold your tongue!" Lady Mary snapped, incurring the old lady's shocked stare. Then she turned to her son. "Nicholas, what could have possibly happened to her between London and Surrey? Do you think highwaymen attacked the carriage?"

"I don't know, Mother, but I am going to find out." Without another word, Nicholas whirled around and started striding off.

"What are you going to do?" his mother asked, picking up her skirts and hurrying to keep up with him.

Nicholas kept on walking. "First I am going to talk to the men to see if they've heard from the drivers, and then I'm returning to London. Perhaps someone there knows what has happened to my wife."

He stopped only when he felt a restraining hand on his arm and looked down into his mother's worried face.

"Nicholas," she said softly, "Aurora loves you. She has not run off with another man, no matter what your grandmother says."

His smile was bitter. "If she has, she had better pray that I never find her."

Then he bowed and left to find out what had happened to his wife.

Half an hour later, Nicholas' carriage was racing back to London at breakneck speed. Several times he almost yelled to the driver to go faster, but he restrained himself. If the horses were asked to run any faster, they would drop in their traces.

Nicholas rested his head back against the squabs and uttered a dismal sigh. Aurora was in danger. He could sense it deep in his gut, a wrenching fear so strong it rose up and choked him.

His ostlers had assured him that although Lady Silverblade might have left London for Silverblade, she had never arrived. Neither had her carriage or the driver and the man sent to protect them.

Where had they gone?

Nicholas rubbed his chin thoughtfully. His men were very loyal. Since he had given them orders to take Lady Silverblade back to Surrey, they would have done so, even if Aurora tried to countermand those orders and have them drive her somewhere else. No, something had happened to them between London and Surrey, and Nicholas feared the worst.

"Aurora, where in the hell are you?" he muttered. But no one answered.

18

AURORA stood at the window and stared out across the fields as a stiff wind pelted a fresh barrage of raindrops against the glass. She shivered and drew her shawl more closely about her to ward off the bone-chilling damp and continued her vigil.

Where was he? she wondered impatiently. Jack had ridden off four days ago on some mysterious errand he hadn't revealed to anyone, even Ursula. No one had seen him since.

Aurora knotted her fingers together nervously as she scanned the landscape, rendered dull and drab by the gray clouds hanging so low they seemed to touch the fields. She felt as though they were weighing her down, crushing the optimism out of her and making her feel sad and dispirited.

She listened, but all she heard was the virulent hiss of rain against the roof. The inn was quiet today. There were no lodgers, so there were no homey, comforting sounds of muffled footsteps in the hall, no echoes of laughter drifting up from the coffee room below. Even the innyard was empty, save for a mangy gray cat darting for a dry bit of cover. The Jolly Wife was hushed and expectant, waiting for Jack to return.

Then Aurora saw the rider.

She blinked several times as the figure topping the rise appeared to be swallowed up by those low-hanging clouds. But just as suddenly, he reappeared, coming into sharper focus as the horse descended the hill. Only there were two horses, one mounted and a second one being led. The one being ridden looked suspiciously like Jack's Blackamoor.

A grin split Aurora's face as she whirled away from the window and went tearing out of her room, her skirts flying out behind her.

"He's back!" she shouted as she dashed down the corridor and raced down the stairs.

Just as Aurora reached the foot of the stairs, Ursula came rushing out of her study, attracted by all the commotion.

"Jack's returned," Aurora babbled. "I saw him crossing the field from my upstairs window."

"Thank God!" Ursula cried, all the tension and worry fleeing from her face. She bustled across the coffee room, with Aurora not far behind, and flung open the door, unmindful of the torrential rain wetting the floor that Ruth and Caro had just finished scrubbing and polishing.

Aurora hung back. Ursula should be the first one to greet Jack, not she. Aurora knew the older woman resented her enough already without her adding to it.

They waited together in silence, shivering and watching their breath turn to white mist in the cold, damp air. But neither of them made a move to don a shawl or close the door.

Jack saw them the moment he rode into the innyard. Ursula was waiting for him as always, framed in the doorway, her eyes locked on his face, her expression hopeful and relieved. He could just see Diana peering over Sula's shoulder, her lovely face radiant with welcome, her blazing red hair as warm and inviting as a fire on a winter's day. Ever since he had rescued the beautiful young Diana, Jack had felt himself irresistibly drawn to her. She was fresh and vital, this sparkling sea sprite, always dancing just out of his reach like some tantalizing vision. Unlike Caro and Ursula, Diana seemed impervious to his handsome face and roguish demeanor, and that perversely made him want her even more.

Jack knew he would have to be careful. He forced his gaze back to Sula and kept it there, lest he rouse her suspicions. If she even suspected he wanted the red-headed waif for himself . . .

"Sula!" He raised his voice so she could hear him over the din of the driving rain.

She came flying out of the inn to meet him, splashing through puddles like a carefree child, unmindful of the rain that soaked her through in seconds and plastered her dark hair to her head.

"Jack, thank God you're all right!"

She would have pulled him right out of the saddle bodily if he hadn't dismounted first. The moment his feet touched the ground, Ursula was all over him, her arms clasped around his waist, her mouth crushed insistently against his.

Jack chuckled as he squeezed her pliant body to him and kissed her back as hard as she wanted, but it was Diana that his eyes sought over the top of Ursula's dark head.

Laughing, Jack disengaged himself from Ursula, who had curled herself around him as tight as an eel. "If we don't get out of this rain this instant, my darling Sula, both of us will catch our deaths out here."

"I am just so happy to see you, Jack," she said, her eyes never leaving his face as he put his arm around her. "I was so worried about you." She looked him up and down like a mother hen. "You're soaked to the skin!"

He grinned. "Then I guess you shall just have to take my clothes off and dry me."

Sula's eye brightened in expectation.

"But first," Jack said, leaving her at the doorway, "I have to tend to my horses." He gave Ursula a resounding smack across her ample bottom. "I'll be right back." Then he nodded at Diana and rushed to take his two horses to the stables.

When he returned, he found Diana waiting for him.

"Welcome back, Jack," she said. "Where did you get that magnificent horse you were leading?"

He resisted the impulse to swat Diana on the bottom as well, for he knew she would never tolerate it. Then he grinned again and lowered his voice. "He's a present for you."

"For me?" Diana's eyes grew as round as blue china cups.

He nodded. "A highwayman is only as good as the horse he rides. That one comes from the Duke of Derry's prime racing stock."

"You stole him?"

Jack shrugged nonchalantly. "Don't look so surprised. How else was I supposed to get him for you? If you're going to ride with me, I can't have you slowing me down, now, can I? Not when our lives depend on it."

Before Diana could say a word, Ursula came striding into the coffee room, her lips pursed into a thin line of displeasure at seeing them together. But all she said was, "There's a fire in your room, Jack, and the water is boiling for your bath. You'd better get out of those wet clothes before you catch your death."

He winked at Diana behind Ursula's back, then followed his mistress upstairs to his room.

Shivering with a mixture of cold and anticipation, they stood before the blazing fire, stripped quickly, and rubbed each other dry with coarse, scratchy towels. Then Jack drew Ursula down on his bed and made love to her roughly, the way she liked, until they were both so hot that steam would have risen from their naked bodies had the room been any colder.

Finally, when they each had taken what they needed from the other, Jack and Ursula lay entwined in each other's arms.

"Jack, you're the best," Ursula moaned against his shoulder.

He smoothed her damp hair and told her what she wanted to hear. "I missed you, Sula. Many were the times I thought I'd die from wanting you."

"Then why did you have to leave me?" There was no mistaking the petulance in her voice.

"I had to get Diana a horse. If she's going to be

riding the high toby with me, she's got to have a fast horse."

Now Ursula drew away from him and propped herself up on one elbow. "Please don't let her ride with you, Jack, I'm begging you. It's madness to let a woman ride with you."

"Not the way Diana handles a pistol," he replied. He couldn't keep the admiration from creeping into his voice, no matter how hard he tried. "She wasn't boasting when she said she can ride and shoot as good as a man. She can. I've seen her. With a little practice, she'd be as good as me."

"That may very well be, but shooting at a target is one thing. Shooting at men who are shooting back is quite another, as you know." Sula looked at him, her green eyes troubled. "Women are soft. What if she loses her courage one night and puts you in danger?"

"I'm in danger every time I take to the road, Sula. Having Diana with me won't make a bit of difference. If she loses her courage, she'll pay the price. I'll not risk my neck to save hers. She knows that."

Suddenly he felt Ursula tremble in his arms, and when he looked down, he saw great tears slide noiselessly down her cheeks. All he could do was stare at her helplessly, for never had he seen Ursula cry. It quite unmanned him.

"What's this?" he demanded, his voice going all queer and shaky on him. "My brave Sula crying?"

"I'm . . . I'm sorry, Jack. I know how much you hate a blubbering woman. But I'm so afraid for you. If you take Diana with you, something horrible is going to happen. I can feel it in my bones!"

Jack had to be stern with her before she broke down completely. "Now, that's enough of that, Ursula Hunt," he said, giving her a little shake. "I need Diana. With an accomplice, I'll be able to take twice as much booty. And the sooner I do, the sooner we'll be able to clear out of this wretched country for good."

He drew her to him again to soften the sting of his words. "We can go to Virginia, Sula, and make a fresh start for both of us. Sell the Jolly Wife and buy us a proper estate, not some plot of ground like my father had. Then you can be the grand lady you deserve to be, and I can be the lord of the manor."

He saw the doubt mirrored in her eyes, but he knew she would never oppose him because she lived in terror of losing him. She was a woman past her prime with never a hope of attracting such a young, handsome man as Jack Pierce again.

"Whatever you say, Jack. Whatever you say." Her words sounded suspiciously like a desperate prayer.

Aurora reined in the bay gelding at the top of the hill and smiled in satisfaction. The horse ran as though he had wings on his heels, just as Jack had promised. She tried to ignore the fact that the animal was stolen, but her conscience wouldn't let her.

"You're a different person, Aurora Falconet," she scolded herself. "You have a different life now, and a different set of values."

A different life. . . . She was no longer a lady of quality. She was a common wench like Ruth and Caro, who shared company with an innkeeper and a highwayman. She was about to embark upon a great, exciting adventure, that of lady highwayman. The Marchioness of Silverblade had ceased to exist. She was Diana Timothy now.

And a bit of Tim Falconet as well.

An ironic smile touched Aurora's mouth. Here she was, impersonating a highwayman, just as her brother had done once so very long ago. They were both so much alike, spirited and devil-may-care, no matter what the consequences. But unlike Tim, Aurora had no intention of meeting her destiny at the end of a smoking gun barrel.

But as she urged the gelding into a walk, Aurora found it increasingly difficult to pretend she had had no life before Jack and Ursula. She found it especially difficult to forget Nicholas.

Did he ever think of her as he lay in Pamela Littlewood's arms? Did he ever regret hiring those men to murder her?

Aurora sighed dismally. In spite of everything, she still loved him madly, still awoke in the middle of the night yearning for his strong, lithe body next to hers, his hunger for her, his tender embraces that made her feel so wanted, so loved. She had stopped counting the times she was on the verge of risking her life by returning to him just to hear the sound of his voice once more.

You stupid little fool! she thought savagely. All the times you've condemned your sister for blindly loving Overton, and you're no better when it comes to Nicholas.

Suddenly she heard someone call her name. She turned in the saddle and saw Jack climbing up the hill on foot. Aurora rode to meet him halfway.

Jack squinted up at her. "Satisfied with him?"

"Most pleased," she replied. "He's fast, but not as fast as—" She caught herself before she blurted out "Firelight."

"As fast as what?"

"Just a memory from my past, Jack," Aurora replied.

He nodded in understanding. "We all have those from time to time." Then he said, "There's going to be a full moon tonight. I think it's time we see what kind of highwayman you're going to make."

Aurora's eyes widened with excitement. "Tonight?"

Jack nodded. "I'll be the one what keeps the pistols aimed at them, and you'll collect the booty from the passengers. Get the gold and leave the jewels, but if all they've got is jewels, then take them."

Aurora frowned in puzzlement. "Why should I leave the jewels? They would probably be worth more than the gold."

Jack shook his head. "You have much to learn about being a knight of the high toby, my girl. Sure an emerald ring or a ruby watch fob is worth more than a sack of gold guineas if you can find somebody to buy it. Gold you can spend with no one being the wiser, but jewels have to be fenced."

As Aurora listened raptly, Jack proceeded to explain that fences bought stolen goods for much less than they were worth, then resold them at a tidy profit.

"Some fences are sneaky two-faced bastards. They'd just as soon set the law on you as look at you. So a highwayman can't be too careful or he'll be dancing from the end of a rope."

"I saw a highwayman hanged at Tyburn," Aurora said, following Jack as he started down the hill again. "His name was Jemmie Taylor. Have you heard of him?"

"Jemmie Taylor," Jack scoffed with a rueful shake of his head. "Everyone's heard of him. A handsome lad, but not very bright. Know how he got caught?" When Aurora shook her head, Jack said, "The idiot took a fancy to a gold watch he stole. Someone recognized it as stolen goods and turned him in."

Now Jack stopped and looked up at her, his expression turning ruthless. "The life of a highwayman is short and hard, Diana Timothy. Most of us are caught and share Jemmie Taylor's fate sooner or later. Some, like me, are clever enough to avoid the noose or the gibbet. Is that a risk you're willing to take? Tell me now before we ride tonight, 'cause I won't stand for you backing out on me at the last minute."

Aurora flashed him a bold smile. "If you're trying to frighten me, Jack Pierce, you're doing a miserable job of it. I said I'd ride with you, and I mean to keep my word. I owe you and I owe Ursula."

His dark eyes danced with merriment and the dimple appeared in his cheek. "Good girl. I knew I could count on you."

Despite Jack's dire warnings, Aurora didn't believe him. He was just trying to frighten her. She trusted her horse and she trusted her own abilities with a pistol. And she trusted Jack with her life.

As they walked back to the inn together, Aurora suddenly said, "Jack, why do you do it? Why did you become a highwayman?"

At first he didn't respond, just walked beside Aurora's horse. Finally he replied, "You could say I owe it to the fine Lady Belcourt. She gave me a taste of satins and silks, and when she threw me out, I just couldn't go back to being a poor farmer like my father. Being a highwayman pays better. Every time I rob some fine gentleman, I see it as repaying Lady Belcourt and her like."

So Jack Pierce had become a highwayman to avenge his harsh treatment at the hands of the upper class, of which Aurora was a part.

She forced such thoughts from her mind and concentrated on her first ride.

Diana Falconet stifled a yawn with the back of her hand.

"Tired, my dear?"

She smiled at the finely dressed gentleman seated across from her in the carriage. "Just a little, Jason. Lady Thorburn can be a bit of a bore."

"That, my dear, is being too charitable." There was genuine remorse in Jason's voice as he said, "I regret ever subjecting you to that horrid woman, but her husband and I have been friends since we were in leading strings. However, from now on we shall curtail our visits."

"You are too kind to me, Jason."

"Nonsense. It is you who are too kind to me, my dear." His brow wrinkled in concern. "Are you sure you're warm enough? I detect a distinct chill in the air."

Diana shivered. "It is, just a bit."

"Then I shall come over there and sit next to you so I can warm you. We mustn't have you catching your death." Lord Jason Barron, Marquess of Penhall, rose to join his mistress.

Despite the swaying of the carriage, he managed to change places without losing his balance. Once he was seated by Diana's side, Jason drew his thick wool cloak over her and his arm along with it. Diana nestled against him like a cosseted cat and rested her head against his shoulder.

As she listened to Jason's even breathing, Diana sighed in utter contentment, amazed at her own good fortune. When Overton had thrown her out, she had been devastated. She had deluded herself into thinking that he loved her as much as she loved him. But it wasn't until she met Lord Penhall at one of Katherine's drums that she realized how very little Overton had really cared for her.

He had certainly proven that by marrying some nobleman's daughter the minute Diana was out of his life.

Jason, on the other hand, simply worshipped her. He was always kind, and forever solicitous of her welfare. If there was anything she wanted, all she had to do was ask and it was laid at her feet. Yet he was not a mindless puppet she could manipulate at will. He guided her with a firm hand and was always quick to let her know when she displeased him. He was a man she could respect as well as love.

She glanced up at his irregular profile silhouetted in the darkness of the carriage. True, compared with Overton, Jason was a plain man—ugly even—with a large lumpy nose and protruding ears. He was also shorter than Diana by several inches and so thin he looked as though a good strong wind could blow him away. But if she had to choose between a handsome man who bullied her and a plain man who adored her, Diana knew now what that choice would be.

Jason glanced down at her. "Admiring my noble profile, are you?" he said with customary self-deprecating humor.

Diana snuggled closer. "Your profile is quite endearing, as is the rest of you. But no, I was just thinking of a roaring fire and our nice warm bed."

"So was I," Jason admitted.

"How long do you think it will be before we reach Penhall Court?" She nipped at his earlobe, causing him to shudder with delight.

He turned in his seat and tilted her face up to be kissed. When they finally parted, Jason said, "I would estimate another fifteen minutes."

Diana pouted prettily, for she knew Jason could never resist her when she pouted. "I suppose we shall have to wait."

He caught his breath raggedly. "I suppose we shall my dear. We don't want to shock the coachmen with our wanton behavior."

Diana sighed in disappointment and put her head back down on his shoulder. She remembered Jason's ardent pursuit of her in London, and how she had agreed to become his mistress only because of his title and wealth, plus the fact that no other man seemed to want her after Overton had discarded her. However, after their first night together, when Jason had displayed surprising inventiveness and prowess as a lover, Diana was delighted to realize there was more to the man than met the eye.

He had gone on surprising her ever since.

Jason Barron's only fault in Diana's eyes was his obsession with his family estate not far from desolate Bodmin Moor in Cornwall. He lived there the year round, so Diana's visits to Aurora and Nicholas would be few and far between.

Diana felt overwhelmed by guilt. She hadn't written to her sister in months. Well, that was Jason's fault. He kept her so busy managing his household, calling on his friends, and wearing out his bed that Diana had scant time for writing letters. Well, she would have to remedy that soon.

Suddenly and inexplicably, the carriage slowed down.

As it rolled to a stop, Diana looked at Jason in puzzlement. "Have we reached Penhall already?"

Jason started, swore angrily, and reached for his pistol. Then he looked over at Diana's frightened face and thought better of it.

"I think, my dear," he said with remarkable sang-froid, "we are about to be robbed."

Through the carriage window and by the feeble light of the lamps, Diana could see a masked horseman brandishing a pistol.

"Stand and deliver!" he cried.

The moment the highwayman spoke, Diana recognized his voice. "It can't be . . ." she murmured incredulously as the blood drained out of her face, leaving her giddy with shock.

"Come, my dear," Jason was saying as he flung open the door and kicked the steps down.

As Diana took his hand and stepped down, she stared at the highwayman. When their gazes met and locked, he stiffened and his eyes widened momentarily through the slits in his black crepe mask. But he said nothing, and his gun didn't waver.

"Just yer gold, guv'nor," he growled, taking off his hat and handing it to Jason.

This time, his voice was different, deep and raspy, not the first voice Diana had heard and recognized. Why had the highwayman suddenly disguised his voice unless he was afraid of being recognized?

While Jason was busy fumbling through his pockets and emptying them, Diana studied the highwayman. He was about Aurora's height, and slight of build, but that didn't mean anything. Aurora had always impersonated a boy with ease. Diana couldn't tell if that periwig hid a mop of auburn curls, either. And the man had an accomplice standing near the front of the carriage with his two pistols trained on the coachmen.

Jason finished and handed her the hat, his expression one of chagrin and embarrassment that she had to suffer the indignity of being robbed while her lover stood by helplessly.

But when Diana begun unfastening the ruby necklace Jason had given her, the highwayman stopped her with a gruff, "I said just yer gold."

Then he took the hat, set it—contents and all—back on his head, and wheeled his horse around. Before Diana could blink, they were both gone, galloping off into the night.

Now the coachmen sprang to life. Cursing roundly, one of them jumped down from the box, grabbed his musket lying on the ground, and fired blindly into the darkness. The sound echoed, then all was still.

"I think I hit one of them, yer lordship," the coachman said hopefully.

"I rather doubt it," was Jason's offhand reply.

"That was the Black Fox himself, I'll be bound," the second coachman said. "Looks like he's found himself a cub to ride with him."

"Who is this Black Fox?" Diana asked.

"Only one of the most notorious highwaymen in these parts, my lady," the first coachman replied. "They call him the Black Fox because he always dresses in black and he's as wily as a fox at evadin' the magistrates."

The other coachman added, with a touch of admiration, "He's been ridin' the high toby for years now and never been caught."

"He will be, one day," Jason said with conviction.

After telling his coachmen to proceed, he turned his attention to Diana. "Are you all right, my dear?" he asked, his voice soft with concern as he put a reassuring hand on her arm.

She nodded. "I . . . I've never been robbed by highwaymen before. Would they have . . . killed us?"

Jason hugged her. "No, no, my poor darling. Only if we attempted to kill them. All they wanted was money, not our lives. I only regret I didn't think of having armed guards ride with us tonight to spare you this unpleasantness."

Diana kissed him on the cheek. "My dear Jason . . . always so thoughtful."

His face twisted, becoming ugly. "I wouldn't have let them harm you, Diana. I want you to know that."

She thought of Jason sacrificing his own life to protect her, and she shuddered. "Thank God it didn't come to that, my love, because I don't know what I would do without you."

Her devotion coaxed a smile out of him. To think that he, the ugly Lord Penhall, had won the heart of such a magnificent woman.

"Come," he said, "let us be on our way before we're stopped again."

But all the way back to Penhall Court, Diana couldn't stop thinking of the highwayman with her sister's voice.

Aurora was so frightened her teeth were chattering, but she fought down the fear and forced herself to keep pace with Jack as they galloped across the moor. The full moon was small and high now, bathing the landscape in its silver light and giving it an eerie, dreamlike quality, full of shadows and shifting light.

The full enormity of what she had done caused Aurora to break out in a cold sweat. Diana had recognized her voice. When she alighted from the carriage, her face was glowing with anticipation, and when she saw a highwayman standing there instead of her sister, she just kept staring. Luckily for Aurora, her sister kept her suspicions to herself and did not betray her.

Now guilt washed over Aurora afresh. She had accosted her own sister. She could still remember the fear in Diana's eyes and the way her hand shook as she began unfastening her necklace. And Aurora was responsible.

She wished she had never agreed to ride with Jack. She wished she were back with Nicholas in those first halcyon months of their marriage, before everything soured. She wished she were a child again, with her father in Ireland. She wished . . .

Tears stung her eyes, but the breeze whipped them away before they had a chance to fall.

Aurora and Jack rode hard and fast, skirting darkened villages and farms with barking dogs. Once they passed a gibbet where a badly decomposed body of a highwayman hung in chains at the scene of his last crime. The skeletal corpse creaked eerily and seemed to moan in torment, seeking release as it swayed slightly in the night air. Aurora kept her eyes averted, but the stench of rotting flesh hit her with stunning force, almost causing her to retch.

Jack just shook his head and muttered, "Poor bastard."

When they were well away from that grim reminder of the highwayman's fate, Jack slowed his horse and looked over his shoulder to make sure they weren't being followed. He nodded in satisfaction, obviously pleased with her performance.

"Good work, Diana," he said with a grin. "You did just what I told you, and you were steady. Now, hand over the booty. Let's see how much we got."

"I've never been so scared in all my life, Jack," she

admitted in a quivering voice as she removed her cocked hat and handed it to Jack. "I don't think my hands will ever stop shaking."

"You need more experience," he said, counting the coins in the hat's crown. "A few more and it'll be second nature to you before you know it." Then he whistled. "Twenty guineas . . . now, that's what I call booty!"

Aurora hesitated, gathering her courage, for she was going to need it. "I've changed my mind, Jack. I don't want to be a highwayman anymore. Once was enough."

Without warning, Jack's hand shot out and grasped Aurora's wrist painfully. By moonlight his face was a diabolic mask of rage.

"After what I went through to steal you a fast horse, you're going to back out on me now?" His eyes glittered wildly. "You're the one who wanted to ride with me in the first place, with your boasts about how well you shoot and ride. And you're forgetting something else, you ungrateful wench. I saved your life, and Ursula's given you a roof over your head. You owe us plenty, and we aim to collect."

Tomorrow she would go to Diana and beg her for sanctuary. She had to escape from Jack Pierce before someone was killed and she became an accomplice to murder. Suddenly being a highwayman was no longer a game.

As if he read her thoughts, Jack shook her arm. "Don't you even think of informin' on me, Diana. You're in too deep to turn back now. You're just as guilty as I am, and if the law catches up with me, I'll take you with me, so help me God!"

She knew he would. She had trapped herself and there was no escape for her now.

"Well?" Jack shook her again. "Are you still with me?"

Aurora sealed her fate with a reluctant nod.

The following morning, Diana left Jason sleeping soundly, and quietly went to her desk. She opened a drawer, removed a sheet of thick, creamy paper imprinted with the Penhall crest, and sat down to write a letter.

When she finished, she addressed it and smiled to herself. Her sister would surely be shocked and amused by her harrowing tale of being robbed by a highwayman she had mistaken for Aurora.

Now, by the light of day, Diana realized it had all been a mistake. Aurora was at Silverblade, safe with her husband, not in Cornwall playing highwayman.

She set the letter out for the morning post, then returned to the warmth of Jason's waiting arms.

19

THREE weeks after he had learned of Aurora's disappearance, Nicholas also learned the fate of his coachmen.

He, his mother, and Wes were in the study of the London town house at the time, examining the sketches of Aurora's likeness that lay scattered across his desk.

As Nicholas stared at one, he thought it was enough of a physical resemblance for anyone to identify her, but it wasn't really the Aurora he knew. The sketches had failed to capture her warmth, her fire, her unconquerable spirit. Nicholas felt a heavy pall of despair settle around his heart again, but he took a deep breath and fought it.

"That was an excellent idea you had, Mother," he said, smiling slightly at Lady Mary, "having these likenesses made from Aurora's miniature. We'll have them posted at the docks, in coffeehouses, at any inn in London where coaches stop . . ."

Lady Mary rose to warm her hands in front of the fire, for it was a wet, raw day outside. "Someone is sure to have seen her and will undoubtedly come forward."

"Especially since you're offering such a generous reward," Wes added. "Five thousand pounds should entice someone to come forward with information about Aurora's whereabouts."

"Five thousand pounds is nothing. I would give

everything I own to get her back," Nicholas said, his jaw tightening with determination.

"Aurora will return to us," his mother said with false heartiness as she returned to her chair. "And soon. Just don't give up hope."

Nicholas walked over to one of the long windows. "Easier said than done, Mother."

He stared out the window, but his weary eyes focused on nothing. Ever since that horrible day when he had learned Aurora never arrived at Silverblade, he had been acting like a man possessed by demons. Once back in London, he had gone directly to Conor Grantley's lodgings and nearly killed him with his bare hands until the terrified young man convinced him he hadn't seen Aurora since the night of that disastrous ball. All that was left for Nicholas to do was to put notices in the papers, notify the watchmen, and hire a small army of men to scour the countryside for Aurora.

By now, there wasn't a person in London who didn't know that the Marquess of Silverblade's wife was missing. But still Aurora had not been found.

"Where *is* she?" Nicholas cried in anguish, slamming his clenched fist into his open palm with a resounding smack.

Lady Mary and Wes said nothing because there was nothing more they could say to him.

Suddenly there came a hurried knock, and the study doors flew open before Nicholas even had time to turn around.

Ollie swept into the room. He looked cold, pale, and exhausted, as though he had ridden through the night, but he wore an air of urgency about him like the wet, muddy black cloak he hadn't even bothered to hand to the majordomo.

Nicholas stepped forward eagerly, not daring to hope. "You've found something."

Ollie nodded as he fought to catch his breath. "We found your coachmen."

Nicholas started, his hopes soaring. "Where are they? Did they come back with you? Do they know what happened to Aurora?" When Ollie just stood there swaying on his feet, Nicholas reached out and grasped him by the shoulders. "Dammit, man! Don't just stand there! Tell me what happened!"

Lady Mary jumped to her feet and intervened before Nicholas could shake his friend senseless. "Nicholas, please! Can't you see the poor boy is exhausted? Let him catch his breath before you go hounding him."

Nicholas smiled apologetically, assisted Ollie to a chair, and poured him a generous brandy.

After he drained the glass, Ollie began. "We found your coachmen all right, Nick, but they're dead."

Lady Mary gasped, and exchanged looks with Wes, who had turned a pasty shade of gray.

"They were buried in a shallow grave in a wooded area not far from the road the carriage usually takes to get to Silverblade," Ollie continued, breathing heavily. "The heavy rainfall washed away the earth, and some village children found them while playing. The bodies were . . . unrecognizable, but they were wearing Silverblade livery. That's how we knew who they were."

Nicholas, who had been sitting on the edge of his desk, gripped it until his knuckles turned white.

"And Aurora?" he rasped.

Ollie shook his head and sprang to his feet. "No, Nick. Aurora wasn't with them. There were only the two men in the grave."

Nicholas slumped forward. "Thank God!"

Now Wes asked, "Was there any sign of the carriage or the horses?"

Ollie eased his bulk back into the chair. "I spoke to everyone in the nearby village. No one remembers seeing any carriage or horses. They seem to have disappeared into thin air."

"Then someone abducted Aurora," Lady Mary said, looking from Ollie to Nicholas. "They accosted her carriage, killed the coachmen, and took her by force. That is the only explanation. Even if Aurora chose to run away of her own volition—which I refuse to believe—she would never have allowed those coachmen to be killed for any reason. Never."

Ollie's head bobbed up and down. "I quite agree. Someone abducted her."

"But why?" Nicholas cried in frustration. "It's been nearly two months since her disappearance, and I haven't received any ransom demands."

Ollie pushed back his wig to scratch his head. "We've been assuming that Aurora was abducted for ransom. But what if we're wrong?"

"What other motive is there?" Wes demanded.

Ollie looked at him in surprise. "Why, revenge of course."

Everyone fell silent to consider this new possibility.

"You certainly have your share of enemies, Nick," Ollie pointed out. "You nearly cleaned out what's left of Portersmith's inheritance at White's last year. And more than one of us has heard Claiborne threaten you when he's in his cups. Or perhaps Littlewood is having his revenge for your . . . relationship with Pamela."

Nicholas laughed at that, a shrill bark that caused his mother to regard him in alarm. "Littlewood? That old man wouldn't have the gall."

But Ollie didn't share his opinion of Littlewood. "All men can find the courage if they feel they've been wronged."

Nicholas fought down the mindless panic threatening to overwhelm him, and forced himself to think clearly. He rose from the edge of his desk and faced everyone.

"Then I shall have to start questioning all those who might bear me a grudge." He thanked them all for their assistance and dismissed them by returning to the window.

Ollie and Wes left, but not Lady Mary.

"Son?" she said softly as she came to stand behind him.

She hadn't called him that since he was a little boy, and it touched Nicholas so profoundly that he found tears stinging his eyes.

He fought to bring himself under control before turning to face her. "Yes, Mother?"

Her pale gray eyes were filled with sorrow and regret. "You must face it, Nicholas. Aurora may be dead."

He stepped away from her, furious with her for

saying what he himself refused to admit. "She cannot be dead!"

"If she were being held for ransom, her captors would have reason to keep her alive. But if someone did this horrible thing to avenge himself . . ."

Intellectually Nicholas knew she was right. His mind could even accept it. But his heart could not. His love for Aurora was so strong it pushed rationality out of the way.

"I refuse to believe she is dead. If I have to spend the rest of my life searching for her, Mother, I will. I will never give up. Never! Even if it costs me my fortune and my sanity."

"I felt that way about your father once," Lady Mary said wistfully. "I loved him more than life itself. And when he died, something inside of me died as well. For seven years I hid myself away from the world, refusing to accept his death.

"Then, thanks to Aurora, I realized how selfish I had been. While I sought to stop life, it somehow went on without me, as it is wont to do. Aurora wouldn't have wanted you to suffer like this, son. She would have wanted you to get on with your life, to—"

"Will you stop talking about her as if she's already dead!"

His cry of anguish rang throughout the room, and his mother recoiled from the vehemence of it. She realized there was nothing more she could do. Without another word, she turned and left her son to his sorrow.

When he was finally alone, Nicholas sank down into the nearest chair and cradled his head in his hands. He was so tired he could have slept for a week, but he had to push himself even harder to go on for Aurora's sake.

He groaned and flung himself back in the chair. He had never known he could feel such pain, this agonizing ache that was squeezing the very life out of him. Oh, he had known great physical pain before, but nothing like this mental anguish that had infected his soul. There was only one cure for it—Aurora.

But what if his mother was right? What if Aurora were dead?

He would never see her again for the rest of his life. He would never hear the lighthearted trill of her laughter, never see her bright blue eyes sparkle at some shared joke. He would never know the sublime ecstasy of her passion as she gave herself so freely to him in so many ways.

Without Aurora by his side, his life would be so empty and meaningless that death would be appealing in comparison.

Nicholas swung his chair around, crossed his arms on his desk, and rested his head against them. Regret and remorse ate at him like acid. If he hadn't been such a proud, arrogant fool, letting that humiliating wager cause a rift between them, Aurora would still be with him today.

For the third time in his life, Nicholas Devenish, the Marquess of Silverblade, wept.

Several hours later, Nicholas was about to go out and continue his search when his majordomo stopped him in the foyer.

"Begging your pardon, your lordship," the man said gravely, "but a letter has come for her ladyship. I thought you would wish to see it immediately."

Nicholas thanked him and took the letter to his study. When he saw the Marquess of Penhall's seal, he knew immediately that the letter was from Aurora's sister. Living in remote Cornwall as she did, Diana would not have heard about her sister's disappearance.

As Nicholas broke the seal, he wondered how he was ever going to explain Aurora's disappearance to Diana. Up until now, he had sought to spare her. Why worry her unnecessarily, especially when he was confident Aurora would soon be found?

But with that possibility growing dimmer by the day, Nicholas had to face the unpleasant reality that Diana must be told.

He scanned the letter. The first few sentences expressed Diana's regrets for not writing sooner, and inquired into Aurora's health. Then Nicholas read something that caught his attention.

"You will be amused to hear, dear sister," Diana had written, "that I have met your twin. Penhall and I were returning from a dinner engagement when our carriage was accosted by two highwaymen. Imagine my surprise to discover one of them sounded exactly like you! He was about your height as well. Unfortunately, it was so dark I couldn't see the color of the bandit's eyes. For one incredible moment I feared my own sister had taken to a life of crime. But I know that is impossible, as you are safe and sound in London with your adored husband."

Nicholas never finished the letter.

He stood in the center of his study as though rooted to the carpet. Aurora in Cornwall, masquerading as a highwayman? Impossible!

Yet the voice and the resemblance had been great enough to make her own sister wonder.

Nicholas shook his head and stuffed the letter into his waistcoat pocket. Then he seated himself, laced his hands behind his head, and began thinking absurd, improbable thoughts.

He left for Cornwall an hour later.

Once Aurora was safe in the stables, she slid off her horse. Her legs were shaking so badly that she had to lean against the stall door until the terror subsided and she was able to walk again. She noticed Jack's horse was already here, cooled down and in his stall for the night. So its rider had made it back to the Jolly Wife after all.

After unsaddling her horse with hands that wouldn't stop shaking and putting him in his stall, Aurora wearily trudged back to the inn. Candles and lanterns were still shining in the windows, making the inn look warm and welcoming, a haven against the chilly night. As Aurora wrapped her cloak more tightly about her, she heard the muffled sound of laughter coming from within. Then she remembered there were patrons inside tonight, so she skirted the building and went around the back, taking care not to be seen.

Once inside, she went directly upstairs to Jack's room. He was toasting cheese before a roaring fire, a tankard of ale in one hand, a clay pipe in the other.

"Diana!" he cried, jumping to his feet at the sight of her leaning against the doorjamb. "You gave me quite a fright, girl. Thought the magistrate's men had you for sure. Glad to see you got away. Come in and warm your bones. This bit of cheese is almost done."

She peeled off her gloves, yanked off the periwig, and shook out her hair until it fell in a coppery veil down to her shoulders. Then she put her hands on her hips and confronted Jack, telling him in a strong, determined voice that tonight was her last night on the road.

Up until tonight, playing highwayman had been a grand adventure for her and a way of repaying the debt she owed Jack for saving her life. She and Jack usually accosted a carriage or a solitary horseman, robbed the traveler without a second thought, then rode off, leaving the legend of the Black Fox and his cub to spread and grow throughout the Cornish countryside. No one was ever hurt.

But tonight had dispelled that romantic aura. Six armed men had been guarding the road, lying in wait for them. When Aurora and Jack approached a carriage, the men came out of nowhere, shooting. Aurora could still hear the ball whizzing close to her ear as she wheeled her horse around and ran for her life, with Jack not far behind. They had separated to evade the magistrate's men, who were breathing down their necks in hot pursuit. Luckily for Aurora, her horse was faster. But she had never been so frightened in her life.

Jack's smile died as he set down the pipe and tankard. "Oh, my dear Diana, you can't mean that."

"Oh, yes I do!" Aurora felt her strength returning as she bristled with anger. "I was almost killed tonight, Jack! Those men came out of nowhere. If we hadn't separated like we did, they would've gotten us for sure."

Jack's smile returned, his voice soothing and placating. "You're just tired and frightened. Once you've had a drink and a good night's sleep—"

"I said I'm through, Jack!" Aurora snapped, her voice rising. "From now on, you ride alone."

Jack approached her and rested his hands on her shoulders, smiling and trying to exert his charm on her. "You can't quit on me now, Diana," he began, his voice soft and beguiling. "Why, you're almost as big a legend in these parts as I am! You're the Black Fox's cub."

She pushed his hands away in annoyance and turned from him. She was not the young, impressionable Caro to have her head turned by his blandishments and a roguish dimpled smile.

He smiled grimly and quickly reached for her, running his fingertips down her throat, tightening his grip ever so slightly on her windpipe, until Aurora couldn't breathe and her blue eyes widened in astonishment.

"I could kill you if you refuse to ride with me."

Aurora boldly knocked his hand away, her breath coming in deep, hard gasps. "You could, but I don't think you will. You're not a murderer. A thief, but not a murderer."

Jack turned away from her and strolled over to the fireplace, his mind racing as he nonchalantly toasted another piece of cheese. He could see Diana was determined to end it this time, and neither wheedling nor threats could dissuade her. But he was a cunning devil himself. He had one last card and he played it.

"One last time, Diana, that's all I ask." When she made a mutter of protest, he quickly interrupted her with, "Hear me out before you refuse. In two weeks, the Duke of Trewen is giving a betrothal ball for his only daughter. I have it on the best authority that all the gentry for miles around will be attending, some from even as far away as London. Think of it, Diana. All those fine gentlemen with their fat pockets, all those fine ladies dripping and glittering with jewels. Ripe for the picking."

She groaned. "I told you, Jack—"

He raised his free hand to silence her. "This could be the haul of my career, Diana. All I need is one last haul like this, and me and Ursula can immigrate to the colonies, to Virginia, like we always planned. We can leave this place and live like kings!"

Jack stood before her like a schoolboy begging for a treat. "But I can't do it alone. I need you to ride with me this one last time, Diana. Do this for me, then you can go your way, and I can go mine. No regrets and no hard feelings. I'll consider your debt to me paid in full."

He held his breath and watched her carefully. He saw a wide range of emotions play across her face like morning light sweeping across the surface of the sea. First there was resistance, then reluctance, followed by hesitation.

"Please, Diana," he murmured. "Do this for me and we'll be square."

"I'll think about it," she said, whirling on her heel. When she reached the door, she stopped and turned. "But no promises."

"A gentleman calling himself the Marquess of Silverblade to see you, miss."

Diana jumped to her feet in a rustle of petticoats and flung her embroidery hoop aside in her excitement. "Nicholas and Aurora? Here at Penhall? Don't just stand there, Chalmers. Show them in."

"Begging your pardon, miss, but there is no one accompanying the gentleman."

Diana frowned in puzzlement. Nicholas without Aurora? She waved her hand impatiently. "Show him in anyway."

While the majordomo ambled off, Diana absently smoothed her skirt and wondered what her brother-in-law was doing down in Cornwall without his wife. Well, she would know in a moment, for she could hear the hurried tap of boots outside the drawing-room door.

The majordomo intoned, "The Marquess of Silverblade," and left Nicholas standing in the doorway.

"Nicholas, how delightful to see you!" Diana greeted him with a wide smile as she glided across the room, both hands extended. "You look—"

Her smile froze as she groped for something complimentary to say, for in truth, her brother-in-law looked ghastly. He was drawn and haggard, with shadowed, bloodshot eyes and several days' worth of stubble darkening his jaw. His boots and breeches were spattered with dried mud, his cloak heavy with mud and dust, as though he had been in the saddle for days.

His lips moved, but no words came out.

"Nicholas, what's wrong?" Diana grasped his hands, so cold to the touch, and led him over to the nearest chair.

After he slid down into it with a weary, grateful sigh, she hurried over to the brandy decanter, poured him a stiff measure, and handed it to him. Diana waited patiently while he drained the glass and composed himself.

"Feel better now?" she asked as she took the empty glass from him.

"Yes, thank you," he replied. "Do forgive me for barging in on you without warning, but it's of the utmost importance."

"You are always welcome at Penhall. But where is Aurora? I thought she would have come with you."

Pain darkened Nicholas' silvery eyes. "It's about Aurora that I've come." He moistened his lips. "She's disappeared."

At first Diana was so shocked she didn't comprehend what he was saying. "Aurora . . . disappeared?"

Nicholas nodded. "She's been missing for almost four months."

Diana stared at him, speechless and aghast.

"And it's all my fault."

Diana put her fingers to her temples to quell the thousands of questions that suddenly rose to her mind, but all she could say was, "What happened, Nicholas?"

He sighed. "Perhaps I had best start at the beginning."

Diana sank down in the chair across from him. She listened as Nicholas told her of some rift that had developed between Aurora and himself, and how he had sent her back to Silverblade in disgrace while he remained in London.

"The carriage never arrived at Silverblade," Nicholas said, his voice dull with anguish. "We recently found the coachmen. They were dead."

Diana gasped and leaned forward anxiously. "And Aurora?"

"There was no sign of her anywhere."

Now she rose, needing activity to keep her wits about her. "But what can have happened to her, Nicholas? Where can she be?"

She listened intently as Nicholas presented his various theories, the most logical ones being that someone had kidnapped Aurora for ransom or revenge.

Diana shook her head. "Who could do such a thing? Aurora wouldn't hurt a soul. She is so gentle, so kind . . ."

"I have many enemies, Diana," Nicholas said wearily, shading his eyes with his hand. "Many enemies."

Cold, stark fear gripped her. "Nicholas, you think she is dead, don't you?"

His hand fell listlessly and he looked directly at her with fear in his eyes. "That may be a possibility we have to accept, Diana."

"Oh, dear God!" She swayed and would have fallen if Nicholas hadn't leapt to his feet to assist her back into her chair.

He knelt beside it and grasped her hands. "There is one last hope and it is my reason for being here." Nicholas groped through his pockets and dragged out a crumpled piece of paper, which he handed to Diana.

"Your letter," he said, "the one you wrote to Aurora."

Diana stared at it. "I don't understand . . ."

"In it, you told of being robbed by a highwayman whose voice sounded similar to Aurora's. Do you remember?"

"Why, yes. Our coachman said it was a man called the Black Fox. He had an accomplice whose voice was exactly like Aurora's. In fact, when I first heard it, I thought my sister was playing some sort of prank on me." Now Diana frowned, then brightened with hope. "You think this highwayman and Aurora are one and the same?"

Nicholas swung to his feet in one fluid motion and

paced about the room in agitation. "Perhaps it is only a coincidence."

"But why would she be here, in Cornwall, posing as a highwayman? She knows I live at Penhall Court. If she were in some sort of danger, why wouldn't she come to me, her own sister, for help?"

Nicholas shrugged. "I don't know the answer to that. Perhaps she is suffering from some memory loss." Now he turned to Diana, his eyes shining. "But I have to try to find her. It's my last hope. Do you remember where you were robbed? Perhaps she is in the immediate vicinity."

Diana rose, fresh determination coursing through her. "Let me find Jason. I'm sure he'll be able to help us."

When he was alone, Nicholas slumped down in his chair, fatigue and mental strain finally taking their toll. He had traveled day and night by carriage through muddy, rutty roads until the turnpike ended in Exeter. Then he took a ferry across the Tamar River, which separated Devon from Cornwall, and rode the rest of the way on horseback, stopping at an inn only once to sleep for several hours before continuing his journey.

Now that he was here, he kept his thoughts focused on finding Aurora, nothing else. Doubt and uncertainty were his greatest enemies, and he refused to countenance them. If he even stopped to consider all the inquiries that had yet to be made in his quest to find his wife, all the villages that had yet to be searched, he would surely go mad.

Suddenly the drawing-room door opened and Diana reappeared with Lord Jason Penhall by her side and quickly made introductions.

Penhall bowed. "I regret not making your acquaintance sooner, Lord Silverblade, but I so seldom leave Cornwall."

"Having seen the countryside, I can't say that I blame you," Nicholas replied, studying the other man and instantly liking what he saw.

The amenities over and done with, Penhall became as eager as a hound on the scent. "Now, let us see what can be done to help you find your wife. Diana,

Lord Silverblade and I will be in my study and do not wished to be disturbed." He glanced at his guest and added, "Except for luncheon."

Diana left to do his bidding, and Nicholas followed his host into the study

When they emerged an hour later, Nicholas' black despair had lifted. For the first time in weeks, he felt confident that he would find Aurora, and it was all because of Jason Penhall.

Briskly and efficiently Penhall had shown Nicholas maps of the area where he and Diana had been robbed, and where he thought two highwaymen might be hiding. He had also mentioned a betrothal ball scheduled for the following night, and explained that guests would be arriving from all over England to attend. "Ample temptation for any robber," he added with a knowing grin.

By the time they had finished the luncheon that Diana brought them, Penhall promised Nicholas to dispatch his own men immediately to search for Aurora.

Rejecting Diana's suggestion that he sleep before starting out again, Nicholas left Penhall to search for his wife.

Ursula stood in the doorway and nervously gnawed on her lower lip as she watched the two horsemen halt their horses on the crest of the hill and wave to her. For one brief moment, the setting sun turned them to gold; then they disappeared as they went galloping off.

Ursula shielded her eyes as she turned to watch that fiery orange ball poised to sink into the sea.

"Damn fool," she muttered with a shake of her head. Then she turned and strode into the empty coffee room.

For once she was pleased there were no guests at the Jolly Wife today, no one to see Jack and Diana brazenly ride off at sunset instead of under the cover of darkness. She never worried when Jack rode out at night. She knew he would always come back to her.

But this was different. It was still daylight, with twilight yet to come, a dangerous time. A coachman would see them coming a mile away and have time to prime his musket.

Ursula clasped her hands tightly together and uttered a prayer with trembling lips. "Dear God, keep him safe for me."

Oh, how she had pleaded with him not to go tonight, but her entreaties had fallen on deaf ears. This was too good a chance to miss, Jack had assured her. This was the last night he would ever have to take to the high toby. After tonight they would have everything they had ever wanted, everything they had ever dreamed of.

If he didn't die in the attempt.

Ursula looked around the room, so empty without the sound of Jack's laughter, and red-hot anger coursed through her veins. It was all that Diana Timothy's fault. She made Jack too cocksure of himself by always playing up to him. She made him think that together they were invincible.

Suddenly the drumming of hoofbeats in the yard sent Ursula racing for the door. Jack had changed his mind. He would not be riding tonight after all. But when she saw it was some stranger, her hopes plummeted.

She studied the man as he dismounted and tied his lathered horse to the hitching post. He was a gentleman, judging by the cut of his dusty clothes, with the look of a Londoner about him. As he turned and smiled at her, Ursula felt eyes as cold and uncompromising as a foggy morning bore right through her, and she had to look away. But he was a handsome devil, the kind of man who could make a woman do anything he wanted. Then he bowed.

"Good evening, madam," he said in an authoritative tone. "May I have a word with you?"

"About what? A room for the night?"

He shook his head, and Ursula felt relieved without quite knowing why. He looked wealthy and was sure to be generous, but the thought of having this powerful, compelling man under her roof made her uneasy.

The man reached into his pocket. "I'm looking for someone. I merely wish to know if you've seen her."

Ursula shrugged. "Many strangers pass through the Jolly Wife on their way to somewhere else."

A friendly smile lit up the man's handsome face. "That's what I'm counting on."

"Come inside," Ursula said. "It's too cold to be standing around outside." As he followed her into the coffee room, she added, "I'm Mrs. Hunt, the innkeeper."

"And I am Nicholas Devenish, the Marquess of Silverblade."

Ursula nodded her head in acknowledgment, but did not curtsy deferentially. When she was behind the bar, she said, "Now, who is this person you're looking for, your lordship?"

"My wife," he replied, handing her a piece of paper. As Ursula unfolded it, he added, "Her name is Aurora, and she has been missing for several months."

Ursula found herself staring at a likeness of Diana Timothy. She prayed her face had not betrayed the astonishment she was feeling and the queer shivering deep in her gut.

But it was no use. She gave herself away.

Lord Silverblade placed his hands on the bar and leaned forward eagerly, excitement in his voice. "You've seen her. I can see it in your face."

Ursula shrugged one shoulder carelessly to cover herself. "I can't be sure. There is something familiar about her, but like I said, I don't know for certain."

"You'd remember her if you saw her. She's very beautiful, with vibrant red hair, blue eyes, and fair freckled skin. She comes up to my shoulder in height."

While Ursula made a great pretense of studying the sketch further, she said, "She's your wife, you say?"

Lord Silverblade nodded. "I believe she's suffering from a memory loss." He spread his hands in supplication. "I must find her. I'm offering a most generous reward to the person who can tell me her whereabouts."

Ursula's ears perked up at that. "Reward?"

"Five thousand pounds, with no questions asked."

Ursula started. With that amount of money, she and Jack could make a fresh start anywhere in the world.

Diana would be returned to her husband and the loving bosom of her family, never to tempt Jack again.

Forgive me, Jack, for betraying you, she said to herself.

Ursula moistened her lips and looked Lord Silverblade squarely in the eye. "I've seen her."

"Where?"

"Before I tell you, you've got to promise me something, your lordship."

"Anything, if only you will tell me where my wife is."

While he listened, she quickly told him how Jack had saved his wife's life and how she was now riding with him as a highwayman.

When she saw those gray eyes grow as cold and implacable as steel, Ursula stepped back and hurried to Jack's defense. "It wasn't his fault! She begged him to let her ride with him. She said she was afraid of her husband and had nowhere else to go."

Lord Silverblade fought to control his rage. "Where is she?"

"I'll tell you, but you've got to promise not to hurt my Jack."

Judging from the man's murderous expression, Ursula realized that the last thing he wanted to do was spare Jack Pierce. But the anger slowly fled from his face as he realized he would have to agree to her terms before she told him anything.

"I give you my word as a gentleman, Mrs. Hunt. Not only will I spare your Jack, I shall see to it that he is spared prosecution for his crimes, and you shall receive the reward."

"You mean that?"

"I said I would give you my word as a gentleman. I don't go back on my word to anyone. I merely want my wife safe and unharmed."

Ursula could hardly contain her happiness. Diana Timothy would be out of her life forever, and she and Jack would be able to immigrate to the colonies.

"They left about fifteen minutes ago." Hurriedly she told him where they were planning to go.

* * *

They waited, hidden by the trees, watching the carriage make its way toward the copse.

"What did I tell you?" Jack said with a grin as he pulled up his mask. "Judging from that crest on the door, I'd say we have a fine lord ripe for the picking."

Aurora followed Jack's example and pulled up her black crepe mask with stiff, cold fingers. She looked at the sky worriedly. There was still enough twilight left to see what they were doing. Still enough light left for one of the two coachmen seated in the box to get off a clear shot at them if they lost the crucial element of surprise.

As she stood there waiting, she prayed the occupant of the carriage was indeed "ripe for the picking." If the booty was sufficient, perhaps then Jack would abandon this wild scheme and willingly return to Ursula with his gold.

"Get ready," Jack murmured.

The sound of hoofbeats drawing closer and the rattling of wheels made Aurora's pulse quicken. Her fingers tightened instinctively on the pistol in her hand.

"Now!" Jack cried, digging his heels into his horse's side.

Blackamoor shot forward with a squeal of protest, and Aurora's horse wasn't far behind. They appeared and blocked the road so suddenly that the coachmen didn't have time to swing the team around and flee. All they could do was rein in the horses and accept their fate.

"Stand and deliver!" Jack cried, aiming his pistols directly at the coachmen's hearts. "And leave your muskets be, if you know what's good for you."

As Aurora started walking her horse toward the carriage door, Jack suddenly shouted a warning and urged his horse forward just as several shots filled the air. Aurora watched in horror as he stiffened and cried out more in surprise than pain, then went toppling from his saddle.

"Jack!" Aurora screamed as she slid off her horse and ran to him, unmindful of her own safety.

She was dimly aware of carriage doors swinging

open, of people shouting, the threat of danger gathering around, but all she could think of was Jack.

The moment she reached his side, she knew he was dying. Even in the dwindling wintry light, she could see his black shirtfront stained darker with his own blood. Aurora placed her hand against one of the wounds as if she could physically keep his life from seeping away.

"Jack," she cried, cradling his dark head in her lap. His eyes flickered open and his lips moved as he struggled to speak. "You . . . you hurt?"

"No, Jack, I'm fine," she replied through the tears coursing down her face. "You saved my life again. Don't try to talk. You have to conserve your strength."

He knew she was lying. He managed a faint smile. "Damned if I didn't break my own rule for you."

Then he drew one last deep breath and held it. When he died, the breath left his body in a long, soft sigh of regret.

As she held him, Aurora thought of his dying words, wondering what they meant. Finally she smiled to herself. He had broken his own rule to save her life. For once, he had listened to his heart instead of his head, and paid for it with his own life.

When Aurora looked up, she found herself staring down the barrel of a musket. The game was finally over for her as well.

A single shot rang out.

Nicholas quickly reined in his horse and listened as the crack echoed eerily through the stillness and seemed to set the very air vibrating. It had come from just ahead, where the road suddenly curved and disappeared behind a thickly wooded copse.

Nicholas dug his spurs into his horse's ribs, causing the animal to squeal in pain and leap from a standstill into a dead run. Nicholas' heart was in his mouth and he prayed that he wasn't too late.

He raced around the bend so fast, his horse slipped on the hard earth and had to scrabble to regain its footing. But it gave Nicholas time to assess the tableau down the road.

Even in the fading light, he could clearly see the carriage stopped in the middle of the road, with several of its occupants staring out the windows. Two riderless horses stood docilely nearby, their heads bowed. Three men were standing in a semicircle looking at something on the ground.

When one of the men heard his approach and started toward him, Nicholas saw what they had been looking at so intently. A man was kneeling in the road, cradling the supine body of another man.

Suddenly memories of another time, another place, flashed through Nicholas' mind, causing him to catch his breath. Only he was the man kneeling there, and Tim Falconet was lying in his arms, bleeding to death from a single shot to the chest.

The sound of someone shouting "Halt!" brought Nicholas to his senses, and he saw that the determined-looking man approaching him was holding a musket aimed directly at him.

"Don't shoot!" Nicholas called. "I am not a highwayman, I am the Marquess of Silverblade."

"Put down your weapon, Parkins," a second man said in a strained, sad voice. "I know him. Silverblade is a friend."

To his relief, Nicholas recognized that voice. "Daltrey?" he inquired as he walked his horse up to the carriage and dismounted before the animal could fully stop.

Daltrey turned to him and bowed, clapping his hands to warm them. "A pleasure to see you, as always, Silverblade, but I could wish for more pleasant circumstances."

"What happened?" Nicholas asked.

"Highwaymen," Daltrey replied with a grimace of distaste. "As you can see, my coachmen spared one the gallows and saved one for Jack Ketch."

Mention of the fate awaiting him caused the remaining brigand to stir. He gently lowered his companion's head to the ground, then rose as if in a daze, unmindful of those around him. He pulled off his cocked hat and periwig, causing a headful of red curls to spring out, then reached up to pull his mask down, smearing his cheek with blood as he did so.

"Well, damn me to hell!" someone swore. "It's a woman!"

Nicholas found himself staring into the same pale blue eyes that had been haunting him day and night for months.

"Aurora!"

She looked at him, but didn't really see him. Her eyes were vacant and unaware.

Nicholas was at her side in three strides, enfolding her in his arms, to the astonishment of all present. He felt her slight body tremble, but she did not resist him.

Nicholas put his lips to her ear and whispered, "Pretend you don't know me."

When he released her, he could see by the blank expression on her face that his warning was unnecessary. She was still befuddled from the shock of her friend dying in her arms.

"Tim's dead," she mumbled, and Nicholas felt a queer wrenching in his heart.

"Silverblade," Daltrey's voice said from behind him, "would you favor me with an explanation for this? Do you know this woman?"

He turned, his arm still around Aurora's shoulders protectively. "She's my wife, Daltrey."

"Your wife!" Daltrey's eyes widened in astonishment as he looked from Nicholas to the woman passively leaning against him, and back to Nicholas.

"As you know, she's been missing for some months. I suspected she was suffering from a memory loss— that's why she never returned to me." When the other man looked skeptical, Nicholas left Aurora standing there and drew Daltrey aside, out of earshot of the other men.

"I need to ask a favor of you, Daltrey," he said simply, placing his hand on the other man's shoulder.

Daltrey glanced at Aurora, then regarded Nicholas with a mixture of sympathy and doubt in his eyes. "You want me to release your marchioness."

Nicholas swallowed hard and nodded. "If you turn her in to the magistrate, she'll hang. Even if she's fortunate enough to escape Jack Ketch, think of the scandal it would cause, the shame to the Silverblade name."

Daltrey did understand all too well. He and Nicholas were gentlemen of the ruling class, bound by shared experiences, values, and traditions. They were united by a common purpose, to ensure the survival of their species.

He nodded. "Take your marchioness and go home, Silverblade. I'll ensure that none of my men ever speak of her . . . activities."

Nicholas could have fainted with relief. "Thank you, Daltrey. I won't forget this."

Daltrey grinned. "I'll hold you to that promise when next we play at White's." When they started back to the carriage, he added, "And don't let your wife out of your sight again."

Nicholas looked at Aurora, suddenly aware of what he had almost lost. "I don't intend to, ever again."

20

WHEN Aurora awoke to find herself in a strange bedchamber rather than her room at the Jolly Wife, she wondered if she were dreaming. Then the events of the previous evening all came rushing back, crowding her mind—Jack dying in her arms, the wild wordless ride with Nicholas to the house of bright lights, a worried Diana silently washing her face and putting her to bed. No one spoke, no one asked questions. Or if anyone did, Aurora hadn't heard.

Nicholas had come for her. Nicholas had taken her out of danger, away from that place of death. She wondered why.

Suddenly her thoughts brought him to life. The bedchamber door opened and there he was.

Aurora stared at him, feasting on his sheer physical presence like one starving. He looked magnificent, so tall and lithe as he stood poised in the doorway, that Aurora felt a lump of unfulfilled yearning form in her throat. She tried to read his face, searching for a softening of the features at the sight of her, a small, tender smile of welcome—something, anything, to tell her that her presence had stirred him in some way, that he still wanted her after all that had happened between them. But his expression was inscrutable, those steel-gray eyes colder than she ever remembered. Nicholas was more like the man she had first met at the Chinese summerhouse, not her loving husband.

He said nothing and waited.

I will not surrender, Aurora thought resolutely. If he expects me to rise from this bed and go to him, he can stand there forever.

She turned her head away, a gesture of rejection not unnoticed by Nicholas.

He took a step into the room, then hesitated. He wanted nothing more than to stride across the room, pull his wife into his arms, and assure her that he would never let her go again. But to his profound astonishment and hurt, he realized Aurora was afraid of him. He had noticed the way she stiffened when she first laid eyes on him, the expression of wariness on her face, like a cornered animal. Except for that initial quiet, reflective stare, she had made no other overtures of encouragement. Just to hear those beloved lips speak his name would have sent him flying to her side.

As he watched her lying there listlessly, staring out the window as though he didn't exist, he sensed with rising panic that he was on the verge of losing her forever. He suspected the cause of her alienation went deeper than the rift that had separated them all those months ago. He opened his mouth to demand the answers he sought, then thought better of it. He would have to proceed slowly. He would have to woo and win her all over again.

Aurora heard his sure, familiar footsteps as he approached the bed, but still she didn't raise her eyes.

Only when she heard Nicholas say, "Aurora, we have to talk," did she turn her head and acknowledge his existence.

He was standing at the foot of the bed, one hand clutching the carved bedpost so hard his knuckles were white. Now that he was standing closer to her, Aurora was surprised to see deep lines of worry etched in his forehead and around his mouth. She longed to reach out and smooth them away.

"What do you wish to talk about?" she asked. Her voice sounded flat and unenthusiastic to her own ears.

"I want to know what happened to you after . . ." He hesitated and swallowed hard. ". . . after your carriage left for Silverblade. Were you kidnapped?"

What game was he playing with her now? Aurora wondered. Why was he feigning innocence when he was the one who had ordered her taken? Suddenly hope filled the aching emptiness in Aurora's heart. Perhaps Nicholas was innocent after all. No man guilty of such a heinous crime could possibly look so innocent right at that very moment.

"Yes, I was kidnapped," she replied.

While Nicholas listened, Aurora told him everything that had happened to her, sparing him nothing and watching him carefully to judge his reaction. When she started purposefully relating her cruel, humiliating treatment at the hands of her kidnappers, Nicholas turned white and slowly left the bed like one in a trance. He walked over to the fireplace and leaned his weight against the mantel, gripping it tightly as though he needed something solid to anchor himself to. His head was bowed as Aurora continued, so she couldn't see his face. But as she enumerated each incident of cruelty she had endured, Nicholas flinched as though he were being flogged.

After she told him how she had escaped by bribing one of the sailors with her sapphire ring, diving overboard, and swimming to shore, Nicholas finally released the mantel and turned to face her again.

"Why didn't you come home after you escaped?" he demanded, his voice hoarse. "Or why didn't you go to Diana? You knew she was living in Cornwall and would help you."

Aurora sat up and propped the pillows behind her. Now that the time had come to make her accusation, she felt her courage deserting her. She clasped her hands together tightly to keep them from shaking, startled to find her fingers so stiff and cold.

"I didn't come home because I thought you had ordered my kidnapping and murder."

At first Nicholas was so incredulous that all he could do was stare at her in shock, his benumbed brain refusing to accept what she had just said. But one look at Aurora's wide-eyed, fearful face told him she had meant every ghastly, killing word.

Finally, all he could do was rake his hand through his hair in frustration and wail, "Aurora!"

She heard the incredulity and reproach in Nicholas' anguished cry and saw the pain twist his features. His whole body went rigid, and he whirled away as though he could no longer bear the sight of her, his shoulders quaking from suppressed anger.

But he turned back, stormed over to her bedside, and grasped her wrist. "Damn you, Aurora! I love you! How could you ever believe I would want to kill you?"

"Because the gang's leader told me so!" she cried, her eyes wild as she tried to pull free. "He said you wanted to be rid of your childless wife."

He flung her away in disdain. "And you believed him? You took the word of a . . . a pirate?"

"I didn't want to," she protested. "But then he showed me your Chinese snuff bottle and said you had given it to him to convince me. How else would this brigand have gotten your snuff bottle unless you gave it to him? What else was I supposed to believe?"

Nicholas was regarding her strangely, a deep scowl between his brows. Suddenly he reached into his waist-coat pocket and withdrew something.

When Aurora saw what it was, her hand flew to her mouth in astonishment.

Nicholas handed her his Chinese snuff bottle. "This is the one you gave me, and I am never without it. If those criminals had one, they did not get it from me."

Aurora's fingers shook as they touched the cool jade, and she kept turning it over and over as if she had never seen it before. But she had, so many times.

She looked up at Nicholas in bafflement. "Am I losing my mind? Th-this was the same snuff bottle the brigand showed me. And since Wes assured me yours was one of a kind . . ."

"Old Immortality was obviously mistaken," Nicholas said dryly. "My bottle must have a twin, and the brigands used it to deceive you."

"But how did they acquire it? They knew so much

about you, Nicholas." For the first time this morning,
Aurora suddenly felt bewildered and unsure of herself, and she looked away from Nicholas' furious gaze.
"And then when I thought of those weeks just before
you banished me to Silverblade, how cold you were
how much you seemed to detest me . . ."

"Detest you?" Nicholas sank down on the edge of
the bed and reached for her at last, wrapping his arms
around her and holding her against his chest. "I don't
detest you. I could never detest you." He took her
face in his hands, caressing her soft cheeks with his
thumbs as he stared deeply into her eyes. "I love you,
Aurora. I have never stopped loving you. You are my
life."

"But . . . but just before you sent me away, you
said if we decided we didn't wish to be married to each
other, you would find a way to remedy the situation."

He shook his head and mentally cursed himself for
ever uttering those hurtful words. "And when you
were kidnapped, you assumed that remedy meant killing you."

She nodded, the look in her eyes woeful and sad.

"Dear God, I have been such a fool. I could kill
myself for hurting you so."

Aurora was silent for a moment as she regarded
him. Then she said, "Nicholas, why were you so . . .
so cruel to me? Why did you draw away from me?"

A sardonic smile tugged at the corners of his mouth
and he rose to walk away from her. "I inadvertently
learned of a wager at White's. Without my knowledge,
several gentlemen placed bets on the date my first
child would be born."

Suddenly Aurora understood only too well. "Oh,
Nicholas . . ."

He stared at the floor and said in a low voice, "I
was humiliated because that event showed no sign of
happening. I feared becoming a laughingstock. The
great Lord Silverblade . . ."

"And you blamed me," Aurora said dully.

Nicholas whirled around to face her. "Oh, no," he
assured her hurriedly. "I blamed myself, Aurora, never
you. I thought there was something wrong with me,

that I couldn't father a child. I felt inadequate as a man and too proud to confess my doubts and misgivings to you."

How well Aurora could believe that, for she knew her husband had enough pride for ten lesser men.

"You must understand, Aurora. Everything I have ever wanted in my life has always come easily to me, except siring an heir. I couldn't accept it, so I made you the brunt of my frustrations." Then his voice trembled with deep emotion. "And almost lost you forever."

Aurora knew what she had to do. She flung back the covers, stepped out of bed, and padded across the floor on her bare feet. When she reached Nicholas' side, she reached up and cupped his smooth hard cheek in her palm.

"Didn't we once promise each other never to let misunderstandings come between us, my love?" she said softly. "That we would confide in each other before they had a chance to tear us apart?"

Nicholas nodded imperceptibly. "And I broke that promise to you, Aurora. I thought I could weather this alone. I don't deserve your forgiveness for all the suffering I've caused."

"And I don't deserve your forgiveness for not trusting you. Even if that pirate presented me with your signed confession, I never should have believed you were capable of harming me." Her smile was radiant as she said, "So we're even."

With a great whoop of joy Nicholas wrapped his arms around her in a crushing hug, lifted her right off her feet, and began spinning her around. When he finally stopped, they were both so dizzy they swayed on their feet and clung to each other, laughing helplessly.

Without warning, Aurora unbuttoned her night rail and shrugged it off, leaving it in a crumpled heap at her feet.

Nicholas choked and his laugh died abruptly when he saw her standing naked before him, her bright hair framing her dear, lovely face and falling down about her shoulders like a copper waterfall. Much as he yearned to take her in his arms again and feel her warm, willing body pressed against him, he restrained himself, letting his eyes leisurely devour every luscious ivory inch of her.

"You are so very beautiful," he murmured, wondering what he had ever done to deserve such a woman.

His fervent gaze roved down her body, resting on her small ripe breasts, their nipples rigid and expectant, then trailing down to her tiny waist and the juncture of her thighs. Just thinking of the tight, silky darkness awaiting his complete possession caused Nicholas to burn with desire for her. He wanted to stay in that bed all day, just taking her again and again until they were both exhausted.

"Take me, Nicholas," Aurora whispered huskily, as if she had divined his thoughts, pressing her breasts toward him until the peaks brushed the front of his satin waistcoat.

Just when he reached up to cup them, Aurora darted away from him with a wicked, lascivious laugh. "If you want me, my lord, you're going to have to come after me."

She ran for the bed, glancing over her shoulder provocatively to see if he was following.

Nicholas felt as if his breeches would explode. As he started walking toward the bed where Aurora now lay in all her naked splendor, he unbuttoned his waistcoat and flung it on the floor. Two steps later and his ruffled white lawn shirt had been discarded as well. Then he kicked off his buckled shoes, which hit the floor with a clunk.

Aurora eyed him appreciatively. "Methinks your breeches are a wee bit tight, my lord."

"I'll have that situation remedied in an instant, my wanton wench."

When he had almost reached the bed, he stopped long enough to slip off the offending breeches and strip off his silk stockings. Now his clothes left a trail that led right to Aurora's bed.

Then he stood before her, reveling in the predatory gleam that came into her eyes when she looked him over like a sultana selecting a male slave.

"You'll suffice," she drawled with a languid, teasing smile.

That inflamed him as she knew it would. With a low growl of outrage mixed with desire, Nicholas slid into bed and gathered her into his arms.

"I'll suffice, did you say?" he said in mock affront. "Oh, I plan to do much more than merely suffice, madam!" To make good his boast, his mouth swooped down to capture Aurora's laughing lips in a fierce, possessive kiss.

After having been separated from Nicholas for so long, Aurora was quite unprepared for the intense response his touch ignited in her. It was as though all those weeks of being kept apart had heightened her senses to an unbearable pitch.

His questing mouth burned as it ground her lips mercilessly, his teeth nipping, his tongue branding hers wherever it touched. The sensation of being kissed with such animal passion left Aurora feeling drugged into senselessness.

She could tell Nicholas was experiencing this heightened desire as well, for when he finally lifted his head and gazed down at her, Aurora could see a wild hunger in his eyes that had never been there before.

He became a savage, pinning Aurora's arms to her sides while he kissed and licked her neck, lazily trailing his tongue over her breasts again and again. Aurora tossed her head wildly from side to side, trying to escape the exquisite torment. She barely recognized her own breathless voice rising in frenzy as she pleaded with him to take her before she died of pleasure.

She wanted to feel him driving into her, filling her, joining with her in sweet intimacy.

When Nicholas entered her, Aurora felt as though she were sheathing a sword of fire. She was so aroused, so ready for him, that the initial possession sent her soaring to the pinnacle of ecstasy. Aurora arched her back to meet it, then cried out Nicholas' name as wave after shuddering wave of delight washed over her.

No sooner had she spent herself than Nicholas followed suit, becoming a slave to his own desires. All it took were several quick thrusts before his body jerked like a puppet on a string and his moaning of Aurora's name caught on a sob.

Later, they refused to relinquish each other and lay locked together, their bodies slick and musky from their exertions.

Aurora sighed in contentment as she rested her head against Nicholas' chest. This union had been like no other. Even on her wedding night, Aurora had never experienced such unbridled rapture, such lusty lovemaking.

They lay quietly for several minutes basking in love's afterglow. Finally Nicholas' chest vibrated as he said, "Who was the man who died last night?"

"His name was Jack Pierce," she replied. "He was the man who rescued me after I had been washed ashore. He could have left me for dead, but he didn't."

Aurora went on to tell Nicholas how Jack had brought her to the Jolly Wife Inn, where she was given shelter by Ursula Hunt.

"He was a highwayman, wasn't he?" Nicholas asked.

"Yes," Aurora replied. She raised her head and looked at him. "And so was I."

Nicholas' eyes were soft with understanding. "Do you wish to tell me why? I must confess to being more than mildly curious."

"One night I inadvertently discovered Jack's identity. He would have killed me to ensure my silence, so I had to do something to win his trust." Aurora shrugged. "In a moment of desperation, all I could think of to do was offer to ride with him. Once I convinced him that I could ride and shoot as well as he could, he agreed to spare me."

"You took a great risk, Aurora."

"I had no other choice."

A teasing smile played about Nicholas' mouth. "And were you a good highwayman, Rory?"

She gave him a look of pure disdain. "Of course." Then she added more soberly, "Until last night, that is." She shook her head, still unable to believe Jack Pierce was dead. "Poor Jack . . . he died saving my life. When he saw someone inside the carriage take aim with a pistol, he rode right in front of me. He took the ball meant for me."

"I owe him a debt of gratitude," Nicholas said.

Aurora looked up at him. "How did you know where to find me?"

He explained how he had come to Cornwall because of a letter Diana had written, and was searching the area when he came to the Jolly Wife Inn.

When Aurora learned of the part Ursula had played in rescuing her, she shook her head sadly. "Poor Ursula. She loved Jack so much. I don't know what she'll do now that he's dead."

Nicholas said nothing, just drew her close and hugged her tightly, thankful that he had been spared Ursula's plight of losing the one person in the world who mattered to him more than life itself.

Suddenly Aurora pulled away, her eyes filling with tears.

"Rory, what's wrong?" Nicholas demanded.

"I've been such a child," she said with a desolate sniff. "I should have trusted you, Nicholas. And I never should have tried to be a highwayman. It wasn't exciting or adventurous, it was frightening."

He grinned. "As long as you've learned your lesson, madam."

"I have. I will never again boast that I can ride and shoot as well as any man."

"Splendid. Now, as much as I enjoy your lovely company in bed, my sweet Rory, I think we had better dress. Then you must tell me everything you remember about being kidnapped. Leave out nothing. Every detail, no matter how small, can be of the utmost importance."

So while they dressed, Aurora told Nicholas everything she remembered about that terrifying time. He listened attentively, his face composed. Occasionally his eyes would darken with fury, but he said nothing, just listened.

As Aurora discussed different elements of her ordeal—the warehouse, the snuff bottle, the ship—everything suddenly came together, and she could have cursed herself for failing to see it sooner.

She looked at Nicholas. "I know who did this to me."

"So do I." The coldness in his voice made her shudder. "'After we go downstairs and pay our respects to Diana and Lord Penhall, we are leaving for London to expose a kidnapper."

A noise aroused Wesley out of a sound sleep. He opened his eyes and listened. Somewhere deep in the house, a clock chimed the midnight hour, then was still. Silence. Suddenly he heard it again, that soft, plaintive sigh like the whispering of the wind as it blew through the eaves. Only there was no wind tonight.

Someone was in the room with him. Wesley could sense a presence. Wide-awake now, he forced himself to lie perfectly still in his bed, arms rigid by his sides. Only his eyes moved, darting back and forth, searching the room for some shadow out of place. His attention was riveted to one of the windows at the farther end of the room. He could have sworn he had drawn the draperies before retiring. Now they were open, admitting a shaft of moonlight floating in a pool on the floor.

Wesley listened again. All he could hear was the thud-thud-thud of his own heart. Nothing. He chuckled to himself. His overwrought mind was playing tricks on him. He was alone. There was no one else here.

As he started nodding off again, he took a deep breath. His eyes flew open. What was that strange smell? His eyes bulged in the horror of recognition. He would never forget the rank, pervasive smell of the crypt after the laughing, jeering village children had locked him in, the smell of damp, moldering earth. Rotting flesh. Death.

Then he heard it again. This time the whisper was a long, drawn-out "Why?" that hung in the air.

Wesley tried to scream, but his mouth was so dry and his tongue so swollen with fear that all that came out was a strangled whimper.

Suddenly he saw it. He watched in morbid fascination as the moonlight shifted and danced, bits of light taking form, growing. He blinked, and there, bathed in moonlight, stood a woman—or what was left of one. Wesley recoiled in horror. Her face was nothing more than three black gaping holes where her eyes and mouth should have been. And the specter was looking right at him.

Wesley tried to run, but he couldn't move. He was paralyzed with terror. He stank of it. Cold beads of sweat rose on his forehead, ran down his temples, and trickled down his neck like icy fingers. His eyes ached from the sheer effort of bulging from their sockets.

The apparition floated toward him. Its shroud hung in tatters, its spectral hair lank and clinging to the small round skull. One skeletal arm was extended, reaching for him, curved fingers beckoning.

Even though the wraith had no lips to form the words, Wesley heard it whisper, "Why? Why did you kill me?" It came even closer.

The same terror that had paralyzed Wesley now spurred him into action. He sat bolt upright and pulled his covers up to his chin as if the cloth were armor that could protect him.

"Wh-who are you?" he screamed witlessly. "What do you want of me?"

The apparition stopped. "Don't you recognize me, Wesley? I am Aurora. You murdered me."

Aurora, back from her watery grave, back from the dead to haunt him.

"No!" Wesley screamed again. He flung away the covers and went scrambling like a madman away from her to cower against the bed's headboard. "You're dead! I paid them to kill you. They told me you were dead."

Suddenly there came the common, ordinary sound of tinder striking. Wesley's attention was momentarily diverted by a glow of light coming from behind the coromandel screen at the other end of the room. As he watched, Nicholas came sauntering out from behind the screen, a silver candlestick in his hand.

The warm, flickering light from the solitary flame banished the darkness, and Wesley eagerly turned to the ghost of his cousin's wife, fully expecting it to be gone as well. He gasped and cried out when he saw it was still there, staring at him out of accusing eyes.

Aurora was very much alive.

As Wesley stared, he saw that the gaping holes had been formed with black lead, Aurora's ghostly pallor nothing more than white ceruse.

"You tricked me!" he screeched, still clinging to the headboard. "You both tricked me!"

Nicholas, who had reached the foot of the bed, set the candle down on a nearby table and bowed his head respectfully toward his wife. "Well done, my dear. That was a performance worthy of Drury Lane."

Aurora grinned and acknowledged his compliment with a graceful curtsy. But Nicholas wasn't smiling as he turned his attention on his cousin.

"Why did you pay to have Aurora kidnapped and killed?" he asked conversationally.

"I . . . I didn't," Wesley stammered, shaking his head. "Someone has falsely accused me."

Nicholas resisted the impulse to wrap his hands around Wesley's lying throat and strangle the life out of him. "Do forgive me, but I seem to recollect your saying several minutes ago that you did indeed pay someone to kill Aurora." He turned to her. "Don't you, my dear?"

"I most certainly do."

Wesley swallowed hard. "I . . . I was frightened. I didn't know what I was saying."

Nicholas' patience snapped. He took a threatening step forward. "Stop lying, you sniveling coward! At least be man enough to admit you did it. We've got you dead to rights, Wesley."

"You can't prove anything against me."

Nicholas raised one brow. "Oh, no? I beg to differ with you, cousin. Aurora's abductors took her to a warehouse, which she has already identified as belonging to your shipping company. The ship she was held on is named the *Silent Sisters*, which just happens to be one of your ships. And I'm sure she could identify its captain and worthless crew when they return from the Indies."

Nicholas stared at Wesley with loathing and contempt. "We know you did it, cousin. I just want to know why."

He waited. Wesley looked like a cornered ferret, his eyes darting back and forth, searching for a way to escape. Sweat poured down his face. His lips moved as if trying to form a fresh set of denials for his crimes.

Finally, when he realized there was no escape this time, he cracked.

"Yes, I did it!" he shrieked. "I paid to have the bitch killed. And you want to know why?" He released the headboard to kneel on the bed, his hands clenched into fists at his sides as he stared at Nicholas. "Because I hate you."

The words were uttered with such virulence that Nicholas was taken aback and Aurora suddenly rounded the bed and stood beside him for support.

Wesley was at full career now. All the hatred, resentment, envy, and spite came pouring out in a bitter diatribe.

"I have always hated you." His voice grew girlish and mocking. "Nick the handsome one, Nick the accomplished one . . . everyone's favorite, everyone's golden lad. Even my own mother used to say to me, 'Why can't you be more like your cousin Nicholas?' My own mother, damn her! But no, I never could be just like Nick. I was always in your shadow, always second best. I never could do anything right. I was a failure. All the women flocked to you, but they sniggered at me behind their fans when I passed. I knew what they were thinking of me and I despised them for it."

Nicholas felt Aurora grasp his hand and take a step closer as they listened to Wesley.

He shook his head ironically. "You were even born the heir to Silverblade, while I had the misfortune to be the child of a second son. You got everything, while I was forced to make my own way in the world like a . . . a common tradesman."

"I offered to help you out of your financial difficulties," Nicholas reminded him, "but you refused."

"I didn't want your help, your . . . your damned charity! I want to be the Marquess of Silverblade. I want everything that you have because it rightfully should be mine.

"But do you know what made me hate you the most?" Before Nicholas could reply, Wesley went on, "The night you and your cronies broke into my house, bound and gagged me, and threw me into that coffin." His voice became shrill and taunting again, while spittle formed in the corners of his mouth. "Did you enjoy seeing me writhe and squirm, Nick? Did you enjoy seeing my eyes bulging with terror? Would you have thought it so droll if I died of fright?"

"No, I wouldn't have, Wesley," Nicholas said softly. "I have always regretted doing that cruel thing to you."

"Oh, yes, you tried to make amends by saying you were sorry, and that was supposed to make me forget one of the most terrifying ordeals of my life. No one ever punished you for what you did to me. No, everyone thought it was hilarious because Nick, the golden lad, had done something so outrageous and novel, so amusing. Well, I never forgot it, and I never forgave you for it. Never, you rotten bastard."

Suddenly Wesley's face twisted slyly. "But I had my ways of being avenged. I worked behind your back, Cousin Nick, ruining your reputation whenever I had the opportunity."

Nicholas had to restrain himself from slamming his fist into Wesley's jeering face. "You sniveling coward! You couldn't confront me like a man, you had to do your dirty work behind my back."

"Some of us aren't as noble as you, my dear cousin," Wesley retorted.

Now Aurora spoke. "Is that why you tried to have me killed, to hurt Nicholas?"

"You were to be my ultimate revenge," Wesley replied, his eyes glittering feverishly in the candlelight. "I was going to take away the one person Nick loved better than himself. You were just going to disappear, my dear, and I was going to take supreme pleasure in watching my cousin suffer agonies wondering what had happened to you."

"You're mad, Wesley," Nicholas said.

"Mad? On the contrary. I thought I was rather clever. I neglected to inform Aurora that the snuff bottle she bought was one of a matched pair. I kept the second one for my own use. Then, when she confided in me that she was being sent back to Silverblade in disgrace, I seized the opportunity."

Aurora's hand flew to her mouth. "I remember now! After Nicholas told me he was sending me back to Silverblade, you found me crying in the study. I told you what had happened and that I was leaving the following day." She shook her head in wonder. "I had forgotten you were the only other person who knew of my imminent departure, Wesley."

That angered him as nothing else had. "Of course," he sneered. "Old Immortality is eminently forgettable when compared with his handsome, charming cousin. He just fades into the background like a piece of furniture. But thanks to that very characteristic, you enabled me to put my plan into action and didn't suspect me of being the one who wanted you dead."

Aurora's voice was icy with contempt. "You were going to let me go to my death thinking that my own beloved husband had ordered it."

Wesley grinned diabolically and jerked his head up and down.

"You poor, pathetic wretch," she said, shaking her head sadly.

Wesley dropped down onto all fours and snarled, "Don't you pity me, you heartless bitch. Don't you dare pity me! You were like all the others, pretending to like me, but you didn't. You laughed at me along with the rest of them."

"I never laughed at you, Wesley," Aurora insisted.

"You're lying!"

Nicholas stepped forward, neatly placing himself between Wesley and Aurora. As he advanced, Wesley beat a hasty retreat back to the headboard.

"Don't you dare touch me!" he shrieked.

Nicholas stopped and smiled slowly. "You know you deserve to hang for what you've done, cousin. But because you are family, I'm going to give you something you don't deserve." He hesitated for effect. "A quick death."

Wesley's eyes filled with terror and his jaw worked, though not even a whimper escaped his lips.

"My seconds will call upon you tomorrow morning," he said briskly. "You may have your choice of weapons and choose the time and the place for our duel of honor." Nicholas leaned over the bed until his face was mere inches from Wes's. "But make no mistake, my dear, dear cousin. No matter which weapon you choose, I fully intend to kill you."

Then he stood back and smiled. "This time you really will be dead when they put you in your coffin. This time there will be no escape."

Nicholas bowed politely, turned, and escorted his wife from the room. As they started down the stairs, Wesley screamed, "No, Nicholas! Please don't kill me."

Even though Aurora hesitated and glanced back over her shoulder, Nicholas hardened his heart and made her keep on walking.

Despite the late hour and the fact that she was mentally and physically exhausted, Aurora removed the white ceruse paint and black lead from her face, bathed and washed the reeking stagnant water out of her hair. Then she slipped into bed beside Nicholas.

"That was a most clever plan you had, my impersonating a ghost," she said. "I must admit that I was skeptical at first. I thought Wesley would unmask our deception right away."

Nicholas reclined against the pillows, his forearm resting across his forehead. "I was relying heavily on his obsessive fear of death to cloud any rational thinking. He was sleepy and the room was dark except for that bit of moonlight. His own imagination did the rest."

Now Nicholas rolled over onto his side and planted a quick kiss on Aurora's nose. "You almost had me convinced you were a spirit come back from the dead."

Aurora sighed. "Diana was right. Cosmetics make all the difference to a woman."

Nicholas chuckled at that. "A very convincing disguise."

Suddenly Aurora's smile died and she grew pensive. "Imagine being consumed by such bitterness and hatred all these years."

"Yes, and hiding it behind a mask of affability." Nicholas shook his head. "I never once suspected Wes of hating me so much. After I apologized for that night, he seemed to accept it with good grace. He always appeared to enjoy coming to Silverblade and being a part of our family."

Aurora shook her head sadly. "What a poor, pathetic, lonely man. I feel sorry for him."

"That's because you have a soft heart, my love. The runt of the litter, a pathetic wretch like my cousin . . . they all find a place in your heart, don't they?"

Aurora nodded. "But you occupy the biggest place there."

Nicholas smiled and drew her into his arms.

She raised her head and looked at him. "Nicholas?"

"What is it, my love?"

"Do you really intend to kill Wesley in a duel?"

"It will be my pleasure," was his cold reply. Now he released her to prop himself up on one elbow and gaze down at her. "When I married you, I vowed to protect you. What kind of man would I be if I can't protect my own wife? After what that bastard put you through, a quick death is too good for him."

"Still, he is your cousin, Nicholas."

"That doesn't give him the license to murder two of my servants and to try to kill my wife!" Then his tone changed, becoming softer. "If it's any consolation, my dear, I'll be surprised if that duel is ever fought."

Aurora wrinkled her brow in puzzlement. "What do you mean?"

Nicholas yawned. "Go to sleep. You'll find out tomorrow when Ollie returns from issuing my challenge to Cousin Wes."

Since he would tell her no more, Aurora resigned herself to waiting.

Aurora and Nicholas were having luncheon the following day when Ollie suddenly came bursting into the dining room, his chubby cheeks flushed with excitement.

"You were right, Nick," he said jubilantly. "Old Immortality has run off. I went to deliver your challenge this morning, and his majordomo told me the master had just left for the Continent."

Nicholas leaned back in his chair and smiled slowly. "I trust he's not expected to return in the near future?"

Ollie grabbed a roll and began buttering it. "Not if he knows what's good for him."

Aurora watched him devour the roll in two bites, then invited him to stay for luncheon.

"Don't mind if I do," he replied, seating himself.

As a footman began serving him, Ollie said, "Old Immortality was a perfidious old bastard, Nick. You're well rid of him. Did you know he was the one who instigated that wager at White's?"

Nicholas' face turned livid and he set his fork down. "How do you know that?"

"Haze found out. He made a few discreet inquiries of the so-called gentlemen who placed the wager. When he became, shall we say, persuasive, one of them confessed it was Wesley Devenish who suggested it."

"He knew how much it would humiliate me," Nicholas muttered with a shake of his head.

"And that's not all," Ollie went on.

Aurora raised her brows in disbelief. "There's more?"

Ollie nodded as he cut his roast quail. "Old Immortality liked to drop snippets of gossip to the Misses Adderley. Do you remember what happened at Tyburn?"

"How could we ever forget it?" Nicholas reached for Aurora's hand and squeezed it.

"Well, Wes told the Misses Adderley that he inadvertently saw both of you together in Nick's bed. Of course, by the time those two old biddies got through with that, Aurora's reputation was ruined."

Nicholas slapped the table with his open palm, causing the silver cutlery to jump. "After what he did to my wife and my coachmen, I feel like going after him and dragging him back to England by his—" He caught himself just in time.

"In fact," Ollie went on, "I would be willing to bet ten thousand pounds that your cousin was responsible for ruining your good name, Nick."

Nicholas shook his head ruefully. "I'm afraid I only had myself to blame for that, Ollie."

His friend shrugged. "In the beginning perhaps, but I think your cousin helped. Think about it. Those rumors about my Pageant of Venus? Wes was there. After Tyburn? Wes was there."

Aurora rose and stood behind her husband's chair, her hands resting lightly on Nicholas' hard shoulders. "Wes was a sick, bitter man, and whatever he did, he's gone now and out of our lives forever."

Nicholas grasped one of her hands and brought it to his lips. "Good riddance."

They left for Silverblade the following morning.

When they arrived, they found a relieved, beaming Lady Mary waiting for them on the front steps. She raced down to embrace both Nicholas and Aurora as they disembarked from the carriage, then drew them into the house to hear all about how Nicholas had rescued his wife and exposed the culprit responsible for her kidnapping.

Lady Mary looked shocked when she learned that bland, self-effacing Wesley was the mastermind behind Aurora's disappearance. Then she just shook her head sadly and said, "He seemed so . . . so good, so pleasant and kind."

"He had us all fooled, Mother," was Nicholas' icy reply.

Then, while Nicholas went to the dower house to tell Lady Vivien that Wesley would never be calling upon her again, and why, Aurora took one of the maids and went upstairs to make a clean break from her past.

She opened the chest at the foot of her bed, took out her father's sword, and handed it to the maid. The case containing her father's pistols came next. Aurora ran her hand over the smooth mahogany in a loving farewell, but didn't lift the lid, even to look at the pistols one last time. This too she handed to the maid.

"See that these are stored in the attic," she said, "in a safe place. Perhaps one day my son will have use of them. They are no longer of any use to me." She was no longer a hoydenish child, she was the Marchioness of Silverblade, Nicholas' wife.

The maid bobbed her a curtsy, then left.

That done, Aurora decided to go down to the stables to see how Firelight had fared in her absence. As she left the house and started through the gardens, she smiled to herself. She hoped he hadn't wreaked too much havoc on the ostlers.

Sudden movement by the Garden of Eros caused her to glance up, and she stopped dead in her tracks.

There was a team of horses in harness, with ropes tied around the statue of Priapus. Nicholas stood nearby, one arm upraised. When he dropped it, one of the men shouted to the horses, which heaved themselves forward simultaneously.

The statue teetered on its pedestal, then toppled to the ground with a resounding crash that caused the earth to tremble beneath Aurora's feet. Then the horses began dragging Priapus away.

Nicholas turned, saw Aurora watching, and just stood there for a moment, his inscrutable gaze locked with hers. Then he grinned and started toward her.

She looked at the retreating statue in puzzlement. "What are you doing to Priapus?"

"Something I should have done a long, long time ago," Nicholas replied, taking her hand and drawing it to his lips. "The other statues will follow suit, and the garden will be redone. The Garden of Eros is no more."

Aurora's eyes misted over with tears as she looked up at her beloved husband. "Thank you, Nicholas."

His gray eyes sparkled with devilry. "What need do I have for provocative statuary when I am married to the most provocative woman alive?"

"You rogue," Aurora murmured with a giggle as she drew her arm through his and leaned against him, savoring his hard, strong body against her own. Then she suddenly grew somber. "What did your grandmother say when you told her about Wesley?"

Nicholas' jaw tightened and his expression turned grim. "What one would expect. She defended him, of course, and claimed everything was my fault. Then she begged me to forgive him and welcome him back into the fold." His eyes darkened with implacable anger. "I refused. There are some things that are past forgiveness."

They walked in silence toward the stables.

Just when they reached the quadrangle, Aurora stopped. Looking up at Nicholas with mischief in her eyes, she whispered, "Firelight can wait. There are still several gentlemen waiting for an outcome to a certain wager that was made at White's. Why don't we return to the house and . . ." She stood on tiptoes and whispered her wanton suggestion into Nicholas' ear.

Nicholas threw back his head and laughed, a hearty, joyous sound; then he scooped Aurora into his arms and carried her bodily back to the house.

Later, as they lay entwined in each other's arms, he nuzzled her ear and whispered, "I do love you so much, my darling Rory."

"And I love you, Nicholas," she replied.

They sighed in contentment and dreamed of tomorrow.

About the Author

Leslie O'Grady was born and raised in Connecticut, where she lives with her husband, Michael. A graduate of Central Connecticut State University, she worked as a public-relations writer for a television station and a hospital before retiring to write fiction full-time. When not writing, Ms. O'Grady enjoys movies, museums, and collecting books about nineteenth-century England and Art Nouveau. Her other novels include *Passion's Fortune* and *The Second Sister* (also available from New American Library).